THE IMMIGRANT MAGICIAN

*An international student's arduous journey
through the rigors of the Great Recession 2008 and
successful achievement of the American dream*

I0662777

First Edition 2017

Copyright © 2017 by Joel Mendonca

All rights reserved

For information about permission to reproduce selections from this book, write to Value Books LLC, 2130 SW High Avenue, # H, Topeka, KS 66611

Cover design © 2017 by Value Books LLC.

Value Books LLC
2130 SW High Ave, # H,
Topeka, KS 66611

This is a work of fiction. Names, characters, businesses, places, events and incidents are either the products of the author's imagination or used in a fictitious manner. Any resemblance to actual persons, living or dead, or actual events is purely coincidental.

Ordering Information:
For details on buying the book, contact the publisher at the address above.

Printed in the United States of America

Publisher's Cataloging-in-Publication data: 2016920989
Mendonca, Joel.
The Immigrant Magician: An International Student's triumph
over the Great Recession 2008/ Joel Mendonca.
p. cm.

Paperback ISBN 978-0-9984471-0-0

Library of Congress Control Number (LCCN): 2016920989

1. The main category of the book —Fiction — Immigration. I.
Mendonca, Joel.

To the man that gave me

So much from so little;

MY DAD

CONTENTS

ACKNOWLEDGEMENTS

This book has been the fruition of several hundreds of hours of deep thought and writing. I wish to thank my greatest supporter, my mother for her unwavering support in helping make this book a reality. And also my father who still blesses us today with his indomitable spirit. This book including the cover design, font and layout would not have been complete without the impeccable graphic skills of my elder brother Angelo.

THE END

THE METALLIC CHAIR FELT colder than normal. Although Ralph had been there only a half hour it seemed like an eternity. *"Am I losing heat or is it just the chill of my thoughts that's making me feel cold?"* he thought to himself. It had been just an hour since he bid farewell to the two old folks who loved him dearly but had come to admonish his naïve actions.

"How long will it be before I see them again? Will they miss me or will they be relieved that I'm gone?" He kept guessing...... *"I hope the journey to the new world is without incident. Or at least very little incident!"* he thought squirming in the chair. This thought would cause him to despise himself later that night.

Things had been rough since his return from the city of Pune. It had been an arduous struggle to make it to the hallowed soil of Duisburg in Germany. And he had still not gotten there. Lots of trials and tribulations had stood in his path. *"I could have prevailed against the circumstances had I persevered,"* he thought. However, parental pressure against a seemingly flailing operation had been too great. "If you can't get admission into a Good university in Germany why are you trying to learn the language? As well you also apply to another country. The US has better prospects for people like you," said Mum in her peremptory tone.

"Yes, but Germany offers free education and living expenses; offers like this are not available in the US," he had countered. "It is still not the best option for us because your progress in Pune is not going well. We don't have anybody there to help you out either."
"I will think about it. Let me see how it goes for another couple of weeks. So far I've had some struggle, but I have held it together" he said positively.
"Ok, try and we will see" said his exasperated mother in a low tone.

1

In Pune, there were a bunch of challenges. He didn't have a kitchen to cook in, no friends to eat with and no independent place to live. Staying with the cantankerous old man Falcao he felt confined to the cold environs of his Pune room. The only contact he had with his family was through the rag-tag pay phone service two hundred feet from the apartment building. It was cheaper than using the relatively expensive pre-paid cell phone, but it required him to get out of his room and brave the cooler temperatures. The cell phone he had was meant to be for emergency purposes and usually served the receiving of calls rather than making outgoing calls.

The food in Pune was the only saving grace though. Sometimes it would be mutton spring roll for lunch; sometimes chicken lollipop. Dinner would usually be noodles or biryani. However, the portions did not match the unlimited quantities that Ralph would draw from the mega vessels at home in Goa. Dad would always be open and generous in allowing him a free hand to the delectable recipes except, of course, if there was a limited amount for everybody. Sweet and sour meatballs, butter chicken, mutton xacuti, what have you. These were some of the outstanding dishes that Ralph would get to savor in addition to the others.

In Pune though, all of these dishes were but a sweet memory. He could only derive pleasure from reminiscing about the food he had enjoyed all those years. *"Wish I could go home and enjoy the food and do this course simultaneously,"* he often thought.

Probably that day was not far off. Among the several north Indians at Max Muller Bhavan there was this freakish, young and apparently quite angry man named Bachitter. He belonged to the feared Rajput tribe in India. He always seemed to have an opinion on everything and would often interrupt people while they voiced their opinions. Unfortunately, he was bunched in a room with another hot head – Ralph!

"Why are you keeping the light on? It's already 11pm," complained Bachitter. "I need to study for the test tomorrow and I haven't finished yet," replied Ralph. "I need to sleep. I don't care if you want to study for the test," Bachitter contested.
"But I haven't completed anything and need to cover stuff before I can go to bed. Tomorrows test carries a lot of weight on the final percentage score. Sorry!" cleared Ralph.

"Hey I am asking you nicely for the last time. Just turn that light off or else I will have to do it myself," Bachitter hollered.

"So you want to push your way through huh. Don't try to touch the light or else I will have to stop you from doing it," said Ralph, trying to sound tough. "And what is the meaning of 'asking nicely' when in fact you are yelling at the top of your voice."

"Turn off the light now!" screamed Bachitter.

"Not until I am done studying you bitch!"

Bachitter began climbing from his top bunk with heated resolve causing Ralph to prepare for a potential fight with a classic martial artist karate pose. Bachitter stumbled off the last two bunk bed steps as he descended to the floor. Ralph was well positioned to attack but held back to continue the verbal argument hoping that they would not come to arms.

"Don't touch the light as I am not going to allow you to turn it off until I finish studying."

"Fuck you! I want to sleep. This is no time to study!" he reached out to the light switch to turn it off.

"Ayyhh don't!" Ralph intercepted him as Bachitter tried reaching for the switch.

Bachitter's Rajput fighting spirit made him go for Ralph's neck. He grabbed it and squeezed hard as Ralph got between him and the switch. The pain forced Ralph to retaliate. He pushed Bachitter hard. The Rajput's head slammed hard against the bunk bed.

He is dazed, not by the pain of the crash against the bunk bed, but by the unexpected action of the seemingly weak kid from Goa. "I am going to report you to the warden" screamed Ralph, his throat still sore from the tight grip exerted by Bachitter. He stormed out of the room leaving the proud Rajput reeling in pain.

"Warden, warden!!" screamed the lad. "I need to report something to you urgently."

He knocked on the door hard as though he was going to break it down. "Hold on! Who's there?" shouted the warden. "It's Ralph. I need to talk to you urgently!"

"Why can't you come tomorrow morning? Don't you know how late it is!" said the warden sounding irritated.

"This is a life or death situation warden!"

3

"What's so life or death about it?"

"That guy Bachitter you assigned as my roommate started fighting and caught my neck. He was not allowing me to study and physically attacked me. I need another room or please put him out of the room," pleaded Ralph.

"I will see what I can do. We can't have wrestling matches here. People come here to study not to fight" he said as he walked towards the room, Ralph following him.

"Hey Bachitter, are you okay?" said the warden, seeing him reclined on the wall in apparent pain.

"He pushed me against the bunk bed bar and I hurt my head," Bachitter squealed.

"Hey Ralph why did you do that?" the warden turned and waited for an answer. "He caught hold of my neck and almost strangled me to death," remonstrated Ralph.

"You two are mature individuals and shouldn't be fighting like this. Not here in Max Muller at least. This is a place where respectable people come to study and achieve their dreams. Shame on both of you."

"He started the fight" exclaimed Ralph. "He tried to forcibly turn off the light. And then was the first to physically attack me. I needed to study for the test tomorrow," exclaimed Ralph.

The warden looked pointedly at Ralph. "Haven't you completed studying for the tests?"

"I have but I need to revise as I have a bad memory. I wasn't feeling too well the last couple of days and missed a few classes. I don't see any reason why I shouldn't be allowed to study particularly since we have no libraries to study in late at night."

The warden stood there in silence as though contemplating the righteousness of Ralph's actions and trying to formulate a possible solution to the issue.

"I can't allow these two to stay in the same room as it might lead to another physical altercation and more disturbances. Better I shift this Rajput guy to some other location where he can sleep in peace. Then this Ralph will be able to study for however long he wants, no questions asked," the warden thought to himself.

"You are going to have to move to the room on the other end of this hall; room number 20A," the warden instructed Bachitter. "That's the only one that's empty right now Bachitter."

"But why should I move? He also pushed me against the bunk bed bar?" objected Bachitter.

"You started this fight so you are going to be the one to bear the majority of the punishment, if not all of it," contended the warden. "The other alternative is I suspend you from the course and send you home. And also send a letter to your parents informing them that you violated Max Muller decorum by attacking another student and starting a fight. Which one would you like to go with – move the room or leave the course?" The warden looks Bachitter in the eyes without batting an eyelid.

The once arrogant Rajput was forced to eat humble pie as he pulled himself up and began to pack his bag. The warden, looking tired from a disturbed sleep sat in Ralph's chair to supervise Bachitter's movements.

After Bachitter was done with the packing, the warden took one telling look at the room. "I presume you won't come here again to pick a fight right?" Bachitter bowed his head and silently walked away. "Ralph you can get to your studies now. Don't interfere or talk to that guy again. Your problem is solved," said the warden as he walked towards his quarters to catch up on lost sleep.

Always having thought that he was very strong, Ralph realized how weak he actually was that day. The altercation with Bachitter was pretty close in terms of advantage and physical superiority. *"I was just lucky today to get away with a minor neck swelling."*

The test the next day was a mixed bag for Ralph. "I could have done much better," he thought, quite disappointed with his performance. He mentally debated if continuing the course was really worth it. After all, admission to a German university is no cakewalk.

"They have asked for above average marks in computer programming languages. They want a minimum of 95%. Also, they want someone with no failed semesters in any of the years in engineering," Ralph had confessed to Mum.

"So why can't you try some other university!" said Mum.

"Almost all universities in Germany want that level of proficiency. They offer education free over there for a reason. You really need to know your stuff" he said despondently.

"So why are you so after that country? If you can't get in there, try the US which I think is the best option" she asserted.

"She is probably right. I need to leave this seemingly impossible dream and get moving in a stable direction" thought Ralph as he came out of the flashback. *"I do have a long way to go in terms of making up for lost ground in regards to starting my US college search. Especially since I lost a lot of time trying for universities in Germany and studying German here at Max Muller."*

As he sat on the bench outside the exam classroom, a familiar voice brought him out of his pensive mood. "Hey Ralph, how was your test? I haven't seen you all week. Is everything okay?" asked Julia. Ralph, almost shaken by her friendly gesture was slow to respond. But he smiled none the less. "I have been kind of busy with classes and tests so haven't really got the time to socialize and meet friends lately."
"You should have come to Sanjay's birthday party. We had a ball of a time. Even Coralie was asking about you. I am going to have some tea at the stall outside. Do you want to come?" she asks seeming eager to have some company.
"Well I am having slight throat pain. Besides I have to go home and get ready for the next class" he said hoping to be left to himself. His throat was still sore from the force of the squeeze exerted by his former roommate Bachitter the previous night.
"Oh, I am so sorry to hear that. The linguistic philosophy class; I am in that class too. Probably I will meet you there. See you at class then. Hope you feel better!" she grinned on her way out of the building.

The class was to begin in one hour but Ralph didn't seem to be in the mood to attend it. He went to his dorm room and hit the sack. With eyes wide open he gazed at the snow white ceiling as though asking it for answers to life's questions.

The bare white wall was as motionless as Ralph's vegetative mental state. He continued to lie there thinking about how to get out of his rather passive situation.

One hour later – it was almost time to get to the linguistic philosophy class and Ralph found himself still lying on the bed, unable to crank out any thoughts, let alone any solutions. He decided against going to the class. *"Rather go and have some of that nice Friday special biryani at the Muslim dhaba[1] outside. That might make me feel better*" he said to himself as he shook off the inertia.

He trotted lazily down the stairs, almost staggering for a second as he missed a few of his steps. The partial fall increased his alertness as he walked steadily towards the dhaba. The aroma of flavored rice invigorated his spirit and enlivened his soul.

"*There are very few dishes like biryani, if any at all. It feels new every time you come close to it!*" he muttered to himself as he hastened in the direction of the dhaba.

With a plate full of salad and another bursting with spicy rice and beef pieces, he gracefully glided to a corner table. As he relished the food he thought about the current state of affairs. "*Should I or should I not quit, that's the million dollar question right now. If I do, I will come across as uncertain and weak in front of Mum and Dad. If I don't, I risk spending more time and money here and not getting anywhere. Even if I do extremely well in the course here, admission to a German university would be near to impossible*" he surmised.

All thoughts were relegated to the background as flavors emanating from chunks of juicy meat passing down his throat put all worries to rest, at least for the moment. Even the pain in his throat seemed too trivial with all the tasty food he was gulping down.

Stomach full, he got up to leave. He felt much better now that he had relieved himself of gastronomical cravings. The short walk home completed, he entered his dank room and took a one hour nap. By now his class in linguistic philosophy was almost done, not that he cared. He slouched in the tousled sheets on his bed.

Not getting any sleep, he picked up a book on German history and started reading through the pages. History and tales of yore gave him a lot of peace and pleasure. He wanted to keep his peace of mind till he spoke to Mum that day and asked her for her enlightened opinion. She had a knack for knowing what decision to make during the most

---

[1] **Dhaba** is a ramshackle, tin roofed establishment that prepares and sells food at street corners. These are widespread throughout the Indian subcontinent.

uncertain times in life. He hoped that her opinion would resonate the force of logical thinking in this time of relative hopelessness. He continued reading the German history text, almost forgetting his worries and problems.

At around 7pm Mum's customary daily call caused his otherwise silent phone to suddenly bristle with life. The buzz evoked a feeling of rejuvenation and vitality in the dejected Ralph.

"Hello Mama! How are you? I am always happy to hear your voice! So how is Papa and everything at home?"

"Everything is fine at home. How was your test and how are the studies going on?"

"Test was okay. I didn't go for the linguistic philosophy class though. Didn't feel like it."

"I had a fight last night with that Rajput roommate of mine. He wasn't allowing me to study."

"Why not? Did he hit you?" she asked sounding worried. Mums seem to be able to tell what has happened when it comes to their children's lives.

"He caught my neck and tried to squeeze it so I pushed him against the bunk bed. His head hit the bunkbed bar and he stopped. I am having neck and throat pain though. What should I take?" he asked plainly.

Worried, mother asked, "Is it a dry pain or shooting pain?"

"It's dry but quite substantial pain."

"Do you have paracetamol with you?"

"Yes, I do."

"Okay. Take paracetamol with food two times a day; mostly after lunch and dinner. And apply Diclofenac[2] cream to the affected area. He must have held your neck quite tight to get such pain!"

"Yes he is quite a strong fellow. But I was quick enough to push him and loosen his grip" Ralph stated.

There was a moment of pre-eminent silence as both mother and son pondered over the strange state of affairs. The silence seemed to speak volumes. Mother seemed to question how is it that fights suddenly arose when he went on a trip with a specific purpose in mind. He seemed to say – "Why does Mum always get puzzled about my troubles and seem

---

[2] **Diclofenac** is the analgesic, topical cream widely available in India and is used to reduce pain for external inflammations.

to despise me after I let her know about them. Why can't she just support me?"

The seemingly long interval of silence was broken by Mum's characteristically poignant advice. "Are you comfortable that you are in the right direction studying German and trying to get into a German university?"

He was surprised and bewildered with her direct question. "Yes, actually I began to feel some uncertainty today after the test. It didn't go so well. Maybe because of the disturbance last night but I am also not sure if I can get admission into a university in Germany. They seem to have high standards in regards to engineering admissions" he confided.

"That's what I thought as well. It's tough to get into universities in Germany with your level of subject matter expertise. Why not try some other country. I would prefer the US" she plainly admitted.

"Baba don't wait there anymore. Just pack your stuff and come home. We can start the process of looking for an American university much sooner if you come home!" There was an air of positivity and confidence in her voice.

"This is definitely Mum speaking with one of her 'smooth decision' oriented caps on. I ought to take this advice" Ralph thought.

"Yes, I think so too. But what should I do about the deposit I paid for the room and the course money?" he asked despondently.

"Just forget it. Simply pack your stuff and walk out of there. That's it" she urged.

"Ok Mama. I will start packing right away and buy a ticket for Margao[3]. Let me see if I can get it today."

"That's the way. Do it as soon as possible."

"Okay."

"I will call you in another two hours to see how far you have gotten," she said in a supportive tone.

Ralph, now shaken from his inertia starts removing the bed sheet covers from the mattress. His spirits were lifted by Mum's clear cut advice and he started acting on the same. There was nothing more stirring than

---

[3] **Margao** is a town in the Indian state of Goa which is known for its proximity to beautiful beaches along Goa's scenic coastline.

Mum's humble and effective suggestion which many times before had more of a semblance of an order. This time it was a picture perfect direction.

"Wait a minute! I better book the ticket first and then do the packing" he said to himself. He quickly put on his jacket and rushed out to get a ticket. On the way out he noticed Bachitter not far away. The two exchanged angry stares. *"That bloody fucker…what the hell is he doing here! Guess he might have to go to Germany to get a beating from those skinheads there"* he chuckled to himself.

As he tried to cross the road a speeding Fiat car almost ran him over. "Bloody bastard! Would have almost run me over," he grimaced. Fortunately his presence of mind helped him stay alert and conscious. *"Mum's 'high concentrate coffee' like advice is strong enough to keep me going for days on end without sleep or rest!!"* he said to himself. He remembered a time when Mum was very angry with his younger brother James for soiling the walls with cough syrup. She gave him such a thrashing that he never repeated the act again.

"C & R Sons Travel" read the signboard. The office was kind of run down in a ramshackle building. "Do you have a ticket for Goa….Margao?"
"When do you want it for?" asked the sales clerk at the front desk.
"If you have anything for today I could do today," said Ralph.
"Let me see…ummmh" he opened the seat register as Ralph looked on.
"Okay, we have two seats available for the 9:30 pm bus today. Like one and half hours from now," he said giving Ralph a suggestive look.
"Would it be possible for you to be here luggage and all in one and half hours?" he asked looking concerned.
"Yes I can manage that. I don't live too far. How much is it?"
"Rs. 350 one way to Madgao" said the front desk agent.
"Okay I will take it," said Ralph as he removed three crisp notes from his wallet.

He took the ticket and rushed back to the dorm to pack up and get ready for the journey back home.

As he grabbed his wardrobe from the closet he felt a sense of hope that the new venture he was going to undertake was going to be successful and stable. *"Mum's advice can't be wrong,"* he chuckled.

The End

From the time he was a child he had come to respect and pay heed to Mum's words. Whenever he didn't, more often than not he would face dire consequences. These were a result of fate or faulty execution. Generally she didn't play any role in trying to make 'him pay for his actions.' Her words before he left for summer camp as a teenager of 14 resonated again.

"Ralph put the pants and shirts in the suitcase first. Pack the undergarments and banians[4] last. That way you can have ready access to the undergarments without removing everything from the suitcase," she had said.
"Why not just pack everything in as I come across it?" he had contested.
"If you do that you will find it difficult to remove stuff from the suitcase. Moreover you won't know where everything is placed" she suggested.

He didn't follow the advice and went to the summer camp with a haphazardly packed suitcase.

On arriving at the camp location all his friends decided to go for a swim in the community pool. As everyone removed their swimming gear Ralph groped through the clutter of his suitcase but didn't find his swimming trunks. *"Gosh, I guess I left it in the adjacent pile when I was busy packing all the stuff. Should have followed Mum's methodical way of packing!"*

He skipped the swimming sojourn and decided that from now on it would be better to consult Mum.

A loud horn from a bus on the road outside the Max Muller dorm brings him back from his flashback. He starts folding his pants first, then the shirts and finally the undergarments. The pants are neatly put into the suitcase first. Then the shirts. The undergarments go in last.

"Umm, there seems to be space in the suitcase to put these books too" he muttered to himself.

---

[4] **Banian** is used in India, meaning wife-beater as in US English.

He quickly removed the topmost layer of undergarments and neatly inserted the five books on German grammar in the suitcase. *"This red book is my favorite. I can't leave it here"* he said as he reverently placed it at the top of the book pile in the suitcase.

A sharp beeping tone from his wrist watch shook him from his reverie. "Gosh, just half an hour before I get my bus. Should be enough time to pack up and get ready" he thought. He quickly put the undergarments in the suitcase and grabbed a tiny lock to seal the zips. *"This should keep it safe till I reach home,"* he smiled. If a thief wanted to get to the stuff no lock could prevent that anyway.

"One done, two to go" he said referring to the other small suitcase and handbag that he needed to get ready. He quickly put aside the newspapers and other trash in the small room and assembled the smaller suitcase for packing. His toiletries, knick-knacks and other items were all neatly dumped in this bag. He then took the clothes he had planned to wear for the journey and inspected them.

"These pants are not well ironed but it doesn't matter. They're just jeans." He quickly took off his pants and started pulling up the jeans over his hairy legs. In less than a minute Ralph was dressed and ready to go.

He picked up his bags and headed to the bus station. *"I think I will read this paper while I wait,"* he said as he picked up "The Muller Times" and leafed through its pale yellow pages.

"Articles on Caucasian girls are always nice to read!" he grinned. Going through the articles relaxed his stressed out sinews and gave him a feeling of calm reassurance that the future was going to be alright.

The bus journey was interesting with a pretty looking girl sitting by his side. Getting off the bus, he could only think of two things though – how to continue his friendship with the girl and the need to get going on his US plans.

A FRESH START

THE COLD FEEL OF the lounge chair along with the surge of rushing passengers brings him out of his daydream and into the real-time task of boarding the plane to Philadelphia, USA. *"Gosh I got to get moving!"*

"Excuse me, is this the plane for Philadelphia, USA?" he asks a friendly looking woman tugging at her baggage.
"Well it's going to Frankfurt, Germany. What does your ticket say?" she asks, looking concerned.

Reaching into his upper pocket he grabs the ticket and reads hurriedly. *"Flight 219 to Frankfurt by Lufthansa"* he says to himself. High up on the airport roof a green screen displays:

Flight	Gate	Time
219	E3	2:30 am

The exhaustion and grogginess are replaced by a sense of purpose and urgency. Like a torpedo homing in on its target he darts towards the E gate. *"Okay, this is C so E can't be far."*

The airport is large with castle-like ceilings. Like a sky opening from under a canopy of green darkness he finds the letter that is going to get him into the land of opportunity – E.

Relieved on having reached the gate he finds a seat to settle in before thinking about the journey that will be the first international flight of his life.

"So where are you off to?" asks the white man to the other. "I am going to Paris" says the man in his typical French tone. "And you?"
"I'm going to Philadelphia. I am from America."

"Nice to meet you. So which plane are you waiting for?" asks the Frenchman innocently.

"Flight 219. I think you are taking the same one too right?"

"Yes the same one. So what you do in the USA?" he asks.

"I work for Temple University in their international marketing & relations department. I came here to conduct a seminar on educational options in the States. What brings you here?"

"I came here to represent my company for a locomotive deal with the Indian government."

The conversation makes Ralph feel like the world is indeed a small place. Here he was going to Saint Paul's University in Philadelphia and just behind his seat was an American from Philadelphia talking to a Frenchman from Paris. He wanted to interject and start a conversation with the American but waited for the right opportunity and for want of not being rude.

As the two westerners continue speaking, Ralph clearly sees the vast difference between the American mindset and that of Western Europe. While Americans prefer talking about general occurrences, events and places; Western Europeans seem to be closer in their thinking to Indians and Asians. When the Frenchman asks the American if his girlfriend works; he ignores the question and continues speaking about the US presidential election. Americans, it seems, prefer non-personal, general topics in regards to conversations with strangers.

When the Frenchman again asks if his girlfriend works, the American is silent for some time and then wearily answers in the affirmative. Ralph is puzzled at first by this and concludes that in American society, acquaintances prefer only superficial interactions. He would, at a future time, come to understand this fact with greater clarity. Realizing that the silence between the two white men is painfully long, he realizes it is time to break the ice with the American by starting a conversation.

"So you are from Temple University huh," he says turning to the American. "I am going to St. Paul's University in Philadelphia," he completes without waiting for the American to answer his first question, albeit rhetorical.

"Oh really. What are you going to study there?"

"I am going to study Computer Science" replies Ralph. "How was your trip to India?"

"It was great. I got to see so many lovely places and meet nice people," replies the American.

Just as they begin to get familiar with each other the announcement that everyone was waiting for is heard from the creaky speaker: "Flight 219 has arrived. All passengers for Flight 219 please get ready to board your plane."

"Well, it was really nice meeting you. Do keep in touch" says the American.

"Do you have an email address?" quips Ralph.

"Oh yeah. I could write it if you want."

"I have a good memory. Just say it and I will remember," says Ralph.

With the email obtained, Ralph decides to keep it in mind and email his new found acquaintance when he arrives in the States.

As he walks into the plane, Ralph is pleasantly surprised to see two beautiful, blond-haired hostesses. He asks for his seat and is directed to the numbers on the overhead luggage compartments. Seat found, he quickly lifts his carry-ons and places them in the compartment above his seat. The aisle seat is always better when someone wants to access the restroom easily. However, it also involves getting up to accommodate the requirements of your fellow passengers sitting in the seats next to you.

Ralph was in such a position. A dark south Indian looking man walked beside him and asked to access the middle seat in the row. Ralph got up and obliged. As they settled down Ralph noticed the Tamilian[5] man gradually pushing his hands against Ralph's flanks trying to take as much arm-rest space as possible.

At a certain point his arms started poking into Ralph's flanks. "Stop poking into my sides. Your elbows are coming into my space" protested Ralph. The man didn't seem to budge. "This is the arm-rest and I am using it" he retorted. "But you can't put your elbow into my side".

The argument reached a point where both parties were contesting petty real estate. However, Ralph's case seemed genuine as it was his space that was being invaded. An air hostess got involved and decided to put

---

[5] Tamilian refers to someone from the state of Tamil Nadu in India

an end to the commotion. "Sir please could you remove your hand from there. That space belongs to both parties and you need to restrict the exclusive use of that space," she politely admonished the man.
He refused to comply. "We might need to call security if you do not remove your hand" she stated firmly.

On this, the man immediately withdrew his hand and Ralph was relieved. The rest of the journey was quite uneventful until the plane touched down on the hard tarmac of Frankfurt, Germany.

Ralph was tired, but relieved to be in the country he would have loved to be in for good but could not. Mum and Dad had won the argument against him on that. For now, he enjoyed the sights and sounds of the country of his dreams. A blond lass walking past him grabbed his attention as he sat down with his handbag. He wished he could go right behind her and make sweet, tender talk with her if not entirely grab her. As she disappeared among the melee of travelers he was left thinking about the probable good times he might have had was he in a university in Germany. At that very moment a slim, Caucasian girl came and stood in front of him. "*Waitress!*" he thought for a second.

Although a little taken aback at first, he maintained his calm as he smiled at her. "Can I take this seat?" she asked.
"Absolutely" he said concealing his ecstasy. "So where are you off to?" he asked.
"I'm going to the United States," she asserted.
"Oh yeah. Me too."
"Where are you going" she asked.
"I'm going to Philadelphia."
"Oh wow. What a coincidence. I'm going to Philly too. You have family there?" she smiled seeing the similarity in final destinations.
"I'm going to do my Masters in computer science there."
"Oh great! Which university?" she sounded more interested.
"Saint Paul's University"
"That's a nice university."
"Yes, it is. My family has a Jesuit background so I thought of going to a Jesuit university. Besides my father has a good friend in that university."

He knew that white people were not easy to befriend. But like all things in life there were exceptions. And if he maintained a decent distance in the initial stages, he would probably be able to start a meaningful friendship if not more. Through tough trials and a million rejections, Ralph had come to understand that friendship with women takes a little time. Unless of course the woman is very friendly and very much "into you." In this case, though, he wasn't sure and was simply testing the waters to find out.

"So is this your first time in the US or have you been here before?"

"No, this will be my first time in the States" he smiled.

"Oh wow. How do you feel?" she says looking concerned.

"A little anxious but also rather ignorant as I do not know much about what's going to happen or what I am going to do. Of course, one thing is certain that I am going to do my studies and get a degree there."

"So how is life in the US different and what can I expect in terms of study help and other things?" he asked, looking concerned.

"It's pretty simple and straightforward. Nothing extraordinary or different from what you have in your country I'm sure. You should be fine," she said in a reassuring tone.

"I tend to worry too much about what I am going to face or have to be ready for. Is there anything in particular that I need to be prepared for, like communication skills, technical skillset, etc.?" he politely followed up.

"Your communication skills are perfect, I assure you. You really don't have to worry about anything. Just go with the flow and you should be fine. I know it can be hard for people coming from a different country to adjust to the States because the cultures are so different. So there is a bit of a learning curve" she said with a tone of solidarity.

"Okay.".

There is a long period of silence as though both are in a trance. Ralph looks down at the glazed cream floor as though pondering what's going to happen. Uncertainty is something that is usually not resolved until you have lived through it. After living through the uncertainty you realize how precarious the different facts in the situation were and which factors had a greater degree of certainty in them.

"So what time is your flight? Oops I forgot same time as mine right. Which is at 11am European time" she said. "We have almost 6 hours to get by, I guess."

"Six hours will go by in a jiffy. Anyways, you certainly seem to be good company!" smiled Ralph.

"Oh that's so sweet of you!" she laughed.

As they kept speaking, Ralph employed his traditional charm to seduce the pretty lass.

"So what do you do for fun?" he asked.
"Oh, I am so occupied with my work that I hardly have much of a social life. But my sister is very outgoing and she pulls me with her wherever she goes. We mostly go to bars, clubs, restaurants and parties."
"Oh nice. What type of restaurants do you go to? As in what type of food do you like?"
"I like Thai food a lot. And Italian also. But after coming to India I think Indian food has won me over. I knew a couple of Indian restaurants in Philadelphia. I will probably visit them when I reach Philly" she averred.
"Yes, I would like to know where these restaurants are as well!"
"Sure. Just email me when you get home. I mean to your university."
"Could I have your email address?" he asked as he pulled out a small notepad from his shirt pocket. Mum had always told him to keep a notepad whenever he went anywhere. That way he could jot down stuff whenever he came across anything. He now saw the value of the pad. *"Mum can help me meet more women and keep in touch with them"* he quipped to himself suppressing a veritable blush.

As she jotted down her email he looked at the symmetric features on her face. She was fair, dainty and nubile. All the characteristics that would make a young man like him swoon. Her slim nose and tender skin made her ideal wife material. But then there is more to a wife than just looks.

"Hey do you cook?" she asked as she handed him the notepad after jotting down the email address.
"Yes I do."
"Wow that's interesting! How did you learn to cook?"
"Well, my Dad cooks since Mum isn't very good at cooking. So I essentially picked it up from him. I was impressed by how he made such terrific dishes so I decided to take his guidance to learn cooking myself." he explained.
"So what food do you cook?"
"I make all types of spicy, curry based meat dishes, beef, chicken and pork. However, in the pork department we have a traditional advantage since I come from a former Portuguese colony in India," he specified. "I make biryani which is a dish consisting of chicken and rice. It is spicy

but can be made sweet depending on your taste preference. Have you had biryani before?"

"No…what bury…aneee…..what is that. What do you call it?" she is at a loss for words. Most Americans not exposed to the Oriental way of life are at a loss to understand or pronounce various words endemic to Asia.

"It's called biryani. The name doesn't sound as good as it tastes" he smiled. "Besides that, I make pork related dishes like vindaloo, sorpotel and a host of others."

"Woah you make vindaloo?"

"You know about vindaloo?"

"Of course I do. It's an amazing dish" she said trying to sound knowledgeable.

"Where did you come across it?"

"I had a Brazilian friend who made it for me and it was amazing. So you make vindaloo huh!"

"Yes we use special types of vinegars and ingredients from Portugal and other parts of Asia and indeed from India to make it. The kind of meat that we get in Goa is terrific because we don't use steroids or any medications on them. The livestock is bred on farms and fed naturally growing hay and fodder. Have you ever heard of sorpotel?"

"No! What is it?"

"Then you are missing something. Sorpotel is the premier Goan dish known for its aroma and mouthwatering flavors. Most people who come to Goa are so enamored with the dish that they stay a couple of weeks; sometimes months longer simply to savor sorpotel a little more. And I am not just making this up. It actually happens."

"I had this friend from Germany who would come every year to Goa in July. He would stay for four months until October and throughout those four months sorpotel would be on his dinner menu. In fact whenever we invited him to our place we made sure we had home-made sorpotel."

"So how do you make this sorpotel?" she asks, looking curious.

"Well every family has a different way of making the dish. And this difference arises from the types of ingredients used."

(Pauses) "But there is a general, signature style of making the dish. It mostly involves marinating the pork for a bit with specific condiments, lots of chili powder, vinegar, garlic and cloves. Then after a couple of hours, sometimes minutes we start cooking the meat with the masalas we have assembled."

She looks a little confused with what he has said. But doesn't question him further. All the talk about the complicated recipe is like wild fire burning through her grey cells.

Ralph knew that pleasant imagination always worked with people. So he decided to embellish the particulars of the recipe. Not that it was entirely fictitious but his imagination made the dish seem even more delectable and difficult to make. The more difficult it is to make, the tastier it is generally considered to be.

The outgoing and passionate Ralph didn't seem to mind the innocuous tales as long as they impressed pretty women. Behind his playful demeanor, there was an element of a go-getter which made him particularly predisposed to taking risks whether it was with opportunities or getting into favor with women. He always seemed to have this intuitive feel for spotting good looking women wherever he went. He seemed to be playing his game now. And it was working so far.

"You seem confused. Is everything alright?" asked Ralph.

"Yes…ummmh you seem to have some interesting food in Goa. I'd sure like to try it someday."

"Absolutely! Probably I can make some for you someday."

"That would be great! Thanks."

"Only problem is I don't have a lot of vessels to make the dish; not to mention the spices. Probably I can cook it at your place if you have a relatively big kitchen."

"Oh yeah, I currently live with my parents and they have a real big kitchen. You should come to our place sometime," she beamed.

"That would be nice. Does your family like spicy food?"

"Dad likes it but Mum is a bit in favor of sweet tasting food."

"Okay. I am going to have quite a time getting adjusted and settled when I come, but it would be a good idea to make the dish and have you taste it," he smiled.

"By the way, do you have ICQ or any sort of messenger?"

"Messenger what's that?" she queried.

"It's a chat service like Skype or Yahoo messenger."

"I used to use yahoo messenger but don't anymore" she replied.

"Man can you believe we have been talking so long. And didn't even exchange names. I'm Ralph. You are?"

"I am Jessica. (She laughs) Nice to meet you. Strange right, we spoke for such a long time and didn't even know each other's names."

"I guess we got so engaged in the conversation that we totally forgot about that part of the introduction. In fact, when two people enjoy the conversation and each other's company you don't really need a name!"

Both of them had a hearty laugh. They continued chatting and only stopped to take a breath or get some rest from the strain of constantly moving their mouths. For a moment, Ralph felt that both of them were in a glass bubble. The whole world with its hustle and bustle and the entire disturbance in the airport was part of some other universe or dimension. He felt a kind of connection with this girl. A kind of oneness. And it was only a couple of hours since they had met.

"How could I be feeling such an intense attachment to this lady? Is it because she is white and good looking?" He was not able to fathom the source of his attraction to her. *"Phew! Let's just enjoy the conversation while I can"* he thought.

As they continued chatting, the beautiful Jessica was captivated by the charms of this fine young man. Not only was he handsome, but so fun to get along with. Kind, considerate and gentle. *"He must have a girlfriend. I mean he's so nice. Any girl would fall for him!"* she thought to herself.

The six hours waiting period seemed like six minutes. And before they were ready to wind up their conversation the announcement is heard. "All passengers on Flight 220 for Philadelphia please get ready to board the plane."

"There it goes. Guess we will be in the air pretty soon. What's your seat number?" she asked looking anxious.
"I am in E14" said Ralph.
"Oh, I guess we won't be sitting close to each other then. It would have been great to have your company."
"Yes of course. But I guess I will don the dress of an air hostess and visit you periodically to serve you drinks!" he quipped.

They shudder with fits of laughter. As they got ready to board; Ralph gently reached out and helped Jessica with her coat and bag. She smiled as she willingly accepted the help. As they proceeded to the boarding gate Ralph noticed the smile on Jessica's face growing wider with satisfaction. He felt certain she was into him. More often than not, it takes a mix of small talk and chivalry to win a woman over.

The flight is long and Ralph sleeps through most of it. Having been exposed to the real deal he doesn't have any wet dreams; just pure rest. The sound of the plane screeching to a halt on the tarmac wakes him from his peaceful slumber.

****

"Welcome to the USA," said the voice over the microphone. He was anxious to find out what the new world looked like and glared through the plane window at the unfamiliar surroundings outside. There seemed to be this air of perfect orderliness in the way everything was arranged on the airport. "*Is this the way it is all over this vast country?*" he thought to himself. "*Is this the reason they call it the most powerful country in the world? Such cleanliness and order!*"

As the passengers gathered in the aisle to alight from the plane, he looked back to see if Jessica was anywhere in sight. In the distance, he noticed her staggering to her feet; handbag on shoulder. He would have loved to go and help her get steady but the mass of bodies between the two of them was too dense to get through; at least during the exit time period. He looked forward and proceeded to take his handbag out of the overhead compartment.

Bag in hand, he proceeded to the exit and thanked the air hostesses for the pleasant trip.
As he walked on he wished he could get to meet the lovely lass again. At least for one last quick minute.
As he approached the immigration area, a greater urgency began to occupy his thinking. The student advisors he had been in touch with had agreed to come and give him a ride to the university campus. "*Where could they be? I guess I will meet them after I collect my baggage*" he thought.

The sign atop read in bold white characters:

International travelers proceed this way

Feeling disoriented, he wondered what the time might be. His black dial watch still reflected the time in India. He quickly hurried up the escalator and stood in line to be interviewed by the immigration officers in black fatigues.

As soon as he stood in line a number of other counters opened up. He decided to proceed to another where he could get through faster. Seeing him vacillate; the officer at a counter with no line motioned to Ralph to come to the counter.

The officer was a young guy and seemed ill at ease that morning. "Where are you coming from?" he asked curtly. Before Ralph could complete his reply he asked another question "What are you coming here for?" The officer didn't even wait for him to answer the first question before asking him the remaining questions.
"I am from Goa, India. I am coming here to do my studies in computer science."
As Ralph was answering the officer asked again "Who told you about this university?"
"My mentor."
"Who?"
"From global hawks in SJU." Ralph was unfazed by the back-to-back questions in quick succession. "When in doubt remain silent" was Dad's advice. Ralph maintained a steely calm in the face of unwarranted and demeaning behavior by the USCIS (US Customs & Immigration Services) officer. His rigid silence forced the officer to rethink his questioning strategy.

Realizing that he was needlessly questioning the young man he stopped the rapid fire questions and asked him for his paperwork. He entered a couple of details into the computer terminal and then turned around to Ralph.

"Do you have any cash?"

Ralph remained mum not knowing what to answer. Mum had given him a few hundred dollars to weather the first few weeks with. But he was not used to this fashion of rapid fire questions.

"Any travelers' checks?" the young officer repeated noticing Ralph's silence.

Either due to embarrassment or mere surprise at the rapid speed of
questions, Ralph stayed mum. Embarrassment as he had not brought any
travelers checks or another form of money with him. Surprise because
so far he had never been questioned by anyone in the way that he was
being questioned now.

The officer stapled a card to his passport. "Go to the immigration
checking in department and get yourself registered there." Ralph asked
him where it is. The officer visibly frustrated either with his job or with
Ralph's silence simply shrugged his shoulders and called upon the next
person in the line.

Ralph proceeds to the broad atrium looking for the word 'immigration'
on any of the signposts. He stops a kindly looking police officer and
asks him what to do in order to get his luggage and other paper work
sorted out. The officer points him in a certain direction. "*Never have I
felt so uncertain!*" he says to himself. Feeling lightheaded he proceeds
to the large counter. The officers behind the counter are quite oblivious
to his presence much unlike the officer at the initial airport screening
desk.

"This bitch doesn't even call me on weekends; nor does she answer my
voicemail messages" says a portly looking police officer to his comrade.
"Well then I guess you are going to have to tell her to screw off!!" says
the other with a wide smile.

Both of them crack up.

Ralph looks silently at both of them and smiles. Seeing the gentle
youngster standing nonchalantly at the counter, they sense a degree of
calmness in him. From behind the desk, the portly officer walks up to
the young man and looks at him calmly.

"Is this the place international students need to come to get their details
sorted out and to start the course?" asks Ralph.
"Absolutely you came to the right place," says Officer Chamar.

In spite of all his apprehensions and uncertainties, for a moment Ralph
feels confident and cool that things will be okay. He had the same
feeling of hope and excitement when he was speaking to Jessica at the

German airport. He hoped this would be the last of the check-ins and procedures he would have to do for the day. He was right.

The officer directed him to the area where the bags were being brought out from the airplane containers. Ralph quickly walked to the area and waited. Seeing a few girls from India he decided to go and say hello. They were the only familiar faces in a sea of 'alien Americans.'

"I guess you need currency to get those trolleys right" he asks a girl.
"Yes. It's one dollar and fifty cents a trolley," she replies smiling at the handsome desi[6].
"Where did you get the currency from?" he asks.
"From home!" she replies still smiling, visibly impressed by the handsome lad.

Ralph senses that these girls are here for a company work assignment. Probably working for Wipro or Infosys or some other Indian IT company. As the two Indian girls begin carting their luggage using the trolley they look to see if the young, handsome guy is going to accompany them or whether they should wait for him. There seems to be this unsaid bond when one meets people from the same country or region. That although they might not even speak when in the same country; on seeing each other abroad they immediately band together. He also had this very same feeling when the two girls waited and looked behind to see if he was going to come with them.

Unfortunately not only had his baggage not arrived on the moving belt; he realized he didn't have the change to get a trolley. So he waited looking for the suitcases with a yellow mark on them. One after another, the suitcases rolled by like large cakes on a conveyor belt. "*Life is one long wait,*" he said to himself.

Then as though like a ripe pod whose time has come; he finally saw what he was waiting for, for what seemed like an eternity. Two black suitcases with round yellow circles on them came rolling by. The yellow ribbon on them seemed like a symbol depicting the new world of America; a symbol of freedom and unbridled opportunity.

---

[6] Desi – is a Hindi word which refers to inhabitants of India; it is also used as an adjective to refer to anything Indian like.

He would need to make great efforts to reap the benefits from these opportunities and be more focused than he had ever been. Pulling the bags off the conveyor belt, he resolved to focus his energies on achieving worthwhile results and dedicating himself to a greater good.

"Okay. Now I've got to go and find those international student advisor guys waiting for me; if they are waiting for me!" he thinks. As he approaches the exit of the airport, he tries to scour the landscape for familiar looking faces but sees none. After waiting for half an hour he begins to realize that may be they have forgotten. He goes to a pay phone but realizes he cannot seem to use it either because the coins he has inserted don't seem to be adequate or simply because he doesn't know how to use the phone. When in a foreign country, a small measure of disorientation gets magnified tenfold, not because it is really complicated but because fear leads the mind to gravitate to a more complex level of reality.

"Okay I better go to that small department store over there and ask for some change or help" he thinks to himself.
"Excuse me do you have a pay phone or something here?"
"You could use that one over there" comes the quick reply.
"I just did. It doesn't seem to work," he says.
"Well it should if you put some coins in it," says the lady at the counter.
"Actually I am new here and am not sure if the coins I have put in are enough or correct. How much does it cost for a local call?" he asks.
"It's a quarter, 25 cents for a call. Do you have change?"
Taking the few coins from his pocket he shows her all he has.
She smiles and says "Umm this is not enough. You just have 20 cents here"
"Would you like some coins?" she asks.
"Yes sure," Ralph says greedily.
"Okay how many dollars of change do you want?"
"Pardon!" says Ralph.
"How many dollars would you like to give to get the change?" asks the lady again, looking puzzled by his hesitation.

Ralph is a little baffled by the question. He thought she would give him the 5 cents he needed to make a call free of charge. He ponders over her question and then guesses. *"Here in America it is a true quid pro quo.*

Nobody is going to give you anything free of charge or just to help you out. Not even 5 cents," he thinks to himself.

Many internationals that come to the States are often baffled by the extent of transactional relationships people have without making the strong bonds that matter. In Asia and many other parts of the world, relationship building is crucial before any transaction or business dealing can take place. Well, at least that's the norm of business in Asia and many other parts of the world. Not that such relationships can be made with every Tom, Dick and Harry that you come across; but in being so robotic while conducting business, people often divorce possibilities of forming strong relationships with people looking to build a strong connection.

Ralph hoped that he would meet people who would be more open to chatting and mingling in the future. "Hopefully the atmosphere at the university would be different!" he thought. But then again, this is just one instance; the first interaction he has had with local America.

Groping into his wallet he hands over a crisp five dollar bill to her. Mum had given him some clear, crisp US currency and he looks at the notes very lovingly as he puts the rest back into the wallet. The lady quickly opens the cash register and dispenses a bunch of quarters to Ralph.

"Wow. Quick service!" says Ralph impressed by her speed and efficiency.
"That's the USA for you. That's how we do it here," she says with a touch of arrogance in her voice. She senses he is not from the US from his demeanor.

Ralph is impressed but says nothing. He walks to the pay phone (which evidently the lady called a 'payson') and puts in a coin. Grabbing the booklet from his bag, he turns to the third page and looks at the number. With Zen-like concentration, he inserts the coin and types the number of the global hawk's mentor he had communicated with.

After a long ring, an Indian sounding voice picks up.

"Hello. Sandeep here."

"Hi Sandy. This is Ralph. I am at the Philadelphia International Airport. I am trying to find you. Where are you?"

"Oh gosh. I guess I forgot about this appointment."

"What!" says Ralph sounding bewildered.

"Yeah we had a long day yesterday with admissions and totally forgot about your arrival. So sorry! Let me contact the other global hawks members and try to get someone to the airport for you," says Sandeep sounding guilty.

"What time do you think you will be able to make it?" Ralph asks sounding worried.

"It will take some time as we need to go to the security office and request the van," says a helpless Sandeep.

"Oh man. Like one hour or so?" probes Ralph.

"A little more than that," claims Sandeep in a weak sounding voice.

Ralph is helplessly silent on hearing this.

"Okay. Well I will wait for you at the entrance of the airport. Please let me know when you reach here. I am sitting next to a store selling water and general goods."

"Yes okay. Thanks. We will come as soon as we can," says Sandeep sounding apologetic for not making it on time and thankful that Ralph maintained his cool.

Ralph feeling dejected manages to scrape just one word "Thanks" as he slides the phone onto the hook.

He goes to a nearby tiled bench and rests his suitcases against it. Then sits himself down as he plainly looks at the alien surroundings waiting for his university mentor to show up.

As he waits, he wishes Jessica would miraculously appear and start talking to him. But she doesn't. He reminisces about the time he spent with her at the German airport. *"Man didn't even get to say good bye to her!"* he thinks to himself feeling dejected.

Seeing the continuous barrage of rushing, weary, beautiful and different travelers passing by he begins to contemplate. *"These people are all rushing as though they have a definite purpose in life. I am sure they have their families and homes here and are rushing to meet up with their loved ones. I have no one here. Not even a relative I can reach out*

28

to! The uncle that I have down in Georgia is a mere namesake. They wouldn't want to have anything to do with me given his relations with Mum & Dad. Nevertheless, it must be nice to have a definite aim in life. Even though I do not have anything at the moment – no wealth, money or family; I would like to have a purpose in life. It would make life more livable and help me feel accomplished" he thinks.

"I need to figure out this purpose before it is too late. Everything else will fall into place once I have a direction. Then I can become like an American rushing throughout the day. This will get me closer to becoming a wealthier person and I will get to hobnob with the rich and famous" he ponders.

His thoughts begin to run wild as he sits in the land of opportunity, no family, and no ride in sight. Ralph's thoughts resemble a strong urge in international students coming to the US to succeed and do well. However, Ralph was of a more enterprising nature. He wanted to do something beyond just getting a degree and trying for a job. He wanted to get as well settled as the normal upper class citizens in the US. America is still disproportionately associated with being a white nation even though you have scores of other nationalities and ethnicities living here. Quite a few things changed after the terrorist attacks of Sept 11th though. With greater security measures put in place and inspections and questioning becoming more rigid, things were quite different than before.

His thoughts didn't factor in the difficulties, though; only the possibilities. As thoughts of progressive growth raced through his grey matter he could feel his soul resolving to work towards his goals. The thoughts made the hours pass faster. When he began to feel that the student advisors from the university might be close by he was grateful that his purposeful thoughts had not allowed his mind to remain vacant.

It would be another forty five minutes before he would actually see them though.

For a moment he thought of taking a taxi and getting to the university himself. However, the $30 ride seemed too expensive when the conversion from dollars to rupees was ascertained at the current exchange rate. Ralph had half a mind to walk to the university. But with two bags and one handbag, and also the jetlag he just wasn't in any position to walk the sixteen odd miles to the destination.

****

A thin-looking guy adorned in a bright red shirt and blue cap walked towards Ralph as though having known him for years. Ralph, who was staring at the ceiling of the atrium, deep in his thoughts, felt the warmth of the approaching silhouette. He hadn't felt this since he had left Dad's embrace back in Mumbai, India. Not even with Jessica.

Before he turned his line of vision the silhouette had got within a few inches of him. There stood a very Asian-looking young kid, slight in built; bold in spirit. He wasn't as well built as Ralph but there seemed to be this unique strength about him that wasn't freely found; not at least in this market dominated, materialistic world.

For some reason, Ralph had an inkling that he had entered an environment where money was valued more than morals, performance more than genuine efforts and power more than ability. "How was the plane trip! You look tired," said the young, smart looking kid standing in front of Ralph. Coming out of his momentary daydream, Ralph felt happy that this Asian youth was there to help him. At least that's what his intentions seemed to be.

"Sorry we got here so late. We had totally forgotten about your trip after momentarily going through that email you sent before leaving India." "That's alright. So how are we going to go to the university?" asked Ralph not wanting to spend more time exchanging pleasantries. "Well we are taking you to the apartment first," said Sandeep. "Which apartment?" "We have a group of Indian students staying in a two bedroom apartment and they need an additional roommate."

Ralph got an inkling of how many Asians stay once in the US. Group sharing is another word for breaking even. Rents can be expensive so there is a need to reduce the burden of costs. This can be done by sharing living space with friends or colleagues.

Sandeep voluntarily grabbed one of the suitcases and Ralph took hold of the other. As they left the airport facility; Ralph followed Sandeep as though a child following its parent. Sandeep led him to a maroon van parked beside the road.

HARDSHIP IN PARADISE

THE DRIVE TO THE apartment which was close to the university was about eight miles. With traffic and other hindrances, it took almost forty-five minutes to get to the destination. In the back of the maroon van, Ralph felt it was like a ride from one time zone to another. As though he was in a time machine, traversing worlds with landscapes that were light years apart. The streets, markets and people were totally mesmerizing and produced more than a fair bit of culture shock.

"Gosh what are these people wearing in summer" thought Ralph, seeing a woman wearing a very short mini-skirt with a halter that seemed as though it would drop from her breasts. *"Why do we need to stop at every cross road?"* he wondered as the driver hit the brakes before every stop sign. Even though he was itching to ask he decided to stay mum to prevent his hosts from feeling the overwhelming feelings he was experiencing. It's always best to reserve your strong emotions and feelings for the appropriate time particularly when amongst acquaintances rather than with family.

"In times of great despair and uncertainty do not forget to keep your calm; no matter how urgent and painful the situation might seem. Your calmness and serenity will defeat the adversity of the situation" said Papa to Ralph when he was struggling to get a job in Goa. Within three months of saying that Ralph had made up his mind to seek greener pastures abroad.

"So this is the place where you will be staying" said Sandeep pointing to the massive building complex.
Ralph was still in his daydream and just looked at the building plainly. It looked somewhat like the buildings he was used to back in India; only bigger and cleaner.

He felt more tired from the forty-five minute road drive to the apartment building than the twenty hours he had spent flying from India. *"Probably it's these varied sights and sounds and of course people that I just saw in the last forty-five minutes that made me feel so disoriented and tired,"* thought Ralph to himself. Culture shock is a major factor that adds to the overall confusion of being in a new country with very different looking people and different looking things, customs and styles.

Reluctantly, he pulls himself from the comfort of the soft seats in the van. For some reason, the van seems like a haven; a source of security, comfort and belonging. Almost like the last vestige of home. As he gets ready to pull the suitcases from the back of the van, Sandeep and the other guy join in helping him unload.

"Pretty heavy suitcase buddy," says the lean looking Sandeep with a wide smile. The other guy pitches in to help Sandeep.
"Yes. Just brought whatever was necessary to be comfortable in the US," says Ralph smiling.
"Well we'll show you where the apartment is," says Sandeep.

They take the heavy laden suitcases and proceed to the thirteenth floor of the massive building.

"There are 3 complexes in this community. But you will be housed in the A complex as we have a vacancy here. Three new guys came here a few weeks ago and they are looking for a fourth person to share," informed Sandeep.

International students, particularly from Asia generally look to share living space with friends from the same country. This arrangement helps to split the cost of the rent and thus reduces the financial burden on each student. It is generally understood that most of the students who come to non-Ivy league universities in the US do not always have extensive means to fund their education. Moreover the courses are amazingly expensive given that the conversion of a weaker currency into a stronger dollar takes a lot of cash out of bank accounts in non-Western countries. They, therefore seek to cut corners and skimp on expenses that are ancillary to living in the US.

In regards to unavoidable expenses like course fees; international students look to subsidize such expenses by seeking assistantships and scholarships. It is no guess why several assistantship positions are occupied by international students in many universities in the US. Financial support is a big deal when it comes to living in a foreign country.

The elevator ride to the thirteenth floor seemed to take forever. Ralph wished it would end quickly. He just wanted to lay his bags down and get used to the environs of the new country he was to spend the next few years living in.

The two young men lead him down a dank, dark corridor into a small vestibule where a faded yellow door masked a story of neglect and poor building maintenance. Sandy knocks on the door once, twice and then four times before a stirring noise is heard on the other end. Just as he is about to pick up his cell phone and call the person on the inside, the door begins to open.

"Hey Sandeep. How are you?" says the slender looking boy inside.
"Hi Rajendra. This is your new roommate from India. His name is Ralph."
With the big suitcase reclining against the wall Ralph wearily extends his hand to Rajendra.
"Nice to meet you. I am Ralph."
"Welcome. Come in. Which part of India are you from?" asks the curious looking kid.
"I am from Goa" he replies plainly not asking Rajendra anything. He is too tired to concern himself with their particulars.
"And what are you here to study?" asks Rajendra immediately.
"Computer science."

A long pause ensues in the communication as Ralph refrains from following up with any questions for Rajendra. A monologue is a sure sign of lack of interest in a communication. Sensing the silence, Rajendra also halts the barrage of questions. After laying his bags down in the hall, Ralph decides to take a few moments for himself.

"Could I use the bathroom?"
"Sure absolutely!" says Rajendra.
"Of course!" says Sandeep nodding his head.

He heads to the bathroom, locks the door behind him and just stares at the mirror. It is quite dark in there so with the light turned on Ralph splashes water on his face. Then looks at the mirror again as though muttering to himself *"gosh what am I going to do now!"*

There is this overwhelming feeling of being lost and alone when you come to the States. It is no secret that most international students without extended families experience this feeling. Not that those with extended families in the US don't experience this forlorn feeling; but those who are here alone feel it way more. And that's just a fact of life of trying to make it in the States on your own.

The joint habitation format of staying has its advantages in that it places students in similar situations in close proximity of each other. Friendships and partnerships develop. The support network helps pull people out of depression or other unhealthy moods. It's not just a lack of resources that plagues several students from foreign countries but the lack of family too. The network of friends and roommates in these cramped apartments serves as a stop-gap support network while degree programs are completed and jobs are found.

It's strange but true that the downsides of several people staying in one apartment are many times made up for by the advantages of better information sharing, stronger relationships and growing camaraderie between the members living in the house. These members are by no means predisposed to friendship with each other, but fostering a good relationship almost always happens as they are brought together by fate and circumstance. It is often believed that while fate brings them together; it is their will to succeed that helps them make it in the US.

Ralph walks into the living room where Sandeep seems to be giving Rajendra some info on the newcomer. Although similar to Ralph in terms of his youthful looks, Sandeep's demeanor is characteristic of a mentor and advisor to the inexperienced students fresh off the boat.

"So boss, take some time to rest. You look tired. Are you hungry?" asks Sandeep.
"Yes actually. A little."
"You got anything to eat man" Sandeep asks Rajendra.

35

"We have some apples. We can show you where we keep them" says Rajendra.

"Ah. He is hungry. Why don't you give him the apple now and then we can do everything else" urges Sandeep.

When it comes to resources; monetary or food, Asian students tend to economize. They come from a mentality of saving as opposed to splurging.

Rajendra directs Ralph to a cabinet in the kitchen and removes one apple from the bowl containing several apples. Ralph eats the apple greedily and goes to the living room where Sandeep and Rajendra are looking at the concrete landscape outside. Although Pennsylvania is a very beautiful state full of green woods and forests; several parts of Philadelphia are heavily built up with tall buildings and factories all around.

As Ralph approaches the two with the apple almost devoured, they seem to be extremely peaceful and pleasant. *"How can these two be so peaceful and calm when I am so anxious and frazzled!"* he wonders.

He would soon realize that it doesn't just take knowledge about everything in your environment. But also a resilient hope that no matter how much there is to learn and cover, one will get there with steadfastness and diligence.

"So Ralph bhai[7] let's sit down and chat for some time" says Sandeep, patting Ralph gently on the shoulder.

All three young men sit on the small couch and adjust themselves.

"So are you taking courses this semester?" asks Sandeep.

"Yes....." Ralph is interrupted before he can complete.

"What! Because classes for the semester start tomorrow," Sandeep says looking worried.

"You came one day before classes! That's a little difficult. Normally students come one or more weeks before the semester starts so they get some time to settle down."

---

[7] Bhai – a word in Hindi meaning brother or "loved one"

"Nobody told me to come earlier. So I took the ticket which was cheapest."

Sandeep and Rajendra look at each other surprised.

"Anyways don't worry about it. What's happened has happened. Can't change that now. Let's see what we can do," says Sandeep on a conciliatory note.

Indians from Andhra Pradesh generally have substantial knowledge of the American system and how it works before they come here. Moreover they plan well before they reach the place; most of the time. There are always instances of those unprepared folks who come to the States on a feather and a prayer. It is God that watches over them.

"Okay, what class do you have tomorrow?" asks Sandeep.
"I am not sure. I think it is an introductory class into data architectures," says a disoriented and bewildered Ralph.
"You have done your four year degree in India right. So I think your first course will be an introductory course. I had that too. It was an introduction to data structures and databases," Sandeep says not wanting to argue.

He pauses a while and says "Do you have your university login and password?"

Ralph is silent. "You should have received it before coming here. It is sent a few days after admission actually," specifies Sandeep.
"I could see what courses you are registered for from your university login. Do you want to see it?" he asks.
Ralph although a little unsure agrees to the proposition. "Sure. I don't have a computer with me though," he says.
"No problem. Rajendra could I borrow your laptop for a while?" requests Sandeep.
"No! Just kidding," says Rajendra as he hands over the laptop to Sandeep.
"Okay, so what's the laptop password? Enter it here please" he says noticing hesitation from Rajendra.

Computer and email account passwords are always prized property as they contain keys to the entire life of people. No wonder people don't generally give this information out to strangers and many times not even to family members.

Rajendra enters the password and gives the laptop to Sandeep. He immediately types in the university website in the internet browser and goes to the login page. Asking Ralph to enter his credentials he looks away as Ralph keys in his password.

"Okay, so you have to go under Student Services tab and check academic profile to see what courses you are registered for. This is the way all students get an understanding of the courses they are taking and how much more they need to take to graduate," he says calmly.
Ralph stares at the screen. "So it shows that I am taking three courses for this semester. Introduction to data structures is one of them."
"The other two are algorithm design and social engineering. Social engineering is a good class. You will have to do a group project for this one," informs Sandeep.
"What textbooks are needed for these courses?"
"The professor usually specifies what textbook is needed on the first day of class. Some professors email the syllabus before the first class as well. Have you received any email for any of these classes?"
"I didn't the last time I checked my email," replies Ralph.
"Don't worry so much. If you don't have the textbooks you can get them from the library or order them through interlibrary loan. Sometimes old students have the books so they can lend theirs to you as well," says Sandeep sensing Ralph's worries.

Textbooks can be expensive and as an international student; one looks to cut costs and economize wherever possible. Ralph was in one such boat.

"Do you have any books for these courses?"
"I will have to check but I don't believe I do since it has been some time since I took these classes. You can always ask other senior students if they have their copies with them. There are many Indian desi students in computer science, so it is generally easier to get books or other material from them," says Sandeep.
"What about white or Chinese students?" asks Ralph.
"Generally white people might not give their books. That's been my experience but there are always exceptions. You could try," shrugs Sandeep.

"And Chinese?"

"I have not really asked Chinese people but you could ask them in Chinese or Mandarin!"

Both of them burst out into laughter. "Well I barely know computer science so maybe I don't have the time to learn Mandarin right now," howls Ralph.

"Don't worry. You will get there," says Sandeep.

"So when are you going to give me a tour of the university. Just so I can see where everything is located and get familiar with the various resources we have."

"Well most of it is self-explanatory but if you want a tour I could give you one," Sandeep assures.

"Yes that would be great. But class starts tomorrow. What time can we do it tomorrow?" asks Ralph.

"Tomorrow morning is a little tight for me. But I could do later in the evening tomorrow if possible. It shouldn't take too long. This campus is relatively small compared to larger universities like Drexel or Temple."

"But I would say for tonight just get some rest so that you are fresh for tomorrow's class and hectic schedule. Things can get pretty hectic here, pretty fast. Have you reported to the international students' office on campus?"

"No," says Ralph.

"Well, that's the first thing you should do when you reach the States. The office will be closed now or going to close so no point rushing there now. What you can do as your game plan for tomorrow though, is go to the office and meet with Sarah James. I guess you were communicating with her right. Let her know where you are currently staying. She will give you the documents that you need to get your social security number. Without a social security number, you cannot work in this country. Not even a part-time job," explains Sandeep.

"So what do I need to ask her?"

"Nothing. Just take your I-20 and passport and any other related documents and go to her. By the way before I proceed, do you have any job lined up or arranged with any department on campus?"

"No I don't."

"No problem. We might be having a vacancy in the office that I work in…..student admissions. I will confirm and check. But in the meantime just go and ask her for the letter by which you can apply for a social security number."

"Yes will do."

39

"All you need to do is get that letter. Bring it to the admissions office and give it to me. I will photocopy it and give it back to you. That way you can start employment before you actually get a social security number assigned to you. It is very important to get a job here as soon as possible so that you can pay for expenses. Outside of course fees rent is probably the biggest of expenses," specifies the well-spoken mentor. "So now don't get too worried about what needs to be done. Just go to bed. Get some rest and tomorrow we will see what to do. It's simple, trust me, nothing difficult. If I could do it, you could too," he says sensing the visible strain on Ralph's face.

"Take care of him and show him around okay," Sandeep requests Rajendra. They shake hands and Ralph is left with Rajendra for the night.

Rajendra shows Ralph the room that he would share with the other person in the house.

"Madhu stays in this room. But he is out of station at the moment. So it will be another two days or so before he comes. Till then you have the room to yourself."
"I think he uses this cabinet. So you can use this other one. Okay, I'll be in the other room if you need me."
"Sure!" says Ralph, seeming grateful he will have some time to himself.

He places his laptop bag in the room beside the bed. Then walks to the living room and drags the big suitcase and places it in the space beneath the dresser. The other suitcase he places next to the mattress. Realizing he would need clothes for the next day he starts unpacking his suitcase and places some business casuals on the hangars in the closet.

With three pairs of clothes on the dressing rod ready he thinks he is ready for at least another two or three days. "*Where did I keep my shaving blades and bath soap?*" he says to himself as he gropes through the well folded clothes in the suitcase.

"*Oh it might be in that black bag of toiletries.*" Quickly zipping open the external compartment of the suitcase he reaches the black bag and finds the stuff he was looking for. Soap and shaving blades.

With the basic necessities for social and school life set aside, he decides to take care of his physiological needs. Still feeling hungry he heads into the kitchen to forage for food. He is surprised when he notices that the only thing available in the fridge is a bottle of orange juice and a half eaten apple. *"This fridge is probably cleaner than any I have ever seen"* he mutters.

Ralph had known that international students are short on many things. He didn't know that food would be one of them. As he stares at the bare landscape in the fridge he hopes he would not have to ever face a situation of no food or rationed food in the future. He resolves to work hard and do well.

The smell of apples leads him to the cabinet and he decides to down another one to get him through the night.

"Hey Rajendra. I am going to bed now. I need to get up early tomorrow and take that tour with Sandeep."
"I think that will be later in the day, right? I could give you a tour in the morning if you like," says Rajendra.
"That would be great. Yes, so let's get up in the morning and plan on it," he says hurrying to his room to hit the sack.

He shuts the door, takes off his sweater and puts on his pajamas and sleeping t-shirt. He apparently hasn't still removed his bed sheet and pillow cover. Fatigue causes him to postpone that until the next day or whenever he gets the time. He will soon realize it was indeed a mistake.

****

As he falls deep into slumber, a strange dream keeps repeating.

A bright light shines through the blinds and begins giving him peremptory instructions. *"Am I still sleeping and is this only a dream or have I really woken up?"* his subconscious says.

The pain from the boils all over his hamstrings and back are too real to suggest a dream. *"What happened last night? Why am I all swollen on my legs and back?"*
As though with lightning agility he wakes from his slumber to investigate the cause of the seething pain in his legs and back. The boils are red and inflamed. *"This could have been caused by only one thing – BUGS! Was this related to the dreams I got all night?"* he thinks.

He investigates the bed and notices that it is quite an old bed. Probably somebody's used mattress. *"This has got to be the source of all those bugs. How did it end up here?"*

"Hey Rajendra. Who bought that bed. I mean when was it bought?" he yells his mouth close to Rajendra's bedroom door.

Rajendra who is still sleeping with the door half shut at this point doesn't move an inch. Ralph enters and shakes him a little to get him to respond.

"Oh man. What's up? It's still too early. The university does not open at this time."

It was 7:30 am and still time left to catch up on sleep. Very few students are actually driven by a purpose that wakes them up every morning with a prayer in their heart and a plan in their minds. Ralph was different though. He always had this urge to explore things and find out for himself. This curious trait always pulled him from bed or from any inertia and pushed him to get on with life.

Today it was the urge to know how bugs had gotten into the bed.

"Hey when was that bed bought?"
"Which one?"
"The one that I slept on last night."
"I think Madhu and the guy who lived here earlier just found it near a trash dumpster and brought it upstairs."
"You mean that bed was supposed to be trashed. In the garbage bin?" he asks mouth wide open.

Rajendra senses an element of fear and surprise in him. He turns from his position towards the wall to face Ralph.

"Well many people in the US throw beds away which are in good condition, well ahead of their useful life being over. So we sometimes find these and bring them to use. Besides it serves to save money that would be used to buy a new bed."

Ralph is a little shell shocked by his plain explanation and wonders how stupid and cheap some people can be.

"But how do you know if the beds are clean or not infected or just not suitable? I mean there is a reason they are being trashed, isn't there?" he asks looking disappointed.
"Well everybody does the same thing!" Rajendra says looking relaxed and calm about it.

Ralph knew that there would be issues for international students with limited resources coming to the US. But using bug infested beds laid out in the garbage bin was a new height in "poverty management" he had never dreamt of in his wildest dreams.

"Yes but there are bugs in the bed dude. My entire back is swollen with bug bites. How can anybody sleep on such beds!" he asks emphatically.
"Sanjay, the guy living there before you came used that bed regularly and didn't have a problem. How come you got bitten?" asks Rajendra.
"I don't know."
"Let's see."

Both of them get up and go to the other room. Rajendra gives the bed a telling look and then says "so you didn't use a bed sheet to cover it?"
"No, my bed sheet is still packed in my suitcase. I didn't have the time yesterday to unpack. And was too tired anyway."
"That's why you must have got bitten. We always use a bed sheet to sleep on any bed. I mean you do that at home too right?" asks Rajendra.
"Even if we don't use a bed sheet at home nothing would happen as there are no bugs in those beds. Beds should be free of such creatures and lice and ticks and all that irrespective of whether you use a bed sheet or not," asserts Ralph.
"Well, that's the way it is here. We don't spend needlessly on beds or other kinds of furniture we can do without. We get it for free. Lots of people dump good stuff here. So we just go and pick it up. It saves money and time too. If we were to go to the store and buy stuff it would not only cost us, but we would have to invest time and energy in bringing heavy furniture and fixtures up the elevator into the apartment."
"But..."
Rajendra continues without allowing Ralph to speak "We are just looking at things from a practical point of view. This works. So we do it."
Sensing Ralph's discomfort with the explanation he says "well this is how it is right now. So get used to it. You will not have to worry so

much if you reconcile yourself to these methods. They have worked for us. I don't see any reason why they wouldn't work for you."

Ralph is bewildered and dumbfounded at the nonchalant response of this Hyderabadi, South Indian engineer. He thinks *"I wonder how these people become engineers in India and are yet so cheap. I mean just because the job gets done they don't mind sleeping on a bug infested bed. I wonder if they do the same once they get a job here as well. I can't live like these cheap assholes."*

India is a land of vast diversity, just as so many other countries in Asia are. It is a fact that several Asians adopt austere measures to get by in life till they become wealthy or are better positioned to meet expenses. There are exceptions of course. But extravagance is not a quality abundantly found among Asian immigrants to the US. Wealthy Arabs and Middle Eastern people fall under a different category though, which can be categorized as rather spendthrift.

Within Indians too, there are divisions based on the geographical regions that people come from. Every region has its own specific habits in terms of thrift, stinginess, food habits and customs that at best would be considered weird in the US by native-born Americans. Ralph hoped that he would not have to put up with too many of these "weird habits" as he started his stay with the Hyderabadi[8] south Indians. After all he was from Goa, a state known for its Indo-European cultural heritage and relatively unique culture from the rest of India. He knew it would be an effort to put up with the habits of these south Indian roommates. He just hoped he wouldn't have to face such 'bug infested bed' situations any more. Only time would tell.

"Okay, I think I will go and get ready. I am not feeling sleepy anymore," says Rajendra sensing Ralph was going to start brooding.
"Yup. I will take this bed and dump it in the trash. I think I have a mat I brought from home," says Ralph.
There is an eerie silence. "Ok, as you wish," says Rajendra.
"Where do we dump these big items?" asks Ralph naively.

---

[8] Hyderabadi – refers to a person from the Indian city of Hyderabad; much like New Yorker is from New York.

"There is a blue color dumpster to the right of the entrance of the building when you go outside. You can put it there."

In India, he wasn't used to dumping large items like these. In fact, on a daily basis, either his brother or somebody else in the household would take the small bag of trash to the main dumpster not too far away from the road. Ralph seldom did any housework. His attitude was one of callous disregard to the operational aspects of running a home. Before he left for the US, Dad cautioned him saying "you will have to do everything on your own once you reach US."

****

Ralph puts on his jeans and t-shirt. Without brushing his teeth or getting cleaned up, he grabs the bed by one end and drags it towards the elevator. He never knew that dumpsters could be this big. How big could the trucks that unload these dumpsters be, he wondered. Suddenly, his commitment for the day begins to nag. He had experienced days when little got done before and didn't want to make this day one of those.

He reaches the thirteenth floor and knocks the door peremptorily for a couple of times.
"Ralph, just make sure you lock the door when you go out. Security can be an issue in Philadelphia."
"I thought it was safe here?"
"Actually this city has one of the highest percentages of murder and crime in the US" clarifies Rajendra.

Rajendra is eating some Parle-G[9] biscuits when Ralph returns to the apartment. His mouth begins to recollect the taste of the yummy biscuit as soon as he sees it in Rajendra's hands.

"Where did you get that from?" he asks pointing to the small biscuit pack in his hands.
"There is an Indian store close to here where all Indian students normally go, to get their groceries" he says.

---

[9] Parle-G is an inexpensive brand of biscuit; known for its glucose content commonly found in stores all over India

He offers him a biscuit and Ralph gladly takes one. By the time ablutions are complete it is almost 8:45am. Ralph removes his mat and a notebook from the suitcase. Looking around, he surreptitiously removes hard currency from the small pouch and stuffs it into his purse. The dollars are fresh notes given by Mum before he left for the US. She had advised utmost caution in keeping the currency safe. Anybody would rob or even kill to obtain currency. Cash is king!

"The university has an interesting layout. Although it is one of the smaller universities in Philadelphia it is neatly designed. I will show you some important places today," says Rajendra.
"Did you have your breakfast?" asks Ralph.
"Yes."
"When?"
"I had it in front of you some minutes ago."
"I had the Parle-G biscuits and gave you one if you remember," smiles Rajendra.
"So that's your breakfast?" asks a surprised Ralph.
"Yup. I've been having that for the last eight months since I've been in the states."

Ralph though shocked, says nothing. *"I can't believe this south Indian has been living on glucose biscuits for the last eight months. How does he get through the morning with only one installment of biscuits until lunch? Does he have lunch or does he wait until dinner?"* wondered Ralph.

"Okay so if you are ready we can proceed to the university. There is a shuttle that takes students from here to the university every fifteen minutes during the semester. At 9am, 9:15am, 9:30 and 10. This is every hour till 8 pm on weekdays. So it's pretty good coverage," explains Rajendra.
"Okay, so we have a transport system in place then. That's great!"
"Do you regularly use it?"
"Yes it's very convenient to reach the university for classes. Besides it's free. Well not exactly. We pay huge amounts of fees for our courses. So in that sense, we pay for the shuttle too."

As Ralph walks out into the open with Rajendra he feels this overwhelming sense of walking into unknown territory. So different, so alien! Yet so well organized; so well defined. The roads are clean and well kept. Well mowed grass and clear sidewalks. But not as many people as back home. The few that you see don't smile unless they know you. *"Are they not very friendly or is it just the way it is here?"* he thinks to himself.

Dad had told him that people in the west, especially white folks might not be very open to conversing with you. The fact that you are colored is an additional reason they might ignore you. *"However, that was way back in the 70s during Dad's time. I am sure there might be some positive changes now. I will keep an open mind,"* thinks Ralph. But deep down he knows that whatever Dad had told him so far in life had turned out to be true for the most part.

Life had been tough, but Dad's ever present wisdom was always near when he sought it. And no matter how much he faulted Dad for his weaknesses, Ralph always knew Dad was a wellspring of wisdom, whether in India or any other part of the globe. No matter how much he tried to face the present with an open mind, something deep down kept telling him that time-tested experience and wisdom is always more reliable than spur of the moment impulses in whatever circumstance or place one might be in.

At the designated shuttle stop he sees a few tired-looking students with small satchels. For a second he felt that they must be working too hard with a limited nutrition base to subsist on. But this is America and people here are generally overweight or over fed; seldom underfed or malnourished. This can't be possible, he thought. But then these were international students waiting for the shuttle early in the morning. They might most likely not even have had a basic breakfast if any at all.

In fact, almost all the seven to eight students at the stop were international except for one lonesome white girl. She didn't look famished and tired, but seemed reserved. Finding her attractive, he thought that she would be a good person to get to know. She had a nice slender figure, delicate hands, and straight flowing hair. Within the short distance he was from her he could see that she had brown eyes. However, since the five minutes they had been there, the girl hadn't even turned to look at Ralph. He had been eyeing her for most of the time, though. Rajendra began to feel ignored.

"Are you feeling strange and overwhelmed?" he asked, being unable to understand Ralph's silence.

"Umm, no just seeing all these things for the first time. It's quite different here, right?"

"Yes, it is. Everything here is well-organized whether it's transport, education, or any other enterprise. Much unlike home, they invest huge amounts in attaining operational excellence here."

Ralph keeps looking around, periodically turning his head to eye the pretty looking girl and her features. Well, the girl at the German airport seemed very friendly. Why is this one so aloof. The Romeo in him would want to walk up to her and find out for himself, but he is with a dark Indian guy right now. So he wouldn't feel comfortable boasting his Portuguese, Goan heritage to her with the other guy around.

Mum had told him that he would be better off saying he was from Goa, which has a European culture, tradition and connection rather than erstwhile India, which is not always viewed favorably in Western countries.

****

As the massive bus comes to a halt in front of them, Ralph looks to strategically place himself close to the white girl so as to start a conversation. His mind tells him to focus on the job he has come for to the US rather than on flirting with girls. But his heart tells him he can probably handle both. He for one knows that he can do both.

However, the dynamics of the current situation are such that propriety would suggest an extreme amount of attention be given to value-generating tasks rather than to romantic pursuits. But Ralph has always viewed romantic pursuits as part of value-creating activities. Unless, of course, Rajendra would mind that he doesn't sit next to him.

As all the students enter, Ralph quickly positions himself to be exactly behind the pretty damsel. Rajendra wonders what has got into Ralph that he seems to be leading him as though he knows his way around. "I thought that this newbie would be following me rather than the other way round," thinks Rajendra to himself. He says nothing, though.

As the young lady takes a seat, Ralph takes the seat exactly behind her. Rajendra is obliged to take the seat next to Ralph on the other side of the aisle. Suddenly for a moment, Ralph begins to feel a power and confidence of the kind he has never felt since he left Indian soil. An exhilarating feeling, a source of strength or Dad's wellspring of wisdom coming into play. He doesn't know how but he doesn't wish to know either. What matters is that he has the strength and confidence from some divine source. Perhaps his own Inner Voice.

When everything in life seemed so uncertain, vague and confusing Ralph feels blessed that it is only "the now" that matters. As an international student in a foreign country, which class to go to, what books to buy, or whom to call a friend seems very confusing. If women could give him this exhilarating feeling then probably he should not shun this activity as a waste of time he thought. After all, he was a young man in his early twenties; strong, handsome and raring to go.

"Excuse me, what time is it?" he asks her placing his hand on the seat in front of him.
"It's 9:15 am," she says looking at her smartphone.
"Thanks."

He pauses a while. Then summons that residual confidence to ask again "Which network are you using?"
"What?"
Sensing she has not understood the question, he says "Which telephone service provider do you use?"

"Oh. This is Verizon," she says with a smile.
"Wow. You seem to be messaging so intently I guessed that your connection might be very strong. So I thought of asking."
"Absolutely," she bursts out with a slight laugh.

Ralph waits for her to further comment but she doesn't. He realizes he is going to need a topic to break the ice further. Her initial reactions to his overtures were positive but she hadn't continued the conversation. Evidently, he would have to push harder in order to continue the conversation. But he seems to lack a common topic to speak about as his approach skills are not all that developed. Moreover, it is that age old conundrum of 'young men getting butterflies in their stomach when faced by a beautiful woman.' Approaching people in the US is a little

49

different from doing the same thing in countries like India. Unlike India where once a conversation gets started, it is easy to continue it; in the US this might not necessarily be the case.

"So what are you studying," he starts again.
"I'm studying criminal justice." He was again surprised as she didn't ask him anything.

Pausing for a bit he began to realize what Dad had told him a few times. They will not interact with you much, unless they respect you a lot or you have done something extraordinary for them. The other possibility is if you have known them for a very long time and have a good reputation in society.

This idea seemed to play out in the current case. Ralph had already tried inciting conversation with her twice. Both times her response had been lukewarm; pretty much unresponsive.

He decides to leave her alone and shift the focus of the conversation to Rajendra who had pretty much avoided any interest in the conversation with the pretty girl.

"So what are you going to show me today?" questions Ralph.
"I will first show you the library and then other important sites on campus. The library is important because you can do your projects there and obtain any study materials you need."

They proceed to the massive building with a beautiful porch and atrium. Although it looks a little dated the building has all the latest technology to facilitate student instruction. The many carrels and study rooms seem ideal for individual or group study. Ralph has never seen such sprawling study surroundings and he is pleasantly surprised that he has such facilities at his disposal. The library back home wasn't this big or spacious. It probably didn't even have the database facilities that this library has.

They look around for a while. "You can borrow books here for around three weeks or so. Books that are not available in this library can be requested using the PALCI system which is like borrowing books from neighboring libraries."

"Oh, so there is a system like this huh."
"Yes. It's very convenient to borrow books from it. Because one library might not have all the books we are looking for," states Rajendra.

They proceed to other parts of the campus.

Ralph knew that the US was large and full of facilities. The tour showed him that it indeed was. He didn't expect to see a student recreation area with free soda vending machines, video game play stations, pool tables and computers to freely surf the net. The preponderance of availability of computers, printers and water vending machines was amazing to say the least. Ralph wondered that in this place of great availability what would be missing? It wouldn't take him long to find out.

"We have a gym here which many students use. I have never used it so I don't know if they charge for it or not. You could go there on your own. It's that building in the corner next to the exit gate. I'll show you the admission offices."

They cross a large road and reach the other side of campus. There they find a couple of offices.

"These are the admission offices. I think Sandeep works in one of these," says Rajendra.
"Oh okay. So they help in admissions huh?"
"Yes, all international and domestic admissions are done here."
"Are part time jobs available here?" asks Ralph.
"I don't know. But there is a place where I know jobs are available."
"Where?"
"The cafeteria"

Ralph would soon learn that places that offer higher wages, quality employment or easy work are not readily disclosed by international students to others like themselves. He would have to rely on just a few trusted, well-meaning colleagues to point him in the right direction in regards to obtaining a job.

They walk to the cafeteria and as they enter it Ralph notices the sheer neatness and magnitude of 'eating' in American style. The tables are so well maintained, neat and clean. He can't remember the last time he saw such a neat, clean place in India or if he ever did. Each table has just the right number of ketchup bottles, pepper dispensers and napkins. The environment in the mess is clean, clear and smells good. Very few restaurants in Goa had such a neat look. Many of them were dank, not well furnished or just dirty. The five-star restaurants were different, though.

However, every restaurant in the US seemed to have a certain standard in terms of layout and cleanliness. Cleanliness is something that is taken seriously in the US.

From the entrance, he could see rows of large trays with food in them. There was chicken, macaroni, spaghetti, dollops of jelly, cream and salads. Each tray hosted a collection of specific dishes. If one tray had non-vegetable foods, the other had sweet dishes and salads. The red, blue and white colored tables were appropriately placed to be aesthetically distant from one another, but not too far away.

"This is where you can get food. I think they have meal plans so you could purchase some for the semester. Let's just inquire if they have job openings," says Rajendra.

On inquiring with the front desk they are referred to the back office where a manager gives them a form to fill out.

"Only he wants to fill up the form since he is looking for a job" says Rajendra to the manager seeking to clarify who the job seeker is.

Ralph wonders where Rajendra is working, but doesn't ask at that very moment. It is considered obtrusive to directly ask a fellow student where on campus they work. Just because getting jobs on campus can be competitive when candidates with similar qualifications are vying for them. In universities having a fixed number of positions and a growing number of international students, it is but natural that competition is likely to be fierce.

He quickly fills out the form and thanks the manager.

As they walk out Ralph sheepishly asks Rajendra where he is working.

"I work outside the university at Dunkin."
"Why do you work there when you can get employment here?"

"Well, they pay more as you don't have to pay for taxes. You get paid in cash. There is no record."

Ralph seems confused about this mode of work but doesn't ask any more questions.

"Have you heard of any graduate assistantships available?"
"No I haven't," Rajendra replies curtly.

Graduate assistantships are usually very coveted and information about them is seldom disclosed between competing colleagues. When it comes to key opportunities; tactical information is not shared; especially between rival colleagues. Anyone who is not a close, trustworthy friend in the same class is considered a rival. The situation gets even more complicated when the parties involved are both international and from economically modest backgrounds.

"So most parts of the university have been covered. You can continue exploring or come to the apartment with me," offers Rajendra.

Ralph opts to stay and explore the university.

As he walks around the computer science building he sees notices saying "Laptops for rent. Contact Student Technology Center." He goes to the Student Technology Center and inquires.

Clean-shaven and dressed in a blue t-shirt and cream pants he is quite a sight, particularly to young women. The young girl at the desk of the 'technology center' attends to Ralph.

"Is there a laptop rental program here?" he asks.
"Yes. Are you a new student here?"
"Yes. I will be starting classes this evening."
"What year are you?"
"First year."
"Which program? Are you a graduate or undergraduate student?" she asks.
"I am in computer science and I am a graduate student."
"Oh, I'm so sorry. The laptop rental program is only for undergraduate students."
"Isn't there anything for graduates?"

"I'm afraid not. Sorry!" she grimaces.
"Okay. Well, thanks."

As he prepares to leave she takes a moment to steal a glance at his shapely chest and clean-cut face.
It is clear, she hasn't seen such tanned, yet light colored guys before. Not white, not black, and not brown either. But somewhere on the fair side with a tinge of olive color. Undoubtedly she finds this extremely handsome if not attractive. Ralph senses that many women in the States would find him attractive.

Motivated with what he has just realized, he proceeds to look around the classes of the computer science program. He would have loved to stand at the technology front desk and continue to chat with the pretty girl. But she would have work to do and if her boss or a customer had come there, it would not have been considered an appropriate place to socialize – not in the US at least.

His goal oriented persona then knocks his door. You can't be trying to flirt here dude. You have a mission to get a degree and get a job. After all, a job had always eluded Ralph in his home country. He would have to prove a point to Mum & Dad by getting a job in a foreign country! "How can I do this," he wondered. But he was confident and ready. That's all that mattered in the end.

He felt a little lost to not have a plan of action in mind. He was comfortable though that things would fall into place and that they had begun doing so. Sandeep had told him about the shuttle service for students. He had miraculously embarked on the East bound shuttle without giving much thought as to which bus he was boarding. How did that happen he wondered. Beginners luck and definitely a good omen.

Mum had always told him to look out for the signs that life provided. "All too often, life is not defined by the theories and postulates that are developed in chemistry labs and research centers but by the very omens and signs that life throws at you!" she would say. He hoped that this would be a sign of the beginning of untold fortune.

He takes a seat at the front of the bus and tries to absorb the surroundings. The bus would make stops at specific places on its beat between the university campus and student housing located all along

East Willow Grove Avenue. The first stop brings in more students to fill the vacant seats. A simple looking, white girl dressed in a pale white jacket enters the bus and heads nonchalantly to the vacant seat next to Ralph.

Although a little taken aback by her plain behavior, Ralph has reason to believe that she didn't even notice him. Dad had told him to try to make friends and develop relationships wherever he went in life. He didn't have much experience interacting with people in the US. But the interactions so far hadn't been too detailed or lengthy. Should he sit and wait for people to start a conversation with him or did he have to go and start talking to others? So far the only people he had walk up to him and start conversations had been the Indian friends who had received him at the airport. *"What should I do with Caucasian, black or any other denomination of Americans?"* he wondered. No one had come and started a conversation with him yet.

As if by serendipity or some other stroke of luck, a voice inside began to tell him. *"Put your hands together and press the fleshy part of your palms against each other."* This was the same voice that had watched over him as he negotiated his way through capricious immigration officers at the airport; helping him maintain his calm all along the way. The pressing of the hands was an exercise he had often used when in a dilemma. He knew it would work now too.

The reply was not very quick but it came without uncertainty. He could hear his inner voice telling him that he would need to put himself out there to try and start conversations. When it comes to Americans he would have to initiate conversations most of the time. This revelation would prove useful as he negotiated his way through American society and culture, and sought to complete the course of study he was here for.

As the bus began moving again, he made an attempt to speak to the attractive lass. The words didn't come out at first until he said, "So what time is the bus expected to reach Henryville Apartments?"
"I'm not sure. But the shuttle driver should have a schedule with him," she replied coldly.
"Actually I am new here and don't know much about this school."

He could sense the distance that people maintain in casual conversations with acquaintances. Probably it was the way that life was in the US. Dad had narrated a few instances of racism in the UK. Although the conversation with the girl wasn't any sort of racism, it was cold unfriendliness or at least that's what it came across as. He nevertheless decided to continue the conversation. Daunting as it was, he realized that he didn't have much to lose from trying to converse and getting rejected in the process. "You got to take the risk and put yourself out there when you want something in life. You might get hurt in the process; but if the universe works in your favor you might get immeasurable results and terrific success," Dad had told him.

****

Risk is the essence of an immigrant's life. When immigrants come to a foreign land with hopes of a new beginning and a new life they think more of hope and positive outcomes than of the massive risks of such a venture. Europeans, Asians, Russians, Africans and all the peoples of other countries that made America their home over the decades had to overcome unimaginable odds to come out successful. It's not about not knowing what to do but about getting up every time a goof up throws you to the ground. To get up every time you fall requires resilience. Ralph resolved to be as resilient as his will could allow him, no matter what happened in the US or the world. After all, Dad had always told him that the world is not what comes to you but what you make of what comes your way.

Many international students coming to the US come with a level of resilience required to make it in this country. They know that the Sept 11 attacks in 2001 gave US authorities enough reason to harden immigration rules against internationals coming here for business or pleasure. Ralph knew it would be tougher than the 70s or 80s to settle down in the US. He didn't have a family here nor a reliable friend, but he had faith.

"Where do you get the shuttle schedule?" he asked the same girl sitting by his side.
"I'm not sure. I don't use the shuttle much," she said.
"So what are you studying?" he says looking to continue the conversation.
"Food marketing," she replies curtly.

He begins to wonder if he should stop the conversation or not. Her replies are now not exceeding three or four words. The resilience he had resolved to adhere to eggs him on.

"I'm Ralph," he extends his hand prematurely.

She extends her hand; reluctantly though. She doesn't say her name.

"So what's your name?" he asks finding her a little laconic. Normally in Goa, people are effusive in extending their hand and making friends. In fact most countries in Asia are rather friendly to locals and foreigners alike. Westerners have the distinction of receiving quality service and VIP treatment in almost all cities and destinations all over Asia. "I'm Ashley," she replies, a puzzled look on her face. She is visibly shaken to be making a friend on the university shuttle. Conversations don't just happen during a short trip in her book. But Ralph is all bluster and bravado. And has no time for shyness. He keeps chatting away.

Though he wonders why she would take so long to just tell her name.

"Where are you originally from?" she quickly asks emphasizing the word 'originally' giving a coy smile.

He thinks it's better to say he is from somewhere in the US as opposed to a foreign country. She doesn't look like someone who would appreciate international diversity much. Ralph had heard of corn-fed white folks who knew the Mississippi as the longest river in the world and America as the biggest country. As it is, he looks like a Latino. And his ample readings and conversations with friends had taught him that at least in the Northeastern US he would be better off trying to fall within the crowd rather than being the odd man out. He didn't mind lying to do so. Many people dodge questions in order to maintain a friendship or even employment. Not out of malice or ill intentions but out of necessity. Helplessness is often what drives them to minor sins.

"I am from Waco, Texas."

His pronunciation is not quite exact and she is quick to notice.

"We pronounce Waco as Waaaaco" she says hoping to corner him into admitting he is not originally from the US.

"Well that's the way we pronounce it down in Texas," he quickly rejoins.

"So how do you like your studies?" he asks seeking to change the topic. She suddenly seems to be silent as if to say "hey you're not from Waco, TX. Don't lie you silly fool! I know where you're coming from."

"So what are your plans for the weekend?" he follows up noticing her silence.

"No plans yet."

He knows he can get her to speak if he starts discussing his dancing skills. This weekend is Valentine's Day and for a foreign student, he feels this is the least he could know.

His uncle residing in the US had sent Mum a Valentine's Day card several years ago. The ensuing conversation helped him understand the concept of Valentine's Day before they started celebrating it commercially in Asia.

"I am going to a dance this weekend. I do tango and salsa. We are going to have a dance competition."

She is still silent.

"Do you dance?" he asks.

"Nope!" she replies quickly.

"I had won the competition last year but this year I won't be able to participate as my partner is out on vacation. But I will be going anyway."

"So you are not doing anything on Valentine's Day right. You could join me for the dance if you like. I could teach you to dance," he slyly slips in the question of asking her for the dance.

"I have a boyfriend!" she says with disdain.

Ralph would later learn that when a woman says she has a boyfriend she means she is not interested in you. Many foreign students are often at a loss to learn the subtle communication hints involved in conversations in the US.

"Well you can bring him to the dance too," he says, not showing any signs of letting up in confidence.

"Well I will be going to meet him. So we won't be here in the area," she counters.

This is final proof that she doesn't intend to do anything with him.

He stays silent till he reaches his destination. He notices she is going to disembark at the same bus stop as well. As they proceed to the exit he decides to muster the courage to bid farewell even though signs of rejection were rife in the short conversation they just concluded.

"Have a good day Ashley," he says as they walk in separate directions.

She simply smiles.

As he walks towards the ghastly apartment he had been to the previous day; he has this untoward feeling of loss and regret. Loss, as he feels so lonely in this alien land where not only the roads, buildings and things are so different. The people also are light years apart in notions, attitudes and culture. He randomly thinks that maybe there are other places in the US where people are more open and caring. He longs to find friends who he can speak his mind to and not fear what they would think of him; people who he could talk and exchange ideas with and get guidance from. He realizes he doesn't have any of these so-called luxuries and can't help but feel regret for not having gone to a better place. "*Is there a better place?*" he wonders. This would not be the first time that he would have such feelings.

As he walks the long corridor towards the apartment unit, he feels this claustrophobic feeling of being caged and watched. Like a thousand eyes staring with strained necks and watching his every step as he treads towards his apartment door. He still doesn't have his own keys for the apartment. Rajendra had told him that he would definitely be at home if not for the other resident. The claustrophobic feeling of the corridor made him wish Rajendra had already opened the door.

International students have to get through a lot to get settled in the US. Apart from the fears of how to get a job, obtain textbooks or do well in their courses the constant need to remain safe always pervades them. Not that security is an issue in the US. But in spite of all the policing and law enforcement there is still a great possibility of things to go wrong. Ralph was in a similar situation and couldn't justify his irrational fears of being alone in the corridor. But he did know that he wanted to be extra cautious about anyone surreptitiously creeping behind him and catching him by surprise. This irrational fear was probably a result of his upbringing. He had been taught there always is an occult element to life. That what people call superstition is not always so. Not just in India but all over the globe people do believe in ideas connected to the occult; although they might not admit it openly. Probably, Mum who always had ideas and beliefs about things like the evil eye, premonition and a higher plan had so ingrained her ideas into Ralph that he preferred to think like her. It was a good way to feel connected with his roots and a surreal sense of safety. *"Mum will be with me in spirit if I adopt her thoughts,"* he thought to himself. Thousands of miles away he felt the only way he could keep in touch with her was through the mysterious application of her occult beliefs. Where physical connection doesn't reach; the occult prevails.

Not noticing any signs of the door opening after ringing the bell twice, he starts hammering away at it. All the while looking back and sideways. No response still. He walks down to the lobby hoping to find a phone he can use to call Rajendra. Being only a day old in the country he doesn't have a functioning cell phone yet. Fortunately he has a diary that he uses to write numbers down in. Rajendra's number is in it. Short on pocket change and eager to get a phone to call from he finds a willing friend in the front desk attendant. "Hello," Rajendra says after a long ring.

"Hey Rajendra, this is Ralph. I am at the apartment and I don't have the key to enter. Are you in the house?"
Ralph senses Rajendra's hesitation in telling him where he is. "I am at the grocery store in the city right now," says Rajendra.
"What time will you be back? I am waiting to get in," pleads Ralph.
"I am done with my shopping. It shouldn't take me long."
"Okay. I will wait for you in the lobby," says Ralph.
"Sure. I will be there soon," says Rajendra, sounding very empathetic.

As he waits in the lobby he feels this overwhelming feeling of being subject to the forces of nature and circumstance in the US. I don't have a house, not enough money, no car, no friends or girlfriend. And here I am waiting for a roommate to come and let me into the house. Isn't that just pathetic! His thoughts can only do so much. Helplessness, combined with anger doesn't help him. It only serves to frustrate him more. "*I need to keep my cool at least for now,*" he reiterates to himself.

International students have several worries in the US. Feeling the blues due to the lack of resources is common among those who do not have many friends in the same boat or those who live by themselves without help or support from anybody. At this point, Ralph seemed to be in the latter category.

****

A slight tap on the shoulder brings Ralph out of his pensive mood. "So ready to go to the apartment?" Rajendra asks with a broad smile. "Sorry, you had to wait so long. I actually had planned to be home much earlier. But traffic was very bad so getting here from the city took more time than usual," he explains.

"Oh...that's okay," replies Ralph.
As he walks with him along the corridor, Ralph doesn't feel the insecurities he felt when he had walked alone. Probably the company of Rajendra, however unfamiliar, is reassuring enough for him to be relaxed and not worry about anything. They enter the apartment. "So how was your day at the university?"
"It was interesting" Ralph replies plainly.
"Great. So did you figure out which classes you will be taking and all that?"
"Yes. I did. However, I am yet to get the textbooks."
"Don't worry. It takes some time. I will introduce you to some second-year grad students who might have the books. Or you could rent them out from certain websites."
"Which ones?" asks Ralph.
"I will show them to you. Let me just put these things in order," Rajendra says as he places some files on the cluttered desk in the living room.
"I will show you around the house again and familiarize you with the rules and norms. Then we can go over the questions you have about the school, courses and other things," says Rajendra.

Placing the grocery bags on the cooking platform in the kitchen, he takes a small bottle of milk and places it in the refrigerator. Then grabs a glass of water, takes a sigh and stretches his arms out wide.

"I guess you don't have a shelf in the fridge right? Madhu and I use the top two. If you like you could use the third one."
Ralph notices some left overs in the third and asks if anybody else is using it. "Well, that container belongs to me. But I will remove it," says Rajendra.

"We generally place stuff in each other's places when we don't have any space left of our own."

Ralph is a bit surprised with Rajendra's declaration of dividing shelf space and nonchalant admission of still using other people's shelf space when enough space is not available. But he chooses to remain silent instead of questioning Rajendra at the outset.

As they walk to the bathroom, Rajendra specifies the need to keep items of personal hygiene separate. "Each of us has separate shaving blades, soaps and shampoos. This cabinet contains mine and Madhu's stuff. You could use the bottom shelf." As they go through the norms of the house, Ralph listens patiently. He is generally not used to listening patiently. But he remembers Mum's advice, "In a foreign country be patient and attentive." He opts to follow it in the absence of no other alternative. Besides, he always preferred to "err on the side of caution."

Ralph knew that he would not have to put up with all these restrictions were he living in his own private space. But that was not the case at least for now. Monetary considerations drove his current circumstances. "So do you eat non-vegetarian food?"
"Yes I do" says Ralph; momentarily shaken from his thoughts.
"Well both Madhu and I are pure vegetarians so if you want to eat non-veg you can bring it from outside. But we don't allow use of the utensils to make meat or any non-veg food."
"No?" Ralph asks looking surprised.
"No. We don't feel it is clean to use the same utensils we use to make vegetarian food to cook non-veg food as well."

Ralph had heard that American folks found it unpleasant to smell Indian curries or dishes. But this was a new precedent wherein people from the same country as he was, were imposing culinary restrictions. He would have to be watchful about their orthorexia-related ideas now in order to preserve harmony. *"Was there a way to get around this?"* he thought to himself.

"We are trying to have a system wherein we do common cooking. As in one person cooks on a certain day. Everyone eats that for a week. Next week another person cooks."
"We even did joint shopping before but because people left the apartment at odd times we have stopped the joint cooking and shopping format" Rajendra says, seeming to look for a reaction from Ralph.

Ralph remains silent not wanting to be part of such a system. *"If I can't cook chicken or beef, no point participating in their crappy system,"* he mumbles to himself.

Ralph didn't like rules, restrictions, or regulations. He saw them as encumbrances on his freedom and creativity. He would need to find a way to get around these restrictions. *"These Indians are dirty pigs back home; but here they act like self-righteous Nawabs[10]. And impose so-called American rules on others,"* he thought.

"Is that all?" asks Ralph sensing Rajendra's silence.
"Well, that's about it for now. But we do have one more rule. Most residents of the house come home by 10 pm. We have had people coming in later than that. However, we prefer if you let at least one occupant of the house know about your whereabouts so if anything happens we know where you are. It's just a safety mechanism to ensure that everybody that lives in the house is accounted for," specifies Rajendra.
"So I guess you must have gotten tired listening to all this," says Rajendra, noticing the weary look on Ralph's face.
"Ummmh…well more tired with the long day," says Ralph concealing his displeasure with Rajendra's briefing of the rules and regulations in the house. Although he does a good job of concealing his true feelings, Rajendra is from the same country and notices the frustrated look on Ralph's face. He decides to not to dig into his thoughts. It is often easy for a person to understand what's going on in the mind of his fellow

---

[10] Nawab is a feudal term for princes in ancient and Medieval India; used to suggest extreme wealth and power. It is a symbol of status and wealth in addition to societal standing.

countrymen. Probably an American would not be able to gauge what Ralph was thinking because the cultures are markedly different. On the flip side, a Chinese or Asian person might not necessarily be able to fathom the thoughts of an American and vice versa. When dealing with intercultural thoughts and feelings, it boils down to the familiarity that two or more individuals have developed with each other. Familiarity helps people better understand the traits and habits of each other. In the absence of a common culture, familiarity is the best way to foster mutual understanding. Familiarity is fostered through fairly regular positive contact and communication.

Rajendra could see the tension in Ralph's eyes and in his demeanor. Indians are very intuitive when it comes to assessing other people's feelings. Ralph would soon realize that in America people are way more intuitive. And they use this to do better in life and business.

****

"Okay, so I will proceed and have some food. Americans call this dinner time," smiles Rajendra.
"So early. It's just 7:30 pm!" asks Ralph.
"Actually many Americans have their dinner by 5:30 pm or 6:30 pm," replies Rajendra.
"But back home dinner is at 10 pm or sometimes even 11 pm," questions Ralph.
"Here it is believed that if you eat late; it's not good for the body and that the food doesn't get digested properly."
Rajendra proceeds to the kitchen to get his dinner ready. Ralph stands there wondering what to do. He hasn't purchased any food nor does he have ingredients to prepare anything. Most of the spices Mum had given him are still packed in the suitcases.

"Hey Rajendra are there any fast food restaurants here?" he asks.
"You should be able to find some on City Line Avenue. I generally go to Wendy's or McDonald's. You don't have any food?"
"No," Ralph says silently and is barely heard.
"You could have some rice and dal with me if you like," Rajendra babbles over the sound of the boiling dal.
"Well I just want to try some fast food since I have not tried it in this country before," says Ralph just to avoid having South Indian cuisine. He hated any non-Goan cuisine and didn't want to try any southern

Indian cuisine of all things. Dal is a pulse used to make a kind of curry in the Indian subcontinent. It is delicious and rich in proteins and is considered very healthy. Most people from the Southern and south-eastern parts of India make a specific recipe of dal as a regular part of their diet. Ralph always abhorred most things south Indian or non-Goan. Nor did they have too many friends from southern India. A select few only.

"How do I get there?"
"The shuttle will be coming here at 7:45 pm," replies Rajendra. "You could also just walk. But it's a bit of a long walk."

India is a land of vast contrasts; both geographically and culturally. Many regions in one part of India will appear so different from the other parts that these might look like a totally different country. Moreover, there are parts of India that were colonized by European powers other than the UK for way longer than when Britain colonized the majority of the country. These foreign governments and rulers imposed their respective ways on the native cultures thus creating new cultures or subcultures.

These differences in language, culture, customs, food habits and the like always create a sense of belonging to the state or region that one comes from. This regionalistic feeling breeds a sense of loyalty and patriotism towards the particular region. Not that this feeling diminishes the love one feels for India as a whole; but it does foster tendencies of regionalism and regional pride. This is a good thing. But when meshed with similar leanings from multiple parts of India it could create a cauldron of opposing views fueled by ugly regionalism. This has in the past led to mass strife and difficulties. Ralph seemed to be experiencing such feelings of regional pride when interacting with Rajendra.

Ralph had a feeling of being lost. A faint sense of being lost in an alien land that made him want his land even more. Like any human being he too wanted to belong and feel wanted. Not to be in some alien land struggling for one meal a day. But he had to remain in the present. He would have to work hard to get along with Rajendra and with the other occupant as and when that person came.

But for now the gnawing pain of his hungry stomach was too strong for him to be able to think of anything else. He grabs his hat and wallet and

65

proceeds to the door. Rajendra rushes from the kitchen behind him. "Ralph, wear a jacket and go. It's going to be cold outside."

Ralph was used to summers as they were in India. Hot during the day and even hotter as it got darker in the evening. Things would only cool down just before dawn. But this was the US. "Okay," he replies just to make Rajendra believe he is going to do as he suggested.

Walking out the door he felt a light chill. *"Guess this is just because the corridors of the building are not exposed to the outside,"* he thought.

Once outside in the open, he waited for the shuttle. The five minutes that it took the bus to arrive seemed like five hours due to dropping temperatures. Philadelphia is known for extreme temperatures. It gets increasingly hot in the morning and quite cold as the evening progresses.

As he sits in the bus he feels a sense of protection from the dark street and the nippy weather. He would need to be more attentive to the weather going forward. He realizes that his t-shirt just doesn't have the needed coverage to protect him from the cold. Rajendra was right. He should have worn a jacket.

The McDonald's restaurant looked like the typical picture he had seen in newspapers, magazines and other media. It was red and yellow and had the ubiquitous 'M' sign splashed all over. Ralph found it very appealing, particularly as he had never seen it first hand in India or Goa.

"I need to go to McDonalds" said Ralph as he staggered. The kindly driver stopped the bus closer to the restaurant although the slated stop for the shuttle was way ahead.

Ralph could see the sense of concern in the bus driver's eyes. Philadelphia, the sixth largest city in the US had long been known to have a high crime rate. Not that criminals and thugs roamed its streets unshackled but the very fact that international students are easy prey was cause enough for the driver to seem concerned. International students are generally not as well versed about the ins and outs of a new city or country and hence are inadvertently rather gullible and easy to fool. Inexperienced or novice thugs would find it easier to steal from a confused international student than from a local citizen. As Ralph alighted from the bus the driver watched him cross the road and make his way closer to the restaurant.

Ralph rubbed his palms against his hands to try and stay warm as he walked the uphill road towards the restaurant. For a moment he forgot Mum's instructions. "Be watchful of your surroundings wherever you go." Then as he saw a faceless, hooded man walking towards him her words struck him like a bolt out of a clear sky.

"Should I cross the road or turn back and walk downhill?" he thought. "There are a lot of passing vehicles on the road and I don't think it's too late for someone to commit a robbery this early in the evening" the voice inside him said.

He opted to listen to the Inner Voice as he proceeded along the uphill pavement. As the seemingly African American man drew closer, Ralph began to wonder if listening to his inner voice was a good idea. Around ten feet away from him, the hooded man began to cross the street. *"Gosh the voice was correct...I got to start trusting it more!"* Ralph breathed a sigh of relief.

He entered the restaurant and was comforted by the heat he felt around him. He was a little preoccupied with the interior layout of the restaurant and took a moment to absorb it all. He noticed people lined up placing their orders. The gnawing pain in his stomach drove him to join the line.

As he waited he noticed the pictures of various items overhead along with their prices. Dad had told him about the Big Mac burger that was so big and delicious. However, the overhead sign board didn't seem to have the famed Big Mac.

"What would you like to have Sir?" asked the girl at the counter.
"I'd like to have the regular burger with French fries over there," he said pointing to the overhead picture.
"For here or to go?" she asked.

Ralph was not familiar with this terminology and he seemed to grope for an answer. Sensing he was lost she asked him if he wanted to eat the burger here or if he wanted her to pack it for him. He decided to eat it there itself. "What would you like to drink?" she asked.

"What do you guys have?"

"Well you can select from the dispenser over there," she said pointing to the machine a few feet away.

Thinking a drink wouldn't be necessary, Ralph felt obligated to avoid the expenses associated with it. "I don't want any beverage. I have my own drink." Most Americans would consider this rather cheap but he comes from a high savings mentality. In his culture, most people are taught to save even the tiniest sums of money.

It would take him a few more years to understand why such penny pinching measures are considered futile and cheap by many local Americans. Generally, Americans work hard and play hard. Or at least that's how they portray themselves to the world. Depriving oneself of basic physiological necessities based on the idea of saving every penny is not considered wise in the US. Not that there aren't people who do that. But you generally won't find this happening unless of course the person is homeless or in dire financial straits. On the other end of the spectrum, there might be people who are health conscious and carry healthy, non-synthetic natural drinks with them wherever they go. They tend to refuse aerated drinks at restaurants or other places; maybe not so much at parties though.

"What kind of sauce would you like?" asked the front desk attendant again.

"What kind do you have?"

"Garlic, blue cheese, teriyaki, barbecue steak, ketchup."

"I'll take the ketchup."

He moved to the side and awaited his tray. As he received the tray, he noticed a large empty paper glass on the tray with a straw in it. It resembled a glass used for Coke. He wondered why she gave it to him even after he told her he was not interested in a drink.

He took a corner seat and casually glanced at the bill. To his surprise, he noticed an extra dollar on it. The attendant had charged him for the drink even though he had specified that he did not want it. That's the reason she gave him an empty paper cup. Seeing that it would be embarrassing to go back and ask her for a one dollar refund he proceeded to the dispenser and filled his cup with Sprite. At first he thought that he could get the drink from the dispenser free of charge.

But soon realized that in America it is difficult to cheat. *"You can't have the cake and eat it too!"*

Generally, in America people are very particular about their calculations. You won't find too many people giving you more money or less money due to a wrong calculation. No matter how much people say that in America, elementary mathematics curriculum is not as advanced as that in Asian or African countries; when it comes to calculating cash they generally have reliable means of determining differences or making additions. Automated machines ensure that all transactions are not just done in a clear and concise fashion but are also recorded for any future information requirement. If things were as systematic in India as they are here, accountability would not have been such a daunting task. Not that things are not recorded in lesser developed countries but the means of recording are not well vetted and are not fail-proof.

As he munched through the burger he tried to discern any specific differences in taste, texture or style of making. Not finding anything special in the features of the cutlet, he wondered what could be the novelty of McDonald's. *"I guess it serves as food to hungry mouths,"* he concluded. In a country where the bulk of the people are constantly in a mad rush to get work done, there is very little time to devote to cooking. Hence they opt for buying a ready-made burger with fries and a drink to satisfy their basic gastronomical requirements. People here are very practical and someone's skill at making a burger fulfills another's need to satisfy his or her hunger. The example of demand and supply theory couldn't be more accurate than in this situation.

He wondered how Rajendra and others like him from India could get so amalgamated with American culture as to feel authorized to start preaching rules to newcomers like him. Back in India, the rules of community living were very different. No one had ever specified to him whether vessels were to be used for a particular purpose or to use only a certain space to keep dirty laundry, personal hygiene items and the like. Not even at Max Mueller Bhavan where he had the infamous duel with Bachitter had he been told specific rules of living.

"I guess when Asians and other internationals come to the US, they also adopt the American lifestyle to a great extent," he thinks to himself. This seems to be a fact of life here. He recalls how Stanley Merchant, Dad's longtime friend from medical school had embraced US ways so

deeply that even when he came back to India you could see prominent traces of US customs. A fact of life for an international in America – you come to America a Chinese, an Indian, a Korean or whatever other nationality; but you leave a semi American or total American depending on how much you embrace American culture. Normally many immigrants are so impressed by the level of organization in the US that they embrace American culture wholeheartedly.

A fact often noticed is that the comforts and conveniences of the American way of life strikes people from other cultures like an irresistible bug. The rigors and drudgery of life in their countries makes them feel like the US is a heaven where convenience, speed and ease of access is magnified to levels not imaginable in developing nations. Probably this is what forces them to embrace American life and America no matter how resistant they might have been to it when they first came to America. Many of them, therefore, decide to continue here in hopes of getting a good job, growing their careers and/or starting a business enterprise; whatever their definition of success may be.

Ralph is brought out of his day dream as a child nearby starts slamming his balloon against the table. "*I could get around the culinary rules imposed by Rajendra,*" he thinks to himself. "*I have two utensils I brought from India anyways which I could use to make my own food and conceal the meat under the curry.*"

His ideas to deceive and evade, however, disingenuous they may seem, give him a sense of freedom and power. He doesn't feel as vulnerable and helpless as before. He quickly finishes the rest of the burger and prepares to head home. Young international students that come to the States are often lost between the twin concerns of uncertainty and fear. Uncertainty as they are not sure what situations or circumstances they might face in a dynamic society like the US. Fear, as many of them do not know the full extent of repercussions of inadvertent or deliberate violation of the rules. Many non-Western, developing countries are traditionally characterized by poor enforcement of laws or legal stipulations. Will the same happen if we mistakenly break a rule here or get into any other trouble? Do I need to keep my guard up constantly and mind my manners wherever I go? These are some of the questions that a lot of international students often ask.

Many international folks always have such conundrums going on in their mind when in the so-called New World. Many learn through experience or have the fortune of being counseled by close friends, be they American friends or friends from their respective countries. Although steeped in controversy for most of his school and college career in India, Ralph had been fortunate to keep his nose clean so far. He wished he could maintain the same record throughout his stay in the US. Though a voice inside him hinted otherwise. *"Wherever you go trouble will follow you."*

He picked up the napkins and the remaining sachets of ketchup and began to walk home. All along he kept turning back and looking. Not for any person walking close to him but for the school shuttle that would stop at the designated stops and collect students. It's a given that travelling by motorized means is not only quicker but safer. With the burger in his stomach now, he didn't feel cold any more.

As he reached the familiar environs of the apartment, the rumble of the bus racing up the hill drowned all other noises of the evening. "Damn, it comes here after I have reached!" he says disappointed with the less helpful timing of the bus. Like many other things in life; things happen when they are not needed.

He quickly charged through the lobby, up the stairs and was greeted by Rajendra. "I guess I am going to need a key for the door," said Ralph. "Yes we can get you one. But it won't be of much use because the lease of this apartment is expiring in a week and we are moving to another apartment."
"Why can't you just renew this lease?" asked Ralph looking puzzled.
"Well this apartment is small for four guys and we might be having more students coming to live with us. So we need a three bedroom apartment," said Rajendra nonchalantly.
"More students? I thought you said we had only one person; Madhu who will be coming to live with us," Ralph asked looking worried.

Ralph had always preferred his own independent space, free of interference and encumbrances. Even at home, he would not allow his brother James to enter his room without a specific reason. Mum and Dad would not be allowed to sit on his bed or touch the computer without explicit permission. How would an individual with this level of control handle such great decentralization of control and loss of authority over private space?

"Well, Madhu will definitely be coming. But we are inviting other students from the new batch to come live with us. We need to reduce and share costs involved in renting this new three bedroom apartment. It is $1050 a month. The more people the better."

Among all Asian and European students, Indian students, particularly from South India were infamous for micro-sharing every aspect of accommodation and expense. "It saves millions" many of them would say with a sly grin on their faces.

"How many more are we looking at?" asked Ralph looking even more worried.
"If we get another one, we would be in terrific shape to get the rent shared to a minuscule amount. If yet another comes we will be saving millions!" said Rajendra not masking his ecstasy.
"But how will six people live in such a small space? I mean even three is too much," Ralph said looking exhausted.

"We have had six people living in two bedroom apartments like this one. Six in a three bedroom apartment is much better!"
Both look at each other, Ralph as stunned as he could ever be. "Don't worry chap, you will get used to it," said Rajendra sensing Ralph's discomfort with the practice of sharing living space.
"I hope so," muttered Ralph as he retired to his room.
He began pulling out the other important things from his suitcase. *"I'm going to need these toiletries and shaving blades in the coming days. These cream-colored pants will go well with this grey T-shirt. I guess I will leave the rest in the suitcase. We might be relocating in a week anyways,"* he thought to himself.
"What's this heavy feeling in my chest," he felt as he woke up the next morning.
"Gosh the orientation session is at 9:30 am followed by class at 6."

Pulling himself from the thin mat he sat with a limp head, still fairly drowsy and disoriented.

He grabbed his toothbrush and headed in the direction of the faint noise of falling water. The door was tightly locked from the inside and

Rajendra seemed to be humming his favorite tune of "dum chika dum[11]" to rhyme with it.

He waited for ten minutes hoping that Rajendra would complete his bath. But he didn't. "*I need to brush my teeth. This son of an ass seems to be taking an eternity*," muttered Ralph, as he proceeded to use the kitchen sink.

He was in the middle of brushing when Rajendra completes his bath and comes into the kitchen. He is a little surprised to hear the dull thud of heavy spit hitting the metallic sink. "What! You are brushing in the kitchen sink," he said, mouth wide open with a feeling of surprise and disgust.

"I waited for you to finish your bath but you were still in there. So I thought of completing my washing in this sink, as it was getting late."
"But we cook our food there. It's not the best place for personal hygiene."
"Oh sorry," said Ralph as he continued washing in the sink.

Though visibly irritated Rajendra maintained his calm.

"You can wash up in the bathroom. It's available now," he said with an air of urgency in his tone.

Ralph completed the remainder of his ablutions in the bathroom. He headed to the university without breakfast and was happy that the discussion with Rajendra didn't escalate into a full-fledged argument.

****

The morning session was relatively light. Besides finding a seat to view the happenings at the front of the large classroom, Ralph looks at the calm faces of a group of Chinese students. They seem very relaxed and assured in their large group. "*Group strength I guess*," thinks Ralph to himself. Watching the lonesome American sitting by himself he is confounded by the vast gap in American and Asian outlooks to life and

---

[11] "**Dum chika dum**" is one of several tunes often sung in the Indian subcontinent

living. The Chinese students, all together in a group, seem to be embracing a collectivistic culture. There is a free exchange of information and ideas between them or at least that's what it seems like. The lone American on the other hand just has the company of his book.

Ralph is alone too. Not because he doesn't have friends, or doesn't want friends. Rather he hasn't yet seen a sizeable number of Indians. Though he wonders if he would be open to going and conversing with the predominantly South Indian community in the computer engineering program. Being of an Indo-European culture he is probably not at ease with their orthodox practices. Never having had an inclination to reading he doesn't even have a book for company. Setting aside the financial resources to obtain a book is yet another issue to address. There are many and multi-dimensional issues that need regular attention.

The head of the computer department, Dr. Barbati, enters the classroom and gives an elaborate talk on the importance and benefits of computers in modern-day society. The man was of medium height, portly and had long ungainly hair. His appearance resonated an outlook of carefree studiousness. But his speech was characterized by deep knowledge.

"You guys, I am sure are distinguished in your home countries. I see most students are from India, China and a few other countries. Here in Saint Paul's University, we have a terrific computer engineering program. And after going through it, you will see that your skills will sharpen and your horizons will widen."
"We cover everything from semantic-based analysis to fact-based decision science. And you have several tools and programming languages to help you in that."
"What programming languages will we be learning here?" asked the American student.
"We will be covering JAVA, Perl and basics of XML throughout the course. But you will have the choice to select other languages to study as well," said Prof Barbati.
"But you don't have to worry. Our curriculum is not just limited to these languages. We have a considerable amount of wiggle room to include top industry relevant subject matter at any time in the coursework. Just feel free to either mention your concerns to your professor or to bring them directly to my office."

Prof Barbati paused for a while, scanning the anxious faces of the students. "I am usually available Mondays, Wednesdays and Fridays from 9am to 12 noon for providing student consultation."
"And since today is the first day you can ask me any questions that you have for the remainder of the class. Or we can start talking about the various classes that we will be having this semester."
"What facilities do we have for international students in terms of help in classes or extra help on difficult course work?" asked an Indian student.
"Ummm, the faculty is generally pretty open to answering questions or helping students with doubts on coursework. Just be bold to go out there and ask the faculty for help. We have great people here in Saint Paul's!" he beamed.

Ralph began to wonder how or why the professor had this aura of calm around him. Was it something about the culture in the States or was it just his personal outlook on life? Did all professors and persons of seniority have this attitude? He wondered if the voice inside him would give him the answers but it didn't. As if to say that you will find the answers on your own.

The discussion on other courses began and Prof. Barbati indulged students with his knowledge about the computer science department and the approach that enterprising students need to take in their studies. The discussion was very enriching. And the one hour that it lasted seemed like ten minutes. "I must say you guys are quite curious and interested in the course. That's a good thing. We are always happy to see students of this caliber in our university."
"Well, the orientation is done for now. If any of you have questions to ask me I will be here for another ten to fifteen minutes. But if not, then it was nice meeting all of you. Have a great remainder of the day. And see you here again at 2pm."

****

Ralph felt the same rumbling sensation in his belly as he did when he first came to the US. He decided to go to the cafeteria and inquire if any positions had opened.

"You can come on Wednesday and speak to our manager for a position. We are looking for some kitchen help. We could use you," said the lady with a smile on her face.

Not wanting to spend $9 on the all you can eat buffet, he walked to Wendy's and bought a $2 sandwich. Sitting alone at the table, he had only his thoughts for company. The most reliable companion of international students in the US is their loneliness. Not because they haven't tried to meet more people or that they are shy. Well, both of those facts might be true to some extent. But even those extrovert students who try to make friends are often conflicted by the gross difference in attitudes and cultures when it comes to befriending American students.

Often times one doesn't know what to say when speaking to an American student and vice versa. Ralph knew that friends are the key to understanding any culture. But making friends here in the States seemed a little different based on what he had noticed and heard so far. Deep down Ralph knew that his Inner Voice would help him understand the things that he didn't know or failed to understand. As he completed the last bits of his burger he felt this urge to start learning and gaining a command of his subject area – computer science.

"To be good in what you do is the ultimate goal of education," he thought. "Character is the goal of all education," Dad would emphatically say. He proceeded to the lab on the third floor of the computer science building. *"Gosh I guess I need an ID card. Sandeep had told me to get it yesterday along with the letter from the international office,"* he said to himself sounding worried.

The one hour before the next class should be enough to get the letter and the ID card he thought. He rushed down the stairs and started looking for a map to find the location of the international office. He knew that he should have done this when he first came to the States. He sought consolation in the fact that he was only one day late on this front. He would later realize that even one day is a long time when paper work is involved in the US.

"These maps are useless," he screamed to himself. Walking a few steps further he saw a tall girl walking towards him. "Excuse me. Do you know where the office for international students is located?"
"Sorry…what?"
"The office for international students. I need to go there."

"I am not sure we have one here. Or maybe you are looking for the registrar's office."
"Where is that?"
"It's in the building behind you," she pointed.

Ralph wanted to believe the white girl. But something told him that that is the wrong location. Sandeep had made a brief mention of the international office being somewhere outside the university campus area. *"So if it's outside the campus area there is no way it can be in the building behind me. I have got to find another person to help me out,"* he thought.

"Okay thanks," he replied to the girl as he headed away from the building behind him.
"It's not that way, though" she replied seeing him proceed in the opposite direction.

He ignored her and proceeded in that direction anyway.
As he rushed along the outer perimeter of the university he came across a genial looking security guard. The guard, seeing Ralph all charged up and adrenaline loaded smiled at him and said hi.

"Everything alright there young fella?" he smiled.
"Actually I am looking for the office for international students. Do you know where it is?" asked an exasperated Ralph.
"I think it is the office across the road from here," he said pointing to the dilapidated building painted in a pale white shade.
"Thanks so much Sir," said a grateful Ralph as he headed in the direction of the international office.

"Gosh good thing I came across him in time!" said Ralph to himself.

As he headed to the office across the street he felt a sense of being exposed – exposed to the road, the people and probably the elements known to mug and rob people. Mugging was one aspect of life in the US that had been a little less pronounced after the frequent on-campus shootings in US universities. "Never roam at night or if traveling be in a group. These thugs always look for weak or lone individuals to prey on," Dad would always say.

Ralph didn't really have a lot to fear as the day was still young and it was bright. But you never know when the unexpected could happen. He reached the office and tried to pull open the door. But it was locked. *"How can the office be closed at 1pm on a weekday?"* he wondered. *"Hope this is not the way they treat international students in this university!"*

Just as he was about to leave a faint looking boy appeared. His upright standing hair and mild demeanor were in stark contrast to that of the adrenaline-charged Ralph. Seeing the well-dressed young man sweating and panting profusely he quickly pressed the switch to open the door to the office. Ralph heard a slight sound and understood why they keep the door locked from the inside. If he felt so insecure when he was on the street it is only natural that they would feel unsafe with doors that could be pulled open. You never know who can walk into the office when the door is not locked from the outside.

He stood there not knowing what to do. As he vacillated, the boy inside gestured to him to pull open the door. He tried pulling the door but mixed up the movement between pulling the door towards him and the boy pressing the release switch at the right time. He finally managed to open the door. As he walked into the office, the abundance of paraphernalia and artifacts from all over the globe provided a great treat to the eyes. For once after setting foot on US soil he felt as though he was at home. Not in an Indian land, but in a multi-cultural setting where all cultures were embraced.

"How can I help you?" asked the frail looking boy.
"I want to meet the international advisor. Molly. Is she here?"
"Yes. She is. Do you have an appointment with her?"

Ralph had not made any appointment but he decided to say yes anyway. He figured it would be better to lie to try and meet her rather than say no and be shown the door right away.

"Ok. Let me go and inform her you are here. What did you say your name was?"
"Ralph. I am not sure if she remembers the appointment, though. We had arranged it a long time ago."

The boy looked puzzled. "Don't worry. Even if she doesn't remember she will still talk to you" he smiled. Ralph felt a surge of positivity.

A pale white woman came rushing out from a cabin. She was tall and well-built and looked very confident.

"Hi Ralph. When did you arrive?"
"Day before yesterday." He doesn't take the time to say hi to her.
"Well welcome to the US. How are you finding it?" she asked smiling at the handsome young man.
"It's interesting" he said not knowing what else to say. Although he felt a sense of being lost, he understood that it might not be appropriate to make his true feelings about America known to his American acquaintances. In true gentlemanly style, he put a smile on his face and maintained it.

"So where are you currently staying?"
"I am put up with a couple of global hawks mentors with whom I was communicating from India. It's kind of temporary right now," he said not knowing the permanency of the accommodation he was currently based at. His continuing there would depend on how he got along with the current inmates of the apartment. The voice inside him kept hinting that "preparation is the essence of hope." Hope that things will work out at the current apartment but prepare to move if they do not. Have a fall back option!

His inner voice resonated the feelings felt by many international students in regards to living in various places in America. Since the accommodations were mostly shared it was crucial that the occupants got along with each other. Not getting along often translated to not continuing to stay in the same place. Many had acrimonious disputes before parting ways. Ralph hoped he would not have to use his muscle power in the event of a separation. "Separations should be made as amicable as possible!" Dad used to say.

"Well I have to discuss some work relating to documentation. Do you have the documents with you or do I have to give them to you?" asked Ralph hoping to change the course of the discussion to more productive matters.
"Yes sure. Did you have an appointment with me today?"

There is a second of uneasy silence. And Ralph gropes for an answer that is not directly a lie but knows it can't be entirely the truth either. He was supposed to meet her the day he came to the US. But there had not been an explicit discussion of an appointment. Which is why she found it odd when the office boy said someone had an appointment with her and it wasn't on her calendar. Americans are normally very particular in regards to planning appointments. And they keep track of all their meetings with people.

"I guess you had told me to just come and meet with you after I reached the US."
"Yup. I'm glad you came," she replied wanting to make him feel comfortable.
"Please have a seat."
"Thanks" he said, glancing around her office.
"So did you bring any documents with you?"
"Oh yes!" He started removing the file containing the I-20 and passport from his bag.

As he removed the file from his bag he couldn't help but notice the extremely well-ordered room. Files were neatly kept in a file sorter. The desk and cabinets were spic-and-span. Everything looked very neat and tidy.

"I bet you might not take too long to find anything in this setting," he said as she removed a few forms from her cabinets.
"Oh I like to keep an orderly office," she smiled.

She opened a file and started writing a couple of things on the form.

"Oh, you write with your left hand. That's amazing. They say that people who write with their left hand are very creative."
"I'm not sure if that's true," she replied plainly.
"Well it was the finding at the end of a research study."
"Then I guess it must be true," she agreed looking uninterested.

As they get the paperwork sorted out, Ralph understands that Americans seem to have a very professional approach. They discuss only work-related stuff and are not content mollifying the atmosphere by doing small talk. In India, in many places, work is regularly relegated to the background in favor of gossip and jokes. But then again, Molly barely knows him apart from the scattered emails they have exchanged during the admissions process.

Although he seems to see the logic of the approach followed in America, his heart seems to crave the ease of conversation in India; that familiar, laid-back feeling. "But this is reality and you are in America!" says the Inner Voice. The speed with which Molly goes about signing and preparing the documents is amazing. She is efficient yet she doesn't make it seem like she is rushing.

All the paperwork gets done in thirty minutes flat. Ralph is amazed. "You should go to the security office and get your id card from them," she says in reply to his question about doors which require swipe access. "Sure. Thanks Molly."
"Oh by the way, will you be working on campus. Have you got a job or looking for a job?" asked Molly.
"Yes, I am looking."
"Well then to start a job on campus you would need a social security number and to apply for that you need to come collect a letter from me."
"Okay, could you give me the letter now?"
"Well, I first need you to get the letter from your employer on campus saying that you will be working for twenty hours. Ask your employer for that and give it to me. I will photocopy it and give you a letter to be presented to the Social Security Administration office. Both the letters need to be given to the office in Philadelphia while applying for your social security number. Without a social security number you can't have a job or earn any income in the US," she explained.
"Yes, I am actually trying for a job in the cafeteria and a few other places. Whichever place has a vacancy I will go for it."
"Yes just make sure you get the letter from them first and then get the social security number. You need it to start work."

The security office had a very efficient system to obtain the ID card and become a registered student. Although it didn't work at the computer lab the first few times, a couple of visits to the security office made the card workable.

The days passed by quickly with Ralph scrambling to attend the morning and afternoon classes. In between classes he struggled to catch up on some homework and nutrition. But more difficult than the schedule and the pace was the adjustment he needed to make at home living with his roommates.

"I need to buy something and cook at home. Eating outside is becoming expensive and I haven't got a job yet." The cafeteria manager had told him that he would give him a job as soon as he got his social security number card. The card had not yet arrived. No job meant no money to buy food. And the cash reserves he had brought from home were depleting rather quickly.

****

One fine day as he traveled back home from class he decided to enter the superstore on the way. He was quite taken aback by the well-arranged assortment of products and colorful packaging. Super markets weren't as clean back home. Let alone so well stocked and neatly kept. All prices were clearly stated on the shelf racks and items neatly arranged. It looked very chic!

Although he hadn't planned on buying anything he decided to buy the sumptuous looking sausages in the meats section. How would he store the sausages at home, though? Rajendra had specified to him that this was a pure vegetarian household and non-vegetarian items would not be entertained. Even if he hid the sausages from view in the fridge how would he disguise the smell while cooking them? Buying the sausages posed a serious challenge but he would find a way to deal with them. "Where there is a will, there is a way," reminded the Inner Voice.

Carefully putting the pack of sausages in a colored bag he placed them in the corner of the freezer behind other packs of groceries. He would come back to cook them at an appropriate time. The following day he got a brainwave. He figured that the best way to fight enforcement was to join it. He would use the same techniques and cooking methods dear to Rajendra to disguise his cooking of sausages.

He started preparing the dish of pulses – spicy dal (a typically vegetarian dish). Inserting finely sliced sausages in the mixture he cooked the meat and had his first home cooked meal in the US. And it was not vegetarian although it appeared to be from the outside. He made sure he prepared the dish in his own utensil so that it would be out of bounds to Rajendra.

A few days later, Madhu returned home from his visit to his uncle's place in Atlanta, Georgia. On entering the bathroom, he noticed an underwear behind the bathroom door. He quickly summoned Rajendra and inquired who it belongs to. "It must be Ralph's," said Rajendra. They requested him to remove it at once and not to keep it there again. "Please don't keep your garments in the bathroom. It's a public bathroom and we want to keep it hygienic," stated Madhu.

The lease was about to expire and they decided to move to a new apartment. Generally renewing a lease is difficult as the condition of the apartment is rather bad after one year or less of staying there. Most Asian students know this. They find it hard to maintain an apartment in good condition because of the transience of their academic and professional lives in the US. Everybody seems to be constantly on the move. Classes, meetings, appointments, group sessions, conferences what have you. Hence, keeping the apartment clean and tidy is the last thing on their mind.

"Hey Ralph we are moving to another apartment. So just pack your stuff and be ready. We are moving tomorrow," said Rajendra on a Thursday.

Ralph didn't answer. "And also we need someone to sign the lease. Could you sign the lease?"
"I have just come to the US. How can I sign the lease? I don't even have a credit card," said Ralph looking surprised with Rajendra's suggestion. "Because our name was on the lease of the previous apartment. We need someone to sign the new lease so they don't figure out that the same people are trying to rent out a different apartment," said Madhu from behind Ralph.

Ralph began to suspect foul play. *"Why would they not want their names to be seen again? Do they want to get me trapped in some sort of trouble? Have they done something wrong in the earlier lease?"* he wonders. Questions of doom begin to haunt him.

"Why can't you sign the lease yourself? Is there anything you are hiding?"
"No. Not at all. You are not going to get into trouble for signing a lease. This is not a jail sentence or something," said Madhu.

Ralph had heard stories of people signing agreements and getting into trouble when they bound themselves to terms they couldn't abide by. Even though the signatory wasn't a direct beneficiary of the contract, the very fact that his or her signature is on the contract documents was reason enough to pursue them to recover the costs or recompense agreed at the time of the contract.

"I have a feeling that these guys are trying to get me into trouble. I mustn't rush my decision just because they are pushing me into it," Ralph thought.

"I don't want to sign the lease right now," he said.
"Then we won't have a place to move into. Where do you want to live? Winter is approaching," replied Rajendra.
"Yeah. This is just a lease and nothing else. Why don't you sign it?" asked Madhu sensing Ralph's hesitation.
"I feel I am too new in this country to sign such a document. If you sign it I can contribute my share of the monthly rent."
"What the heck man. Even we contribute our share of the rent. There are no more marks for doing that. By signing the lease you would make it possible for us to have a nice apartment. Why don't you understand that!" hollered Madhu.
"We just need your signature on the lease. You don't have to abide by it," seconded Rajendra.
"And what if something goes wrong? I would be responsible for it since the landlords would see my name on the lease."
"Not at all."
"Who told you that?"

Rajendra and Madhu reply in quick succession. They begin to pile the pressure on Ralph using a combination of threats and peer pressure. They know he is new to the country and doesn't know much about the legal implications of contracts. They feel it would be easier to get him to sign the contract. By this they don't intend him any trouble. But should any one of them have to move for any reason they would not be obligated to find a substitute tenant. In fact, they wouldn't be responsible for breaking the lease or have to be involved in any hassle concerning the lease. Breaking a lease involves a penalty. The penalty could either involve paying two month's rent or forfeiting the security deposit or a combination of both. Generally, landlords have specific measures to secure their earnings. You are lucky if you have easy terms and conditions. The person who signs the lease contract generally has his or her social security number associated with the lease. Non-payment of the entire lease amount causes the rental company to file 'damage claims' on the individual's credit report. Having a clean credit report is important to get proper access to loans, credit cards or any sort of financial assistance in the future.

"If you don't sign the lease we might not be able to keep you in the apartment. You would need a new place. And it's hard to find one these days. Just think about it," replied Rajendra sternly.
"Yes and you don't get as good rents as living with us gets you," said Madhu.
"But you guys have so many sharing the same apartment. The rent reduces because of the crowd in the apartment. That's not a very good thing. You barely have any privacy and room in the apartment. Moreover people seem to keep coming and going," countered Ralph.
"You have come here to study; not to find a place to live. The way we stay helps us save a lot of money. It creates a lot of unity. I recently got an interview for a position at Siemens. It was because of a contact I had met through group living. He was living with us for a short time but we became good friends. You think this way of living is bad?"
"Madhu, you might have benefits of group living. But what you are asking me to do is not possible. I cannot sign this contract. I already have enough problems of my own and don't want more," explained Ralph.
"You need to stop looking at things as problems. We are doing this so we can have a nice place to stay" replied Rajendra.
"We can have a nice place but not at my expense."
"Okay if you are adamant we will have no choice but to leave you to find a place for yourself on your own" stated Madhu.

Ralph didn't flinch but knew that the arguments with Rajendra and Madhu were going to continue and probably escalate in intensity. Both Rajendra and Madhu leave the room and go into Rajendra's room. Ralph is left dumbfounded in regards to their apparent threat. But he resolves to stay his ground no matter what. "Always be prepared!" reminds the Inner Voice.

The hours and days in the apartment get tense as the end date of the lease draws closer. Almost every night after Ralph came home from classes there used to be an argument in regards to getting the new lease signed.

Five days before the lease was to end, Ralph realizes that the acrimony towards him has reached boiling point. He knew that his international student advisor ought to help him. He goes to her office without an appointment and asks to see her. His sense of urgency is too deep for the office boy or her to ask him if he had an appointment. Not that he cared if they did.

"I need a place to stay. The lease of the place I am currently living at is about to expire and the roommates don't have space for me in the new place where they are moving," he hollered.

"I think there is a place not too far from here called International House where they have rooms for rent," replied Molly. He kept standing there in front of her motionless. "You could go there and find out," she said seeing him still standing in front of her.
"Where is it located?"
"Let me see, ummmh; it's straight down Overbrook Avenue on 6305 Lowerbrook Avenue. Go and check it out. You can't miss it. They always have a room. In fact, the director recently called to inform us they have more rooms getting empty in a few days."
"Thanks," he said as he dashed towards the door.

Molly sensed his urgency and silently seemed to hope for the best for him.

****

The friendly Nigerian guy at International House seemed extremely happy to have a student inquiring for a room in person. Normally they had phone inquiries that never materialized into appointments or if they did folks rarely showed up.

Ralph saw the well decked room and was happy with the size of the house, its layout and the privacy it afforded. The house didn't have too many rules and best of all, they allowed consumption of non-vegetarian food. In fact Kuda, the easy going director did all the grocery shopping for the whole house. All the tenants paid was the rent. Kuda also liked the Indian who had shown up at the house with such interest and vigor.

They shook hands and signed the lease. Ralph paid him the security deposit, agreeing to pay the remaining amount towards the first month's rent on his return.

The accommodation issue out of the way, Ralph now had to figure out how to move his stuff from the shared apartment to the new room at International House. He rushed to the security office and asked the attendant there if they had any special service to help international students to move house. He expected to use the fact that he is an international student to come to his aid. Maybe they would feel bad that he didn't have a car or any mode of transport other than public transport and give him a ride along with his stuff to the new place. Or he could talk them into providing him with a ride along with his baggage.

He just had two suitcases, though. He figured if he didn't get the support of the security office he would have to use the shuttle service to move his stuff. "Hi Sir, I am Ralph Coelho. I am a new student at St. Paul's. I have been looking for a place to stay and I finally found one. But I need to move there and I don't have a car. Would you be able to help me with an escort van so that I can load my two suitcases and reach the new place? I currently live at the Henryville Apartments."

The attendant kept looking at the computer screen he was looking at when Ralph entered the security office. Only momentarily had he paused to have a glance at Ralph. Something seemed to be telling Ralph that this guy might be friendly although his outward demeanor showed otherwise. But it wasn't his inner voice that suggested this.

The attendant's face was very chubby, yet stern. His demeanor though reflected geniality. Something about the way he looked at the computer screen and typed on the keyboard reflected a sense of calm and kindness.

After a slight pause, the chubby attendant turned to Ralph and asked him if he had any friends. "No I don't," replied Ralph. "Why?"

"Just wanted to know if you would have anybody to help you bring the suitcases from your apartment to the van," replied the portly attendant smiling.

"So that means I am going to get the escort to help me move?" asked Ralph half smiling.

"You got it young man!" smiled the portly attendant. "When would you like to have the van come to take you?"

"Would it be possible today at around 3pm noon time?"

He looked through the van schedule and looked for an appropriate time when the escort service would be relatively less occupied. "Okay we cannot do 3 pm but 5:30 pm would be a possibility."

"5:30 pm would be fine," Ralph blurts not wanting to miss the opportunity to get the ride.
"Okay so where do you want to move to?"
"I am moving to 6305 Lowerbrook Avenue."
"Cool so just give a call at around 5:15pm to ask for the escort" said the chubby attendant.
"Thanks so much Sir. Appreciate the help!"
"That's what we're here for. All the best with everything," smiled the genial man.
"Absolutely," said Ralph as he gestured the thumbs up sign.

Ralph didn't think it would be that easy to get a ride to the new place. But probably fate wanted him to get to the new place as easily and comfortably as possible. The omens were definitely showing positive signs.

As he got busy packing his stuff in the suitcases, Ralph got concerned about his academic conduct. Since school had started he had simply been shuttling between school and home; doing some grocery shopping and trying to catch up on homework assignments. Between all these things, there were the periodic disturbances caused by arguments with the loathsome roommates forcing him to sign the lease contract. He hadn't been able to do any measure of meaningful studies. Computer science was a rigorous field requiring a deep understanding of concepts and diligent practice. How could he continue like this?

If his grades dropped or he slipped in his understanding of core material, his academic prowess could be hampered. He feared poor grades. He had heard that poor grades of C or below in more than two courses would mean expulsion from the program. He would have to complete the transition to a new place, get a job and get settled before time ran out for him in terms of his academic obligations. He would soon realize that it was not 'catching up' that was needed now but rather damage control.

At 4:45 pm he remembers that he needs to make a call to the security office. But doesn't have a phone to do so. He had used the apartment reception once before and he figured one more call for a good purpose wouldn't be too much to ask for.

Seeing the packed suitcases, Rajendra asked him what's going on.

"I am moving to a new place" Ralph replied curtly.
"Oh when?" asks Rajendra looking surprised and worried.
"Now!"

Rajendra is dumbfounded. He didn't think in his wildest dreams that Ralph, the newcomer from Goa would be able to find a new place in less than two weeks. As Ralph carted away the second suitcase, Rajendra felt a stab of shame. For six days in a row they kept arguing with him to obtain his signature on the lease contract and for six straight days he struggled against their recalcitrant demands. In spite of being new and lonely in a foreign land, he held out. They were supposed to be his guardians and mentors here but instead they chose to harass him to serve their selfish ends. Although it was Madhu who initiated the idea against Ralph, Rajendra was guilty of supporting Madhu in his aims.

Rajendra could not help but console himself. He wanted to make up with Ralph but feared rejection from the empowered fella. If he was capable of finding a place for himself so early in his stay in the US; what more could he be capable of? I ought to make amends with him so I can stay in touch with him, thought Rajendra to himself. But it was too late. Ralph had already carted out the last of the two suitcases. Through the window he could see the lad lugging the suitcases into the maroon university escort van. "Could I have offered to help him with the suitcase? Probably if I reached out I could have helped foster a rapprochement with him after the alienation of the last couple of days," muttered Rajendra to himself.

In an alien land, it always helps to have strong allies. Capable and willing friends are one of the best resources any person could have, not just an international student.

****

The sweat on Ralph's neck began to evaporate with the cool breeze blowing through the window. As he relaxed his stressed sinews he could feel the comforts that would come his way as he began his stay at the International House. He hoped that the stability gained through a nice place to stay would translate into advantages in terms of better study time and better grades.

On arriving at International House, he immediately opens the suitcases and dispatches the contents to the appropriate cabinets and cupboards. He has a desk and a table lamp. The house even has wireless internet. However, he deeply feels the absence of a computer. He knows he needs a laptop. But does he have the money to purchase it? With his reserves of hard currency dwindling, he is not sure. Moreover, his social security number hasn't arrived which means he can't start the job in the cafeteria.

He needs to conserve his monetary resources to pay the rent and keep some for any unforeseen contingencies. But without a computer, he is subject to the timings of the computer lab and the library. It is a common fact that computer science students need to have 24/7 access to a computer. How am I to get out of this situation? *"If I am to buy a computer immediately I might have to borrow a relatively large amount. I wish I had a credit card."*

One week races on and the mid-term test he answers reveals to him his weakness in computing concepts. It is now clear that he would need nothing short of a miracle if he is to get through the selected courses successfully. A personal computer would have been a tiny step in the direction of that miracle although an expensive one, he thought to himself. A friend had told him that a Toshiba laptop was one of the premier models of laptops available. In terms of durability, performance, and few other factors it scored extremely high.

He decided to conduct his own research too. For some reason, Ralph had this uncanny ability to condense results and understand things quickly. Probably it was from his ability to talk to multiple girls in online chat rooms at the same time. Or probably from his ability to constantly mine the internet for information. He wasn't sure where his searching skill set came from but he knew it would have to get better in the US. He had tons of curriculum related information he had to mine anyways.

Fridays were supposed to be the best days to purchase electronic items. Firstly, retailers would push leftover stock before the start of the next week. And they needed to make room for the incoming stock for the coming week so they were more likely to give discounts on various products. Kuda knew of a place in the city where laptops were being sold. He agreed to give Ralph a ride there.

Ralph was amazed to see the wide assortment of laptops and cell phones on display at the store. He opted for the Toshiba A65 model. Although it was almost $680 he was confident of its capabilities and potential to help him get through his computer science course. He had heard from several friends that a Toshiba is among the better of the laptop brands and can take a lot of punishment in terms of long working hours and great speeds.

"This model is a good one. Only thing it is pricey," said Ralph pointing to the Toshiba laptop.
"You should buy a laptop that will serve your requirements in the best possible manner. Don't go to look at the price. If you pay a good price now you will end up with a good product. But if you try to save money, you might not end up with the quality you want and then spend more on repairing it," counseled Kuda.
"But I don't have that much. I just have $550 and it costs $680. I'm short by $130."
"Well, I can pitch in $130 for you. And when you get home you can pay me."

Ralph is silent as he looks at the ground.

"Or if you don't have it you can pay me whenever you get the money," said Kuda sensing Ralph's monetary predicament.

Ralph was visibly grateful with the extent of Kuda's benevolence. He couldn't remember if he had ever received this level of gratitude and appreciation since he arrived in the States. He began to feel a great sense of fulfillment at having found the International House and at having found Kuda. He looked back at his short stay in the Henryville Apartments and remembered the agony and pain he had to go through at the hands of his fellow countrymen.

But seeing the effusive graciousness of Kuda, he felt that the conflict with the "south Indians" was a blessing in disguise. He wouldn't have searched for a new place if it wasn't for that conflict. And he wouldn't have had the need to become resourceful if all had come to him nice and easy. In the process of trying to find a new place he had to go through struggles that taught him about unseen hardships that life throws at you. At home, protected by Mum and Dad, he had no idea of the perils and pressures that exist in the world. He had his first experience with real life. Life in a foreign land where all he could fall back on was his head, his heart and the omnipresent Inner voice.

As they drove back home, happy with the new laptop he had just bought; a sort of calm descended on the two men. While they had been focused to the point of being agitated while driving towards the store; the purchase had given them a feeling of accomplishment. Almost like the fulfillment a mother feels when a baby is born. Deep down Ralph resolved that although Kuda had been kind enough to help him with the extra cash, he would not take advantage of the man's kindness. He resolved to get the campus job and repay Kuda as soon as he could.

They arrive home and Ralph waited for Kuda as he parked the car in the garage driveway. As Kuda approached Ralph, he smiled and looked at the young man with a mix of admiration and amusement. At one end he was amazed at the level of initiative and foresight Ralph had; on the other he was kind of amused that he took only $550 with him to the store. But Kuda is familiar with that situation. He remembers how he came to the United States as a refugee fleeing the sectarian violence in Nigeria and barely had any money to live off. He worked in a local Presbyterian church as a clerk and on the weekends helped with the soup kitchen. With the meager earnings he made, he managed to scrape a living. The tragedies he witnessed in Nigeria and the hope and solace that Christ gave him strengthened his faith in Christianity. He started taking a course in theology at the church and was referred to the Presbyterian seminary for further studies by a pastor who saw a lot of promise in him. Through diligent study and dedicated efforts he completed the theology program and became qualified to minister in the church.

"Ralph, now you have a good computer. Make the best of it to get where you need to," said Kuda with an air of seriousness in his tone.

"Yes, I have a lot to cover since I am getting this laptop late. I am going to have to work against time to get things done. Thanks for your help," replied Ralph gratefully.

Deep down Ralph had an inkling that although things had been rough thus far; this was the start of the upswing. He would need to apply himself very diligently though to see things through to fruition. Somewhere he heard his Inner voice saying that things would be hard, but if he persevered in spite of all the tragedies he would see light at the end of the tunnel.

Ralph thanked Kuda again for all his support and proceeded to his room. He began to set up the laptop. He was happy to receive a mouse. It was part of the complementary sale. But along with the mouse he had also received a MS-Office CD at a discounted rate. He always thanked his stars for taking him to places at the right time, for showing him the right direction. He always believed he had pretty good luck on the whole except for the venture that led him to the US. In spite of all the minor blessings he had received he still believed he had to endure tremendous hardship to continue his stay and study in the States. A lot of students did have a similar feeling of dissonance after coming to the country that was believed to have the foundation of innovation and enterprise.

Was it his lack of work experience and indeed experience in self-life in India that was responsible for his hardships or was it just his fate that wanted him to bear such hardship. "*Why would fate want me to bear such troubles?*" he often thought. "*Probably to help me learn about life and to dream in spite of all of life's tribulations.*" Dad had told him that life was hard and that you would need to struggle through it to find what you want.

"The journey might take you far and wide but you will eventually find your calling," Dad would often say. *Ralph thought that life was not about finding what you want, but rather finding what God had sent you to the world to find.* "God always has a plan for everyone. It is God who shows you the direction when you feel you have none" Mum would always say to him.

The other things that come in your way on the way to your destiny are but distractions. But even distractions have a purpose in life. They are meant to teach you how to get focused. Ralph knew he hadn't seen as many distractions as he had expected in the US. He knew that there would be more opportunities to get distracted and lose focus. For now, he wanted to start setting things right. "The path to grand success starts with small steps," he remembered a phrase he had read a long time ago.

****

He starts preparing for the final test the next day. He has eighteen topics to complete and he knows only two. The computing skills he acquired in his degree program in India seemed like a cropper compared to the material he is going to need to get through for this course. To add to his predicament he doesn't have the money to buy the textbooks. Normally, international students borrow textbooks from the previous batch of international students. Or they simply download textbooks online. Ralph had neither. He had only the meager notes given by the professor. He had no textbook, no friends to ask information to; no Godfather. All he had was faith in his heart. All along the Inner voice kept telling him to be steadfast in spite of seemingly insurmountable odds. He was beyond late in his preparation for the final test but he had hope.

Trying to contact his Indian friends from the class was subject to his relationship with them. He instead decided to google concepts and information concerning the test the next day. Pulling together all the nerve, strength, and will he had he motivated himself to sit the entire day in front of the new laptop. He read and read. When he couldn't read he went downstairs and prepared a small meal. As he had the meal, he tried to narrate some concepts he had learned to himself so as to strengthen memory and recall.

He quickly washed the plate and proceeded to his room to study. "*If the professor himself had seen these efforts, he probably would have exempted me from taking the exam,*" thought Ralph. But that was merely wishful thinking. No amount of effort justifies a poor result. However, a great showing generally overshadows a meager effort. For some reason, the Inner voice kept telling him to do his best now even though he knew he had not covered a lot of the curriculum all these weeks.

The test the next day was sordidly difficult. Fifty percent of the test was objective and the other fifty percent involved writing code. Ralph groped for the answers but was happy that he had done his best to bridge the herculean gap between what he knew and what he needed to learn.

Sometimes it is hope for a better future that eggs us on in spite of difficult circumstances.

A week later he would have his results. He knew what he needed to do in the meantime, though. He went home and started researching various topics relating to computer programming. As he got increasingly familiar with the laptop he began to assimilate various search techniques using Google and a host of other online search engines. A sense of confidence began to resonate in his entire being.

He kept hitting the keyboard and clicking away at the mouse. He didn't have a specific purpose for doing what he was doing. But he just wanted to learn all that he did not understand. He would later realize that sincere dedication to learning always pays off even though you might not see immediate results.

****

One week went by in a jiffy. The maroon and white webpage of the university didn't seem like much to look at but he had reason to ponder over it. Out of the three courses he took in the first semester of his time in the US, he had managed to scrape through two and had failed the third. A 'fail' designation in India is equal to a 'C' grade in the US. The email from the professor suggested he would have to take the course again. Taking the course again meant paying for it all over again. Not something that a lot of international students are comfortable with. In fact, most people would balk at the thought of spending a few thousand dollars for the same purpose again.

Since he was still without a job and without a graduate assistantship, Ralph had to suffer the infamy of narrating the disappointing news back home to Mum. "Okay, no problem. Don't lose heart because of this. I will wire the money tomorrow," said Mum. Although she was taken aback she concealed her disappointment. She voiced her concerns to her husband. The perennial optimist that he was; he told her that better times were on the horizon.

The rupee to dollar exchange rate was pretty high with one dollar valued at approximately forty-five rupees. Failing a course meant paying money for the same purpose without any value derived from the money already spent. It was definitely a huge drain for middle-class Asian parents who earned every penny through sheer hard work.

"Be strong Ralph! Don't give up in spite of all that happens. Study harder and success will be yours. This is just the start so don't blame yourself for failing the course. You will do well," she urged her eldest son.

Though dejected he started the course again along with courses he needed to take for the other semester. There would be times when he would be sitting at home trying to study and loneliness and dejection would overtake him. He sought refuge in the library to get away from his blues and maintain his concentration. But his inner voice once again came to his rescue. "*Failure is only a distraction from the fortune that awaits you. Do not give up no matter how distracting the circumstances or how painful the situation,*" the Inner voice kept reiterating.

A ROAD LESS TRAVELLED AND LOVE

THE SECOND SEMESTER HAD started out on a positive note with a terrific test result in all three courses. The laptop and his new found expertise in optimizing its use began to make things flow faster. He wondered if this is the upswing the Inner voice had been talking about all along.

One day as he was sitting in the Social Engineering class the professor announced that the course would involve working in two team projects. The teams were assigned by random numbers repeated in a sequence. When the teams assembled, Ralph was surprised to find that there wasn't a single international student in his team. He was a little disappointed that he didn't realize that he was in fact the only international student in the class until then. He wondered how he could have been so oblivious to the happenings around him. "Guess it is a lack of sensory perception," suggested the Inner Voice.

"Probably that's something I need to learn. How to be more aware of my surroundings," he said to himself. He didn't feel any overt hostility being directed toward him due to his apparent minority status. But wondered how he was going to interact with his teammates as easily as he did with his friends when in India. For one, he still found it a little difficult to understand some terms and clichés used by his American colleagues. Even in the first semester, he was lucky he didn't have to work in a team. In fact, most of the classes had a majority of Chinese students. Not this one though. Being a non-programming class, most American students preferred taking it to get enough credits to obtain the degree or simply to avoid taking programming-related courses.

Not to say that Americans didn't like programming courses. But it was a commonly believed truth that most people who join computer science are international students from China, India, and a few other parts of Asia and the Middle East. Most Americans opt for management-related

97

positions and even those that opt for computer science are generally content with taking non-programming courses or courses more related to the business aspects of IT.

A clear advantage enjoyed by American students over their international colleagues was their employment status. Most American students had full-time jobs and usually attended the courses because their employers paid for them. Many of them attended with the sole aim of obtaining a degree to show to any prospective employer or simply for access to 'bragging rights.'

Ralph sometimes wondered what would be his situation if he had been a green card holder or a citizen. Getting a job would be easy for one. But the freedom of not being tied down by his paperwork would afford him the chance to explore other avenues for greater opportunity or business ventures.

"Okay so I guess we have five individual projects to get done and three group projects," said Dan. "Pretty short time period within which we have to get these things done. And then it's the three group projects that need to get done as well...phew!!"
"Well, time pressure is a good thing in a way because if we didn't have that, we would probably wait until the last minute and hurry up towards the end anyways. Why not just scramble right now!" counseled Ian. Denise and Bob were quite non-committal during the entire conversation. Ralph stayed mum not knowing what to say. He had faced a bit of an issue trying to understand the American accent very early in his stay in the US. Now he was a bit confounded with the varied topics that they would discuss. Sometimes he thought of them as rather trivial; at other times he was astounded by the level of importance and value they placed on the smallest of things in life. He had not experienced these types of in-depth discussions at home. In fact, Mum and Dad barely spoke enough at home. Not in the least, of daily things in life or about the things that mattered. Conversations would generally be about where are you going tomorrow or did you get that done today and other ordinary daily life things.

Something about American life suggested that valuable time to sit back and reflect on the happenings of the day or the season was a necessity. They would always assign time for thinking and analysis, however busy the day might be.

The first three individual projects consisted of extensive research and Ralph was only too happy to crunch through them. Over the last couple of weeks, he had developed this expertise in searching for varied documents and to source information from diverse websites. In fact, continuing his work on doing the course projects gave him a great sense of fulfillment because of the opportunity to put his hard earned online research skills to work.

The projects that would have normally taken two to three days, he completed in a mere one day using his newly acquired skill set. The other two individual projects involved a little more of analysis and thinking than mere research. He was not much experienced in doing analytical related work. He had scraped through his engineering degree back home and couldn't even find a job. His understanding of the course material was very poor. *"How am I going to manage these analysis intensive projects here,"* he wondered.

However, he took consolation in the fact that he was way ahead of schedule with the other projects and the other projects wouldn't be due until the three that were completed were submitted. For now he would have to regain some of the energy he had expended doing the first three projects and just pray and hope that the anxiety within him would subside. Ralph became anxious when he landed in the States; seeing the big buildings, big roads, and multiple differences in the place from things in his home country. He would regularly feel a sense of confusion mixed with a loss at the idea of not having achieved his full potential in studies back home. Now he would have to work very hard at doing well in the States. How much he wished he had gotten more out of his education back home. He did realize though, that his efforts were sublunary and way below the mark needed to understand the concepts that he was being taught.

****

At the JAVA II programming class, a sense of calm seemed to dawn upon him. Firstly he had completed the complicated assignment relating to his social engineering class. The group dynamics in the team were more complicated than the subject matter itself.

JAVA II was a cake walk particularly since his grades in JAVA I were stellar. However, he would prefer not to be explicit about the third reason for his calmness. A female interest had recently piqued his attention. Matilda came to St. Paul's University for a semester. Hurricane Katrina had devastated her hometown of New Orleans and among the network of Jesuit universities in the country, St. Paul's had offered to accept students from disaster ravaged universities around the country.

"Do you have an extra pen?" she asked plainly looking into the young man's eyes. He didn't have one on him but didn't feel like turning the sexy damsel down. Ralph knew that women have a tendency of getting close by asking for help. When you help them willingly they like it. Then they ask you for more help. When you help them again they become comfortable with you. And the cycle continues. And what is the key to a successful relationship with a woman? – service with a smile! Well not always. But at least if you are there for her when she needs it most, you will have a good chance of striking it big with most women.

As he rummaged through his bag, he realized he didn't have another pen. Rather just a pencil. He quickly dropped the ball point pen from the corner of his left hand into the bag and pretended to have an extra pen.

"Woah! Your lucky day. I have one," he said. She smiled as he stretched out his hand to give her the pen.
"Thanks" she gushed.

Ralph was of medium height, but broad and well built. His black hair and tawny skin tone, coupled with a smooth swagger made him seem like an uncrowned actor. No wonder Matilda was quite impressed with Ralph. The entire class goes by and Ralph tries to hide his pencil from her so that she doesn't think he gave her the only pen he had. Moreover, he didn't want her to know that he wanted to satisfy her request so bad that he gave her the only pen he had on him.

Once the class was over he waited for her to come and return his pen. But she seemed to be taking her own time. He figured it won't be good to go and ask her for the pen. So he packed his books in the bag and prepared to walk out. He turned to exit the door. At that very moment a soft voice from behind him said, "Hey there, hold on."

He turned around to the sight of a slim, svelte girl. She had a wide smile on her face and seemed elated that the young man was so helpful, yet so simple.

"Thanks so much for the pen."
"Oh no problem."
"Did you take down everything?" he smiled.
"Oh yes," she gushed.
"This class is a little intense so I tend to be slow for its pace; but your pen definitely helped. Thanks so much!"
"Sure. I'm Ralph by the way."
"Oh. I'm Matilda. Nice to meet you."

Both of them smiled at each other with glee. He was seemingly more excited than her.

"Well, look forward to meeting you in the next class," she said, sensing a kind of unsaid attraction between them.
"Me too," he replied with a feeling of cool confidence.

****

The day of reckoning finally arrived. That Wednesday evening, Professor Panini declared that groups would need to start work on their projects as the deadline for the first group project was one and half weeks to the day.

"Hey why don't all of us meet up for five minutes after class. Let's discuss the project outline," declared Dan to the group. None of the members replied. Dan is a short, portly man with small eyes and a cherubic face. He has bushy eyebrows and a large jaw which gives him a fiendish look. He is confident and brash and seems to communicate openly leaving nothing to doubt. He seems to have many years of experience behind him to suggest the least.

The group convened around a rectangular table at the end of the classroom. Dan took the center seat usually characterized as a leadership seat. He sets himself down heavily on the thin wire frame chair. It squeaked as he sat on it. The other team members were a little amused by his uncouth behavior, though no one said anything.

"So we have this project on developing a situation in an IT company where social engineering can be easily facilitated. Anybody have any ideas?" he asked.

"So I guess we need to have a situation in which IT systems are so designed as to allow IT malpractices and data insecurity. How many places like that do we have these days?" asked Denise.

"Quite a few unfortunately," replied Ian. "We had this situation in a financial company; I won't name which one, where a clerk had access to the banking account numbers and credit card details of investors. The glitch wasn't found until a team lead began examining the system when it went down one day. He came across it by accident while trying to repair the system."

"Wow that's so outrageous. Banking details and credit card information being open to others!" balled Denise.

"Anyway, so there definitely are such instances. In fact, why don't we put this particular incident in the project? It would serve as a good example. Besides you would be a good resource person to give information on this case," suggested Dan.

There was a short silence.

"Yes I think this would be a good way to go about it," seconded Denise.
"Absolutely," that's the only word Ralph said in the entire conversation. He remained mum not knowing what to contribute. And he preferred staying that way fearing the older, experienced folks might see through his facade and find him lacking in experience and full of fear and insecurity. He knew that his previous educational record was out of their reach. But whom could he confide with in regards to his lack of work experience or lack of knowledge in regards to how systems actually work?

"So how do we divide the parts about who does what?" asked Dan again.
"We'll divide them in the format in which each one is comfortable with the respective task," said Denise.
"Good idea!"
"Anybody have any other suggestions on how we should go about this?" asked Ian realizing that Dan didn't ask if there was a counterpoint.

Ralph would have preferred to first discuss the entire project and then divide it into parts. However, he didn't seem to find the courage to speak about his opinion. Hence, no one knew. He had serious doubts whether they would even consider his opinions if he were to voice them.

"It is better to ask and get an answer then to assume a 'no'," Dad had said so many times in the past.
"Okay then who would like to do the introduction?" asked Dan in a peremptory fashion.
"I can do that" Dan answered noticing hesitation.
"Okay, the second part ought to be a brief on the types of social engineering possible. Who's gonna do that?"
"I could do that," said Bob.
"Hey are you sure the flow of the report needs to be in this manner?" asked Ian sounding a little worried with the way Dan seemed to be listing out a range of subtopics.
"Yeah I think we ought to discuss the sequence more" said Bob.
"I agree," replied Ralph seeing he had a small majority that he could fall back on.

He was always shy to speak about his ideas and since he arrived in the States, had been skittish in the presence of working class Americans older than him. He often wished he had gained work experience in India which would have helped him understand and learn more quickly. It would probably even have taught him to handle work-related pressure, deadlines, and produce high-quality output appreciated by colleagues.

But that was an improbable possibility now. He would need to juggle many responsibilities and play hard to keep up with the rigorous curriculum of the computer science program at Saint Paul's University.

As they discussed the roles of each person, Ralph was afraid to speak up and volunteer. He waited for everyone to select a role. Dan finally asked "we need somebody to send an email to the professor asking him a few questions regarding which organization we can talk about for this project. And hopefully, we can continue with the same organization in the next project as well."

"So you want to do it?" asked Dan looking Ralph in the eye.
"Sure. I can do that" replied Ralph a little shaken.
"So could you send the email by tonight. We need to get the professor's feedback by tomorrow."

"Yes I will send it today," replied Ralph. He was a little worried about the speed that he was expected to follow up with. In India, things were generally slower paced. He would need to get used to the American pace of doing things.

Immediately after winding up the meeting, Ralph walked to the library and was surprised to see quite a few of the computers occupied. Not having a computer to surf, he waited for someone to leave.

He saw a girl who seemed to be leaving. He quickly approached her.

"Excuse me. Are you leaving? I just needed to use a computer," he said.
"Yes sure. I just need a minute to pack up and then I'm out of here" she smiled.
"Okay. Thanks"
"No problem" she gushed seeing the simple looking young man so genial and smooth.

Ralph moved to the side and behaved as though he was looking at the reference books on the shelves. He knew that women needed their privacy and it would seem awkward if he were to simply stand behind her like a statue. As she picked her bag up he graciously looked at her.

"It's all yours!" she said.
"Have a good night."
"You too," he whispered.

As he opened his email to prepare the text of the communication to the professor he had a feeling that he would need to make this one accurate and effective. An MS Word document would be better to first draft the email, make edits to it, and then email it to the group for verification. He wasn't confident of his ability to communicate well. For one, he wasn't much the English professor and secondly being an engineer he had more of an affinity for mechanical things than for linguistics. He always preferred the urge of working with his hands to repair and fix things instead of reading a book or writing an essay. This correspondence work was indeed difficult stuff for him.

"Dear Dr. Panini,

Our group is working on the social engineering project concerning Blue Danube Realty Services that almost went bankrupt after a former employee used social engineering to obtain account passwords and penetrate their network. We were wondering if we could include information concerning this live example in the first project. And were thereby hoping we could continue to use the case of the same company in the second project as well. Please would you be able to clarify on this doubt?

Thanks.

Kind regards,

Dan, Denise, Bob, Ian, Ralph"

He looked at the draft of the email again and checked to see if there were any typos in it. Not finding any, he sent it to the group, requesting their feedback on whether it was appropriate for sending to the professor. Having done the first part of the work for the night, he opened the documents discussed during the class. He quickly printed them out and headed home.

The ride on the shuttle was slow due to the traffic. He could feel the rumbling in his belly. But more than that he felt the uncertainty of his situation in regards to completing the course and getting along with his colleagues. He had never faced a situation in which he had to actively work and contribute to a team. This country demands that the contribution is of acceptable quality. Mere attempts will not earn you any respect least of all a grade. In America, people view you through a "crystal of micro-judgment and scrutiny." *No matter how much they might say they don't judge, the reality is that they do.*

Everyone from the president to the janitor is judged for standards. *"Is that the reason this country is so perfect and powerful,"* Ralph wondered. Probably! However, for a person from a totally alien culture where people are not judged at every step in life; adjusting was definitely an uphill task. Although he had thought that the adjustment process would end in the first two months, this had not been the case. It was not just the school curriculum, housing and interaction norms that he had to get adjusted to. He had to learn and get acclimatized to the work culture, the attitude required to succeed in professional

105

organizations and of course, the approach normally followed to resolve conflicts.

Ralph knew he had none of these skills and would need to develop them or empirically learn them. In India, people were open enough to tell you about your mistakes or how you should approach different situations. At least that's the experience that Ralph had faced. He had not been fortunate enough to come across any mentor in the new country who could show him the ropes or guide him on how to go about things. He would need to be a mentor and a comfort for himself at least for now.

****

Matilda is a ravishingly attractive and voluptuous girl. But Ralph found her attractive for one more reason. She had heart-melting humility and was always very approachable. As he prepared for the social engineering class the next day, Ralph was pleasantly surprised to see Matilda working in the library. He wanted to go to her and start chatting. "*But I don't have a good reason to talk to her*," he thought. He headed back to his desk and tried to come up with a good enough reason to chat up the beautiful damsel.

As he gazed at the screen and then at the beautiful blonde in the near distance, he asked his mind to come up with a reason. And it needed to be good; genuine. He managed to sneak a few stares into what she was reading and realized she was doing some computer related reading. "*Cool, she is reading JAVA-related stuff. I am good in that and could easily talk about it.*"

A good reason is always followed by confident action. "Hey Matilda! How's it going? What are you doing?"
"Woah! Angelo, great to see you. What are you doing here?" she said ecstatically. For a moment it seemed she was expecting him as much as he was wanting to talk to her.
"I just came to get some reading done for the social engineering class tomorrow."
"What are you reading?"
"I am reading some JAVA, to do better at the JAVA course I am taking. I am not too good in programming," she said.
"Have you done a lot of programming?"

"Yes I have. JAVA was one area I was good in and I found it fun," replied Ralph confidently.

"You found it fun!! I can't imagine anyone finding JAVA fun, particularly as you get into the advanced programming phases of it. You must be having a great deal of patience to learn the language," she smiled.

"Well I guess it's just a matter of sticking to the course when you think it's getting tougher. Just like anything in life – practice makes perfect!"

Matilda felt a wave of wisdom resonate through her body as he said that. She felt she was with one of her favorite uncles whom she adored greatly. But she maintained her calm and tried to focus on the conversation, not overtly showing her growing interest in the person with whom she was conversing.

Something about this tawny skinned guy was irresistible. His tone, warm attitude and conversational style seemed very congenial and magnetic. Needless to say, he was very attractive.

"You got it. Well now I know who to go to next time I have a question about writing any script or developing a program," she gushed.

"Absolutely. I can help you with whatever I know about it. So feel free to ask."

Both of them stared at each other with emotions that can only be categorized as affectionate.

"So what were you studying before you came to Saint Paul's University?"

"I was at Loyola University in New Orleans, Louisiana. Hurricane Katrina caused the university to literally shut down and the computer science program had to be transferred elsewhere. Fortunately, Saint Paul's University was the only Jesuit university that offered displaced students from Louisiana the opportunity to continue their education. Thank god for that. Else I would have to start looking for a job to pay the bills. The hurricane devastated more than just property. It took lives and destroyed livelihoods" she said in a melancholic tone. The pain and hurt of Hurricane Katrina were still clearly visible on her face.

"Well that's why you are here. To not allow the hurricane to continue to hamper your life. And we are going to help you overcome the pain that Katrina brought!" said Ralph putting his hand on her shoulder.

"Oh you are so sweet!" she said lunging at him and hugging him.
"It's okay. Don't worry. You are fine now," said Ralph patting her lightly on the back.
"It takes a strong person to go through the disaster you went through and still come out alive and sane!"
"What about your family? Where are they?" Ralph asked.
"My Mom and Dad are divorced. Brother ran away from home and doesn't communicate with us. I live with my Mom. But she moved to Florida to live with my uncle as our house was heavily damaged during Katrina."

There is a sudden silence. Both of them seemed to question as to why God would allow such a thing to happen to anybody.

"Whatever has happened cannot be changed. But you can look to the future and try to change that. What attitude you have towards your experiences will determine how you use them to get ahead in life," Ralph asserted.
She looked at him with glowing eyes. "You are so deep and understanding. Your family must be very lucky to have you," she said with a twinkle in her eyes.
"Well, I hope everyone were to feel the way you do," he quipped and both of them burst out into hearty laughter. Although Ralph would want to tell her about his exit from India, he reserved the narration of the acrimonious events for another day. "In fact, those events are not worth mentioning," he felt.

They chatted a little more until Ralph felt the need to go back to his studies. "Well, I guess you need to complete your JAVA reading and I need to do some reading and research for my social engineering class. So I'll just go to my desk now," said Ralph lightly.
"Oh sure. I really liked talking to you. I'd sure like to talk to you again."
"Me too," said Ralph.
"I come here almost every evening," replied Matilda in rapid fire mode.

She is clearly smitten by this handsome, suave young man. It is evident that she wants more of him if not all of him.

"Yes. It would be great to meet you again!" exclaimed Ralph.
"By the way, where are you from?" she asked as he turned to head towards his desk.

She is surprised how she didn't ask him about his origins before. He seemed so different and genuine. So different from the typical American male. "Hey is he American. He can't be – American guys are not so nice!" she pondered.

"I am from Goa, India. Have you heard of the place?"
"No. Not quite" she smiled.
"Well just to give you a brief overview it is one of the top tourist destinations in India and even in Asia."
"Wow!"
"Yup. We have a large coastline. My house is not too far from the beach."
"You should come there sometime. I am sure you would have fun!" he said calmly.

Matilda seemed to be on cloud nine on having this soft conversation with him. She felt the urge to talk more. Ralph knew he now had a fair amount of rapport with her. He knew he wouldn't have to struggle much going forward.
"Okay, I'll probably just complete some of the research that I need to get done. It was great talking to you. Hang in there Matilda," he said giving her a thumbs up sign.
"Absolutely. Same here," she gushed as she raised her thumb acknowledging his encouragement. He felt positive until the next day.

****

The next day Ralph is unpleasantly surprised to see a rather confrontational email from Dan. Dan disapproved of the text of the email that Ralph had drafted. He chided Ralph in the email and insinuated to his lack of experience in communicating via email.

"Hi,

Ralph, the email you sent is not very appropriate for our purpose. The text of your email is not effective in addressing the professor appropriately. Please send the following email to the professor:

"Dear Dr. Panini,

Thank you so much for the opportunity to work on the project concerning Blue Danube Realty Services. I am sure the energy and enthusiasm with which you assigned this project to us will go a long way in helping us learn from this assignment and contribute greatly to the class. We were wondering if it would be appropriate to use information concerning the company in the first project and thereafter in the second.

I know this might be pushing the envelope in terms of using the same information in two projects. But if you could help us identify if this is possible and how to go about it, we would be most grateful.

Thank you.

Sincerely,

Dan, Denise, Ian, Bob, Ralph"

"Please would you be able to clarify on this doubt" sounds as though the professor is at fault or hasn't done something correctly. If everyone is okay with it, I would like to start sending all outbound communication concerning the group's projects here on.

Regards,

Dan"

Ralph went through the entire email with surprise and wonder. He was amazed to see how pugnacious Dan was over something as basic as an email being sent to the professor. He didn't expect to see this level of granularity and attention being given to an email. Guess this is the way they do it in the States, he thought to himself. Although a little unnerved by the language and directness of Dan's communication, he decided to keep the peace by not contradicting him. He replied in the affirmative to his request to conduct communications for the group.

Little does Ralph know that Dan's confrontational attitude is not considered so in the States. It is a mere representation of the hire and fire policy so prevalent all over corporate America. He would come across such situations again. For now, he was content that what had to happen had happened. The pain that had been caused would be replaced by the lull that would follow. Many international students in the US took life in this fashion – hoping and working; taking life one day at a time. Confronting peers or local citizens on any issues is fraught with various dangers. You might not know the law well enough, you might not have the monetary resources to back your claims, you might lack the confidence and the communication skills needed to substantiate your claims. Ralph did not want to get himself embroiled in a fight before he had the basic means to be strong enough to take care of himself in the States.

The classes were a drag from then on. Dan looked to browbeat the team member he considered lesser than the rest. Ralph's dressing style consisted of jeans and ordinary t-shirts. The others were working professionals with full-time jobs. They dressed in the pure corporate style that corporate America required. Obviously, it wasn't difficult to find the odd one out in the group.

In every group interaction, Dan would take the lead in discussions or in suggesting approaches. Many of the group members did not appreciate this but restrained from confronting him to preserve team cohesion.

"So does everyone have their roles for this project," asked Dan one evening following class.
Everyone seemed to nod. "Okay. And what about you? What are you doing?" he asked pointing to Ralph.
"I will be writing a brief on the technical aspects of social engineering," replied Ralph plainly.

Dan slightly nodded and then looked away as though brooding about Ralph not doing more work for the team. It seemed he was thinking about what move to take that would effectively eliminate Ralph's position in the team. It's weird that sometimes no matter how much you do or try to do; you are judged by the relevance of the work rather than by the efforts invested. No matter how good the work, if it does not relate very explicitly to the job being done it is considered useless. The work Ralph had done, although good, was met with bland recognition from the team and would not be given its due worth. Recognition is only obtained when performance meets the need.

Ralph wondered why his role in the previous work effort had been undermined by the mere fact that the work had not been directly relevant to the project being done. "*They could have just told me what to change,*" he thought to himself.

Samarth had told him how he had got into trouble when he had started his program in the US. He would develop content that was either too technical or not directly relevant to the work they needed to be done. He only wished they had given him a chance to do things again or correct the things, not in sync with the given assignment. But second chances are hard to come by in project-based scenarios in the US. Ralph wished he would not have to face a similar situation again but so far it had played out by the book – the US book.

Would he get a chance to prove himself or to redo an assignment? The circumstances were increasingly pointing in the negative direction. Ralph decided to look on the positive side of things and do the best he could on the assignment currently at hand. He scoured the internet for information on social engineering and related topics. Whatever he found he would keep in a document and take only important parts of the same to include in the project document.

He often wondered if this was the same methodology used by his American teammates to do the assignments. Did they do their research as extensively as he did and then type stuff out on their own or did they directly type prose with their ideas incorporated in it? Could they have a method of study more suited to getting work done quickly, he wondered. Why did he feel that they viewed his work as subpar? Was it really? Although he was not adept at the American way of life, he sought consolation in the fact that he was an engineer with a degree. This no one could say he was not; nor steal from him. It was not a possession that someone could take by force but an intangible asset that had tangible connotations.

International students come with their education and expertise from foreign countries, bringing with them diverse experience and varied skills, histories and attitudes. When in America, they are required to quickly adapt to an American way of life at least as far as the basic ways of interaction, living and completing work are concerned. This definitely places a huge stress in terms of adaptation and making sure they learn all that is being taught without getting overwhelmed.

Apart from the requirements of having to adapt to the curricular requirements of their educational programs, they face significant challenges understanding that America is not essentially what they had seen in Hollywood movies. Realization of this does create significant amounts of frustration and stress. Frustration because they came to the US with a fixed idea in their minds. Stress because they need to adapt to new ways and ideas. Often the mere thought of having to learn new things and adapt to new ways causes them to give up and lose commitment. Many Americans view this loss of interest and commitment as a sign of laziness. But that is not the case.

Ralph, in the depth of his being, felt this loss of commitment and a foreboding sense of laziness. As he continued completing the assignment, he hoped that this work would help him get the much needed approval of the team.

****

He made all the nice decorations on the file and sent it across to the team, fingers crossed and full of hope. A day later he is unpleasantly surprised to see an email from Dan curtly brushing aside the work as full of grammatical errors. It read "Ralph, your work contains a lot of grammatical mistakes. It is quite large for us to go through it, so it would be better if you redo it without the grammatical errors."

Given the more face saving cultural background that he is used to Ralph felt the stab of arrogance in Dan's communication. He wondered what grammatical errors could be there as he had already checked for that before emailing the work. "Okay I might not have done the spell check" he said to himself. After doing a spell check in Microsoft Word, he hardly had any error corrections to accept or reject. Having done so he emailed the corrected piece to the group.

In a matter of a mere one hour, he received a response citing way too many grammatical errors even after the spell check. Who is the email from....none other than Dan! One part of Ralph's being made him feel that Dan is out to no good. The other part forced him to look on the positive side and ignore the overt signs of challenge and hostility that Dan was exhibiting.

Ralph resorts to using a grammar textbook from the library to try and see what errors he might find in the work. He simultaneously requests the group to help him out with any suggestions. The other members help out eagerly. Dan's suggestions border on the brink of suggestion and insult. Ralph bears the affronts but he knows his patience is running thin. He decides to make the document in compliance with the suggestions and send it across. On several occasions, Dan emails him with concerns that are not in the remotest way his fault. On every occasion, he diplomatically defends himself without coming across as defensive. Being strong yet measured is a difficult quality to have but his 'inner voice' keeps telling him to strengthen it. Practicing it is the only way to strengthen it. All types of abstinence; be it for anger or habit require a strong will and even stronger motivation. The motivation here was to get the job done while trying to learn the ways Americans do business or go about doing their work.

Two days later, Dan and the rest of the group are in the class. Ralph tries to ignore and avoid Dan given the relative lack of warmth in their relationship. Seeing that Ralph did his part in the assignment well, Dan realizes that he shouldn't be fighting with Ralph. He tries to mend fences by starting a conversation with Ralph.

"How's it going, Ralph?" he asks.
"Great man. You?"
"Good."
"Thanks for your help in correcting the grammatical errors!" says Ralph.
"Oh. No problem. It was easy," says Dan.
"I also used the grammar book from the library to correct the mistakes," says Ralph.
"Oh yeah! That's great. All I was trying to do was just help. And you threw the book at me," replies Dan.
"No offense. I was just combining the feedback you gave with the information in the book. So that the prose looks and sounds as perfect and as complete as possible."
"But thanks for your help anyway," says Ralph smiling.
"We will be having another assignment related to this one so we might be able to use that grammar book" replies Dan as if to show his support for Ralph's practice.

Though communication between them seems direct and not very hostile; underlying signs of dissension are rife. Americans are known to bring matters of concern to people's attention in a very polite manner. And though they might not be overt in expressing frustration and anger, this doesn't mean they don't feel strongly about an issue that matters to them.

Many international students figure this out for themselves after landing on US soil. Ralph had too. One day as he was preparing an Indian curry, the American lady sitting in the living room of the International Student House walked up to him and asked what he was making.

"Indian chicken curry" he replied.
"It stinks!" she grimaced.

Though he was taken aback by her direct assertion; he didn't retaliate. What he found most bewildering was how she regarded the smell – 'it stinks.' Most Asians and even Europeans would regard the smell as an aroma and probably have mouthwatering fits, but this wasn't the case with her. She merely saw it as an olfactory nuisance.

The impressions of quality, penury and fun can be markedly different between Americans and non-Americans. Ralph wanted to dig down and understand the norms and styles of Americans. But to do so he would have to go through the labor pains of seeing what he did differently. How did these different ways compare with the ways of Americans? And why would someone look down upon the practices he was used to.

Thousands of international students in the US face this very dilemma. In trying to mingle more with Americans, they are always faced with the question – should they entirely adapt themselves to American customs and traditions at the expense of their indigenous ways or should they continue with their ways which would probably make it difficult to gain American friends.

Many international students who return to their countries do take with them a substantial chunk of American ethics and values. On reaching their homeland they realize that American ways are neither entirely good nor entirely bad. They are just the ways that the inhabitants of the US thought were best to go about their lives.

It is then they figure that probably a mix of American habits and those of their native lands would be the best way to not only go about their lives in America but any part of the world. Attitudes and traits learned in one place may serve one's purposes well in other lands as well. Or they could hamper one's cause. It all boils down to discovering and understanding what works and what doesn't. Life is a continuous process of discovery and learning.

Ralph wanted to know what would work for him to get along better with Americans, make more friends and be more successful in school and later in his profession. And he wanted to get this understanding fast. International students seeking to understand and adapt to the American way of life are often faced with many hurdles. Not having an American mentor to guide them through the intricacies of American society is probably the biggest of them. Ralph knew he needed a mentor. The Indian colleagues who had provided him with startup guidance from the airport were not always available now that he lived in a different place.

Not that relations between them were strained after the move to a different place. Just that the lack of touch bred a lack of familiarity. Whether in the US or most other parts of the world, people gravitate towards people they know or meet on a regular basis. I guess it's just part of human behavior.

****

The assignment was well received by Dr. Panini and received an A grade. Ralph breathed a sigh of relief considering the relative turmoil he had to go through to complete his part.

"The third project is more analytical and will be quite a challenge for us," said Dan at the end of the Thursday class.
"It relates to the analysis of the causes behind social engineering, right?" chimed in Denise.
"Yes. But we also need to include charts concerning the incidence of social engineering crimes in the US and the world," said Dan looking serious.
"So Ralph, what part of this assignment would you like to do?"

Ralph looks at Dan plainly; wondering why Dan always asks him stuff and not the others.

"Or you could do the whole assignment," replied Dan sensing Ralph's confusion. The confused silence is broken only by Dan's artificial laughter. "I'm just kidding. What part would you like to do? Once you select the part you are comfortable with then the rest of us can take the other parts."

Dan's words smacked of arrogance and sarcasm. "Yes, sure. I could do the analytical part of why social engineering is so widespread and what are the causes behind it," said Ralph keeping his cool all the while.

"Okay. Great. So who wants to make the charts and statistical diagrams?" asked Dan with a presumptuous air.

"I could do it," said Denise as she raised her hand calmly.

"Great! So what parts do we have left?" he asked.

"I guess we could do a section on the effects of social engineering on business and society," suggested Bob.

"So would both of you be able to do it," suggested Dan pointing to Bob and Ian.

"Yup that would be great! Bob can do all the work and I just put my name on it," laughed Ian.

Bob joined in the laughter too. Dan eyed everybody with an air of suspicion. Ralph noticed this and tried to avoid locking eyes with Dan as his gaze reached him. There seemed to be this overarching feeling of suspicion and worry in most of Dan's dealings with team members.

Ralph wondered if this was Dan's attitude to his dealings with everybody. "*Does this lumpy guy have corrosive feelings towards everybody or is it just his behavior in the team?*" Ralph wondered.

In the centuries when colonialism ravaged the so-called third world; the natives often found it difficult to understand the motives of white explorers. They came as traders and used goodwill garnered by providing the conveniences of western products to penetrate the ranks of local peoples. Deceit and trickery were used to divide tribes and clans with an aim to controlling the local politics and eventually the territory.

The indigenous peoples often failed to understand the true intentions of these white Europeans who came as traders but sought to become rulers. After they did become rulers they were called as colonial masters. Ralph was also feeling a loss. A loss in understanding Dan's exact intentions. And although he knew for a fact that the other team members didn't particularly like Dan; he often wondered why they didn't show overt signs of their dislike.

I guess when you are domineering, outspoken and overconfident; you give people a feeling that you know everything. You might not even know the basics but people tend to be so much in awe of a "loud mouth" that they simply shrink into a shell of compliance. The strong and furious dominate in society. But not everyone notices that those who only show themselves as strong also get to influence the way fear and respect gets passed around. Advertising is definitely a great deceiver, not to mention those who use it effectively.

Dan was definitely a shady individual. He didn't have the qualifications or credentials needed to be a successful project manager or leader. He wasn't intelligent or at least didn't seem so based on his contributions in class. But somehow when he was with the team he would try to throw his viewpoints all over the place. In the absence of a clear leader to lead the discussion, group members would accept his version of lopsided leadership and control. The dynamics of business teams in America were varied and at best complicated.

Ralph realized that it would be a while before he got adjusted to the idea of group politics. For now, he would just see how he could best complete the given task at hand.

****

As he surfed the net, he was amazed to find exactly the answer to his questions. He started putting stuff into his article piece from various websites. He carefully formatted for errors and mistakes. *"Gosh this wasn't so difficult after all. These folks will like what I have done,"* he said to himself.

"Dear All,

This is my work for the part of "causes that lead people to resort to social engineering." Please feel free to go through it and let me know your feedback. I would be glad to accommodate any changes.

Thank you.

Ralph"

Ralph happily clicked the Send button as he dispatched the email to his team members. He hoped he would receive a response pretty quickly just as he did in some of the previous projects. He waited and waited. And waited a little more. He doesn't hear anything for a day.

"No point thinking and waiting for their response. When they see the quality of the work they will come to me," he thought.

As he heads to the library to check his email he feels that he is getting somewhere. At least in some intangible fashion.

"Woah. These people have still not replied – what's going on with them," he thought, not finding any email from his social engineering class teammates. In spite of all his hope and urge to think positively; the inkling that something was amiss was quite resounding. *"What could have happened? What could have gone wrong! Why haven't these people replied?"* he thought to himself.

Fear turns to suspicion as he begins to doubt if Dan is playing any game to undermine his efforts. *"I can't hear what they speak. I don't know how they think. So I can't really say!"*

When one is international it can be challenging trying to figure out American thought processes or work-related attitudes. Ralph had noticed that his team folks were particularly unfriendly and distant from the very beginning. As the course progressed they began to have an indifferent attitude towards him. The indifference was later replaced by a feeling of despising and loathing. It wasn't openly said but he could sense the negative feelings radiating.

Negative feelings have a tendency to poison a clean atmosphere; to deprive the energy and vitality of people. Ralph had known and experienced this before too. "Ways of making friends in the US are very different from that in places like India, China or other parts of Asia. Even the attitudes towards friends, acquaintances and lasting relationships are unbelievably at odds with those in many other parts of the world. Even the very practice of maintaining friendships is so infused with practicality that many international students find it hard to understand. Is it a fallacy or a mere fact in the US that Americans tend to be very career focused and intense in any endeavor that they undertake? Well, at least that's the impression they have created the world over.

The need to be focused and directed causes them to become very practical and driven. Maybe that's what causes them to be so distant and business-like. Ralph's thoughts were interrupted by a call from a friend he knew while working in the cafeteria. He opted to not pick the call but was a little surprised at the time. It was already 9:45pm. *"Gosh I got to get home and cook something,"* he whispered to himself.

Quickly shutting down the computer he was overtaken by the need to catch the shuttle bus to get home. He rushed towards the dorm gate to wait for the 9:50 pm bus. As if by serendipity, it arrived exactly after a minute of waiting. A good omen! "They might be up to something," the Inner Voice tells him. As much as he wants to be positive, the inner voice has never been wrong so far. It was with him from the day he fought two strong guys at school and emerged victorious. It had been with him during the worst crises in his life and it was there with him in the US. Between a trusted voice and a need to have a positive attitude at the expense of ignoring the dangers out there; which would you choose?

I think opting for the Inner Voice would be the right option. Only thing Ralph didn't have the wherewithal to doubt his elusive team members and emerge victorious. Not so early in his time in the US at least. He was dependent and weak. It is important to get independent and strong quickly when in a foreign country. But external support is important to achieving this. This external support does not come readily though. Exceptionally lucky and endowed individuals could catch the attention of a powerful patron and do well.

The other way to get lucky is if some hotshot feels pity looking at your condition. Yeah, unless you are the son of a millionaire in your country or have Father Time on your side, you would need nothing short of a miracle to transform from a needy international student to an independent, self-sustaining individual.

Visceral rumblings of hunger forced him to quicken the preparation of the dish. He gulped down most of it and headed to his desk to complete the two chapters of JAVA II reading for the next day's class. Vagrant thoughts distracted him. Matilda, the controversy surrounding the social engineering class and the mere struggles involved in being an international student and doing well pervade his mind.

"God help me just clear my mind of all these distractions and concentrate" he prayed. Somewhere close he heard the inner voice promising him three hours of undisturbed concentration. The two chapters were read and digested rather quickly and Ralph wondered if he could keep doing this in all his courses and studies. The social engineering class could definitely do with a greater degree of relevant involvement and concentration. *"Is it too late for that though,"* he wondered.

****

At the beginning of the course, Dr. Panini had said that the third group project would be due two weeks before the final presentation. The third group project would be like an icing on the cake for eight weeks of team related project work. It was now only one day from that day. The inner voice had cautioned Ralph about ornery consequences and about a probable backlash from the team. Though he had an inkling that things would pan out the way the inner voice said they would, he continued to remain positive. He didn't quite feel ready to take on the burdens of fighting these individuals who had been in America since birth; who had a color which the West would normally identify with; who had financial and human resources that poor Ralph lacked.

More than anything else, they had an understanding of the cultures, traditions and norms of the US. Was there a shorter, quicker way to learn these things other than to spend a decade's worth of time here. Google, the internet and acquaintances can teach you only so much. There hadn't been an ounce of valuable communication between the team and him. And it was clear that something was brewing. Ralph only hoped it wasn't in a crucible.

"Hey Ian, how's it going man," said Ralph as Ian stood far away from Ralph outside the classroom. "Hey" responded Ian dryly. A moment of silence ensued. "So did you get a chance to go through the article I wrote?"

"Not really?" replied Ian looking at Ralph with a mix of suspicion and anger.

"Where did you get the information from?" he asked in a probing, serious fashion.

"I got it from a number of websites. Some of the stuff was my own too."

Ian remained silent as he gazed through the long, bright corridor. The other team members stayed at a distance and seemed very solemn. They stole suspicious glances at Ralph and avoided eye contact. Dan spoke on his phone and behaved as though Ralph didn't exist. Bob was less hostile and managed a hello.

Ralph now asked his Inner Voice to not give him ideas but to be with him in the raucous trauma that seemed imminent. During the class, Dan eyes Ralph with a sense of loathing and mistrust. Ralph could clearly sense that a wedge had been drawn between him and the group. He only wished the inner voice would tell him the reason why.

But there is no clairvoyant voice talking to him now. As though saying "I told you before, why didn't you heed my warnings! I am not going to help you now." All he felt were rumblings of disturbance and trauma. No reassuring proverb to go by, no friend to fall back on, no nothing. Ralph's "total loss" situation was quite symbolic of many international students who do not know what to do and where to go when they realize their American friends have discovered a goof-up attributable to them.

Ralph, like the so many other internationals, only wished he knew what this mistake was. Did all Americans start ignoring and neglecting the guilty to make them realize that they were at fault? Or was there another different, less painful way to do it? In the absence of a clear answer, Ralph could only speculate.

As they take their seats, Dan sat the farthest away from Ralph. Ian also placed himself at the farthest point along the table from Ralph. Only Denise and Bob were closest to him, sitting beside him. None of them said a word to Ralph. It seemed like the lull before the storm. It is clear that there are underlying signs of hell going to break loose. Just a matter of time before it does. Ralph breathed deeply to try and calm himself down. He needed all the peace and calm he could find in this lonely land to keep sane. Deep breathing always helped him stay away from the extremes of anger or fear. He prayed that it would keep him from extremes today too. "Even in adversity, it is important to keep yourself composed!" Mum would always say.

And way too often he had broken her principle by losing his temper, having boisterous fights, or getting into other sorts of trouble. Mum knew he would eventually learn the importance of her principle. Ralph hoped he internalized the principle well enough to stand his ground with dignity in the face of what was to happen now.

Through the sides of his eyes, Ralph could see the sign-based communication taking place between Dan and Ian. "*It was awful*" he thought. He wished they had connived in a more noble fashion. But connivance is not a trait of the noble. In spite of all the bad things in the world he wished that the "live and let live" nature in their conscience would make them do whatever they were going to do as peacefully and painlessly as possible. But possibility reels with imagination!

As the class wound up, Ian made an announcement that made things clearer than clear. The team would be having a meeting. Ralph could see the same fate as that of a lamb being taken to the butcher. What charge would be slapped on him, he could only speculate.

Ian and the rest of the team raced ahead with war-like enthusiasm as they headed to the top floor for the meeting. The warning of what was going to happen suddenly stopped altogether. A mysterious calm came upon Ralph. As though God Himself had descended to Earth to help the young man weather the imminent storm. "You need to be optimistic. Just stay positive" said the Inner voice. "God will protect you!"

Confused, fearful and still positive he made his way up the stairs. Surprised to find everybody take seats so quickly, he took his seat opposite Ian. All of them were seated opposite Ralph with the exception of Bob. It seemed almost like an inquisition. It seemed as though the other four members had a chemistry of connivance going on between them. Although Ralph wished he knew what it was about; he didn't care anymore. "What is going to happen will happen! But God will remain with you throughout it" said the Inner Voice.

Ian seemed very focused and angry. His face was hard set and emotionless. It was now clear what the group was going to do. "We have a set of issues that we have to discuss today. But the first issue is the instance of plagiarism by Ralph," said Ian with a sneering look in his eyes.

The words hit Ralph like a bolt out of a clear sky. "What!" he exclaimed in his customary innocent fashion, looking very shaken. In fact, he was. He didn't quite understand what had just been told to him. All he knew about the word 'plagiarism' was from an article on it several years ago. Michael Jackson had been accused of plagiarism in regards to some of his song tunes. When he looked up the meaning in his dictionary it read "unauthorized copying or duplication of someone else's work without giving credit to the original creator of the work."

"Am I being accused of this? Am I actually guilty of this? What did I do that would qualify as plagiarism?" wondered a disturbed Ralph. For several moments he couldn't even comprehend what the team was talking about. The aggression with which Ian had confronted him came as a rude surprise.

"Your entire file contains stuff from various websites and sources that have not been documented," said Dan.
"What do you think. You can just put stuff from anywhere in your documents!" asked Ian.

Denise wasn't vocal but showed covert support for Dan and Ian. Bob was silent and seemed supportive of Ralph. It was evident that Dan and Ian had formed an axis to get rid of the innocent international. The rest of the team would follow their lead.

"What do you mean by plagiarism?" Ralph could barely mutter the words. "What is plagiarism?" he asked in rapid bursts. Ralph was nervous and scared. This was evident from his voice and demeanor. But things weren't going to stop just yet. At least it didn't seem like it was. "You mean you copied stuff from all those websites and you don't know what plagiarism is?" said Ian; his voice drenched with an air of disdain. "Ralph your contribution to the group has been very poor. In fact, you have hardly contributed anything. Besides that, you now go ahead and plagiarize stuff!"
"You can't just have the other team members do all the work and you get the grades right. So we are thinking whether we should keep you in the group or not," said Dan in a non-stop train of words. It was clear

now. They wanted to remove him from the group and had already set their minds in that direction.

"But I did do the report and made other contributions, right?" said Ralph calmly. "But that was of subpar quality," dismissed Ian, sneering again while saying so.

It seemed as though nothing he could do to explain would change their minds. But that wouldn't stop him from trying. Ralph now heard the Inner voice telling him softly "Try your best to retain yourself in the group. Your grade depends on it." In spite of all the disturbances in the group meeting, in spite of all the tension; the voice deep down had just drawn Ralph away. Away from all the confusion, distress, and hurt and into a place of safety and security. A refuge from the dangers of the world; a bubble that was of iron-clad resilience. The voice which had forewarned him of dangers in the past was now giving him solace and peace as he prepared to weather a new storm in the American wild west. A storm bigger than many others he had been through. Probably one he would come out of a changed man.

After the class, the team approached the professor and requested him to remove Ralph from the team on the charge of plagiarism. The exchange between them was quite acrimonious and Ralph wished he could put it behind him. The professor indicated in his judgment that Ralph would be removed from the team and would not be graded for that assignment. He let the whole class know about the verdict. The judgement was pretty severe and Ralph felt the sting. He never knew that an inadvertent mistake like that would invite such condemnation and shame. Justice in the US seemed infinite and harsher than the alleged crime.

The manner in which the team approached the issue of his inadvertent mistake of putting in the material from the website was not very straightforward. It was conducted in a way to trap him and to not allow him any recourse to explain his action.

If you have poor relations with people, little opportunity for explanation will be allowed to enable you to recover from a mistake you committed. In a professional environment, if your colleagues feel you are not very competent or not showing much interest than they would certainly try to remove you from the team.

****

Two days pass and she didn't see Ralph in the library. Wondering what's wrong she decided to walk by the computers and stake him out in case he is buried in his mountain of research or studies. Still no sign of the handsome lad.

"Why isn't he here? Hope nothing's wrong," she thought.
"I should have at least taken his number" she rued.

Then suddenly in a distant carrel, slumped in a chair, she noticed him seemingly buried in pensive thought. He didn't look tired or hungry, just worried. While she wondered where he had been all these days, she was happy to see him in the library again.

"Hey stranger! Where you been hiding all these days" she said gently tapping him on his shoulder.
He turned his head from his lazy concentration and looked at her with droopy eyes. He was obviously tired and seemed depressed. But still, put a smile on his face.

"Ooh! Look at you. You look tired. Is everything alright Ralph?" she asked looking concerned.
"Oh yes. Sort of. Just been dealing with some assignments and a crazy group."
"Ooh, poor thing. Stressful group project huh!"
"Oh yeah! Very demanding!"
"What did they make you do?" she asked intently.

Ralph was still in the middle of the recovery process after his excommunication from the team. He seemed to be smarting from the pain and agony of being humiliated and removed from the team. It's not easy when you are an international student barely four months in the country to deal with the pressures of a crazy workload, distant team mates and literally no friends.

To top it all off there is a huge race to learn new laws, rules and norms in the US of A. Often times, the pressure to accomplish so much in so little time is so great that prioritizing is the only recourse to getting anything done. If it is effective that is!

Very few students actually crack the formula of balancing school and social obligations while maintaining emotional equilibrium when still only a couple of months in a foreign country. Then there's the conundrum of maintaining health too. Culture shock aggravates matters beyond measure although if you are a hillbilly kind of son of a bitch who cares two hoots for society then you should be fine.

The US is well known for its emphasis on quality and high standards. Whether it's the roads, buildings, institutions, or people; in general everything follows a standard. Such standards are set by society or by the government. Trying to fit into the system is not the most straightforward of processes when one is a gauche yokel from a developing Asian country; callow and fairly inexperienced in the ways of the world.

Ralph didn't have a mentor either. He would have to navigate this entire American theater on his own, at least for now. It's tough when you're in a new zone on your own. A new country, new challenges, new jungle. Old ways need to be adapted to suit current conditions and new learning's need to be assimilated quickly.

"All sorts of crazy stuff. But it's all good," Ralph muttered, not wishing to go into the sordid details of the entire social engineering excommunication episode.
"How have you been?" he asked gently.
"Ooh! This school work keeps you so busy. It's crazy. Good to see you though," she sympathized.
"Always good to see you," he smiled.
"I do need to get away from all this and take a vacation for a while," she said as she grimaced.
"Only thing there isn't any time for a vacation!"

There is a long pause and both their youthful bodies seem to be in a pensive trance for a good number of seconds. The seconds almost seem like hours.

"Well you could take a short vacation in that case," quipped Ralph.

Both of them burst out laughing.

"So what are you doing on the weekend?" she asked.

"You mean like Saturday and Sunday?"
"Yes the weekend, Ralph!" she emphasized.

It does take a while for international students in general to familiarize themselves with terminology and institutions common in the US. The 'weekend' is an integral phenomenon of American working life. After a long five-day work week, most working people look forward to a relaxing Saturday and Sunday. Many times, Friday, Saturday and Sunday constitutes a weekend for some working people either too well off to have four-day work weeks or disadvantaged at not having enough work to do.

Ralph felt a light bulb turn on in his head. *I guess having American friends is the best way to learn about American culture and traditions,"* he thought. He always knew this fact. But now it seemed to be working. Heck, he just learned the actual meaning of weekend without opening a single web page. It's true, what Americans born and raised in the US take for granted, takes effort to learn when one is an international.

Though one brings a lot of broad-based global experiences from places like Asia and the Middle East; in America you have to know and act like Americans. Knowing the norms of the country and culture is crucial to making more friends.

Though he often felt cynical, Ralph knew he had to stay positive. But this opinion was held not just by him, but by many international students he had met before. "Well what are you doing on the weekend," asked Matilda again.
"Well I will be completing some assignments and cleaning my room."
"Umm. And?"
She looked at him hoping to elicit some more "to do's." He said nothing.
"Oh wow! Sounds like fun."
"That all? What about something fun?"

She kept looking at him intently.
"Umm.....oh yes. We will be having a party for international students."
"Now that sounds interesting," she smiled.
"Yeah. This international house has a terrific director who organizes many events."
"So what are you doing the weekend?"

"I was planning to go to a cousin's place in Lancaster. But we had to cancel as she will be having her boyfriend over. So right now I don't have any plans," she said plainly.

"Oh. So you will have lots of time on your hands then."

"Yup. I guess so."

"Hey why don't you come for the international student party on Sunday?" said Ralph after a long pause. He was thinking if it would be appropriate to call her for the party.

"Is that an invitation?" she played.

"Of course it is. What else did it sound like?" he smiled.

Matilda starts laughing. "Yes. But is it open to everybody?"

"Yes it is. Anybody who is a student can come. Even if you are not a student you can come." Both of them begin laughing at Ralph's characterization of invitees and non-invitees.

"That's very nice of you to invite me over," she said.

"Well, you said you didn't have friends here right. So I am trying to be your friend. That's if you allow me to," he grinned.

"Stop it!" she blushed feeling him flirting with her.

"So anyway. I'm going to go and get some work done," she said.

"Well, make sure you do the work and don't think about me" he quipped.

She gives him a stare and smiles coyly.

"Oh Matilda. The party starts at 2:30 pm tomorrow, so make sure you wear your best dress and come."

"Sure. Don't think about my dress while doing your research," she retorted.

"Hahaha," Ralph felt jubilant and for once after the painful experience of the social engineering class he felt there was hope. Hope to make friends and continue with his quest of the American dream.

PAIGE PARTY

As he arranged the cups and plates, he couldn't help but be distracted by the pristine white silhouette of the gracefully walking damsel. Through the tainted glass window, she looked like a smiling angel about to give a blessing and a wink.

"Oh my! Is that Matilda. It sure looked like her," he said to himself.

Ralph rushed to the door as her silhouette whiffed by towards the porch of International House. He yanked open the heavy door with uncharacteristic ease and peered through the flimsy screen door into the green sea of grass ahead.

"Hey, Matilda! You found the place alright?" he gushed suppressing the exhilarating feeling that is racing through his head and gut. He had felt such a feeling only twice before – once when he saw Mr. Costa's daughter, the talk of the town in Goa; the other when he sat behind Rajeshree on her scooter to go home from Maxmueller Bhavan in Pune.

But this time something felt different. The feeling was much stronger and energizing. As the smiling lass climbed up the few stairs to the porch, her svelte and curvy figure was accentuated by the light September breeze blowing against her body.

Her medium height, page boy hairstyle and glowing face made her seem like an angel from heaven above. Though he wanted to suppress his feelings, he knew it would be hard. But he did. As she reached the edge of the porch, both of them instinctively embraced each other with a tight hug.

It was as though some unsaid chemistry existed between them. Something that wasn't easy to describe, but which they knew was a little more than friendship. Universities can facilitate education and learning. There is some learning though, which only life and experience can give you. Ralph always valued this alternative learning. And made no bones about looking for the new experiences and acquaintances that would facilitate it.

He had always been interested in fostering friendships with women. What eluded him was how the friendship can be made strong. The only strong friendship he had so far was with Rajeshree, the precariously skinny girl from Pune.

She found the young lad extremely attractive. More than anything else, he was so open, approachable and fun to be with. "So how have you been?" she asked running her hand over his arm.
"I've been good. But I feel even better now that you are here," he smiled as he felt the ecstasy of a lover in the midst of passion.

The words seemed to rub a warm touch on her lips as she giggled with glee. "You look different," he said as he led her inside the house intermittently glancing at her dress. "Well I'll take that as a compliment," she gushed.

"We are going to make you a celebrity," he declared as he handed her the name labels and diary to have her enter her name and contact details in the International student house guest list.
"Wow this is so cool." He delicately placed the label on her left upper shoulder.
"Yeah, you're official now!"
"Stop it!"
"So how was your day?" he asked.
"Oh boring. But I did get some stuff done."
"Well, you came to the right place for some quality fun."
"Yeah. I knew. That's why I came."
"Let me show you around the house," he said as he held her hand.
"This house looks so big," she said.
"Yes it is. But not bigger than my room!"

She giggled.
"Let's go on top and then we can come to the first floor."
"The third floor up there is no man's land. I've never been up there and not sure if anyone is allowed. Though I think nothing's up there to see. Hopefully, no ghosts either."
"This room belongs to Kuda. He is the current caretaker of the house. Actually more like president of International Student House."
"Two Korean students live here," he said pointing to what looked like a hole in the wall.
"You mean two in this tiny room?" she asked looking surprised.
"No. No way. Even if they were married; the two would not be able to live there," he said giving her a clever look.
"Yup right," she blushed.
"And finally the room we've all been waiting for – the best room in the house, my room."
"Doesn't look too big, though!" she quipped.

He rushed towards her as though to affectionately strike her. But both of them just embrace.

"You've kept it really clean and neat. Do you spend a lot of time in the room?"

"I didn't before. But once I got my laptop I did most of my work in here."

"Besides its convenient and distraction free to sit in your room and have the world at your fingertips without having to actually travel there. The laptop makes many things possible," he added.

"Umm."

She looked around the room like a mother surveying her children's activities. He watched her and experienced the feeling. The feeling of being thought about, cared for and loved. He hadn't had that feeling in quite a few months; though it seemed longer than that.

Deprivation can have a greater impact on the psyche than satisfaction and love. Ralph had begun to get toughened and insensitive with the lack of love in his life. His insensitivity was more towards his own feelings rather than a negative form of insensitivity to others. Bereft of close friends in a foreign land it is difficult to share emotions and feelings except with near and dear ones over the phone. Making friends is important in a foreign land. How close they become is a function of one's personality and fate to a great extent.

It's dangerous to live without love. For one gets used to living in solitude. Solitude's control can be so great that when love is at one's doorstep, it is difficult to recognize it. Ralph could feel this same thing happening to him.

First, a feeling of being horrifically lost overcame him. It led to despair and desperation. Fears of being left behind shook him from his inaction. He struggled and tried to work hard to make a change. He would try to reach out and make friends with people. Not just once or twice would he be rejected. Not seeing instant gratification, he was obliged to give up. It is hard to maintain momentum when one is alone without anybody else to provide external motivation.

Without support, moral or monetary, life can be daunting. Not only in the States but in any part of the world. You need all the support and encouragement possible to be successful.

"Ooh! What is this?" she asked pointing to the small doll with its hands on its heart.

A calm smile adorned Ralph's face. "That doll belongs to my mother. She gave it to me so I would know she is with me wherever I went. That doll has an amazing story. My mother received it from her best friend on the day they were going to part ways. Both of them were going to different universities for higher studies. She kept it close to her. Then one fine day when she was returning from a long trip to a neighboring city, the strap of her carry bag broke and she didn't realize it. There was nothing important in it. Except for this doll of great sentimental value."

Matilda is amazed by the level of detail and concern Ralph exudes as he narrates the incident. She looked at him with tender affection.
"Mum realized she had lost it only after coming home. She was upset and in despair on losing the doll. She didn't want to believe she had lost it. That it was only misplaced. So she continued to second guess herself and look around the house."
"The search made it burning bush clear to her that she had indeed placed the doll in the damaged carry bag. The bag was light and she had lost it once before; only to be retrieved by a handsome young man walking not too far behind her."
"This time though it was different. There was nobody behind her or looking out for her. She realized she might have lost it on the packed bus while trying to get out the door."
"Follow-up inquiries yielded no results from the unhelpful bus conductors. And then fate took over. A kindly old lady noticed the bag under a seat. She opened it and saw the doll with my Mum's name inscribed on it. She happened to be a good friend of my grandmother and had sure seen the doll and the bag when she visited home. The next evening my Mum saw her lost doll on the vanity table in her room. She couldn't hold back tears of happiness as my grandmother reached out to hug her. They embraced as the kindly lady who had found the bag looked on and smiled."

Matilda seemed to be in a deep trance. Ralph, not saying anything now seemed to be deep in thought pondering that day when fate and destiny conspired to get the doll back home.

Both of them look deep into each other's eyes but neither looks away. A strong bond seems to be underway. The feeling and atmosphere are so deep they fail to recognize that they are staring. It is clear that they no longer consider the trivial things concerning manners or proximity any more. Their relationship seems to have transformed into something much deeper, much more profound than a friendship.

The beautiful damsel felt at ease with the young man now. "Not many people are so deep as you." Matilda seemed to be convulsing with affection. The silence and understanding filled gaze continued. "Yup I'm like that," Ralph smiled.
"I guess the best test of whether something really belongs to you is when you lose it and it comes back. It wouldn't come back if it didn't belong to you or was never yours!" The words resonated as though from the Bible or some other holy book.

Matilda smiled, affection in her eyes and reached out for his hand. He clasped her hand tight and they embraced. He almost shook with the emotion but controlled himself. Her hug was warm and for the first time since stepping on US soil he felt wanted, loved.
As she felt his muscular build she couldn't seem to resist the feeling of protection. The feeling of being taken care of by a male companion.
"These international guys are quite a handful. I wish we had more like this one though," she thought.

Their memorable time together is disturbed by the sound of the director of the house walking up the stairs. "Ralph….Ralph? Where are you?"
"The party's going to start," he hollered into the partially open door and walked away after delivering the message.
"Woo….looks like somebody's looking for you."
"He's just Kuda. The director of the house. I was helping him the whole day so he's looking for me."
"You seem to be quite popular here!" she said giving him a telling look.
"Well I try!" he smiled.

She bursts into laughter.

"Come I'll show you the other places in the house," he gently extended his hand as she placed hers in his.
"So as we go down the stairs we come to the common areas. Here on left is the study and living room area."
"Oh there you are" said Kuda wearing his infectious Nigerian smile.
"And this lady here is?"
"This is Matilda. We study computer science together."
"Hi!" she said in her typical American accent.

"Nice to meet you. Welcome to International Student House!" he said extending his hand.

"Thanks."

"Make yourself feel at home. I'm sure Ralph might have shown you quite a bit of the place already."

"Oh yeah. He's amazing. He does a great job," she said with a twinkle in her eyes.

"Enjoy the party," he said as he proceeded to the living room; tray full of pastries in his hand.

"Kuda's a very jovial guy. He used to be in Africa. He wanted to be a pastor so he came to America to study and he's been here ever since."

"Oh."

They descend the steps. "So on the right here is the kitchen and the dining room. We use it more as a buffet area, though."

"Woah! This is a nice kitchen!"

"Well, Theresa takes care of it. I'll probably introduce you to her too."

"We all take turns to keep the kitchen clean and tidy. And generally, everybody is quite cooperative. So it works out."

"We have two ovens. The girls make good use of them to bake stuff. Besides, Theresa is here pretty much for every event to guide the girls on what to bake, how to bake and what attire to wear when doing so. She is amazing."

"Cool. I'd really like to get to meet Theresa. It'd be great to learn the art of cake making from her."

"She would love to have you as a student!"

"She must be in the living room. I'll introduce you to her."

"What's that area?"

"Oh, that's where the director lives. We also have a mini-botanical area back there. I'll show it to you once we get to the end of the party."

They head to the living room. Ralph spotted a corner sofa to sit on as all the places had already been taken. "Sorry there's not enough space to sit on."

"Oh stop it, Ralph! We can share the seat."

He makes her sit and then tries to take a spot next to her. Seeing him moving farther, she huddles closer to him. *"Gosh this is more than I bargained for!"* he thought feeling the warm touch of her body.

The only warmth Ralph had experienced thus far had been that of his mother and the puny girl from Pune, Rajeshree. But this warmth was of a woman from a different culture; a wholesome, untouched and ravishingly pretty young damsel. Kuda started giving the welcome speech to all the international students, well-wishers and supporters of International Student House gathered in the living room and the study.

There was intermittent chatter among the people gathered but all Ralph could think about was the pretty young thing sitting close to him. As Kuda gave the speech, people started clapping, laughing and smiling throughout. Through all those moments Ralph could see the surge and crests in action. But he couldn't hear the content of the speech.

His attention was imprisoned by Matilda. He began to daydream. He and Matilda were running in the middle of a park holding hands and periodically stopping under trees to hug and kiss. Her long, blonde hair kept blowing in the wind caressing his cheeks.

"So you wanna go grab some punch and appetizers? Ralph, are you awake?" she gently caressed his arm.

He is woken from his daydream by the same creature that caused him to have it.

"Wow. What a lovely speech. Although I heard nothing of it," he humored.

She burst into rapturous laughter. He felt he needed to make her believe that he was listening even though he was totally distracted.

The fruit punch is in a wide glass bowl and looks like a mini, maroon colored-ocean of froth. Fruit punch is a typical American drink – what Ralph would normally call a soft drink. It is usually drunk without alcohol in it, though some people do mix and match based on personal preferences.

"This is so cool. Who made these tiny ships and birds," asked Matilda referring to the decorated items on the table.
"I made the paper birds. The ships were brought from a local craft store."
"Woah, I didn't know you made items like this."

"Well let's just say I am a man of many talents," he smiled. "I used to do these things for a long time in my country so it's no big deal doing it here."

"That's so cool!"

"Well, today is going to be a day of many cool things. Wait till you meet some folks I am going to introduce you to."

"Have you tried this Matilda," said Ralph pointing to the assortment of Asian ethnic appetizers on the table.

"No. What is it?"

"It's called a samosa. It's a traditional Indian appetizer and is common even in other countries like Nepal, Sri Lanka and Pakistan. You should try it."

"By the way. Do you like spicy food?"

"Oh yes. But probably not as much as you do. But I sure would like to try the samosa!" she smiled.

He placed a samosa on her plate. And she shyly appreciated his care.

"Oh yeah. This is the way we do it in Goa. Even if you don't want to eat it we are going to put it in your plate. Then if you don't eat it I will eat it myself."

"Oh gosh. You're a handful" she laughed.

"Oh here comes the person you have been waiting to meet."

"Hi Theresa!" Ralph said as he embraced her in a bear hug. "I have someone here who wants to meet you."

He puts his arms around Matilda. "Matilda, this is Theresa – our God Mama."

"Hi Theresa! Nice to meet you. I'm Matilda."

"Ralph's told me a lot about you."

"All good things I hope!"

"Haha. No I was telling her how mean and angry you always are!" joked Ralph.

"Oh stop it!" said Matilda as she tapped his arm.

"I was telling her about your baking skills and how you teach the girls so many things," he said looking at Theresa.

"She could certainly be a good student and provide you with cheap labor in the process."

"Oh Ralph! She's so sweet, I wouldn't want to make her work like that. If there is anyone I'd like to get cheap labor from it would be you!"

"Oh I'm scared," he said shrugging his shoulders to dramatize.

"I generally bake on Saturdays so that we can enjoy the fruits of our labor on Sundays! You are welcome to join us and learn if you like dear."

"Oh I'm so thankful," replied Matilda.

"And Ralph. Why don't you introduce her to Lily and Siona and the others so she can get information on when we plan to have long baking sessions like the one we had yesterday."

"Definitely! I was, in fact going to do that but I had to have her meet the master of all baking – You!"

"Very good," smiled Theresa as she looked in the direction of the living room.

"Well nice seeing you as always Ralph. I'm going to head to the living room and meet the other guests too. Great meeting you once more Matilda and please do come again for more such parties and baking sessions."

"Same here Theresa. I look forward to it."

"By the way, could I call you Matty.?" asked Theresa.

"We generally have family names for all our occupants and baker students…haha" she said sensing a blank from Matilda.

"Oh absolutely. I would love that. Matty sounds nice," said Matilda recovering from a temporary daze.

"Yeah I like it too. Sounds sexy!"

Both women punch Ralph in the arm.

"What do you call Ralph, though?"

"Don't tell her," interrupted Ralph.

"I think she already knows."

"I usually call him Ralphie."

"Ralphie huh!" she smiled slyly.

"Oh gosh Theresa. You've given her something to tease me about."

"I thought that was the objective. Why should only you have the privilege? Let her have some fun pulling your socks too!"

"Well, hey it was nice meeting you Matty…….Matilda. I'd really like to see you again."

"Absolutely, right Matty!" quipped Ralph.

Theresa laughed and proceeded to the living room giggling with mirth.

"She's so nice!" said Matilda.

"I live with nice people! Remember what I had told you that day in the library!"

Seeing Ralphie with the pretty young thing, Kuda felt stimulated. He knew Ralph had a penchant for getting along with people, particularly the ladies. But he had never actually seen any of his exploits. Today seemed different though.

"Hey. How's your party going? Enjoying yourselves! Ralph and Matty......umhhh?"
'Matilda...hhh. I'm Matilda!"
"Oh, I'm so sorry. Now I won't forget your name though. It takes only two times to remind me of a name. Then I don't forget" he smiled.
"Kuda is the man when it comes to remembering people and names. He has taken care of International Student House for two years now. And taken care of me for three months," Ralph asserted.
"Well, I try to be the care taker. But in reality, it's the students living here who take care of me!"

The trio laugh.

"See, this guy can never stop being jovial. He is a mood elevator."
"I am sure he is," Matilda seconded.
"So where are you from Matilda?"
"I'm from New Orleans, Louisiana."
"Okay. French influence city huh!"
"Yes. You know it?"

"I had a friend in Texas who used to visit Louisiana often. That's how I know about it."
"So you came here for school?"
"I used to go to Loyola University in New Orleans when Hurricane Katrina struck. The university was damaged quite a bit and had to shut down. Many classes were not restarted. We were offered the option of continuing our studies in other Jesuit universities in the US. Saint Joseph's offered many facilities which I didn't find other universities providing; so I opted to come here. And anyways our home in New Orleans was all but destroyed. So even my mother recommended that it would be a better bet to live and go to school in Philly while things gradually return to normalcy in New Orleans. "

There is a momentary pause as Kuda, Ralph and Matilda recount the long time it might take for the devastated city to return to normalcy after the massive scale of the destruction wrought by Hurricane Katrina.

"There is still a lot of construction work to do."
"Hey I think lunch is ready. Let me go check. But why don't we continue the conversation over a plate of burgers, fries and lasagna, haha."
"That would be great" says Matilda.
"You need any help Kuda?" asks Ralph.
"Oh. I'm fine. Thanks," says Kuda, winking at Ralph. Ralph suppresses his smile knowing why Kuda winked.

There are few things that most men cannot resist. Conversing with a good looking woman is probably one of the most potent of those few things; if not the most potent.

"Why don't we go sit there and wait for lunch. I think we'll have more people I could introduce you to," Ralph suggests.
"Head to the shore, Ralphie!" she gushes.

Ralph gives her the look and puts his hand on her shoulders. As they take their seats Matilda cuddles up closer to him.

"This cushion is so soft," she exclaims as her smooth buttocks almost rub against Ralph's thighs.
"Not softer than you though," he mumbles.
"What!" she gives him a look of surprise and wonder.
"It's nothing," he says slyly, suppressing a naughty smile.

She tries to make sense of his statement but lets it go thinking of it as a boyish prank. She always finds this handsome guy very friendly and funny.

Ralph doesn't need the inner voice to tell him how Matty feels about him. Her response to his actions gives him clear indication that they are at a higher level of trust. A trust that often exists between people who are more than friends. It's obvious when what you say would normally make a stranger get upset; but the person in question laughs instead. That's when you are in a high trust relationship.

The same seemed to be the case between Ralph and Matilda. And Ralph had reason to believe it was true. As they get cozy, Ralph is clearly in a cupid mood. "You have to maintain your calm Ralph; don't blow it," he heard the Inner voice say to him.
"So you have such parties quite often here huh!" she asks smiling.
"Oh yeah. But this one's a special just for you."

She looks at him and gives him a slight nudge with her elbow.

"How long have you been living here?"
"Since the last one and half to two months approximately."
"Ummhh"
"You like it?"
"Oh, it's a nice place!"
"Hey guys, lunch is ready. Please come and help yourselves in the dining room," announces Kuda.

Ralph secretly cringes, hating Kuda for always coming in and making announcements at critical times.

"*I was in the middle of getting even closer to this chick and the Nigerian charlatan barges in. Gosh! Horrible luck!*" he thinks.
"There's terrific culinary goodies waiting for us. Let's go and have some. Come!!" Kuda is all smiles.

Ralph eyes him with cupid disappointment.

"Great! I can't wait," she says as Ralph hands her a paper plate.

Ralph curiously looks for signs of people in the dining area. Not seeing anybody he then looks at the array of multi-colored dishes laid out on the table. A dining room bereft of people is always prime hunting ground for grabbing the best portions of the food. The table is an interesting mosaic of ethnic Chinese and American food. There's Chinese rice dumplings, orange colored rice with chick peas, luscious bean sprouts rolled in boiled green leaves, grilled chicken legs, semi-fried French sprouts, roasted potato slices and of course the all-American pumpkin pie. There also is cake - marble cake, coffee cake straight from Starbucks and bundt cake.

"I guess you know most of these dishes right."

"Yes. They look delicious!" she replies.

"They're meant to be so. If you like I could guide you through the Asian recipes."

"Oh. That would be great," she can't suppress a grin appreciating his chivalry.

"I think the best ethnic dish here is the Chinese rice dumplings. They go well with soy sauce or ketchup."

"I think you are pretty familiar with the rest right."

"Yes. Anything I don't know I will taste first and then ask."

"Hahahaha! That's the way to go!" he agrees.

They start tasting each dish. "Ooh, this egg rice is so colorful."

"Well so many things in Asia, China and India are so colorful by the mere fact of being Asian. I mean the spices, people and culture involve so much variety and color."

She takes some fried bean sprouts.

"I guess it's just that different civilizations have grown in different parts of Asia and they happened to do different experiments with cuisine. Moreover, I guess they had more time to experiment with cuisines because these are like three thousand or five thousand year old cultures. Especially when you talk about Indian or Chinese civilizations," explains Ralph.

Plates full with multi-colored dishes, they proceed to the living room to chat and enjoy. The large sofa seems conspicuously empty.

"Let's take that place over there," she says with an air of confidence. Ralph follows suit.

"Ummhh!! Good place selection. You have good spatial orientation," quips Ralph.

"Well, the sofa looked bigger than the other one back there. And also feels quite comfortable."

"Well, it is. However, not as warm as the previous one." Ralph is actually referring to the warmth he felt when both their bodies were close to each other.

"Excuse me," she looks at him in a queer, amused manner.

He digs his face into his plate smiling.

"So how's the food?"

Matilda's mouth is full and she struggles to push it down so she can speak and not look like she's talking when eating.

"Tasty...not tasty?" he continues.
"Sorry. Uh....it's delicious!" Her pre-occupation with eating the food leaves her little time to reply.
"I can see that!" he smiles.
"Yeah. I'm not going to mind my manners today."
"I was going to say, you shouldn't. This is a party to enjoy, make friends and of course eat to your heart's content."
"The only American food I've tasted is pizza. It's very colorful, very red. Is American food colorful and spicy?"
"Well I don't know about spicy but we might not have as many colorful dishes as in Asia."
"What's colorful in American cuisine is definitely the sweets, though."
"Oh yeah!"
"Yup. We have candy bars, candy cane and different types of cakes. These have a lot of color in them."
"What types of colors are mostly prevalent?"
"It's a lot of chocolate; so brown, dark brown. We also have multi-colored icing, cream toppings, blood red cherries and a host of other colored cherries. I once had a candy cane with yellow, red, blue and white all rolled into one stick."
"Amazing. I wonder how they do that?" Ralph asks.
"Well, they have mixtures of melted sugar in each color. They have machines that mix these sugars in the right proportion and shape them as canes. They are mostly seen during Christmas time when everybody wants to hang them on Christmas trees and give them to children."
"I remember as a child I would eat so many candy canes that my Mom would be worried that I'd ruin my teeth."
"Now that's something that's common all over the world – children ruining their teeth by eating too much sugar and chocolate."
"I love chocolate and candy a lot," Ralph says.
"Most people do right!"

The differences in culinary practices between the East and West are evident not only in the types of spices and ingredients used; but also in the colors of the food. Indian food, for example is rich in a reddish green, brown tinge due to a high content of peppers, chillies and spice in it. Generally, Americans seem to patronize a lighter food color due to a preponderance of pasta or bread in their food.

Similarly, the sweets have bright colors like blue, red and orange in them because they follow the European tradition of bright colors in sweets. Bright colors are attractive especially for kids who identify more with such colors.

"But what about the packaging?" asks Ralph.
"I guess bright and colorful packaging also plays a role in promoting sales of candy and other sweet products right?"
"Packaging is a central part of American business. Any business' marketing efforts would be incomplete without packaging," Matty emphasizes.
"Yes. The packaging I have seen here, I have never seen back home except maybe for in Europe."
"Yes. We make our stuff as attractive as possible so people buy as much as they can and thereby increase business revenues."
"Businesses and organizations in India could definitely learn a great deal from the strategies adopted by American businesses," Ralph says.
"So are you a heavy shopping person?"

She looks at him as though not knowing what he just said.

"As in do you shop a lot?"
"Yes, I shop for groceries."
He smiles. "No, I meant like actual shopping for clothes, perfumes, those kinds of things."
"Well, I do go like twice or so in a month. But haven't been doing it lately. Why do you ask?"
"It just seems like you got pretty good taste."
"Oh really! You think so. How come?" she questions.

Ralph is put on the spot when she asks him the question.

His speech is shaky but he manages to gain composure. "Well your dress looks classy and you have put on an irresistible perfume. Besides you seem to know quite a bit about marketing, packaging and other facets of American business practices."
"All these things point to the fact that you might be a connoisseur of style. Which is why I am wondering if you go shopping a lot.

Something tells me you know your way around the boutique or fashion store!"

She smiles and takes a deep sigh.

"Well. It's just my Mom. She had such an amazing fetish for dresses, shoes and all things that make up a female wardrobe. I think it kind of rubbed off on me."
"My Mom had an entire cabinet full of nail polish, lip gloss, mascara and eye color. The cabinet was placed just beside her vanity table. Whenever she dressed I would see the vast quantities of make-up she would use. She had an amazing collection of dresses too."
"Okay, so that's where your amazing sense of style comes from. I will believe that because even in my household, my mother is the epitome of style," Ralph says.
"Was your Dad also very stylish?"

She grimaces and balks. Ralph suspects he asked the wrong question.

"Are you alright?"
She shakes her head a little and then forces a smile. "Oh yes. I was just thinking about something else. Sorry about that!"
"Oh no. It's good to have thoughts about other things and diversify your thinking," he says seeking to change the subject of the conversation.
Apparently, she doesn't seem to have a good reaction to questions about her Dad and Ralph didn't want to open skeletons from the cupboard this early in their developing friendship.
He tries to change the topic. "So do you cook?"
"Yes I cook," says Kuda interrupting the conversation.

Matilda bursts into mirth filled laughter.

"Sorry to interrupt your conversation. But could I join you guys?" he asks.
"Oh absolutely!" beams Matilda.
"Sure," seconds Ralph.
"Thanks."
"So you all were talking about cooking. Why don't we finish that topic before we go to the other ones."
"Oh gosh. I was happy when you came cause I thought I would not have to talk about my hopeless cooking skills," Matilda says.

"Well. Why don't we torture you a little and ask you exactly about that," Kuda smiles.

"Or maybe ask her a lot," adds Ralph.

"Yeah that sounds fair!" laughs Kuda.

"Oh gosh, you guys are incorrigible!"

Ralph and Kuda look at each other and wink. It's always nice to get mushy with a pretty looking girl. The African knows how to sweet talk and the Indian 'playboy in development' knows how to make women feel cozy.

"Well.....?" Kuda poses a suggestive question.

"Okay. I won't resist anymore. I'll tell you what I can't cook first and then you can guess what I can cook."

"Okay. We don't mind playing 'guess the animals.' So shoot!" Kuda says.

"Well I don't make Chinese rice dumplings, I don't make pizza, roast beef, noodles or hamburger. But what I do make is KFC steaks, McDonald's burgers and Pizza Hut pizzas. Which unfortunately you get at each of these stores so I don't have to make them. I just buy them when I feel hungry! Any questions?"

"Okay. Having said that I would like to ask you guys what you cook?" she smiles triumphantly feeling she has pulled off a smart move on them.

"Hold on! Not so fast. We got a little more probing we need to do first," Kuda smiles fiendishly.

"Probing! Hahaha," laughs Ralph.

"That would be fun."

Matilda looks at both of them with friendly suspicion. "You guys are up to something, with Kuda as lead henchman."

"Okay, so first question – how often do you eat out?"

"Umhhh....wait a minute, I'm not telling you that! What's up your sleeve?"

"Well, we answered your questions and will be open to answering any more you have so you better be open to answering ours now," Kuda smiles.

"Be a sport Matty!" Ralph giggles.

"Okay. I guess most of the time. And anyways we don't have a very nice kitchen in the dorm that I am currently in. The other girls usually want to go out and eat so they ask me. I go with them. It's not like I always like to go and eat at McDonald's or Burger King."

"So what do you eat when you don't go out?" Ralph asks.

"Okay. That's enough. We're just trying to get under your skin," Kuda interrupts seeing Matty glare at Ralph.

"Well, we have just one proposition, though. If you like you could always come here and help us out with cooking, baking, or decorating. We always have plenty of stuff to do here. And your skills would be a great help!" Kuda looks at her with gentle caring eyes.

In truth, Kuda knows that her cooking skills are abysmal if not non-existent. Ralph suppresses a snicker.

"That would be great. Thanks so much for offering," blurts out Matilda.

"Yeah. I learnt my cooking skills in the US. As in I knew how to cook back in Nigeria but the practical learning came in the US. I think that's what this country teaches you – practical learning derived from practice!" Kuda beams.

"It must be so different though right coming from a different country and trying to stabilize yourself in the US. What's the most challenging part?" she asks looking concerned.

"Well, I came here for pastoral studies. So I had the support of my church here. In that respect, I would say I was pretty fortunate to not have to go through some of the things that probably other international students have to go through."

"What might those other things be?" Matilda asks.

"Good question. Well I know about them but haven't actually gone through them. So I'm not sure I am a good person to ask that question. But Ralph here has gone through quite a lot in a short span of time. He'd be able to give you a first-hand account of what it's like to be an international and inexperienced in the US of A."

"What do you say, Ralph?"

"Thanks for making me a consultant on the life of international students in the States, Kuda."

"Well, you know when Kuda talks about the problems international students face here he refers to a lot more than just getting used to the cuisines, customs or styles in the US. He is talking about many other things. Those other things are many and numerous. But I could give you a visual into it."

"Being an international student in the States definitely has a lot of benefits. But there are responsibilities and duties that come with it.

There are aspects of being here that you just can't deny. The very endeavor of making friends and staying is different here than it is say in India. In my personal opinion, making friends in Goa was quite a cakewalk. Here it is more of an effort. I guess this effort teaches you how to reach out to people who might not have a reason to talk to you. It teaches you humility and how to not let your ego mess you up."

"It is a fight more against reforming oneself than against the circumstances that exist around one."

"Having liquid cash is a great help when you have just arrived in the US. Cause credit cards are not easy to get, especially when you have no credit history."

"Credit history, umhhh, I never knew about this concept before I came to the US. And then I wished I had not known of it. Cause I got turned down by more than four credit card companies before I applied for the fifth and they told me I could apply after three months. Which meant all expenses were supposed to be met using cash. That was difficult cause I wasn't all that educated about which areas of the city to avoid especially when you are carrying cash on your person."

"Did you ever feel scared walking alone on the street?" Matilda interrupts.

"Well, I would have to be extra alert at night walking on the street or even on the streets within the college campus. And it wasn't even that I had to but rather wanted to. There is always a sense of self- blame when you get robbed and you weren't watchful. As opposed to getting robbed, when you are watchful, that's a different scenario."

"Ummhh, so coming back to the point of international students getting adjusted in the US. Every act right from making friends, getting bank accounts, filing for work related papers, or even signing a lease for renting an apartment are procedure and paper intensive tasks. These need getting used to. Especially when one is coming from a place where these things weren't as detailed or procedure-oriented."

"Did you feel lonely?"

"I guess you must have," she says noticing his silent gaze.

"Loneliness is a part of daily life in the States!"

He pauses. There is this forlorn feeling so visible in his eyes. They look like a deep abyss of darkness. An abyss which preserves secrets of a difficult past and an uncertain future. While harboring a wellspring of bright ideas and ambitious ventures. There seems to be this shallow hollow resembling a cave with white walls that holds a glowing secret. But the secret is only his for now. He knows that he can't let this secret out to everybody. That God has kept a special person out there who will be a party to the secret. And that day will come.

"Having been brought up in a communal setting it takes a while to get adjusted to the individualistic culture in the States. We normally just talk without having a specific reason to people. Here in the US, it seems as though you need a purpose and a reason to speak to somebody. Life's pretty regimented. Similarly, it can be pretty fluid provided you are wealthy enough to be able to make changes to your schedule, lifestyle and work."

"But what I never stop finding amazing is the tremendous level of organization you see in the US. Everything is so well laid out, organized and planned. You hardly have any plans or activities which come all of a sudden or do not have a significant amount of planning behind them," says Kuda.

"And that's where the first signs of stress begin to appear. Many international students come from countries which are considered developing or underdeveloped. Compared to US standards, these countries could often be considered anarchical. Often times they are called third world countries. Organization is conspicuously absent in these places. Administrative ineptitude is glaring. So obviously when you see this level of organization and planning, a lot of stress is created in the minds of callow international students."

"Why so?" she asks. "Is it because they're scared of order and organization?"

"It's more because they're unsure if they would be able to adjust to this level of organization and planning actually."

"High standards require certain amounts of commitment. This need for commitment might not always be forthcoming when one is from a different setting," seconds Kuda.

"And I am not saying it's good or bad. It's just the situation most of the time," completes Kuda.

"Yes. That's an amazing point you brought up Kuda. It's very true and I couldn't agree more. However, many ambitious students also get so anxious trying to catch up with the norms and practices in the US they do themselves a great deal of disservice. Worry seldom helps unless you have the right plan to eliminate the cause of your worry."

"So yeah those are just the tip of the iceberg when it comes to problems faced by international students. There are many others which I don't have at the top of my head right now."

"I must say though life in a foreign country can be challenging as well as interesting. The very fact of going to a restaurant and finding cuisines that one has probably never heard of. Or going to buy a ticket and being oblivious to the courtesy of standing in a line. These are some of the basic things that the so-called 'culture shock' begins to show up in."

Culture shock is the feeling of disorientation a person might experience when in a foreign country. Such feelings are caused by being exposed to alien surroundings, people and norms. Usually one feels totally out of place. Feels lost and alone. These feelings tend to be so strong sometimes that they are categorized as a shock arising out of cultural differences.

"So this culture shock – How long does it last?"

Ralph and Kuda look at each other in surprise.

"Well I don't really know but it could last anywhere between six months to one year. Though of course, there are instances in which some people simply don't adjust to American culture. They keep struggling," Ralph says.
"Ohhhh....!" she gasps.
"Yes, there is a certain degree of letting go that is involved in trying to get integrated into a foreign culture. It is as much a function of self-effort as it is of meeting the right people who will be sympathetic enough to explain to you the various nuances of American cultural norms and traditions."

Matilda's eyes grow wide and she looks dazed. It is evident that she finds the entire topic of culture shock and international students adjusting in a foreign land more than interesting. Ralph senses her interest, amazement and extent of confusion in trying to make sense of immigrant-related issues and concerns.

"Yeah. It can be challenging. But that's the fun – doing things you don't know or are not good at on a regular basis. Having done more of theoretical stuff all those years," quips Kuda.
"So tell me about you," he looks to change topics and focus on the woman in consideration.
"You said you are from New Orleans right."
"Yes. New Orleans, it is? The French, Creole land."

"So do you speak French?"

"Well, I used to when I was little. But then became a victim of the 'use it or lose it' theory. I understand more than I speak now. But yes in some households in Louisiana, French is spoken as much as English. In New Orleans though this tradition is being increasingly replaced with a greater use of English."

"I had studied French for three years in Nigeria. Then the communal violence started and there was civil strife, so all public institutions started degrading in quality and service delivery."

"And?" Matilda looks worried.

"We had to leave school and stay at home."

"Ooh that must have been difficult. How did you manage?"

"I guess it's just one of those things. You know you feel miserable when all of the violence starts. Then despair overcomes you and shakes you from your inaction. You begin to think survival. And then endurance keeps aiding survival. You begin to pray and strengthen your faith. Faith, in turn strengthens you."

She continues gawking.

"And that's essentially what happened to me. When in school I could safely say I didn't have faith. Then the violence began and all hell broke loose. At the end of it, I had lost a couple of family members but my faith was stronger than a rock. I don't mean to say it's okay to lose your family in exchange for faith. But that is what happened to me. My suffering had made my faith unshakeable. Faith is what got me out of the violence and the danger. It helped me heal and taught me to forgive."

"How did you come to the States?" she asks with concern.

Ralph notices that the Nigerian man has a great deal of depth in him. And the pretty damsel is totally enamored by his genuine personality and frankness. Kuda has, in fact, begun to look handsome for the first time since he has been in International House; for the first time in several months. "Charm is what makes someone handsome and good looking; not just looks!" quips the Inner Voice.

"I could develop this type of style. I might not even have to ask Kuda how. Watching his living example could teach me how to," thinks Ralph. He continues to listen intently.

"Well during the period when violence was rampant in Nigeria, even hospitals would not be spared from attack. Hence many of the wounded would sometimes have to be treated in churches or make-shift shelters close to the Church. We had faced many further casualties transporting patients to and fro from the hospital."

"I was a regular helper at the medical outpost in the church. During the day, I would be as busy as a worker ant, constantly tending to the injured and the ill. At night I would pray to the Lord to give me strength to carry out my duties selflessly."

"A Christian missionary noticed my fervor and tireless efforts and felt I had all the qualities of a fearless preacher. I guess he felt I could become a good missionary. So he offered to sponsor my education in the States. I couldn't believe at first that I would be getting a full scholarship to complete a Masters in Theology. Of course, after I came to this country and completed my Masters, I was urged to go in for a Ph.D."

"So that's where I am today."

"Oh! That's so cool! A story of overcoming suffering and human cruelty in spite of all the odds."

"Umm, you're an interesting person. You regard a difficult life as cool. Ralph, see you could learn something from her!" says Kuda sounding appreciative of her compliment.

"Hahahaha....!"

"Stop it!"

"I always knew there was something weird about her," Ralph smiles.

"You....." she tries to retaliate.

"Cool cool!" Kuda reassures.

"Well anyways, I think it was great that you came to the party and we got to meet you. You should come again and I don't know if this guy has already introduced you. But do meet our in-house baking specialist Theresa if you can today."

"Yup, I already did. She's great."

"Oh cool. Well, I got to just go and catch up with a couple of other guests. Do stay for the rest of the party. We've got a lot more fun and games coming."

"Thanks so much Kuda! It was so nice meeting you."

"Same here Matty!" Kuda gives a gentle smile.

Ralph looks at him with surprise as though Kuda taught him a thing or two about speaking to people and making a connection with them. He knew it was probably the Inner Voice guiding him to such situations to learn what life really is about.

"Nice meeting you too Ralphie!" Kuda says as he rushes out the living room. Both of them exchange friendly glances. Both of them know what Ralph's objective is. Probably Matilda has the same objective too.

As lunch time wears down, people begin to gather in the living room as though an unwritten rule exists prodding them to assemble there. Noticing the winding down of lunch, Kuda signals to his right hand, miracle man – Ralph.

"Could you go into the kitchen, the study and the porch and round up people from there. We are going to have some games."

"He always interrupts at strategic times. I was in the middle of getting close to the chick," Ralph exasperates silently.

"Sure!" says Ralph as he hurries to complete the rounding up as soon as possible. After all duty comes before everything and above all. Though, girls kept waiting for too long are girls lost – he knows that.

"Hey guys, we are going to have games in the living room. So if you all could go there that would be great," he blurts out to a group of Korean guys.

"Yoy, yoy!" they say indicating approval.

His personality and look give him an uncharacteristically familiar sense of command and authority. Needless to say, people interacting with him feel in awe of him. They are obliged to pay heed.

"Wow, that was fast!" He can't believe his own speed in getting the job done with such blitzkrieg.

As he hurries back to Matilda, she looks at him with childlike wonder. It's symbolic of a woman looking in awe at a young man; strong and capable, going about his daily tasks one mountain after another.

****

"We are going to have some games in a while."

"Oh wow. But I really need to go home and meet one of my friends. She's coming from Ohio. And we were planning to meet for a long time," says Matilda.

"Can't you wait for just a short while. It will be great," pleads Ralph.

"What games are they playing?"

"I don't know but they are going to be a lot of fun. Kuda keeps them a secret until it is time to start playing."

"Well, I could wait for a couple of more minutes and sample them."

"Cool! Once you see the games you will feel like staying longer. I would have told you about the games but that's one part of the party I didn't help organize."

"Okay. Sure."

Kuda comes to the forefront of the room and asks people to huddle close together to easily form teams and play the series of games they have planned.

"Dumb charades would be the first in our lineup."

"Woah dumb charades!" she exults.

"See, I told you you'd like it."

"What is dumb charades?"

Matilda raises her eyebrow, squints and then bursts into sarcastic laughter looking at the callow young fellow. He's so self-effacing and innocent though that she feels like hugging him instead of mocking him. "You seriously don't know what dumb charades are about?"

Ralph's blank stare assures her that he doesn't know about it.

"It's a game in which you pick a paper with the name of an actor, character or action and then act out the part in front of the whole crowd."

His stare is still as blank as it was before.

It is not common knowledge that many games and norms considered widespread in the US are not well known in other parts of the world. Hence, many immigrants and international students often don't understand references to historically Western games and recreational activities. Whether it is dumb charades; rock, paper and scissors or even activities like a cookout; all these are generally unheard of by people in other parts of the globe.

Other countries have their own types of games. The ones that are played in a group require people that know or understand these. Ralph had often noticed that not many international students are comfortable enough to open up about their native customs, traditions including games to Americans. What holds them back?

Probably that their English might not be up to the mark and prevent native English speakers from understanding. Hence they hold back from saying anything. Or that they might simply lack the accent. Or more terrifyingly, that the game itself might not be well received. That the local Americans who hear about the game might disregard its value, because American video games and cultural pervasiveness is so widespread that anything other than Zynga, Sony, Facebook or any other American brands is no brand at all.

Ralph knew that each of these factors if not a mix of all of them contributed to the relative shyness of quite a few international students. He had come across a case where a Chinese student would play a game of zeros and crosses only with fellow Chinese students since he had had poor prior experiences with American students.

Uniformity in language understanding more than makes up for a large amount of clarity of the subject being discussed. Nevertheless, the mere fact of speaking a language that is pretty much the standard in the developed world and indeed in most parts of the developing world, reduces the acceptance curve that ideas and people need to go through to gain popular approval.

So when two people proficient in English discuss a game and agree; the 'not so proficient speakers' of the language usually have little language fire power to defend their ideas with. Even explaining their ideas becomes difficult.

Hence, a group think tends to form. The collection of English speakers bolstering their agreed ideas and the non-native, poor speakers merely accepting what's been said to prevent rocking the boat and all the time second guessing themselves.

"You'll understand how it's played when the game starts," says Matilda.
"Okay is everybody ready?" Theresa calls out.
"Yeah!!" the crowd is unanimous to acknowledge.
"As many of you might know, we will be playing 'dumb charades' today," Theresa announces.

"I have been playing this game for thirty-five years. Now I know many of you or rather most of you (she probingly looks at the bevy of students and International House patrons) are from different countries and have not heard of this game before, let alone played it. I would urge you to not feel shy or restricted by that. This is an easy game to play. You don't even have to learn it."

Theresa has this great capacity to understand what's going on in the heads of students, especially the international ones. She's American but it's strange how deep her understanding of Asian and 'international student thinking' in general is. Ralph has never stopped being surprised with her insights and clairvoyance. Behind her steady, delicate figure there is a treasure of experience-laden learning, though.
She looks and sees surprised, worried faces.

"Trust me people. If I can play it you can too."

There's something about Theresa's manner and attitude that Ralph can't seem to understand. She always seems to have the tender ability to put people at ease no matter how apprehensive they might be. Ralph has had the direct opportunity of having her counsel him about the things he did wrong on so many occasions. Any other person would in all fairness be right to take his head off. But she didn't get all huffy and puffy about it. Her calm composure was the key to making him reconsider his behavior rather than the single misdemeanor itself.

He remembers the time he forgot to turn off the flame in the kitchen and the pot got burnt. If it wasn't for Theresa, the smoke detectors would have gone off.

"Gosh! What explanation would I have given had she not turned off the stove and agreed not to complain to Kuda!" Ralph wonders.

****

"Okay so who'd like to volunteer!" she announces.
"You Ralph?"

He is shaken from his day dream into reality. Theresa is a little puzzled to see the normally alert Ralph in a pensive mood. "Hope he's not distracted by thoughts about love and the pretty lass sitting next to him!" she thinks.

The glass bowl looked immaculate and clear. Its shiny surface reflected the light from the fluorescent light bulb making it resemble a bubble. Mum asked Ralph to come dance with her but Ralph wasn't feeling much in the mood to dance. But realizing that the evening wouldn't be enjoyable for Mum he decided to shed his inhibitions and don his dancing shoes. Classy weddings were prime hunting grounds for Mum to shake a leg or two. And this wedding was one in which Mum didn't want to be left behind. As she positioned Ralph to make the right moves, he could see that he was being trained in the fine Goan art of dance. As they danced through the night, Ralph could see that Mum's energy was boundless and that he was finding it hard to keep up. But he knew he had to.

Ralph didn't want to get into any more daydreams. He had dreamt quite a bit for the day. An enthusiastic voice brought his daydream to an ungraceful halt.

"Okay...okay. I guess I put the cart before the horse. There are names of activities on papers inside this glass bowl. The player needs to pick a paper and try to depict the action or role stated on the chit of paper," states Theresa.
"Questions?....Anybody!"
"Well, either you have understood everything or understood nothing. Which one is it?"

Still silence.

"Hey, Theresa. I think the best way to find out is by putting somebody in the hot seat," galls Kuda.

The crowd follows Theresa's screeching laugh and the collective laughter seems more like a bunch of football fans gone crazy.

"How about Ralphie!" Kuda grins. The crowd bursts into rapturous applause.
"Yay! Good choice," yells Matilda.
"Go on, you have a show to attend to," she prods a hesitant Ralph.

157

He is shy and unsure of how to play the game.

"Come on dude. You can't play the game from your chair," exhorts Theresa.

Sitting cuddled up on the sofa, Matilda by his side; there seems to be this overwhelming sense of calm that beseeches him. The crowd all around is charged and full of glee. Yet he seems to be in a bubble of peace and composure; untouched by the happenings around him. He knew that it was in settings like these that jewels of wisdom often struck him. The inner voice often spoke to him in situations like these.

"You can do it bud!" the Inner Voice said.
"Okay, okay if you don't want to go I will. You can watch me and learn," she gestures.

All the while, Matty had been calling out to him into his ear and he hadn't been able to hear. His peace and calm had been unshakeable. He secretly hoped this composure would take him through other less fortunate situations! The problem with the social engineering class team was one of the foremost on the list. Although they had already taken action against him; he needed to brave the class the last few days of the semester. That meant seeing his irreverent former teammates who threw him under the bus.

"He has given his turn to me," Matilda says to Theresa.
"He is not scared, but only wants to give me a chance to lose!" she gives him a coy smile as she walks to the center of the room. Theresa is all smiles at the humor of the pretty, intelligent damsel.

****

Putting her soft, pale fingers into the bowl she reaches for the chit of paper and hands it over to Theresa. Ralph is surprised to find a look on Matty's face somewhere between embarrassed and blushing. Theresa sees it and covers her face with her palm not to give out any clue of the role.

"Groovy, groovy.....da da da!" Matilda begins gyrating her torso; then her voluptuous hips. All the while her hands are high up in the air, palms rolling up and down in supple movements resembling the grace and beauty of a Hindu deity.

Gosh what the heck is she doing. I never knew she could do such seductive movements. "*Hmmmm.....what was on the chit of paper?*" Ralph thinks.
"Can anybody guess," Theresa interrupts the crowd giggling with rapturous squeals.
"It's a cabaret," shouts Ralph.
"Wooooooooooooooooo!!!" crowd.
"Close but not close enough" replies Theresa.
"An Arabic belly dancer," Kuda says.
"He got it!"
"And oh yes. Anyone who gives the right answer will get a prize."
"Candy cane for the starters!!!" Theresa hands Kuda a candy cane for the right answer.
"Hahahahahahaha," laughs the crowd.
"I think this was a particularly difficult role to play and she handled it amazingly! And I hope you thought so too. A big hand for Matty!! Woohoo!!"
"Matty, Matty, Matty....Matty!!!" the crowd erupts in thunderous applause.
"Now I know whom to ask when we are looking for a belly dancer for a bachelor's party," Kuda thunders.
"Oh yeah. Well you're gonna have to get through me before you ask her Kuda!" Theresa states in a matter of fact manner.
"Another round of applause for the newest member of International Student House, Matilda!"
"Yay!"
"You go Matty!" shouts out Ralph.

She comes and crashes on the sofa, half on his lap.

"Phew! How did I do that! Belly dancing!"
"What's your part-time job?" Ralph kids.
"Oh, you are always so ....," she pokes his slim belly.
"Oww, oww....umhh. I got to see your resume. You seem to have an interesting past given the way you danced."
She gives him the look. "Alright, alright, I'm gonna stop. I don't want to get a black eye after the party. Though I must say I'd like to get a candy cane by giving the right answer."

"I could help if you agree not to ask for my resume," she jokingly glowers.

"I'll try to…..hahahahaha."

"Okay, so who would you like to select Matilda? You need to pick a person to play the game after your turn," Theresa informs.

"Oh yeah! Sorry, I skipped…well, the person next to me would be fine."

"Yay, that's great Matty. Now you're getting the hang of putting Ralphie on the spot!"

"Come on young fella! We're going to make you do something more than dance like a belly dancer," Theresa says.

"Woohoo," the crowd cheers in unison.

On stage events were always panic inducing for Ralph. He remembers the time when he was selected to make a speech in school on "time management."   The thought of standing at the podium and delivering the speech made him so uneasy that he ended up passing the opportunity to another student.

"I have a sore throat," he told his instructor, to avoid the effort of having to drum up the courage to deliver the speech.

"What am I going to do now! No way to get out of this situation. At least none I can think of!" Ralph thinks as he slides his tawny-colored hand down the bowl of choices.

He knows that he is now in an international, western setting. Not enough room to give excuses or evade responsibility, unless of course you die. *"Death is not an option at this tender age. What do I do?"*

He feels the external world suddenly closing in and the bubble forming around him. "Balls up and just do it. Don't run away from this!" says the Inner voice. One of the few times he had heard the voice so clear, so direct.

The bubble suddenly breaks as he feels a warm, soft hand touching him.

"Ralph, Ralph…..is everything alright." Theresa reaches out for his hand to see if he is alright and in the present.

"He's just stunned with fear," yells Matty from the gaudy sofa at the back.

"Oh yeah. He can't move because he knows he can't dance and can't talk," guffaws Kuda.

"What is he going to school for! He looks unable to read! Well are you going to open the piece of paper and tell me what it is," grins Theresa.

At first Ralph dangles like a puppet doll from left to right as though not knowing what to do. But he knows. He knows that the Inner Voice can't be wrong. That it has led him in the right direction when he was in India and will do the same in this country too. Through all his deepest fears and most recalcitrant anxieties, the protective bubble of the Inner Voice has been a stable harbinger of the best course of action.

"Ooh….you're in business," says Theresa as she reads the piece of paper he handed to her.
He squats and places his hands in a cup like circular fashion over his mouth. Then like a roulette wheel starts circling around a central point. All the while holding his hands to his mouth and squatting. Concentrating at the point on the ground, focusing on it with maternal affection.

The crowd stops laughing and wonders what role could possibly be assigned to him. There is just one person desperately trying to suppress her laughter in the back of the crowd. Matilda and Ralph seem to have developed this special connection which permits her to snicker at him without feeling bad. Or without worrying about making him feel bad.

But right now he is not concerned about who's laughing and who's not. Dumb charades is to be played with the actor not making a single sound. Ralph's total and complete silence makes it difficult for the non-Indian crowd to guess the act.

"Okay stop! Anybody with answers?" Theresa blurts.
"You"
"Pole dancer!"
"Yeehee…..nope but good try!"
"I wonder why we're having so many dance roles starting with Arabic belly dancing and now this!" Theresa humorously thunders.
"Grind dancer!" says another student.
"Sorry!"
"Five, four, three, two, one…..and we don't have an answer!"
"Anybody? Last try."
"No? Great. So the actor gets to tell what the role was."
"It's an Indian snake charmer," says Ralph.

"That was an interesting act, I must say!" Kuda acknowledges.

"Probably Ralph came up with it himself!" quips Theresa with a smile.

"Well, he gets a candy cane for his act since nobody could guess the right answer."

"A round of applause people!" says Theresa.

"Yay!" Ralph notices Matilda slamming her palms like little cymbals. She is obviously very impressed with his snake charmer, dancer performance.

"Woah! You were like a God back there. I didn't know you knew to dance," Matilda galls.

"Trust me, lady. You don't know many things about what I'm capable of."

"That's right. Could you give me your resume? I'd like to see what you've done in the past!" she chuckles.

He gives her a look somewhere between smarty and 'you have timing!'

"Yes, I sure will. Only after you provide me with yours, particularly the activities you do outside of curricular work," he flashes a naughty smile.

"Okay so how long is the game going to last?" she smiles not ignoring his earlier statement.

"Oh yeah. You're getting late right. What time do you need to get home?" he asks seriously.

"Well, this friend of mine will be coming at around 4pm. So I wanted to be ready with some lemon juice and cookies for her. We've been friends for a long time!"

"Ummhh, I wish you could stay longer for the other games."

"How long does it take to make lemon juice?" he asks hoping to change her mind and make her stay longer.

Lemon juice and cookies are a cultural trope in America. It wouldn't take a whole lot of time to make lemon juice and cookies. You get lemon juice concentrate in the store and freshly baked cookies are sold in almost all bakeries throughout the US. It takes like max ten minutes to purchase these two items. "*Why would she want to go home so early?*" Ralph wonders.

Well since these two items are crucial to have in most meetings involving near or dear ones; an additional element of care is involved in such situations. Usually, once the juice and cookies are ready, people spend some time getting ready; bathing, doing makeup, nail polish and essentially getting pretty. The idea is to be as well-groomed and done up as to have the right mix of goodies to eat and drink.

Being from a different country, Ralph isn't all that familiar with this mode of operation. Back home Dad would cook everything with a little help from Mum. Then he would have a shower and get dressed while Mum put the dishes in nice containers and cleaned up the kitchen. Immediately after Dad was out the bathroom, Mum would head for a quick shower leaving the well-arranged dishes to cool down.

The kids would be instructed to get dressed if they weren't already. In fact, this is how it worked in most middle-class households in India. But in America, with most houses having more than one bathroom and encouraging independent thinking, things are different.

People value their looks a lot. They tend to dedicate equal amounts of time to work and play. Sometimes, it's more to play depending on how wealthy the person is. Matilda wanted to go home, get the cookies and juice ready and then prepare herself to meet her longtime friend. As per her estimate, she needed at least an hour to do this. Sensing her impatience, Ralph acquiesced to her urge to leave the party. He didn't understand why, but he wanted to show that he was fine with her leaving. Just to seem flexible and not clingy.

But he did not actually understand the reason why she wanted to leave – the way an American person would have looked and understood the situation. Herein lies a core difference between people born in America and those that come to the US from a different country and a different culture. The difference might not be as much in the dress, the food or the color of the skin. But rather is very pronounced in the mentality and the thinking.

Even though a person might learn American customs and norms relatively quickly it takes time to understand American logic and reasoning. What understanding is present usually is of a more superficial nature. Superficial understanding is rarely internalized and people don't tend to take ownership of such an understanding. More so in the absence of an American friend or chaperone. It is an open secret that it takes a long time to adopt the rationale that Americans use to go about their day to day activities.

People often come to a new country leaving behind the old. But just by getting a person out of a country you can't get the country out of the person. That process of emotional and social gentrification takes a lot longer. Which is why culture is such a widely discussed topic today. Even companies have their own culture. Personnel recruited in a company are often taken through a long period of orientation to indoctrinate them with the culture of the organization and wipe out traces of an earlier organization's culture.

When responsibility for adapting to a new culture rests solely with oneself the process of social and cultural gentrification involving adoption of new ideas, concepts and ways of thinking is usually more laborious. New immigrants essentially have themselves and may be a few committed friends to engender the learning and internalization of practices followed in a foreign country. It is a daunting challenge, but not unachievable; with hard work and dedication.

****

"Yup sure. If you want to go and get ready that's fine," he says gently.
"Well it was really nice of you to invite me over. I hope you can call me again."
"It was nice having you. Let's go before Theresa calls you again for a belly dance," he guffaws.
"Haha. Wait. Let's say bye to Kuda & Theresa."
"Oh you can do it from here. Kuda's pretty cool when it comes to goodbyes."
She waves out to Kuda and Theresa.
"Thanks for coming Matty. Next time we will have a belly dancing competition," Theresa grins.
"I'm up for it!" Matilda says.
"Thanks for coming Matilda. See you again soon!" Kuda shouts.
"You too Kuda!"
As they walk outside the door and the porch, an uncharacteristic silence seems to dominate the previously gregarious couple.
He's wondering how important she regards him compared to her female friend. A sense of insecurity or a mere craving for love? Or more like jealousy in regards to love. Ralph knows that women in general and American women in particular can't be pushed around or forced to do something they don't want to do. Western nations are known to have

equal rights for all its citizens irrespective of religion, gender or sexual orientation; at least that's what it is on paper.

"So till what time are you going to be here?" she asks sensing the silence as they walk towards her car.

"I don't know. I want to go to the library and get some research work done. So I'll probably scoot off in a couple of minutes or so."

"Oh ok."

Silence again. She gets into her light sea blue colored car and lowers the window.

"Thanks for everything today. I really enjoyed myself!"

"Thanks for coming."

"Hey do you want a ride to the library? I will be passing that way on my way home."

"Ummhh."

"I mean if you want to attend the game go ahead. But if you want to go I would love to give you a ride."

"Yeah. I guess it's better that I start my research as soon as possible so that I have enough time to complete it. I'll grab my books and bag."

"Oh great. I'll wait for you."

"Thanks."

He rushes up the stairs with less vigor than he had at the start of the party. While at the outset he had thought that he could use the party to get closer to Matilda he now settles in for a more realistic scenario. That scenario seems to be of slow friendship and gradual attraction. A ride to the library is not quite his idea of getting close to somebody of the opposite gender though. But hey it's something. And something is always better than nothing.

As he gathers his books and laptop in the small duffel bag he notices the glowing image of the Our Lady in the center edge of his desk. The Our Lady was his mother in this country and in any country he would go to in the future. He knew he always had her to watch his back and guide him. But he was grateful also for the earthly mother he had been given. However strong, strict and tough she could be and was, there wasn't a match for her love in the world. Through the meshed wireframe door she seemed the same angel she was a couple of hours earlier. Sitting in her car, as though in a verandah, Ralph didn't feel any sort of anxiety or trepidation approaching Matilda.

He avoided locking eyes with her as she kept staring at him admiring his checked black on a white shirt and blue jeans.

"Ready?" she smiled as the engine revved.
"Yup."
"So what are you going to research at the library?" she asked seeing him in silent contemplation.
"Social engineering dynamics and neural networks."
"Ooh, sounds complicated!"
"Well, I'll be doing only preliminary research."
"Teach me about it sometime!" she winks.
"Oh sure. I'd be happy to teach you just as soon as I'm done with it!"
"Here you are," she says as they reach the gate of the university.
"Thanks for the ride."
"Have a great time with your friend!"
"Thanks."
"We should meet again if you like."
"Yup. That would be great!" says Ralph sensing a need from her.

She looks at him expecting him to say when. But he seems dazed and just affectionately smiles at her. He is actually disappointed that he couldn't influence her to stay longer at the party. It is difficult for people who are lonely and friendless to understand that people have a lot of friends and tend to have many commitments besides the one with you. Ralph was probably in this situation.

"Well, I saw your place today. Do you want to hang out at my place this week?" she asks, wanting to make sure they can meet up.
"Oh yeah. That would be nice. Where is your place? Around this area?" he asks wanting to know how he could get there.
"Well it's a hop, skip and a jump from the library," she says to assuage his logistics related concerns. Both of them laugh out loud.
"Let's text."
"Absolutely," he replies.

As her light blue Chevrolet Aveo slides past him he can feel a sense of belonging. Belonging that he hasn't felt since he set foot on US soil. Though the Inner voice and the Our Lady were always there watching over him and his every move; this girl represents a type of belonging in the flesh and the blood. He does not know if this feeling might last long. But however long it lasts, he wants to savor every second of it.

Relationships whether good or bad, I guess were meant to be. Every relationship serves to teach, educate and to be a memory on the mosaic of experiences that life is.

He enters the dignified library with a sense of fulfillment and happiness. In spite of all the upheaval going on in his dealings with the social engineering team and the personal adjustment problems in a foreign country, he feels a certain sense of being complete. This, in spite of all the incompleteness surrounding him. The research work proceeds quickly with great internet speed, a nice study environment and a clear mind.

****

Although one would not want to judge people by the sound of their sms messages; there is something very unique about Matty's messages. Ralph feels they are so genuine that they are a reflection of her true self.

"Have a good night. Sweet dreams – not about me, though!" was her message on the night of the party.

There is an underlying tone of flirtatiousness in most of the text messages. Ralph knows too well that they are beginning to be more than just friends. But what does she actually think? He couldn't know for sure.

"So do you have a girlfriend?" says another text.
"Don't know!"
"Ooh! What a bummer. I have a lot of boyfriends, though!"
"Hahahaha!"

It is clear she is trying to get under his skin.

"Good for you. Are they handsome," he texts back.
"Not as handsome as you!" she keys back.

You don't have to be born in the US to know that such sentences are clear indications that she's into you or trying to get closer to you. Ralph has had Indian girls hitting on him. But this is the first unique experience with an American Caucasian girl showing overt signs of interest. Needless to say, he likes it but still finds it strange. Why is this girl so into me or showing that she is, he often wonders.

(Text-Ralph) "Hahaha…well, I'd like to meet your boyfriends and see for myself how they look."
(Text-Matilda) "Sure. On one condition."
(Text-Ralph) "What's that?"
(Text-Matilda) "Could I introduce you to them as my special boyfriend? ☺"
(Text-Ralph) "Hohoho…..I don't see any reason why you can't! So do you have any girlfriends? How many?"
(Text-Matilda) "I have a couple. Why?"
(Text-Ralph) "I was just thinking I'd like to meet them and then do some pick and choose. ☺ [wink]"
(Text-Matilda) "Ummhhh…."
(Text-Ralph) "Don't worry, it's not intended to make you jealous!"
(Text-Matilda) "Well my girlfriends live far away and they already have boyfriends, so ….."
(Text-Ralph) "Oh really! Special ones or non-special ones? ☺"
(Text-Matilda) "Stop it. You're teasing."
(Text-Ralph) "That's my profession….hehehe"
(Text-Ralph) "So you want to meet up? I might tease you less in person! Cause then you have a chance to beat me ☺"
(Text-Matilda) "Sure. What are you doing this evening?"
(Text-Ralph) "I'll be busy with research. How about tomorrow?"
(Text-Matilda) "Yeah. Tomorrow would be fine."
(Text-Ralph) "Where do you want to meet?"
(Text-Matilda) "We could meet at my place. You haven't seen it have you!"
(Text-Ralph) "Okay. But I don't know where it is. And I don't have a car to get there."
(Text-Matilda) "No problem. I'll come get you. Does 5:30 pm sound okay?"
(Text-Ralph) "5:30 pm sounds great."
(Text-Matilda) "Great. See you then."
(Text-Ralph) "You too."

The trauma of the night before was painful. There's something about this girl that makes him feel comfortable, though. Puts all his worries and anxieties to rest. Is it because she's non-judgmental, playful or just likes him. He doesn't really know. But he believes that he likes her or at least is beginning to. It's difficult to differentiate though; if this is love or mere infatuation. That's a major conundrum about youth....you never know for certain. And even if you do there is reason to ask if experience would have made you think otherwise. Anyways, he prefers having a person to talk about non-work or non-school related things. Someone who helps to off-load the stress he is enduring. A temporary stress buster in this time of great chaos in his life. He is grateful for this God sent person.

****

The red traffic sign is blazing brightly on an uncharacteristically sunny November Friday and he doesn't feel the hurt of the social engineering team expulsion. Not as much as he does the urge of spending time with a beautiful lass. The wind seems crisp and calm. The atmosphere inside the car is comfortably warm. She is partly blushing, partly smiling. And he can't seem to place her feelings.

"So do you have a lot of friends here?" she asks.
"A couple."
"Have you been to their places or spent a lot of time with them?" she asks sensing his casual answer is an indication that he has only school-based professional relationships with people.
"Well, a lot of the people I've met have been through International Student House where I live. We have parties and get-togethers where people from different places come. It's a great way to meet people. Non-stressful, casual setting."
"Yeah, I thought the party we had the other day was very nice. One of the few parties where I have met so many people and got to talk to them so much," she smiles.
"Yes. Isn't it! I myself haven't got an opportunity to get to know people so well at many other parties I've been to" Ralph seconds.
"Oh. So you go to a lot of parties outside of International Student House?" she asks curiously.
Pause.
"I've not been to a whole lot. But been to a couple – mostly student parties."
"Oh....nice!" she seems to contemplate something. Her coy smile gives away an embarrassing intention but Ralph can't seem to place it. He says nothing.
"So have you been to like frat or sorority parties?" she slowly asks.

169

"I know kind of what frat parties are. What's soro..soro..that party?" he fumbles as he tries to pronounce the word.

"Oh. Sorry. So if you know what frat parties are you shouldn't have much of a problem understanding what sorority parties are. A fraternity is a society whose members are all male, whereas a sorority consists of all female members. Usually, frat parties invite women also. But you might not always find guys at sorority parties. So yes it's a typical American college concept."

"So are these fraternities and sororities only at the college or university level?"

"Yes. Typically they are. At the high school level, we might usually have clubs or groups."

"So what are these fraternities and sororities formed for?"

"You don't know!" she looks at him surprised. But stops short of saying anything more to avoid bringing his ignorance to the fore.

"Oh, they're just groups of like-minded students. More so.." Her speech is cut short by a pedestrian crossing a street while the yellow light is still active.

"Damn, a light breaker."

"What's that?" he says, not understanding what she just said.

"Oh, that guy who crossed the road did so without the green signal going into effect for his side of the road. Else we would have been able to get through the yellow signal. Now we got to wait till the red traffic sign passes. I wonder why they do that. It's not like he would not have a green light for his side of the road."

"Phew!" Ralph sighs.

"Well, can't you cross now. It's still yellow."

"After we've come to a dead stop on a yellow light its best to stay put. Cause yellow means a warning that the red light is round the corner. So you are typically expected to stop. If a cop car sees you crossing on a yellow after stopping they will follow you and give you a ticket."

"So traffic rules here are pretty strong huh."

"Strong on those who violate them," she laughs.

Ralph had seen from the very day he set foot on US soil that bending of rules wasn't generally the norm. People would try their best to stay within the rules, going the extra mile to prevent bending or breaking the law.

Those who flouted the rules and were caught would be prosecuted like the man in a speeding car who was detained by the police on Thanksgiving Day. He broke two red lights and then tried to evade arrest by making two police cars give him chase. Nobody is above the law in the US. Or at least that's what they claim. Why else would President Clinton have been pulled up for potential impeachment for a matter which in the case of any ordinary man have been considered a mere case of infidelity!

Ralph notices the raggedly dressed young student looking much older in his filthy clothes. Definitely, that guy's not American. Not Caucasian American at least. He could either be a Mexican or Asian. The strong November wind blows his hoodie a little to reveal a couple of facial features.

"Nah, that guy's definitely Pakistani, Bangladeshi or Indian," he lightly mutters.

"What!" she asks.

"No. It's nothing. Just thinking out loud."

Ralph now understands why the pedestrian must have crossed the street prematurely. Most cities in the Indian subcontinent have a glaring absence of traffic lights. Why? Firstly, it's cost effective to not have them. Secondly, even if they are present there are always going to be undisciplined people who would flout the lights when no one is watching. Quite a few considerations weigh in on the authorities involved in making these decisions. Lack of budget or administrative ineptitude are not exclusive to these list of reasons.

Major intersections in large cities (known as metros in traditional Indian English) generally have traffic lights at all major intersections in the 'heart of the city' areas. '*Heart of the city*,' would translate as 'downtown' in North American vernacular.

"Interesting terminology conversions!" Ralph thinks.

But here there is a 'stop' sign or a traffic light at every crossing and intersection. Back home only the major intersections in big cities (metros) have them. Goa, the tourist state Ralph hailed from barely had any.

The understanding was that drivers on two wheelers or four wheelers would see each other coming in varied directions and stop or allow the other to go. But who would go first or wait was a matter to debate.

In the US, the driver who arrives at the stop sign first is the first to get the right of way to leave or cross the intersection. Back home, there are no ubiquitous stop signs. People rely on intuition and intra driver understanding to coordinate who waits and who gets to leave first. From the viewpoint of the systematic, organized system present in Western nations the Indian system of traffic flow besides being disorganized would seem deadly and dangerous. A veritable war zone!

"No wonder when Western tourists come to Goa they are appalled by the traffic, the stray dogs, the cattle and the vehicles moving within inches of each other."
Unfortunately, the concept of lanes or orderly traffic movement is not uniformly present on local roads and even city roads. More so it is absent in the psyches of the people who use the roads. Absent from their psyches and absent from their needs to ask the administration for better organized roads. Bicycles move alongside motorbikes, scooters and cars in a humongous, zigzag of sorts. Even the minutest of vacant space is considered as fair territory to place one's rubber on. Through gaps and clever maneuvering if you can get your vehicle out of a traffic jam, you are considered smart. Not at all like the organized traffic flow in the States. Accidents occur at the drop of a hat in such disorganized settings. However, they are often blamed on the individual driver's lack of dexterity or quickness or simply inadequate driving aptitude; rather than on the improper traffic system.
It's interesting to note that the system of vehicles squeezing within a narrow road hardly receives any criticism from the authorities that are responsible for ensuring proper transit systems. Only a bunch of educated folks will occasionally upbraid the system. Some may write articles on it, but that's about it. Coming to the States from that kind of background, Ralph feels liberated. Almost empowered for not having to deal with the petty issues that should never have been occurring were the system organized enough.

The youngish looking man abruptly crossing the street before his turn reminds Ralph of the huge leaps that his country needs to make to reach the level of preciseness existing in the States. He shudders to think Matilda got so harried by the mere fact of this guy crossing the street out of turn. What might have happened if the same girl was driving on a crowded road in India where hundreds of vehicles might be jammed adjacent to each other on a strip of road equal to half a lane in the States. And that's not all. Along either side of the road, there are stalls selling eatables, cheap jewelry, clothing and other knick knacks. People often use the traffic jams to do their shopping whether grocery or other. Time management is what they would call it.

"Americans would probably call this necessary downtime to prevent a 'traffic induced' personal meltdown," he silently thinks. But then with the vendors trying to pull a fast one on unsuspecting tourists, most westerners would probably stay away from such cheap deals with street hawkers. It's kind of rough but it's a fact of everyday life in India. Though Western eyes would find this system haphazard, crazy and dangerous; nobody would be able to find a smile that's artificial or pain that is not real. It's strange but true! In spite of all the inadequacies in infrastructure, administration and government, it is a remarkable work of attitude when you see the people who should ordinarily have been huffing and puffing with anger are in fact smiling and laughing. Boldly brushing off the material weaknesses of their society as a work in progress rather than an endemic malaise.

"I guess there is so much of work to do, so much that is incomplete that it is best to keep oneself positive, avoid the customary depression and achieve what is within reach," thinks Ralph about the attitude of so many people in India and many other developing nations in the world. Sometimes trying to be oblivious to the cloud of problems around you is the best way to stay sane. In a world where even basic human needs like sanitation, healthcare, clean food and drinking water are hard to come by it is important to consider first things first.

Do I indulge in self-pity and lose what is within striking distance or do I compose myself and address the problems head on? Trying my best to resolve solvable problems properly and systematically. And even if I try to solve the problems by not giving room for self-pity; is there a guarantee that the problems will go away? Well, only a guarantee that I tried!
These are some of the questions that the middle class and upper and lower middle classes in Asian countries debate. The hope of trying and winning against the daunting despair of utter loss – both of time, effort and the illusory joy of surpassing difficult issues.

****

In America though, he realized the issues were quite different. Generally, the government takes good care of matters like road construction, infrastructure maintenance, building water pipes and the like. Or there are private companies that make profits building this infrastructure, through contracts from the government. Construction of facilities or other infrastructure maintenance issues are not considered issues at all. They are considered work that's going to get done by business organizations that have been given charge of getting it done. And these people will be held accountable for the work getting done.

173

Generally, such work gets done without asking twice. In fact, without even asking once! An employee assigned a certain job is required to do it. Else, he or she would generally be reassigned or fired.

Attitudes to work in America, Ralph realized, tend to be apolitical. People come to the workplace to get a job done, get their money and go home. The work needs to get done quickly and fast, consuming only the correct amount of time needed to get the work done.

"So do you drive?" her caring voice distracts him from his thoughts.

"I used to drive my uncle's car a little, when I was back home. But that's about it."

Pause.

"I guess for everything here you require a car right."

"Well cars are part of everyday life here. Nobody thinks about them until their car breaks down," she states in a matter of fact manner.

"In my country, cars are not used as much as they are here. Mostly people who have businesses or more money purchase cars."

"Oh really."

"Yes. There was a time when cars were considered a luxury. However, with greater economic liberalization, enterprising people are finding it easy to do well. The new found wealth helps them purchase expensive, luxurious cars."

"Nowadays, it's becoming more like cars are a necessity. Somewhat like here. But they're still not there yet."

"So what do people mostly use to get from point A to point B in India? Public transport?" she asks.

"Public transport is used quite a lot. In fact, the majority of the people use it. However, most of the middle class people use scooters or motorbikes. Scooters and motorbikes are to them what cars are to people here. It's as common as that."

"So you must have been riding a motorbike right?" she smiles.

"A scooter actually," he blushes. "My parents were more comfortable having me ride a scooter than a motorcycle."

"Motorcycle, scooter....?" she looks puzzled.

"Oh a motorcycle would be called a bike here," he says sensing her confusion with the terms.

"Have you heard of scooter?"

"Well...umhh," she fumbles.

"I don't know if you have them here. But I saw a moped-like vehicle that's smaller than a motorbike. It has room for 2 people to sit and ride. If you have seen an Italian Vespa, that's what a scooter is," he states.

"Okay. So how are they to ride? I mean fast, comfortable?"

"Oh yes. Scooters are among the most comfortable of two-wheeled vehicles. They have a lot of room to store and carry stuff and have good fuel efficiency. More than motorbikes."

"Really!"

"Yes. Motorbikes do not have as much storage space. Besides, many of the mechanical components are exposed. Scooters, on the other hand, have all their mechanical components inside a covered compartment. So they don't come in contact with people sitting on the vehicle. Also, there is not as much of a chance for garments to get entangled with the moving components of the machine. Motorbikes are also safe. But I've had instances wherein ladies' garments have got entangled in the wheels or other moving parts while riding a motorbike."

"Oooh!"

"Well it doesn't happen all the time. Just have to be careful that you are sitting properly on the vehicle. A good thing about motorbikes is they have a good center of gravity. So it's easier to ride them since they tend to have good balance."

The car takes a sharp right. "Oooh. You're strong on the steering wheel. Have you used a scooter or motorcycle before…sorry motorbike?" he asks.

"No. My sister would drive a rag-tag motorcycle when we were kids. She was better at most things physical. Very athletic."

"Strong kid huh."

"Well, just that she tended to be more outgoing and boyish. She even had tomboy type hairstyles throughout her teenage years!"

"What kind of bike did she ride?"

"It was a bike in which there only seemed to be an engine and a fuel tank. Nothing else. And she rode it as though it was a horse. She would offer me rides often. However, most of the time I would refuse."

"Nice!"

"Well, sort of. She can be pretty rough sometimes. And doesn't generally take a no for an answer; particularly not when she is trying to get you to try her bike."

"How did she learn to ride it?"

Ralph knows that riding scooters or even motorbikes isn't as common in the US as it is back home. Riding a bicycle is more noticed than a motorbike or a scooter. The scooter population is a minority in the States.

"Well, the bike belonged to her boyfriend. He is the one who taught her how to ride."
"Wow."
"Yeah. They would spend a ridiculous amount of time together."
"In fact, at one point, the bike would be parked in our garage throughout the night and at the break of dawn, Shannon and Jay would be off riding the bike."
"Where would they go so early?"

"No idea. But the neighboring town had many bike races in which couples participated. She was a free spirit and still is. She enjoyed the races, the bikes and of course the bearded men!"
"What kind of men do you like?" Ralph sneaks in a question.

At that moment, the car veers sharply right and screeches to a dead halt. Her eyes turn hawkish as she shoots an angry grimace at the nonchalant lad.

He feels a moment of regret for having said what he did and appears alarmed. *"Probably I should have waited for us to settle down inside the house before trying to get under her skin,"* he surmises.

"What do you mean?" she questions with a tone sharper than the tip of a knife blade.

He looks at her with a look of surprise and reverent fear, hoping that it might placate the stirred lass. He only meant to tease her with the comment but it seemed to have opened a can of worms. This was the last thing he wanted. Probably the last thing any guy on a "girl baiting mission" would want.

She keeps staring. Angrily.

"Oh sorry, I was just, umhhh…"
"Haha. I got you there!" she cracks up.

As he looks at her with surprise, he is dejected that he couldn't see through her façade. He feels stupid that she was smart enough to trick him with her external behavior.

"Ummhh! You have good humor. Hahaha," he says without laughing. "Ooh. Mr. Sensitive! I was just doing reverse teasing. Sorry if you fell for it without a clue!"

He still shows as though he is offended.

"Come on. Cheer up. I was only kidding." She gives him a friendly tap on the arm and presses it.

She feels a muscular arm. Finally, he puts on a smile. "You're quite a jester! But I'm better than you."
"We'll see. Let me show you the house."

They leave the car and walk towards the elegant looking porch; he's looking at the place with interest and she is clutching her little purse.

Her delicate, slim figure is accentuated as she climbs the steps, stretches and stands upright. Her jean skirt seems very well chosen to match the white blouse. A cool combination. Ralph loves good combinations. *"Hope this woman is not reading my mind!"* he thinks.

As they enter through the screen door, he feels a surge of leather polish smell. Somebody's either bought new leather sofas or coated the existing furniture with a leather scent. Or probably everything's new in the house.

Suddenly a kind of silence befalls them and he wonders what he needs to say. "Don't do anything extraordinary. Just go with the flow," says the Inner Voice.

"So this is my place! We have the living room here – my best part of the house!" she giggles.

"That's the kitchen over there. Oh, and in case you need it, the bathroom's over here." She points to a vestibule in the corner of the living room.

"Where is everybody? Seems like you live here alone."
"Oh three of us live here. But today everybody's out on their own. So the house is all mine," she gets a dimple on her cheek.
"And mine too," he raises an eyebrow, suggestively.

She taps him on the arm and he follows up grabbing her by the arm pinching her on the shoulder.

"Owwh......you're strong and rough," she howls.
"I like it rough! Hope I didn't hurt you dear!"
She moves back. "Ummhh...want me to get mad at you again," she sports a naughty smile.
"Hahahahaha!"
"Come let me show you my room. Oh, are you thirsty, hungry,...angry?"
"Well, I could do with a glass of water! Angry, umhh, not yet." He gives a slight smile.

She rushes to the kitchen and grabs a glass. Fills it with bottled water from the fridge. Then rushes back to him. She has a broad smile on her face. It is amply clear to Ralph she is ecstatic that she is alone at home with him. Or so it seems.

"Here you go."
"Thanks. I could do with plain water from the faucet. You didn't have to take out the bottle from the refrigerator."
"No worries. Bottled water is cleaner than faucet water. It's good for you."
Ralph always wondered why so many people bought bottled water in the States. "*Why don't they just use tap water or better still, just a water filter to purify the water from the faucet!*" he often thought.
"But why don't you just use a water filter to purify tap water and use that. You won't have to buy those cartons of bottled water every time."
"Well, it's more convenient to get bottled water from the store. All you do is just put the carton in the cart, bill it and then transfer it to the back of your car. It works out well. Besides bottled water is cheaper than faucet water if you do the math. Why would one want to go through the trouble of filling bottles of water when you can easily have a pre-filled bottle of fresh, mineral water for like two or three dollars a carton! One carton had like 10 or 12 bottles of water."

Ralph is confused but decides not to argue. The land he comes from people think differently. They think in terms of saving money rather than mere convenience. Don't get me wrong. Convenience occupies a high priority on their agenda too. But saving is also deemed very important. Those folks don't mind going through a little discomfort or lack of convenience to save some money. "Small amounts of money saved today will form part of a large pool in a couple of years" is the normal thought process.

This pool of cash could be used for education, marriage or in the case of any contingency. Extra reserves of cash are always helpful. Such ideas to saving and convenience reflect the fundamental differences in attitude and thought processes of Asians vis-à-vis Americans. Not to say that Americans don't save or that they don't have a Scrooge mentality. Rather Americans have a very covert Scrooge mentality. But the ratio of those Americans that penny pinch is far less than that of Indians or Asians who do. At least that's the impression that is held the world over.

"So are you going to keep looking at that glass. Or you want to see my room too!"

She stands at the top of the stairs and grins at him. Her calf muscles and thighs look rounded, smooth and curvy through the faint light coming through the painted glass on the upper level of the stairs. Her short skirt and curvy figure make it hard to resist her call.

Ralph seems confused what to do with the empty glass in his hand. "Just leave it on the table. Come on," she hollers noticing his hesitation.

His vigor replenished; he rushes to set it on the table and then heads upstairs.

She unlocks the door and thrusts it wide open. "Welcome to my humble abode," she laughs.
"It's an abode alright," he says looking at the well-arranged furniture in the room.
She goes into a corner and gazes at him standing and observing her room.

"Nice. You have decorated it well."

He looks at her observing him and she continues to look, nod and bite her lips. Although Ralph is a bit of a horny guy, he is not quick when it comes to getting cozy in bed. He blushes and looks away.

"Thanks for the compliment!" she says sensing his shyness.

Women tend to have this sixth sense that helps them understand or decipher facial and emotional cues.

"So who is this?" he points to the photo of a girl on the dresser.

"That's me."

He looks at the photo, then at her trying to draw a similarity. "Doesn't look like you!"

"Of course not. I was kidding. Remember!"

"Oh gosh. I keep getting fooled!"

"Don't worry. You'll get used to it! I have a knack for conning people."

"So who is that?"

"You like her?" Matilda gives a naughty smile.

"No!" he smiles too.

"Then why did you ask? I can understand you are trying to hide your feelings in keeping with traditional reticence!"

"But anyway. She's my long gone sister."

"I'll tell her you have a crush on her the next time I meet her," she grins again.

"Where is she now?"

"I don't know. She's been long gone for a couple of years now. Way too long. We're no longer in touch. She ran away from home when she was seventeen."

"Alone?"

"No. With that biker boyfriend of hers and the motorbike of course." She laughs. It doesn't seem genuine. And Ralph wonders whether to regard it as one of disappointment, forgiveness or happiness. *"No, it definitely can't be happiness. I didn't see the slightest glint of joy and happiness there,"* he thinks.

"Oh yeah. You were saying in the car that your sister was a free spirit and enjoyed bikes and restaurants," he says.

"And men too," she twitches.

"So do you miss her?"

"At first I did. But not anymore. Wherever she is, she is probably happy."

"Sorry to hear that."

"What? That she's happy."

Ralph gets a little pissed off with her kidding but maintains his composure.

"No. That she ran away from home and didn't come back."

"Oh. I'm not. Given the circumstances we were in I wouldn't blame her for what she did."

Ralph senses there is something more painful in her history than mere family issues. He decides he doesn't want to go there just right now. Not so early in their friendship at least. He changes topics. The feeling of pain, loss and residual hurt is clearly shown on her face. He takes a seat on the couch.

"So you were telling me that your sister was very smart and strong right?"

"She did well at school even though she barely studied. And had quite a few boyfriends."

"So did you guys get along?"

"We did. Although she could get bossy sometimes."

"So is that the reason she ran away cause you resisted her bossing?"

"That's not funny."

"Sorry. I'm just ..."

She cuts him. "You're fine!"

She only has her sister's photo in her room. The parents or relatives are nowhere to be seen.

"So tell me about you," she shakes him from his thoughts.

"What'd you wanna know?"

"Start with your blood group and move onto your height, weight and other essentials, including your appendages."

Ralph rolls his eyes. "Well I could start off with my education and my background and follow-up with any other questions you have. I'll leave my height and weight for you to guess."

"I forgot to ask your age!"

"Okay, do you have a TV or something here?"

"You saw it in the living room."

"How about we talk while watching a movie?"

"How can you watch and talk at the same time?" she retorts.

"It's called multi-tasking and we do it all the time!"

They walk downstairs, hand in hand.

"Gosh, the couch had begun to get warm when he asked for the freakin movie. If only for a few more minutes of cozy time!" she thinks. Sex is always at the top of your mind when you get close to somebody of the opposite gender. Watching a movie together is one of the instances of getting close.

As they walk down the stairs, Ralph is occupied in a mini-dilemma. A dilemma of whether to do or not to do. The girl in question seems very horny, very forward. Should I keep her at bay or go along with her. Her agenda seems to be one of falling in love and getting laid. If I don't go along with her plan I risk alienating her. Ralph knows there are very few entities as disgruntled as a woman whose sexual needs are not met. "Hell hath no fury like a woman scorned!" – William Congreve didn't write this for nothing.

On the other hand, if he acquiesces to her overtures, he risks making the friendship a lot more than 'just friends.' He compromises his principles and home bred motherly advice. "No sex before marriage. No girl can be yours until marriage!" was what she always said.

"Go with the flow," says the Inner Voice.

He doesn't hear anything else. "I guess I'll just do as it says," he thinks. When Mum is not around the Inner Voice is the guiding light.

"Anyways, I've never had such a one on one experience before. So it wouldn't hurt to allow the experience to happen. Why change fate by artificial intervention. I've been doing that quite a bit following advice from others. But in the bargain I lost important opportunities to grow. Let it flow now!!" he thinks.

"Hey where you running," she calls out. In his thoughts about the propriety of being with the pretty girl he had sped down the stairs without her.

"I guess I'm looking for the best spot to watch the movie from. I need to get to the spot before you do!" he jests.

"Haha. And you think that's going to be possible?"

"You never know."

"You better not. Cause it's always me who calls the shots around the living room. Even when my roommates are around."

"Cool, cool. I was just kidding."

"I know," she smiles as she catches up with him.

****

"So what movies do you have?"

"We got a couple. Depends on which you like."

"I was going to ask you that actually. Which one's your favorite?"

As she opens the drawer beneath the fixture holding the TV set, a wide array of DVDs and cassettes are seen. The DVD casings look like narrow black keys on a piano; though in a continuous array without any white key in between.

He wonders why the girl has been having a naughty smile on her face ever since she sat next to him on the couch upstairs. Although he can

182

feel the rumblings of a casual flirtation getting deeper, he prefers to stay calm. After all, go with the flow was what the Inner Voice had said.

"You got an amazing collection there!"

"Yes. But I like just one movie the most from all of these."

"Oh yeah. Which?" he asks wondering what kind of movies, blonds like her tend to like.

She grabs a DVD from the array of DVDs and flashes it across her face.

"No Strings Attached!" she winks at him.

"Have you heard of this one?" she looks at him with a glint of panache in her eyes.

"If you like, we could watch it!" she says without waiting for him to answer.

He tries to conceal his underlying excitement to her seemingly flirtatious behavior. He has heard that in America, freedom is defined by your attitude to life. If you are open to opportunities in general then that's what you need to become successful. Probably that's what you need to become successful anywhere right - being open to new things! According to several studies, teens in the US become sexually active or are exposed to stimuli that cause sexual activity a lot earlier than in many other cultures.

"I need to be cooler about this," he tells himself.

Ralph knows that 'No strings attached' sounds very slutty. But prefers to experience it with her rather than shy away from it. Not only because of an underlying meaning that refers to 'sex without commitment' but also the cover picture on the DVD case. The cover shows a half-naked woman with a man putting his pants on.

It's a no brainer what the contents of this movie might be. However, he wonders what intentions this girl has behind selecting this movie on this day. Is it because they are home alone that she decided to make the movie her 'favorite movie?' he wonders.

"Whatever might be the reason for her selection, just go with the flow!" Ralph tells himself. The Inner Voice would not have had it any other way.

She switches on the TV set and presses a couple of buttons to get the movie playing. Then presses 'pause' as she turns to the young man making himself comfortable on the soft sofa. Their eyes meet and she continues looking at him.

"What!" says Ralph.

"Just wondering if you'd like something to munch on while we see the movie."

"Umhhh."

"There's popcorn in the kitchen. I'll go get some," she rushes into the kitchen.

She walks gently by, all the while keeping her eyes on him with a smile meant more to seduce than to convey approval. He turns his eyes away from her and tries to suppress a blush.

"Gosh things are definitely heating up here!" he mutters to himself. He slides back into the couch and decides to get some rest before she comes back. He realizes he might need it considering that things seem very likely to get steamy.

****

In the background he can hear popping sounds and the microwave beeping. Loud sounds created by utensils clanking against each other. His eyes shut and he falls into a snooze. Suddenly he sees an elderly priest dressed in imperial yellow and white garments reading out a sermon. It sounds a lot like a sermon of love. A wedding sermon. He doesn't know why but he is dressed in immaculate black - a black suit. Beside him stands a lady in total white – a wedding! But whose getting married? To who?

As the priest reaches the end of the sermon, he asks Ralph to face the bride. Everything becomes crystal clear now, as the lady he faces looks no different than the beautiful Matilda. In her tiara and white dress she looks the part. Her smile is infectious. In a moment all that changes as the woman in white bends and reaches for his family jewels and pulls them hard. The priest and the entire congregation laugh and seem to enjoy as she tries to detach his testicles from the groin.

"Hey….hey.." he feels her tugging at his shirt. "Did you fall asleep?"

"Oh….umhh…no." He is glad to be awake. He didn't want to witness his castration with several dozen people jeering in a church, even though it was just a dream.

"We still have a movie to watch!" she smiles.

"I was going to say you have a beautiful smile."

"Thanks," she says looking a little perplexed as to what has gotten into him to give her an off the cuff compliment.

"Woah. That 5-minute snooze was heavenly. Got my brain cells recharged," he quips.

"Well the popcorn is right here, so feel free to grab," she says as she places the bowl of popcorn on the table in front of him.

"There's something more than popcorn I'd like to grab," he mutters.

"What?"

"Nothing!"

She presses the 'Start' button and the movie starts playing. Ralph is calm and confident as she jumps onto the soft sofa close to him. He puts his right arm on the couch just skirting her shoulders. The movie starts as most normal movies do. Life description, lead character, boyfriend or girlfriend of the lead character. But as the movie progresses into savory tidbits of no strings sex, the chemistry between the only two members of the audience begins to change dramatically. *"She's probably trying to seduce me,"* he thinks.

Ralph's arm gets closer to Matilda's shoulders and she draws closer to him. They can now feel the warmth of each other. The two central characters in the movie are Emma and Adam. As Emma and Adam get together every night for steamy, no strings attached sex; Matilda begins to bite her lips and Ralph tries desperately hard to be composed. At one time he tries to focus on preventing an erection. She's too close to him to allow his little brother to rise ninety degrees anyways.

His Asian, Catholic upbringing creates a mental barrier to making out with a girl. But there are a couple of things in life that discipline can't always prevent you from. Making love to a seductive woman is probably one of them.

"So do you like the movie?" she asks as she feels Ralph getting increasingly agitated.

"It's great!" he mumbles as he tries to force down an imminent erection.

"Just great?"

"Umm…it's fantastic!"

"What's fantastic about it?"

She can feel him getting sweaty. But he doesn't seem to be taking any action. No first move. *"Hope it's not that Indian conservative dogma bullshit,"* she thinks to herself.

"Well what's fantastic about it?" she repeats not having received a response from him.

He hesitates at first. Then realizes that it's not propitious to feel backward and shy. Not of new experiences at least. *"Go with the flow, that's what the Inner Voice had told me,"* he reminds himself.

"Well?" she continues.

"Well I thought it's amazing how two people can have sex without having any commitment. I mean sex for the sake of sex; just physical interaction on an intimate level. No emotions or attachment involved."

"Yeah. You're right. Isn't that great!"

"It is…yeah. Sort of."

He doesn't know what to say. If he says he patronizes no strings attached love making she might make a certain judgment on him. If he condemns it then also she might feel he is not very forward and not be happy with his outlook on love, sex and life. Girls can be very judgmental and choosey. He knows that. Moreover, he has heard and seen in various places – American girls always look for a handsome, manly jock. Usually, the relationship goes on till she is happy with what she is getting – the fun, the tequila shots, the sex, the parties. Or till he gets tired of servicing the same girl. And she might be saying, it's great just to try to figure out what kind of guy he is.

These girls are quite shrewd and they have a specific thinking that they apply when they want. To guys they want to apply that thinking to. He didn't want to be judged through a feminine magnifying glass. So he decided to stay as politically correct and cautious as possible while being friendly.

"Sort of? I guess you don't know what it means to have somebody hug you tight and kiss and cuddle you!"

"Of course I do. I've had my parents kiss and cuddle me."

"Have you had your girlfriend or boyfriend kiss and cuddle you?" she retorts.

"Well I'm not gay, so boyfriend is out of the question. Girlfriend, umhh, kissed but not cuddled much."

He knows that's a lie, but he feels like a loser saying he never had a steady girlfriend. Most guys would prefer pretending they have or had a girlfriend rather than admitting they never did.

"Oh, so you did have a girlfriend then," she says sounding surprised.
"Yup," he doesn't sound very convincing and he knows that. But he goes with the flow none the less.
"How long did it last?"
"You mean the relationship?"
"Yeah."
"It was an off and on kind of thing. Not very serious."
"You mean you were not serious or she wasn't?"
"The relationship wasn't serious."
"So you shouldn't have much of a problem adjusting to a 'No Strings' kind of relationship since you were already in a non-serious kind of relationship before right?" she guesses.
"Haha. Well this no strings movie we're watching is a little steamy. My relationship was more of a friendship kind of thing."
"Oh friendship huh," she has a naughty smile. Deep down she feels that there can never be much of a friendship between men and women. Because the sex always gets in the way.
"I can't believe this Adam character is so strong in bed though. Seems like he's got boundless energy! Wonder where he gets it from."
"Probably it's that pretty looking girl he's with that's getting him that energy!"
"Probably. Or might be that he's just interested in sex a lot."

Ralph maintains perilous silence on hearing these comments. For some reason, he senses where she's trying to go with her extremely forward, 'bordering on the edge of seductive and involved' remarks.
She feels the silence and realizes she would need to push harder, more directly to get this guy out of his shell.

"So are most men interested in sex?" she asks playing casual.
There's ice cold silence in the warm room.
"I'm talking to you!"
"Oh sorry. What'd you say?" he feigns paying total attention to the movie when in fact he is not.

His plan to seem too involved in watching the movie serves to strengthen her resolve in unmasking him and seeing his manly innards.

"I was wondering if all men like to have sex?" she reiterates.

"I wouldn't know. You're gonna have to ask all the men in the world," he gives her a wise smile.

"Haha. So you're getting wise huh," she says affectionately.

"Well trying to! Next question."

"Well then you should definitely have the answer to this one."

"Oh yeah. What's that? Nothing too direct I hope."

"No I was just wondering – do YOU like to have sex?"

He appears frozen at first. Then recovers and regains his composure.

"I don't know. I've never asked myself that question before," he looks at her with an air of having dodged her question.

"Well, you've never asked yourself that. But now I'm asking you that question!"

Still silence.

"So do you like sex? Or don't you? I won't mind if you say yes or no; the answer is immaterial. But staying mum is not an option."

"Why not?"

"Cause it gives me the wrong idea."

"Wrong idea?"

"Yup. Makes me think you are either gay, celibate or simply scared to reveal your sexual orientation."

"So, which one of these applies to you?"

"I'm somewhere between heterosexual and too scared to reveal my sexual identity. Thanks for giving that option in your list of answer choices!"

"Okay. Nice to know that you are straight. I've been coming across a lot of people with alternative tastes lately."

"Oh really. How come?"

"Just come across them at different places."

"Then you're probably hanging out in the wrong places!" he grins.

"I guess!"

"Like which places?"

"Bars, bowling alleys, theaters, other fun places."

"So are you lesbian or something? I mean it seems so since you come across such folks quite often!"

"Sorry to disappoint you. But no. I am not lesbian."

"No disappointment at all!"

"You still haven't answered my question."

"I just told you I was heterosexual."

"My question was 'do you like sex; are you interested in sex'?"

Ralph knows there's no point evading the question this time. It would take the fun out of the repartee and probably get her pissed off as well. And the last thing you want is an irate woman.

"Well if that's the case and you really want to know then yes, I like sex," he admits.
"Great. Now how difficult was it to say that? You made me ask you so many times," she snaps.
Ralph unfolds his lower lip in a sign of shame.
"It's nothing secret or confidential about sexuality. So don't feel so sheepish to talk about it. At least in this country, everybody talks about it openly."
"Oh. We talk about it openly in India too but not as openly as you do here. And it's mostly the younger generation that talks about such things openly."
"Do you prefer talking about these things openly?"
"I don't have a problem with it."
"Okay. It's always good to be open to new ideas. You never know what you might stumble upon," she squinches.

****

Ralph remembers the time when mother would tell him to stay away from girls. Mother was protective of him and didn't want his future getting messed up due to any involvement with a woman.

"So aren't you going to ask me about me?"
"What about you?"
"Like what's my last name. Whether I like sex or not etc., etc." she smiles playfully.
"Oh no. That's okay. I'm fine knowing as much about you as I do now. I'll leave those questions for some future time."

The movie reaches its climactic stage and he feels the heat inside him as well as with the girl inching steadily closer to him. It's too late now.

Her hands are on his thigh and she is so close to him he cannot extricate his arm from around her without she moving back. He doesn't want to push her away as that would come across as rude. Moreover, he is in her house.

"Don't blow this up," comes the quick advice from the Inner voice.
"*Yup I shouldn't allow my conservative nature to break the flow of this experience*" he thinks. He decides to stay put and enjoy.
"So do you like to have se se sex?" he almost stutters.
"What!" she gabbles.
"I thought you didn't want to ask me about that?"
"Now I do. I just changed my mind," he snaps.
"Well I hope you don't change your mind so much when you're actually doing it!" she quips.
"Hahahahaha" he can't seem to stop laughing realizing how witty she is.
"And yes I do like sex!" she declares.
"Great!"
"Great and ....?"
"Great and what?"
"Aren't you going to ask me out?"
"Ask you out to what? To sex?"
Heheheheheheeeeee.....both of them burst out laughing.
"Something tells me you haven't had a relationship."
"Why is that?"
"You're just so simple, straight forward....unpolluted!"
"So what does that prove – NOTHING!!"
"Well it proves that you haven't experienced the heat of sexual relationships, the throbbing of one heart for another or the rapture of a first kiss!"

Ralph is shell-shocked by her comprehensive analysis. Never had he imagined that in the third or fourth meeting would a girl be able to know about his past without him telling her. He hadn't told her. She had analyzed and deduced, almost mind read! Girls do have a strong sixth sense. But this was his past. How could she have read him so deeply?

Then again, this was an American girl. In America, women are taught from childhood to look deep into a man's past; to analyze and look for red flags. The results of this analysis serve to caution or assure them about the relationship. Continuing the relationship or not is a function of this composite analysis.
Some of his male friends had told him that women in America, particularly Caucasian ones tend to be very judgmental. Although on more occasions than one they might show otherwise. They use their analytical sense to sift through potential partners. It's a sieve that men are put through to eventually find the best man. The best fit for them. In

the process, they come across men that are to be discarded after one meeting, maximum two or three. Such certainty and confidence in continuing or stopping communication with people arises out of a comfort with one's analytical abilities. Analyzing people is considered a forte in America. As also it must be in other parts of the world.

Ralph knows this could just be somebody's opinion. But he sees the part about analytical skills playing out in front of him.

"There's only one way to ascertain if you're right," he asserts.

"What's that?"

"Do it."

"What!"

"Yes. Let's have a kiss and I'll show you how good of a kisser I am. So good, no first-time kisser would ever be able to do something like that!"

She flinches at first. Then covers her lips with her palms, inches closer to him, keeping her lips covered all the while. He can see her ever increasing cheeks bulging with a blush behind her palms. The laughter coming from behind her palms sounds muffled. Almost like a sparrow's chirp.

They inch closer to each other as the climax of the movie they are watching plays on. The movie is no longer the object of their attention. It never was. It was only meant to bring them closer to where they are now. Closer to their first kiss. Matilda probably knew she would reach this place with the movie serving as a catalyst.

He is dangerously unsure of what to do now. His face is inches away from hers. Does he dive in like a swimmer and reach for her lips or does he allow her to come closer to him and then lock lips. He shouldn't rush, else he might blow things up. "Don't jump in like a savage!" reminds the Inner Voice.

She inches closer to him and stops. He needs to take decisive action now, else nothing's going to happen. He pushes his face closer to her and places his hand on her wrist as he pulls it away. Her lips and his face are now diametrically opposite each other. He moves in for the kill. She hesitates and then pushes forth too.

The love lock is intense and both of them have their eyes wide open as though electricity is passing through their bodies. Although this is not her first kiss she can't resist the convulsions. She feels the power in the young man. "He's got great sexual power in him!" she thinks.

His hands reach for her ears and then her hair as the kiss stretches into two minutes since inception.
And then one of the worst things happens!

****

A cling and clang on the heavy door alerts Matilda to a foreign presence in the house and she pulls back from the kiss. A startled Ralph draws back his hands and tries to pretend as though he has been looking at the movie on the screen. For a moment he thinks the odor of his mouth has caused her to break the kiss.

"It's Shala, my roommate" she thunders with pretentious delight.
The tick tock footsteps reach the living room. "Hey Matty! How's it going?" Shala smiles.
Matilda smiles back trying to pretend as though it's like any other day. Except this day involves the company of a handsome hunk by her side.
"And who is this?" Shala asks, visibly surprised at the sight of the muscular body next to Matilda and eager to know who he is.
"This is my friend Ralph," she says, suppressing any signs of what was going on just before Shala walked through the door.
Couples need privacy at least in the initial phases of their relationship; most of the time.
"Hi Ralph! I'm Shala. Nice to meet you," she extends a hand.
"Same here," he replies.
"Okay well, I'll allow you two to continue watching the movie. I've got some school work to do. See ya later," she says as she turns and gives Matilda a wink as she leaves the room.
It's no secret that most women find Ralph attractive. He has a light wheatish color, is muscular and confident.
"I think the movie is almost done. You want to go out and have a stroll or something," Matty suggests.

She feels uncomfortable now that there is another person in the house. Intimate time with Ralph will have
to be at some other spot. Some spot isolated. Both of them agree as though they seem to have this psychic connection between them. They walk out and take a stroll towards the park down the road. The park is a

queer natural fortress. Entering it involves walking over a bridge with pristine effervescent water flowing through the 'vein like rivulet' beneath.

"Wow this place is so serene!" he remarks.
"It is, isn't it. My roommates and I come here often to have a picnic or just to hang out. It's amazing during the summer when the trees are full of green leaves and birds singing everywhere. And best of all there's so much of privacy here. Nobody to bother you or see what you are and are not doing."
"It definitely looks private and secluded!" he says looking at the lonely surroundings.

For a moment he wonders why she brought him here. It's very bushy with no moving soul in the vicinity.

"How come this girl is so bold to come to such lonely areas alone. I've never seen or heard too many girls go to such lonely spots. Hope she's not thinking about something else while thinking about this place" he ponders.

As they cross the bridge, a tiny log cabin appears. It is covered quite densely with vegetation. It looks pretty rundown and it's evident that nobody has been using it for quite a while.

"Woah, looks like a park ranger cabin. Only thing no ranger in there. Looks like no one's been in there for a while," he comments.
"Yes. Whenever my friends and I come here that place is always locked up. I think somebody used to be posted there; using it a couple of years back. But the economy the way it is now, I think they have cancelled funding for a ranger to be posted here. Besides it's a very tiny park with hardly any wildlife except for squirrels and rabbits. The year was 2007 and the first signs of the recession were already being felt. I guess this ranger lost his job to that," she comments.
The grass and stone covered path leading into the park resembles something out of a story book. As they get deeper into the park, trees envelope them on both sides. The sun's rays turn into a divine green and he feels a warm, soft touch on his palms.

He looks at her in surprise as she clutches his palm tightly. "It's always good to keep close and hold each other in case one of us slips," she smiles.

"Good idea!" he suppresses a blush. He can feel vibratory sensations running through his chest, his torso and reaching down south closer to his groin.

"*Keep calm Ralph, keep calm!*" he reminds himself.

As they proceed along the path, the vegetation gets denser. Ralph normally feels claustrophobic in enclosed, densely wooded areas. But right now he doesn't seem to have a care in the world. He seems to enjoy the feminine touch that he hasn't had in so many months. Mum would hold his tiny hands and pull him swiftly as she walked him to elementary school. That was several years ago when he was a tiny youngster. He felt a sense of being protected, cared for; away from the worries and the dangers of the world. Protected by a bubble that was Mum.

He had a somewhat similar feeling here too. Although, this time he knew that he was being regarded more as a source of protection than the other way round. At least that was what he thought she would think.

"Hope you're not scared of the dark and the woods!"

"No, I'm not. I guess you've been here before so you know where we're going right!" he says.

"Yes. Unless of course we get lost!" she laughs.

"Like you would want that to happen at this time."

It was 3 pm in the afternoon. But it was autumn and the days were getting shorter. The sun wouldn't stay up for too long.

"Okay, we're almost there."

A well-rounded boulder with a flat base and rugged sides sat in the middle of the grassy field. It was greyish black and had distinctive spots of white scattered all over its surface. It looked like a large flint stone with a greyish black coating over it.

"We place our barbecue grill around this rock when we have a cookout. It is also a good place to sit and hang out."

"Yeah it looks like a nice perch."

"You got to get on top of it and sit!"

She places her leg on a small stone at the foot of the boulder and tries to sit on the large stone. Seeing her try to climb it Ralph offers a hand. One hand on the boulder and the other in Ralph's palms she rises to the relatively flat surface atop the boulder. The hemline of her short skirt rises high as she works to get to the top. A distracted Ralph tries to stay focused on helping her.

"All set?"
"Yup. Thanks!" she says as she settles herself above the boulder.

Ralph athletically climbs to the top of the boulder in one easy stride. Atop it, there is a feeling of being away from the reach of ground crawling insects, centipedes or any other creature that could probably get on your shoes and pants.

Ralph perches himself close to her. "Wow. This place is like a sofa. And a pretty high one too. Quite high above the ground!"
"It's my choice. Could it be any less!"
"Don't you think it's comfortable too!"
"Oh yeah. It sure is. I'm glad I came."
"Yup. It's hard to resist me anyways," she grins.

Though the mutual attraction between them is obvious, they haven't yet reached the point where they openly talk about it. It is more subtle at this stage and they exchange repartees and suggestive innuendos to voice their respective attraction.

"So what do you do during your free time?" he asks.
"Ummhh, watch movies, knit, cook, have fun!"
"Knit and cook?...I thought the only thing you could cook was McDonald's burgers?"
"Hhahahahaa," he laughs as she agreeably acknowledges.
"So what'd you knit?"
"Oh I try to but really end up playing with long needles and thread."
"Something told me you did that!"
"Well the next time you say that I'll make sure I put a long needle into you!" she pokes him in the side with her finger.
"Hehehehe."
"What do you do?"

"You mean during my free time!"

"Yup"

"Oh, I hardly have any free time since I came to this country. Though I usually help out with parties at International Student House or watch a movie when doing nothing." Ralph feels a sense of guilt when he has free time. Cause there are so many things internationals need to get done in the States that having free time means you are not making good use of your time. On the other end of the spectrum it means you have achieved everything. Many driven and ambitious individuals feel this way too.

"Then you ought to make time for free time. You do know that all work and no play makes Jack a dull boy right."

"Yes, I do. But all play and no work makes Jack a stupid boy as well," he smiles delicately.

"No. But seriously, you need to have some downtime. How are you going to enjoy the fruits of your labor then!"

Ralph is surprised to hear someone telling him to essentially rest and make time for relaxation. Since he's come to the States it's been all work and more work. Getting even the simplest things completed involved substantial reinvention of the wheel. Like starting from a scratch. Getting a place to stay, obtaining text books, making friends, what have you.

"Yeah. Probably I need to work on that!"

"But one major thing I do when I have even five minutes is calling home. I always keep in touch with my folks at home."

"Okay."

"You must be missing them quite a bit right."

"A lot!"

"So do you call your folks often?" he asks.

"We're not quite in touch. Sis was in touch for some time after she ran away from home. But not anymore."

Ralph looks at her curiously expecting to hear about the other family members. But she doesn't appear to say anything.

"Well?"

"Well what?"

"What about your Mom?"

"Oh yeah. I talk to her occasionally. But she's busy with her life too."

She seems to have a forlorn yet toughened look on her face. Ralph feels puzzled how she doesn't seem to show a feeling of being homesick. Is it because she's in the same country as her folks. Is it because reaching home is a matter of a two to three-hour flight? Or is it that she just doesn't miss home; but misses just the idea of home?

He couldn't place it but knew for a fact that American teens leave home early. His professor in India had told him that by the age of eighteen many American kids opt to go solo. They decide to go live with their boyfriend or with their girlfriend or simply move out of the house to some place where they feel free and independent. There are those who stay till their mid to late twenties as well but the increasingly prevalent trend has been the former.

Ralph also embraced a lifestyle of independence and freedom. However, he couldn't imagine going a single day without calling home. The international calls were expensive and did consume time but his urge to hear Mum's voice and get an update on family affairs was also great.

"You mean she doesn't call you?"
"Our relationship is kind of off and on. It's been that way since I left home a few years ago."
His ideas about 'teens moving out of homes' is confirmed. But he only wonders what the reasons could be for this widespread trend.

"But I'm pretty sure you're in touch with your Dad right."
A bolt of lightning suddenly seems to have struck Matilda. She turns a pale blue, her hands cold. Ralph notices and looks closer at her thinking the weather might be getting colder.

"Are you okay Matilda?" he touches her shoulder.
Still silent.
"Matty?......Is everything alright?"
She shakes herself a little.
"Yes of course," she visibly tries to regain her composure. "Oh sorry. I think it's getting cold," she breathes deeply.
The sun was still a little bright. "We could go back to the house if you like," suggests Ralph.
"Oh no. Please no. I like it here. I'm just, I just got occupied!"

"Oh. With your Dad's memory huh. Oh man, Daddy's girl!"

She gets even more upset. "Ralph please! Stop it!" she sounds serious as she says it.
"Sorry. What! Did I say anything? Oops. No. I didn't mean to offend if I said anything offensive."
"No. No. It's not you. I'm sorry, I can't hold back some emotions."
"Oh. Please. I want you to vent. Please don't let me hinder you."
She covers her face with her palms and weeps. He pats her back saying it's okay.
"No it's not okay" she sobs.
"It'll be alright," he looks at her with caring eyes.

She wipes the tears off her face and takes the piece of napkin he hands her.
"So want to tell me what's on your mind?"
"I don't know if I should?" she says as though she is questioning him if her secrets are safe with him.
"Well then you don't have to. I thought you might want to get it off your chest. And you don't have to do it right now. We can walk back home and do it in the house."
"No! I think it's better I do it while we are out here. The elements here will take away the grief and the loss!"
"Okay! So what's up!"
"It's just this thing about love."
"What about it?" he peers at her attentively.
"I don't know if anybody truly loves me!"

Ralph is clearly confused by this statement. But he doesn't make his confusion obvious. In India, or at least in his family, love is not openly stated. It is shown though. It is implicit. He wonders why she thinks love is missing in her life, but says nothing in order to allow her to vent without being encumbered by questions or fear of judgement. She looks at him as though he ought to say something instead of plainly looking at her. She continues to stare at him bewildered, no smile, no acknowledgement.

"I like you!" he puts on a coy smile.
"That's not the point Ralph. I've had a lot of loss in my life. And besides my sister leaving and all else I think the greatest pain of all is

being abandoned and abused by the people who should have been protecting and loving you."

"I don't understand!" he questions.

"Please don't call me Daddy's girl or even Mommy's girl ever again!"

"Okay. Why not?"

"Cause I much hate and despise both of them. Particularly the man who used to be my Dad."

"The man who used to be your Dad?"

"Yes, he's no longer my Dad. At least I don't consider him to be so," she sobs again.

He looks at her with sad concern. He doesn't know her entire story; doesn't even know little of it. But yet something about her situation makes him feel bad for her. He empathizes wondering what he would have done were he in her shoes. Even though he still doesn't know what being in the shoes of a local American girl is. It's not just the 'understanding gap' in terms of the gender but also in terms of the nationality.

"Why not? Why are you so against your folks?" he asks gently.

"They never cared for us. Never really loved us. (Pauses). That's why my sister left; ran away from home!"

"You mean they never showed their love for you?"

"It's more complicated than that Ralph!"

"See I know not all parents can be perfect. Hence not all can show their love explicitly. That doesn't mean they don't love you!"

"No. You don't get it you....uh!"

"Okay. Then could you tell me what it is."

"I don't know if I should."

"Why not?"

"I don't know how you'll perceive me after I tell you. Don't know how you will judge me!"

"There is only one person who can judge others in this world. And that person is not a person, it's God! If you don't feel like telling me, you don't have to. I would just like to have anything that is burdening you come off your chest. That's all. It's not force, it's not that I won't be your friend or anything."

Her tears run dry. The pain seems to cease and she looks at Ralph with deep, caring eyes. "Oh Ralph. That's the sweetest thing anybody has said to me in a long long time."

He extends his arms around her and they embrace each other in a tight, warm hug. Ralph doesn't feel titillated nor excited hugging such a lovely damsel. He just feels the warmth of love. He wonders how he didn't get an erection in spite of being not only close, but in a warm embrace with the pretty damsel. But this embrace is not of a sexual kind although it might lead to that later on.

"Could I ask you something?" she slowly says.
"Ask whatever you want Matty!"
"Do you like me?"
"I sure do! Do you like me?"
"Oh. Of course. You know that right!"
"If I told you about my family and the relations we have; would you stop liking me or like me less?"
"Oh come on Matty. I've already told you. Nothing you tell me about your life will cause me to hate you or like you any less than I do now. If anything it will make me like you even more for having the courage to tell me."

He pauses. A delicate smile shows up on her face. It's more a simper though.

"Thanks so much."
"Unless of course you've killed somebody in the past!"
"You haven't done that, have you?" he looks at her seriously for a moment and then gives off a slight laugh.
"No. But I will do it for the first time now if you don't stop." She punches him lightly in the stomach.
"Oh God. Please give me strength to talk about this!" she says to herself.

The happy frolicsome atmosphere suddenly turns as solemn as the darkening sky.

****

"Well it's about my childhood and teen years. Everything seemed okay until I turned fourteen. Mom was caring and Dad regularly played with us. He took us on vacations and dinner outings. Life seemed happy!"

Ralph felt that it was normal for parents to be caring and loving. What's so different or new in that? My folks were very loving and I would be the same if I was a parent or became one in due time. *"I think in America probably love is not as freely available as it is between relations and within families in India,"* he thought to himself.

"Then?"

"Then strange things began to happen. Dad got involved with another woman for a year or so. Mom got suspicious about Dad's changing behavior. My sister and Mom were close. Mom used Shannon as her spy to snoop on Dad."

"And?" he asks, eyes wide open.

"That's how she found out he was cheating on her."

"The family atmosphere began to get very sulky and sordid. Mom and Dad would have long, heated arguments and then wouldn't converse for days on end."

"The tension and acrimony between them began affecting us. We couldn't concentrate on our studies. We would think about the difficult situation at home while sitting in class. Wondering what we could do to change it or could have done to avoid it in the first place."

Ralph was as silent as the night sky all this while. He was seeing a family drama unfold before him but couldn't understand how or why things couldn't be compromised towards a reconciliation. Probably the same reason reconciliation was hard to come by even in his family. Families always have some underlying issues brewing. The sooner they are addressed and resolved the better it is for everybody concerned.

"During this time, Mom was constantly using Shannon to spy on Dad. Shannon would try to listen to Dad's conversations in his home office, record times that he left the house and came back in. And also smell his coat for any alien, sweet smelling perfumes. All the information gleaned would be conveyed to Mom."

"Apparently Dad didn't relent in his philandering ways in spite of all the bitter arguments and fights with Mom. Then one day, Mom found out the cause of her consternation."

"Dad and his lover had been spotted in a lonely, corner table in a restaurant. Shannon had not made any bones in specifying the physical attributes of the woman my Dad was seeing."

A tear rolls down Matty's cheek like a thick white pearl. She stops talking and tries to wipe the tear from rolling down her cheek.

Ralph gently caresses her. "You don't have to go on if you don't want to!"
"No. I better get this out of me else it's going to smother me."

Ralph knows that it is better to purge pent-up feelings through catharsis rather than stuff them in. But he doesn't want her to feel vulnerable by telling him everything in the name of catharsis. He doesn't want her to regret exposing all her secrets to him. However, when you share somebody's darkest fears and tragedies you grow closer to them.

"My Dad was having an affair with a woman, a little older than Shannon. She might have been twenty something. Shannon had seen them at that restaurant when she had gone there with her boyfriend for a romantic evening. On seeing Dad with his paramour, she turned around. But not in time. Dad managed to get a glimpse of her boyfriend and figured Shannon would be around the corner. She was with that boyfriend of hers almost twenty hours a day anyway. Dad's doubts were confirmed when he saw her auburn hair blowing in the wind as she grabbed on to Jay on the speeding motorcycle."
"Was he pissed or surprised?"

Matilda doesn't acknowledge his question. But seems to continue with her regular train of thought.

"Dad didn't have much of a rapport with my mother anymore. But after that day he began to act differently towards Shannon and me as well. He began to be angry at the both of us for no apparent reason. It seemed like he would be taking out the anger of the arguments he had with Mom on us."
"He wasn't a bad man. But after that day he became paranoid; suspicious of every small thing we did. He had sufficient reason to believe that Shannon had been spying on him. She was on terrific terms with Mom. And would do most of what Mom told her to. Except of course to ditch her boyfriend!"

For a moment, it appears as though Matilda's somber mood is replaced by a welcome smile. But she quickly gets back into the melancholy of a funereal narrative.

"It didn't take Dad long to figure out that a friend of his enemy is his enemy too. Our family had been disintegrating for some time. But after that realization by Dad, things took a turn for the worse."

"He began yelling at us for the smallest of reasons. Began prying into the smallest of activities we did. We no longer felt safe being around him. Felt he would lash out at any instance. He just needed the smallest reason. We would be on edge when he was around, always on guard," she laments.

"The family was no longer having dinner together. Each of us would microwave our own dinner, go into our respective rooms and have it. The dinner table was the cleanest those days because it was essentially not getting used. Mom and Shannon would have dinner together when Shannon was at home. Shannon's boyfriend would join sometimes. Mom really didn't want him there but couldn't object for fear of alienating Shannon and losing her support and help in combating Dad."

"I was pretty much left to fend for myself. Even food in the refrigerator began to be marked with names of people to designate ownership."

"What! Marking food items as they do in shared communal living while living in a family. Gosh, that's absurd!"

"Yes, it was. But we didn't have a choice. Mom and Dad would go days on end without even saying a few words to each other. I began using the money I made from my part-time job as a waitress to buy food and other necessities. During this time, Mom was sleeping in the guest room, Dad alone in the master bedroom. We had our own rooms, but were always worried about fights erupting in the house and our peace being lost."

"And then one day, the thing that should not have happened, happened! Dad thinking that nobody would be at home brought his lady love home for dinner. Mom unexpectedly walked in and saw what was happening. She broke into a frenzy and drove Dad and his lover out. I guess Dad had told the young lady that he was divorced and not living with his wife. But that day she got to see for real. Personally, I didn't think it was right for Dad to bring his lover home when things were already sour between Mom and him."

"A couple of weeks after that incident, Dad was seen more often around the house. We understood that his paramour had dumped him for lying to her. He was a family man yet lonely. I felt bad for him until the transgressions began!"

****

"Transgressions?" he asks wondering.

"Dad suspected that Shannon and I probably had a role in the incident involving Mom coming home when he was with his paramour. He felt that we had somehow got wind of this fact and had tipped Mom about it. The hate that he already had for us began to simmer to boiling point. And then the abuses began. First it was just verbal. As days passed by it began to get more vicious. Shannon was three years elder to me so she could kind of resist it. Besides she had a boyfriend to protect her. She was a free spirit anyway. Moreover, she had Mom's explicit support. And Mom would always intervene when Dad targeted her. She was the one who had done the spying in reality."

"But who got trapped? Me!"

"Seeing Shannon impervious to attack, Dad turned his attention to me. I was only fourteen when the abuse began."

"Abuse?" Ralph's eyes flash fire.

"Yes. It started off with verbal abuse and then took a physical dimension."

Ralph began to get a gist of the abuse when he heard the word physical. He had seen a couple of movies involving similar situations in India. He dared not ask her what the abuse involved in physical terms. Unless of course, she told it herself.

"I was only fourteen – too young to provide meaningful resistance. The abuse continued for almost nine months. After the breakup with his lover, Dad took to alcohol on a daily basis. Alcoholism made him more violent. I don't even feel like calling him Dad cause his behavior was not at all like one."

"Well couldn't you tell your mother. Didn't she protect you?"

"This is precisely the reason, I think my Mom is a bitch. I told her about what was happening and she acted as though she was listening when in reality she was ignoring it. I figured the only person she was really concerned about was Shannon. Because Shannon did the spying for her. There was a quid pro quo there. Mom had approached me with a request to spy on Dad for her. But I had not understood it back then. I guess my response made her feel that I didn't really understand what she was hinting at. After that, she didn't really pay me any mind. All my needs were relegated to secondary, sometimes not even that. Since I was of no use or consequence to her I was considered expendable."

"What did you do then?" he asks intently.

"Well, my sister Shannon ran away within a month of realizing that Dad had become belligerent and was growing more violent by the day. Something tells me she had Mom's support when she ran away."

"Support?" he wonders.

"Yes. Mom would send her money and other goodies. Mom knew where she had run away to. Besides, she ran away with her boyfriend. So she had pretty much all the help she needed – Mom's and her boyfriend's."

"My case was not the same. Since I hadn't taken up on Mom's offer to spy on Dad in exchange for undeclared, intangible support, I was essentially a persona non grata. Mom thought she just had one child from then on. It's strange isn't it. You don't play a role in family politics and you get excommunicated!"

"But did you tell her that you were being abused?"

"Yes. I did."

"And?" Ralph's eyes widen with curiosity and anger.

"She acted as though she didn't; didn't want to hear or simply didn't believe in me. Mom was so hell-bent on getting even with Dad for cheating on her that she only saw and valued those who would help her in her fight against him. She virtually forgot that we were her kids; at least that was her response to me."

(Pauses) It's visible that she's fighting the urge to cry. For a moment, it seems as though anger overtakes grief and she feels a vengeance towards her parents. More so towards her Mom for having willfully turned a blind eye to the abuse she was suffering at the hands of Dad.

"All love that was present in the family until then seemed to have evaporated in thin air. My mother wanted to get back at my Dad for cheating on her. My Dad wanted to get back at her for destroying his relationship with his extramarital paramour. And there I was, drawing indiscriminate fire from both of them. A silent sufferer!"

Ralph couldn't fathom that parents would let their own children suffer for the sake of getting even with each other. Worst of all, he was appalled to know that a mother would ignore her own daughter's pleas that she was being abused by a man who should have been protecting them. Just because the girl wasn't cunning enough to accept the spying offer doesn't mean that she be punished with neglect. Of all the things, how could someone, especially a parent ignore claims of abuse? And a mother of all the people! These thoughts pervaded Ralph's mind like a recalcitrant oil slick.

He knew that a lot of relationships in America are business oriented. In fact, the majority tend to be so, unless of course, you have a blood relationship with somebody. Your colleague likes you if you help him or her. Your boss likes you if you do all the work you are assigned and more. People in general favor you if you are of some benefit to them. But how could this business rule apply within a family? It shouldn't ideally.

For example, a disabled or paralyzed child might not be of any help to the parents. In fact, he or she might be a severe liability. Does it mean that the parents dump the child or stop caring for the child! However grave the problem; in many countries in Asia, Africa and several others, taking care of a non-productive child is considered a duty. Ralph realized that in the USA, things work differently. If a child wants a bicycle or a toy, they would be encouraged to take up a part-time job to earn some of the money to buy the item. They are encouraged to spend summer vacations doing part-time work or volunteering in various initiatives at Church or local county organizations.

Parents encourage their kids to take increasing amounts of responsibility and share in task completion in the States. Not all countries in Asia or elsewhere have such practices. Families and people in the USA, in general, favor a lifestyle of self-sufficiency and independence. Not that people in other countries in Asia or Africa don't but it's more prevalent in the States. It's rightfully a part of US culture and so much a part of being American. People coming here from cultures that don't essentially embrace self-sufficiency find the equal sharing of work responsibility within families very business-like; almost uncaring and unfriendly. In reality, it's a mere difference in looking at things.

"So what did you end up doing with all this abuse and pain?"
"I figured there would be only one way to get away from the abuse, the hurt and the rejection." (Pause)
Ralph's eyes widen with suspense laden concern.

****

"I ran away. Went to a neighboring town in Louisiana where I had a friend and stayed with her for a couple of days until I got a job. I didn't have a car of my own so I had to go by bus. I managed to sneak away with some cash from Mom's purse. Took some of my clothes and

essential items. Wrote a tiny note to Mom and then walked out of the house early in the morning. Not that she deserved the note or anything."
"So how was life after that? Must have been rough?"

A relaxed smile appears on Matty's face. It seems as though a heavy load has been taken off her chest. A great relief!
"Actually no! It was extremely relaxing and free of tension and worry. Being on my own had its challenges but it had great rewards as well. I felt liberated that I was no longer in that house of horror. That I had taken the bold step of running away. That was what made me feel so liberated."
"There were times when things got a little tough. For example, when we had stormy showers and the roof began to leak. But at least it wasn't anything like the suffering I had to undergo in my parents' house."
"Sophie and I were very compatible too. She had a boyfriend who she would spend a lot of time with. I was essentially left to myself in the house so I could concentrate on my studies. No wonder, I ended up acing my classes most of the time."
"How'd you pay for school?"
"I didn't!"
"After I started living with Sophie, I couldn't continue school; didn't have the money for it actually. So I went and got a job as a waitress in a local restaurant. I worked there full time for a year till I had enough money to pay for school. With Sophie's help I enrolled in a couple of vocation-based courses while waitressing part time."

Ralph seems impressed by the level of initiative and independence this American girl has to leave home and settle in a different city pretty much all on her own. Till then he thought there were very few people as smart, aggressive and independent as he is. Matty was probably one of those few. He begins to feel a great awe and respect for her.

"It probably wouldn't have been as easy to leave one city and settle down in another in India," he thinks.

Having a friend is great but the part time jobs in India are not so easy to come by. Often you need to have a certain degree of rapport with the owner or manager to land one or know somebody who knows the manager or job creator well. In that sense, it is easier to get a job in America where the level of partiality or favoritism seems to be much lower than that which exists in India. At least that's the case for part time jobs or jobs of lower pay.

"So how did you do in those courses?"
"I did very well. The days were fun as I had great colleagues to work with and a stress-free home environment. Everything was going great guns until I had to move to New Orleans for university studies and Sophie moved to Ohio. I began living in another rented room in New Orleans close to Loyola University. Sophie is at Ohio State University. She asked me to come with her. But I had a full scholarship from Loyola University."
"We kept in constant touch. Life was busy, but it was good."

Long silence. It seems she is finally feeling better. No tears. No grief. Just a pleasant smile.

"And then what?" he asks feeling a conspicuous suspense.
"And then God sent Hurricane Katrina!" she sighs.
"I guess there needed to be somebody to get jealous of my happiness. And who better than nature!"
"I have a question though. Didn't your parents know that you were going to Loyola University and try to contact you?"
"Oh I guess I didn't say. After I left home leaving a note for Mom, she filed for divorce. They no longer live together. Mom's in the same house I guess, but he left. Don't know where. Probably rotting in some hole."

Pauses. Ralph continues gazing at her, expecting more information.

"And no they didn't try to contact me. I wouldn't have wanted them to either!"
"Poor girl! It must have been tough on you. All this and then Katrina!" he caresses her hand.
"Not really. The family part was the toughest. The rest was just part of everyday life, even the hurricane."
"I think that things happen for a reason. If it didn't happen you wouldn't have come here and we wouldn't have got to meet!" he quips with a smile.
"You bet. Say, how long have we been here?"
"Like over an hour."

They had been sitting there on the boulder cuddled up for over an hour. But it felt like five minutes since they had got on top of the boulder.

"I must say you are a terrific listener. Do you have a girlfriend?"
Ralph looks at her with a naughty smile and remains silent.
"Or rather did you ever have one?"
"I do now," he lightly grins.
"You....!" they spontaneously hug.
"It's okay honey. It's alright!" he says as he gently caresses her back.

He looks straight at her and pushes his lips towards hers. They lock lips in a rapturous kiss. Forgetting all the pain, hurt and grief; wrapped in a swirl of love and affection. All the shrubbery and woods around them seem to disappear. They seem ensconced in a bubble of bright light surrounded by darkness. His hands reach for her hair and her neck as he feels her tender skin on his palms. They lay on the flat rock and continue kissing.

"So you want to go home. It's getting dark," he interrupts noticing the darkness enveloping them.
"Sure. We could go and sit in my car if you like," she suggests.
"That would be great," he says not wanting to end the passion.

He hasn't had this level of passion and engagement any time before. Why would any guy in the right frame of mind want to let go of it? As they walk towards the path they entered the woods from; it is clear why the area offers such seclusion and privacy. Both sides covered by thick trees and shrubbery. Smoothly shaped rocks and soft green grass to pad one's feet and deny any sound or motion. Not a trace of movement, yet the woods are teeming with peaceful life forms that call the thicket their home. As the evening matures, the car seems like a welcome shelter to continue their conversation and exchange some affection. The cool evening breeze getting colder makes Ralph feel a lot more exhilarated. He is anyways full of energy – he's just wound up a spell of lip service with a pretty damsel. That's more energy than hot tea or soup anyways; at least for him.
As they lock the doors inside the car, a sense of being safe and protected envelopes them. "Umhhh, this place is even better. At least, we're inside the car and warm too," she suggests.
"Oh yeah!"
"So you feeling better now?" he asks.

"Yes. It's warmer in here."

"No. I mean now that you've unloaded the stuff from your chest do you feel better? I guess you do right."

"Oh, of course. Sure I do. I needed that. And I am glad I can share these things with you," she says gratefully.

"You're a good kisser by the way," she compliments.

Though he's a little taken aback by her forthrightness, he thanks her for the compliment.

"In spite of everything about you, I can now safely say that you probably did have a girlfriend. Else how would you know how to kiss so well!"

"I don't know. It's just beginner's luck" he shrugs nonchalantly.

"There are many other things that can or cannot suggest if you've had girlfriend experience or not," he seconds.

"Like what?"

"Umhhh, it's a little embarrassing to say."

"No. I won't judge you. And don't feel embarrassed."

"Well you know. Things like caressing, fondling, cuddling, running your hands over somebody's soft areas, what have you."

"Well then, why don't we see it."

For a moment, he is gob smacked. But regains composure.

"You mean you want to see me caressing and fondling you?"

"Not just see. I want to feel you caressing, fondling and cuddling."

He hesitates.

"Come on. Don't feel so shy. You know all about me now. I told you all about my family, my background, my problems. What do you have to hide or be ashamed of now!"

"Yes....yes" she encourages as he inches closer to her as they cuddle up in the back seat of the car.

As he caresses her arms, his palms move to her back, her flanks and then her midriff. She feels his warmth and the soft smell on his neck. His palms slide along her shoulders, her neck and then begin rolling downwards. He stops and wonders whether to proceed down south or stop right there. He has this fear from back home; that if you take liberties with a woman without her express approval you could end up with nothing less than a tight slap. Sensing him stop, she wonders what got into him. She wants him to continue and feel the tender love and affection she has been craving.

"Can I touch your chest," he shyly asks.
"Absolutely. Go for it!" she gushes as he lightly begins to fondle her breasts and takes the strap of her tank top off. The soft, moist tissue of her breasts feels like heaven. He just can't resist the temptation to take off her bras. As he gently scoops her breasts out of the A cup bra holders, the lightly colored nipples bounce out like smooth domes of a building.
They are so smooth, silky and white with a few dots here and there. As he lightly squeezes them, it seems as though milk could gush out of them any moment.

"Ah…..ah…uh" she lovingly groans as he fondles her anatomy.

It seems like she has never felt a guy touch her so lovingly. He wonders if she ever had a boyfriend. Sexual abuse victims often have massive problems returning to their sexuality and living a sexually productive lifestyle. "Could this be Matty's case?" he wonders. And why did she open up so much to him about her past, the abuse by her father? People generally tell such things only to spouses or definite girlfriends or boyfriends, not just to friends. Unless of course, she considers me her boyfriend. The feeling is too much to hold back.

****

As they continued hurling blame after blame at him, the discussions started getting increasingly bitter. Denise, Ian and Dan didn't seem to let up in their criticism of Ralph's innocent, ignorant conduct. "Well we just can't have a few people in the team work while others get the benefit. And that's fair right. So we are thinking whether to keep you on the team or not!" said Dan in a crude fashion. His emotionless face was red with anger and deception and almost stone like.

Ralph had heard that not only Americans but all people involved in business keep emotions away. Hence the terminology "I am all business!" This indicates that even if you try to chat me up or make me mushy, I won't budge from my professional, business-like demeanor. Dan's and Ian's behavior wasn't only core business, it was bordering on the edge of anger and war. They seemed to have pre-planned answers for every reason that Ralph gave for his so-called poor performance.

And that surprised him more than anything else. That someone would disregard all his initial quality performance in a desperate bid to prove their need to remove him from the team.

"Why would these people do this?" he thought. I have contributed in the past. Do they have a hidden agenda in trying to supplant my earlier contributions? Though the direction all this was heading in was apparent, Ralph wanted to believe there was a silver lining somewhere. The interactions by now had become very acrimonious. And salvaging any honor would be difficult. Ian seemed to go on and on about how Ralph's poor quality work and conduct, in general, was a bad influence on the group.

Ralph wondered what "bad influence" his jovial Goan, fun loving conduct could have on the group. He had fun when the time was right and was serious when the situation demanded it. *"What else did they want?"* thought Ralph. He wished attitudes and hints weren't as subtle as they are in the US. In Asia and most other places people tell you if you are offending them directly. He wondered why these so called 'courteous' Americans didn't open up about what he was doing wrong or not.

But they don't. If they are not satisfied with your skill set they indicate the same to you through hints or rude behavior towards you. In some cases, the concerned employee is fired[12] without warning. Ralph hoped his fate wouldn't be as bad. All indications were pointing in that direction though.

"You haven't even apologized after we brought this to your attention!" erupted Dan looking at the others in the group. "We need to talk to the professor!" said three of the four members in unison. Only Bob kept mum, not seeming to appreciate the uncouth manner in which the entire matter was being handled by the rest of the team members.

As all three members storm up from the roundtable, Bob is gradually obliged to follow them. It's an unsaid rule of team dynamics that the minority has to follow the majority decision. In this case where the minority was one versus three and Ralph was the sole defendant against

---

[12] **Fired** is a term regularly used in US corporate culture which refers to removing an employee or worker from the job.

the four; there was very little Bob could do, although he did not overtly agree with the way the expulsion was being conducted.

The group walks down to the second floor of the building and gathers and waits. To Ralph this seems so needless and wanton. All of them waiting to meet the professor, waiting to build up a case to throw him out of the group. For what! A mistake of taking stuff from a website and putting it in the project. Something that Ralph did all along in India. Something which was not even thought of as punishable. But in the US this action is given the elaborate name of 'plagiarism' and is severely punishable.

In India, using various online resources to get school work done is considered innocuous in most educational institutions. The attitude is a carefree, relaxed one. Not in the US. In the States, everything is critically evaluated and measured to understand what is the core contribution of the student. The level of understanding and work put in by the student is measured and held to account when assigning a grade. The reason the US is such an advanced country is because all aspects of profession and career are taken very seriously. People's work efforts are monitored and they are held accountable for their results. One thing difficult to find in the US though is a lackadaisical approach to work. Their 'no-compromise' attitude in regards to quality leads to a standard of delivery that the world aspires to have. Collectivistic cultures like those that exist in India and are generally more forgiving and easy going find it difficult to measure up to this level of standards. Why? Because they simply don't follow a philosophy of pushing their workers hard enough or are forgiving of mistakes that might not normally be excused in the west.

Not to say that it is bad to not forgive. But the results you get are proportional to the strength of the philosophy you preach. A philosophy that preaches strong work ethics, honesty and care of thy fellow human is worth more in gold than a philosophy of self-preservation. But this was not the philosophy that was being used to penalize Ralph.

It was more a plot to get rid of the weakest member in the team. Why should he get such a high grade equal to the rest of us when he hasn't really contributed quality stuff. Or he doesn't have an understanding of the work that's needed to be done. This guy can't even afford a car to visit the client team. That was the thought process of Dan, Ian and Denise; the all Yankee team.

They stand outside the class looking to hurl accusations on Ralph's reputation. It is a surreal scenario of character assassination at its worst. Ralph walks slowly towards them not knowing what to do to change the course of events. Their angry glares and almost threatening stance is something out of a horrific Hollywood movie. A movie whose plot is centered around pain and cruelty.

The only difference here is that this is not a movie. This is real life persecution. Persecution for a mistake that Ralph didn't even know was considered a legal offense. Internationals not accustomed to the ways of the West often face a downward curve when it comes to adjusting to life in the States. Interactions with Americans are fraught with risks involving verbal innuendos, miscommunication and misunderstanding. Relationships and connections take time to build. Life comes to a screeching halt as areas of common interest are very few if non-existent. And that's true even of the people brought up in households that espouse western values.

"Hey, Ralph. Please leave. We don't want you to be here," says Dan in a peremptory tone. The idea is that the defendant shouldn't be present when the complaint is being filed. That way the complainant can spice up the story and enhance the scope of the transgression to the person in authority.

Kind of unfair, considering fair trials ought to take place with the defendant in court rather than in absentia. "Yes. I think you should leave," seconds Ian.

Ralph continues to stand outside the classroom putting forth a brave face. Deep inside him though lurk undiscovered fears. Fears of being in a foreign country with no great help. Fears of not having extensive monetary resources. Of being an unrecognized, nameless entity in a sea of overwhelming competition from well-established people and the procedures they have put in place. In spite of all the fears prevalent, Ralph was worried that he would be deprived a chance of a shot at the American dream. A chance he had not even got with all the rules and insurmountable paperwork applicable to immigrants abounding in this land.

Ralph wondered what he could do to change the course of events unfolding before him. But it seemed futile. All his prior attempts to bolster strong relationships with his American counterparts were met with lukewarm responses, if no responses at all. It seemed for a while that he was a non-existent entity. Someone who didn't have a role in the team or in the progress being made. And although the group had made material progress; this progress was characterized by a conspicuous gap. A gap in which not everyone in the team was made to feel included. Ralph strongly felt this discrimination on several fronts. And was disappointed that he had to face this in spite of his perpetual efforts to contribute greatly.

Ralph had felt this idea of exclusion being thrown at him time and again. More so he felt its stab now when the entire team was looking to get him excommunicated – an international in a foreign land being treated like a pariah. What could he do to change this? The lack of information and ideas caused him to wonder about his "no ideas, no options" conundrum. But he could only guess. Action was something that did not come easily to Ralph. Nor did anger. That was a good thing, particularly in a country where any sort of action if on the opposite side of the law can be penalized severely.

In this country, you can get away with anything only if you are one of 2 things – *a politician or a millionaire*. For the others, it's luck or fate that determine most things. As the professor comes out of the class, Dan moves forward to approach him as he had done all through the class, while it was in session. "We can meet in that area over there," says Dr. Panini pointing to the small area in the corner of the upper level atrium with a couple of chairs and tables in it.

"So are you gonna leave or what?" asks Dan again. This time in a more irritated tone. Ralph doesn't look at him; says nothing either. "I guess not!" verbalizes Dan.
The foursome walk towards the sitting area. Dan mutters something to Ian cautiously watching Ralph trailing them. They seem to be partners in crime orchestrating an expulsion that is rooted more in hate and disdain than in mere wrongdoing. Moreover, the action smacks of a lack of cultural neutrality particularly since Ralph is from a different culture. The proceedings taking place are entirely one sided with Ralph seeming

like a hapless victim and the four trying to show that in fact they are victims.

They select a table and take seats. All along Dan and Ian keep telling Ralph to go away. It's clear they do not want him to be a part of the disciplinary action they plan to initiate against him. Why? It probably helps to have a mute defendant in a case that's not strongly in favor of the plaintiff. Moreover if you are an international in a foreign land, they know they can concoct a rule against you that you might generally not be able to fight. The reasons for not being able to resist range from not having adequate knowledge of the law to not having enough courage and resources to continue the fight against unfair treatment.

Ralph continues to sit around the table waiting for the professor to arrive just as they wait alongside. He knows whatever that is going to happen now is but inevitable. It was all coming right from the time he joined the group. Although he had tried his best to adjust to the group; a sort of maladjustment continued to plague his presence in the team. He tried with limited success to understand what was the cause for his low stature in the team. His deliverables were regularly ignored no matter how good a product he tried to render.

The present situation seemed like an unwarranted prosecution. The professor arrives in his English suit and sits beside Ralph. "Ralph, please could you leave the table," says Ian his eyes closing; discontentment and anger writ all over his face.

Ralph ignores it. Finally, the group asks the professor in unison to ask Ralph to leave the table. "Could you wait over there while we talk?" the professor says gently. Ralph complies and walks toward the bench in the corridor. He can hear screeching sounds of the others negotiating and pleading with the professor that he be removed from the team. Or so it seems.

Ralph can't bear to hear the accusatory comments from a distance and the worst part is he is not allowed in on the discussions to defend himself. After around 15 minutes of wait, which felt more like thirty; Ian asks Ralph to come to the group table with a thumbs up sign.

Ralph is a little surprised with his aggressive stance a while ago and the thumbs up now. He proceeds to sit at the table. Americans can be quite a chameleonic bunch when it comes to acting and shifting from mood to mood. As far as violation of even the smallest law is concerned; if you are a nobody then you are penalized to the hilt. If you are a person of stronger means and high connections then you can get away with things either by using your money or your connections. "Private meeting huh!" says Ralph.

"They just wanted some private time," the professor says lightly. His slight smile betrays a disagreement with the way the rest of the team members requested a private meeting with him. But it seems his old age wants to maintain the peace and just do what is needed to get the team back on track.

As Ralph takes a seat, the professor struggles to tell him what the issue is. "They have an issue with you. They think you haven't been giving as good of a performance in the team as they would want."

"Firstly, I haven't heard anything that they have said since I was asked not to be here. Secondly, I don't know what this is about but I strongly believe it is a ploy by Dan to throw me out of the group," Ralph shoots back.

Then what happens is history. The back and forth between the team members and Ralph; now considered a pariah keeps getting increasingly acrimonious. They complain and howl about Ralph's callousness in regards to including stuff directly from the website in their project assignment. The professor leaves intermittently to send out some emails. But Ralph senses that he has in fact gone to escape the bitter argument unfolding. "You guys just see how you can negotiate this," he says as he walks to his cabin.
When he returns, it is evident that things have gotten quite worse. "He still thinks that we are accusing him because of personal reasons rather than performance," utters Dan with an air of contemptuous anger. Dr. Panini remains silent.

"I believe this is being done in a very partisan fashion. So that is evidence enough that your allegations are but a pretext to throw me out of the group," replies Ralph.
"Partisan – it's we four against you!" Dan responds furiously.
"I wonder why he is behaving so furiously! Is it because I am not allowing them to have their way or questioning their rationale behind

wanting to kick me out of the group or just because I am resisting?"
Ralph says to himself.

"I would have been thrown out of the course were this discovered by the professor and we hadn't complained about it," screams out Dan.

"I don't believe that is the case because you were always very belligerent in almost all matters concerning me. Moreover, your angry emails are proof of the same," counters Ralph.

"No. I would have complained against him too if he had done it," says Ian pointing to Dan. He is trying to sound fair in his approach to the situation.

"Are you sure?" asks Ralph suspecting foul play between them.

"Hey, I don't need to play partial here. I am not in favor of anybody," emphasizes Ian with a peeved tone.

"No. I still think this is a witch hunt without providing me an opportunity to justify myself."

"Sir, he is not agreeing to his mistake," avers Denise.

"Now what we heard are opinions. Let's see the facts," responds Dr. Panini.

"I'll forward the email he sent us to you," hollers Denise.

Ralph now knows that his fate is close to sealed. They had set on a path to excommunicate him from the group which is why they had started talking to him with an aggressive stance right from the outset. There hadn't been any intention of negotiating or retaining him in the team. His fate was doomed from the outset of the current situation.

"Ok send it, send it," says Dr. Panini with a sigh. He eyes Ralph with a peeved look. There seem to be overt signs that he would willingly support the other American team members since he identifies more with them than with the Asian Ralph.

Ralph doesn't want to continue the fight any more but Dan keeps coming at him.

"So you will now see who is right and who is wrong," says Dan, anger writ large on his face.

"You are the one instigating this so I have nothing to say to you," says Ralph.

Ian makes a guttural sound as though condemning Ralph.

A Road Less Travelled

****

The feel of her breasts combined with the thought that she probably regards him as her boyfriend gives him a stronger than usual erection. She unconsciously realizes it and drags her hands closer to his groin area.

"Are you feeling woody Ralph?" she purrs.

"Woody?" he doesn't feel assured he has heard the word before.

"Are you feeling your instrument getting harder!" she clarifies.

At first, he thinks she doesn't mean what he thinks she means. But as her hand inched closer to the male bull's eye, he realizes that she, in fact means what he thought she didn't. As her fingers reach into the crevices of his zipper and try to pull it down there is a sudden reflex action from Ralph. He releases the breast from his hand and pulls back sensing the disturbance down under; as she gropes to squeeze her fingers through the opening in his pants.

As he tries to put space between their two bodies; Matty is temporarily shaken from her trance-like drive to reach his prized family jewels.

"What happened Ralph? Are you okay honey?" she asks looking worried.

"Ummhhh…yes."

"Okay," she smiles as she lunges forward to continue her escapade deep inside Ralph's lower half territory; breasts still hanging out of her bras.

He pushes himself back again and struggles against the rubbery upholstery of the car. There's nowhere more to move back, though.

"Wha, what, what are you doing?" he asks a suppressed question.

"Ralph, you know what we are doing right!" the answer is intended to admonish rather than educate.

She sees him as a willing partner in the foreplay. But apparently, he doesn't have his mind on sex. Not this early in the relationship at least. The conservative culture he harbors from India seems to forbid him from pre-marital intercourse. And although the hormones in his body are pining for sexual activity, his mental and cultural propriety is pushing for carnal restraint.

"Well, I don't know if I can do it!" he says sounding exasperated as she keeps groping inside his pants.

"What you mean you can't do it. Your wee-wee is harder than wood right now and you say you can't do it! Gosh, I know you're turned on. You don't have to lie to me."

"No. I'm not lying……"

(she doesn't allow him to complete) "Then what is it? Oh, I know this is your first time. You are just too scared of doing it cause you've never done it before!"

"Noooo!"

"Ralph, is there something you're not telling me? Listen I know guys are shy. And probably you are too."

"It's not that!" he shakes his head from side to side.

"Oh okay. I know what it is. Don't worry. I won't laugh at the length of your wee-wee[13]. I won't judge your anatomy. It all depends on how much force you put into pumping, not necessarily the length. You don't have to feel shy that yours is small or short. I promise I won't laugh," she holds his palm.

Something about her demeanor tells him she is sincere; her intentions are pure. He doesn't feel she is mocking his wee-wee size.

He was afraid to tell her the actual reason for his sexual restraint for fear of making her feel bad. Now though he worries that she might think his reasons for keeping sexual distance concern anatomical inadequacy or doubts about potency. When it comes to sex, he wonders if female thoughts are universal throughout the globe. He remembers having a similar situation in India when a few female physicians in the hospital Dad worked in were talking about a new male doctor who had just joined. They were gossiping about his good looks and muscular physique. Matilda's perceived reasons for his sexual hesitation seemed to echo the conversations he heard back in those years when he sat in an outpatient department close to the female physicians enjoying a conversation about a new good looking male physician.

Full of energy and excitement, they seemed to project an image of sexual democracy and independence. They were so much in heat that even the suggestion of an orgy or any of the oddest positions in the Kamasutra would have seemed to be agreeable to them. Matilda was American. She was a young woman brimming with sexual power and energy. The abuse from her father might have led her to hate men. But

---

[13] wee-wee is American slang for 'small penis'

when you meet the right man, the dynamics of the ball game change entirely. She had a man she considered suitable and the right fit now. And there was no doubt, she wanted to hit the jackpot with him.

Ralph continues to hesitate and vacillate. "Okay, dude. You're not shy, you say your wee-wee is not geometrically challenged, so what is the issue? Why you so scared and hesitating? There's absolutely no reason to be. I know what you got down there and you know what I have down here. The only difference is I am a man and you're a woman."
"Ummhh…..actually it's the other way round Matty."
"You know what I mean Ralph!" she exasperates.

They stare at each other for a while.

"Hey, I told you about my deepest of personal secrets. Even about my abuse and running away from home. You haven't told me much about yourself. So at least you shouldn't be shy to do this. Anyways, I'm the one with my breasts out right now!"

He gives a suppressed laugh as she smiles. Her pleadings touch a chord with Ralph. All questions about her past seem to go away in an instance of burning bush clarity. But then again Ralph wasn't concerned about her past. He valued more what she was as a person. He figured now why she had been so open to him. Sexual abuse victims crave real love. After enduring abuse at the hands of those who were supposed to love them, they lose faith in near and dear ones. They start viewing everybody through a prism of suspicion. And then when they find somebody who harbors genuine love they open up, hoping to elicit a reciprocal love as sympathy for the abuse they have suffered in the past.

Ralph figured this was the reason Matilda told him about the sexual abuse by her father. She saw that he was caring and kind. And wanted his sympathy, love and care. Moreover, telling him her innermost secrets helped her offload the burden of sexual abuse and incest. The only other person she might have told this to may have been Sophie, her sister, he figured. And Sophie was probably the only person beside him to believe her. But he could only speculate this possibility. God knows what other reason she might have had behind telling him about her abuse at the hands of her father. Was it to gain his sympathy and love which she hoped would probably translate into sexual affection? He couldn't say.

"Well I like you and value you a lot but we generally don't have sex until after marriage in the culture back home. I know it's weird and I don't entirely agree with it but my mother holds me accountable for it."

Matilda slides back and begins putting her bra back on and getting her tank top back into shape. She is visibly disappointed and Ralph does see signs of resentment. He doesn't wish to invite her wrath on him. So he neither consoles her nor says anything. He doesn't wish to indicate that his principles are not worth standing by. The silence is disturbing. And he strongly feels that he blew a chance for free sexual gratification. He assures himself that sticking to his principles is worth more than sexual gratification.

She tries to show that things are okay by putting a smile on her face. Deep down she realizes that he is a nice guy. However much she would like to have some sexual release, she is happy to see that he is a person who upholds his values. She would not have realized this had he gone ahead with the love making. She probably wouldn't have missed it either. But she now has more respect for him even though the respect is not of a sexual variety.

"Okay. Well that's good. But I hope we can continue to be friends," she says in a conciliatory fashion.
"Oh come on Matty. Just because we didn't hit the jackpot today doesn't mean we aren't friends. I think we're the best of friends and will continue to be!"
"Not so fast dude. The 'best of friends' title is reserved for someone else in my book. I prefer being something more," she says trying to regain some lost ego.
"Hahahaha" he laughs as she begins to smile.
"Hope you're not missing me sugar lips," he says in an apparent reference to her rosy red lips.
"No. But how about we meet again. Is going to a bar against your culture too?" she asks.
"Nope. It's not."
"Great. So would you like to meet again at a bar? Don't worry, it's not too far. And I'll drive you there," she says trying to assuage his worries of transport and general logistics. He doesn't have a car and doesn't much have the need for a car. The only time a car comes handy is when he goes to the grocery store.
"That would be great."

"Aren't you going to ask about which day and time like you normally do?" she inquires.
"Yes. I almost forgot. Which day?"

Ralph seems to be in a hurry to get out of the car. He feels claustrophobic having got close to getting undressed in the car.

"How does Friday evening look for you? This Friday?"

Ralph had already completed all the painful requirements of the social engineering class including the alternative assignments and coursework[14]. Thursday would be the day of presenting material for the social engineering class so he was essentially free the whole Friday.

Mum would normally have recommended him to be at home and work or study. Going to parties or hanging out wasn't her cup of tea. And she didn't expect it to be part of her children's either.

But Ralph had gone through a lot since he had been to the States. The struggles of finding a place to stay, making friends, not being a 'nobody' were beginning to diminish. New challenges were taking the place of old ones. The new ones were more formidable.

The incident with the social engineering class team was definitely a new challenge. A challenge on how to work and deal with an all-American group of teammates. He felt anything he could do to reduce the stress or get rid of it was welcome. Mum's advice was good, but it was probably better suited in a different context. In America, bars were a good place to meet people informally and also to beat the stress. Logic suggested that he go with Matilda to the bars she wanted to.

"Yes, Friday would be fine."
"Great. So I'll come to your place to give you a ride then. 5:30 pm okay?"
"5:30 pm is great!"
"So I guess I'll just head out now and let you get on with your other stuff."
"Do you need a ride home?" she asks.

---

[14] Ralph was given a separate assignment to do in lieu of the allegedly plagiarized work.

"Ummhh. I think I know the way. And anyways I can go to the
university and call the school escort service from there."
"Well give me a call if you get lost," she smiles softly.
"Sure! Thanks for offering."
"You're always welcome," she presses her gaze on him as he zips his
pant back up.

He draws forward, kisses her on the cheek and begins to close his jacket
for the walk home.

"Good night Matty," he says as he gets out of the vehicle and walks on.
"Good night Ralph. Sweet dreams!"

She looks at him with queer surprise as he struts along the street with a
swagger. "I've never seen anybody say no to sex and sexual
gratification!" she thinks. "This guy's different! Probably that's why I
need to pursue him. I don't think it would be a good idea to drop him
like a sack of potatoes. I'd be losing an opportunity." And so she tidies
up her cardigan, locks the car and goes into the house.

****

"I'm outside your place on the porch" reads the text. She is already in
the car with him when she reads it though. Being a girl she takes her
time to get dressed. And although she is good at texting she doesn't
allow it to interfere with getting glam.
"You're pretty good in texting it seems."
"Oh yeah. Thanks. Why you say so?" he wonders.
"I guess you sent me the last message as you were walking towards the
porch right. Walking and texting. Wish I could do that too. I usually
need to be sitting or in a stationary location to be able to text. Can't do
both simultaneously," she smiles.
"It's just practice, I guess," he assures her to make her feel better about
her abilities.

She drives briskly. As she swivels the steering wheel it is evident she
has had quite a few Christmas' of uninterrupted driving experience. The
car begins to feel like a ship, with her artful driving and negotiating of
long trucks and small cars trying to get ahead. The road ahead is lit with
multi-colored lights of various cars. The tail lights seem more colorful
than the yellow headlights though. Blue, green, orange, red, even

magenta is visible. Almost like a rainbow at night. As she negotiates the vehicles in front, Ralph can't help but compliment her driving skills.

"Just like your texting skill, driving comes with practice too!"
"You mean nobody taught you?"
"Well, my friend gave me an introduction into it. But the rest was trial and error."

He wishes he could drive as well as she does. He knows that someday not far away when he gets his own car he will. He watches her hand and wrist movements intently. The endeavor seems effortless for her. He hasn't seen this level of expertise and strength in women at home. They seem so subdued and submissive compared to the hard hitting and almost boyish lasses in the States. Her hands and fingers seem so flexible and strong.

The roads are quite a work of engineering marksmanship as well. They are designed to minimize accidents and you got to be an utterly crazy driver to have an accident. It's mostly drunk driving that gets people into accidents on US roads. The roads appear to be designed with an aim to reduce casualty in spite of driver mistakes and oversight. As they close in on the destination, Ralph notices quite a few bridges and flyovers ahead.

They are apparently crossing city limits and entering a zone outside of the city. She had told him about her Friday night exploits and her wide knowledge of local bars. He hoped to see this first hand.

As they proceed, the road full of cars gradually turns into a serpentine sea of pedestrians and a dwindling number of cars. They are in Greater Philadelphia on Friday night – a day of party and fun. She parks close to a line of four pubs. As they enter the door, soft Bob Marley music is playing in the background. He was expecting loud music to be blaring. What's wrong with this bar? The people also seem to be rather gentle. They are sitting on tables, on stools along the bar table and sipping their shots and cocktails. Everyone seems to have company. It's not like the typical 'young crowd' bar.

"Oh, you have nice taste. I thought a bar would be noisy around here."
"There are plenty of noisy bars. I just wanted to start off with a quiet one so you get a feel for the night life," she says.

In reality, she didn't want him to feel overwhelmed or outraged at the crass behavior in a typical teenage or student patronized bar. The idea is a gradual introduction into a bar environment. The same principle that is used to introduce captive wildlife back into the forest.

As he prepares to head to a table in the corner; Matilda reaches for his arm. "Hey do you want to take a seat at the bar in the front over there?" she suggests.

He looks at her with a little awe and reluctance. But agrees to go with it none the less. He doesn't want to be a boring and self-opined date. He had seen bars like this in Hollywood movies. It feels different sitting in one, though. More so with a beautiful chick by the side pushing herself on your arm.

As Ralph steadies himself on the bar stool, he is pleasantly surprised to see an all-female crew of bartenders manning the bar. They have an interestingly attractive attire too. Knee-high length shoes, hip high miniskirts and red tank tops. Most have their hair in a simple ponytail. Although there is one with a page boy hairstyle and yet another with auburn piled hair divided into two bulbous sections on the head. With her tiny round glasses on she almost looks like a college scholar. "Strange attire for a college scholar though," thinks Ralph. Her tank top is much smaller for her anatomy. And the garment seems to struggle to contain her odds and ends.

As she surveys the scene her attention is drawn to a young bespectacled guy in a crisp white shirt. She almost doesn't notice the voluptuous, blonde girl sitting next to him.

Her hair, tied into scallion like balls, seems to get bigger as she approaches. For a moment she looks like a real life version of cat woman from the Batman series of yesteryears. "Hey there! How you guys doing," she erupts as she looks straight into his eyes.
"Good," he replies in a subdued fashion. He's never been to a bar and doesn't really know how he should come across. "*Should I be lively and flirtatious, just lively; serious and measured or just myself?*" he wonders.
"Great. What about you?" comes the American accented statement from the girl beside him.
Noticing the differences in accent the spritely bartender turns towards Matilda.

"Fantastic! Great to have you guys here. I'm going to be your server tonight. What would you like to have?"

"What's the special?" asks Matilda.

"We've got a black wheat beer and Bailey's tonight. Many of the other beer brands also have a special price today."

"Oh great!"

'Yeah! So do you know what you want to get or would you like a couple of minutes to think."

"I'll take the Bailey's with the black beer."

"Do you want it together or separate?"

"Separate, of course!"

"And what could I get you, Sir?"

"I'll take what she's taking minus the beer, though," he says politely.

"Cool. I'll be right back." She disappears into the melee, her shapely rear dangling as she struts off.

"So you like our bar server?" Matilda asks softly.

"Ummhh…she's helpful," says Ralph as he tries to mask his feelings.

Matilda had seen him looking intently at the bar tender. She didn't know he had never been to a bar before. Or even that he might not have seen scantily clad women before. But something about being a girl informs her that he is straining his eyes trying to study their server in anatomical detail. If not all of the bartenders.

"Why do you ask?"

She looks at him and doesn't seem to respond. "You don't have to deny your feelings. I know what's happening down there. I won't feel bad if you tell me!" she smiles seductively as she runs her hand over his thigh.

"I was just looking at her!" he gasps.

"You were actually ogling her!"

He shoots a tender smile. "So you like those kinds of girls huh," she follows.

"Don't you?" (Pause) "I thought you were a lesbian."

"I don't mind being one if you tell me the orientation details about you," she retorts.

"I would love to but this place is rather loud to talk and too crowded to afford discretion," he says referring to the three overhead TVs playing music videos and baseball games.

"Oh, this is one of the quietest pubs in the area. There are others with six to seven TVs and tons of people. It's even difficult to get a seat there. We'll probably go there before the end of the night."

He acquiesces and looks around at the crowd. Interestingly the bar stools are well spaced and though the pub is pretty full it's not packed to capacity. She seems to have made good choice coming to a less densely populated pub early in the evening. A sober start to the evening is always nice.

Amanda approaches with a tray. Two shiny glasses with what seems like a small ocean of icy foam and a towering beer bottle.

"Bailey and beer for you Ma'am," as she lays down the glass before Matilda.
"And a Bailey for you Sir."
Ralph and Matilda individually thank the server for her prompt service as Ralph again gets temporarily distracted by her attire.

"I saw that!" Matty again teases him noticing his slight smile.
"So what is it with you, looking at my every move." He doesn't care about people looking at him but everybody is wary about being constantly followed at least at some point in time.
"I am just observant!"
"Same way as I am."
"I am the same too……But I think you were gawking right."
"Well, I can be voyeuristic sometimes I guess."
"Sometimes huh….umhhh!"
"Oh, I'm just teasing!" she says noticing his frustration.
"I've never tasted this before. What is it?"
"It's a bailey. It's made of alcohol and sugar and a little chocolate."

He looks into the frothing surface of the cocktail glass. Having had a father steeped in the traditions of alcohol intake, he is opposed to consuming alcohol. Mum forbade it due to the frequent conflicts she would have with Dad owing to his alcoholic-like habit. He ponders taking the sip.

The question is whether to do or not to do. The inner voice often helped him in difficult situations when he didn't have the slightest clue on what to do. This was not a situation like that. Here it was more a question of minor compromises concerning home-endowed principles versus the situational dynamics of socializing in an American pub setting. The same kind of mental and moral conflict he faced when in the car with a half-naked Matty trying to seduce him. He didn't expect any help from

the Inner voice in this minor dilemma of conflicting principles and
actions.

"I know it looks good. But why don't you take a sip and actually taste
it," she suggests.
"Oh yeah," he gulps a small bit.
"Ummhh."
"Good?….tastes like chocolate, doesn't it?"
"Yes. It's sweet and like chocolate flavor."
"Where did you hear of it?" he asks looking curious.

In all the years, Dad consumed all types of alcohol, Ralph never learned
about the different brands. Mum regarded drinking as a vice. And
exhorted Ralph to never take it up; to stay away from it at all costs. The
need to uphold Mum's teaching had led him to totally blindside himself
to any knowledge of alcohol or alcohol-related matters.

There was only one type of information that he needed to know about
alcohol – stay away from alcohol, drinks and drinking-related company.

But in the US, a good way to socialize is to meet up at a pub or bar. A
drink or two later and the ordinarily reserved, 'hard to get to know'
people become mellow and friendly. Conversation begins to flow like a
river. In the heat of conversation, attraction could also arise. Hugging,
cuddling, smooching and PDAs[15] become commonplace. One-night
stands are a regular byproduct of a quick and exciting rapport developed
at the bar.

Could he just leave the bar and walk out. Or would it be practical to
compromise between homegrown principles and some harmless
socialization? He decides to opt for the latter.

"I come here quite a bit. That's how I know their drink specials and the
drinks they offer in general."
"Oh so you come here with your friends or boyfriends?" he asks.
"Both!" She gives him a suggestive look.
"You jealous," she shoots a triumphant look.
"No. Just jealous of the amount of knowledge you have – drink-related
knowledge. I'm going to have to learn it all to keep up."

---

[15] PDAs – public displays of affection

229

"It's easy. You'll learn if you come out more with me," she smiles.

"That would be great!"

"So how many boyfriends have you had?"

"More than you can count on your fingers."

"So you're experienced then!"

"Depends on what you mean by experienced," she says in a matter-of-fact manner.

"The same thing you do."

"Oh yeah. By experience I mean meeting new people, exploring new mindsets, hearing of new places. What's your interpretation of it?"

"Really. Is that your interpretation of it? Because what you said was, in fact, my understanding of experience. Hope you didn't steal it from me."

It is evident that the American lass understands the country bumpkin from India pretty well. So well that she knows where to place his ideals and definitions or where they would be.

It's interesting how people in the US tend to be so shrewd and insightful. A knack for reading between the lines. They judge you based on how you look at the froth in your drink or how you swallow a sip of sweet brew. Or even on your conversational skills, Ralph thinks.

You know a person is lying when he answers you while sipping his drink. He figures she's seen his true self and made a mental picture of him.

"Nope. I'm not a mind reader!" she replies.

(Pauses) "I wish I was though," he says.

"So is that the motivation to have boyfriends and relationships. That you get to meet more people and explore different mindsets by getting intimately involved with them?"

"Well having a boyfriend or a girlfriend doesn't mean you get intimately involved with them. It's just company. Helps you keep away from loneliness. Coming to the part about mindsets and meeting new people; you don't have to make boyfriends or girlfriends of people to meet and explore new mindsets. You can just as well be good, close friends and get to know each other that way."

"I mean, let's face it, you walk into a pub and grab a drink at the counter and start enjoying it. If there's someone sitting by your side, you're not going to be uncouth and just stare at them. You will obviously say hello, won't you. That's the way to make friends. From there if your

interaction clicks or you guys hit it off, then the relationship can always progress to something more. I believe relationships happen by serendipity. They grow by work. Very few are pre-planned."
Ralph sits there patiently listening. He is so taken aback by the seemingly profound wisdom this girl has that he can barely say anything for a while. He wonders how this hippie looking and sounding girl has this much of wisdom and knowledge. He had noticed many Western tourists coming to India had an outward persona of being funny and cheeky. Very sociable.

However, when you come to the West; not everybody might be as effusive and convivial as when in the Orient. Guess when in Rome, do as the Romans do would be the appropriate dictum applicable to this scenario. It's quite a perception that many Americans can be very business-minded and logical while outwardly showing they are carefree. That's a good quality to have because you don't let the stress of being calculative ruin your chances of being sociable and friendly.

This girl was the same. Fun, outgoing and carefree on the outside, but had a lot of knowledge and depth. Americans tend to be informal and congenial while being sharp and business-minded. An eclectic mix of smart and fun. Ralph had seen this quality in an overbearing number of Americans that he had come across. He knew that it would be wrong to categorize in this manner. But in the absence of a different understanding, he had little else to go by.

One aspect of relationships in America was same as in the rest of the world though. Relationships take time to develop. More so in the States. Sustained communication is required to build a strong relationship over time. In the midst of analyzing all the differences between life in the US and life in India, Ralph feels a sense of security in knowing that of all the varied differences at least one basic aspect – relationships, has a semblance to the way it's done around the world. However, it might be easier to chat someone up in Asia. It is easy in the US too, but not in all parts of this vast country.

"So now that I've told you about my boyfriends, you want to share a little more in detail about your invisible girlfriends!" she interrupts his thoughts.
"Sure."
"Well?"

"Yes. I had good friends when I was studying in India. One of them was very close too. Good friends as in they would call home and stuff, go around eating, hanging out and stuff."

"And?" she focuses her eyes.

"And….umhhh…have fun."

"Fun huh!"

"Not the type of fun you're thinking about. More platonic fun."

"So like you guys went to the pool together, swam together, ate and umhhhh…s-s-slept together?"

(He suppresses a shy smile) "Well, we ate together, hung out but didn't swim and definitely didn't sleep together. We slept alone at home. Swimming is something which is usually done in Goa but not in other parts of India. Most of the invisible girlfriends I had were in other parts of India."

"You mean you were a girl deprived single guy in Goa?"

"No. Just didn't have as many girls as friends to whom I was close in my home state" he clarifies.

"So are you sad that you didn't have as many girlfriends when you were back home?"

"Ummhhhh…."

"You seem to have a forlorn feeling as though you missed something. Something nice!!"

"Not really. Friendships weren't as easy to build always; so it was a question of serendipity or mere coincidence."

Ralph can sense that she sees through his explanation. That deep down he too feels that there might have been ways to foster stronger friendships and relationships with colleagues back home. This fact is accentuated by how complex relationship building can be in the States. But sometimes it's mere inability to overcome shyness and meet people. I guess true grit and resourcefulness is evoked when one is thrown from the frying pan into the fire. The crucible of the melting pot, which is the US has already begun to show in Ralph's outlook to relationships, work, people and to the world.

"When you no longer have people that were always by your side; you realize how foolish you were to have taken them for granted. You see their value after they are gone" he ponders.

"So missing someone special huh!" she states sensing his thoughts. All he can do is smile. "That's a yes!"

This would seem weird but there's something similar about being in a pub and being at mass in a church. While there is a ton of activity going on around you in a bar, you still find the inner calm to think about the things that mattered most or that still do. Just as while the mass is in full session you still find the inner peace to delve into the tragedies and missed opportunities of your life gone by; of the romances and dalliances that could have been more than just casual affairs; of the relationships that could have been strengthened but were waylaid by one's self-centered greed and short-sightedness.

Ralph wishes he came to a bar before. And resolves to come again and again. He is happy to have met the young, beautiful lass. He would not have been in the noisy bar if it wasn't for her. For once in the whole night, he is sure that he is doing the right thing. In spite of all the homegrown programming of 'no late nights', 'curfew by 7 pm' and other military type rules he knows that life is much more than that. You don't have to be in the US to realize that. But sometimes it takes a journey of a thousand miles to meet that someone who can show you the world; show you parts of yourself you never knew existed; show you You!

****

"Missing me!!!" she interrupts with a low pitched screech.

Both of them burst out into amiable laughter. They spontaneously hug and start kissing. It usually doesn't take too long the second time around. And it's always easier when you are kissing the same person.

"So you want to try out another bar?" she suggests as they engage in more lovey-dovey actions.
"We haven't spent much time here have we?" he asks curiously. Ralph seems to be of a school of thought that engenders staying at a place for a longer period of time.
"Normally I am in and out of a bar within 15 minutes. We have already been here around half hour or so."

In reality, they have been there for only 20 minutes. She wants to move up the chain and get him into the wilder bars so he can loosen up a lot faster, a lot easier.

"Well let's finish the drinks and we can move. Sound good?"
"Sure thing!"
"Wow, how did I say that so calmly," he wonders. *"The drink is probably having an effect on me or maybe it's the bar environment. I have already begun to take more decisive action"* he tells himself.
As he tries to gulp the drink down the fizz in the Bailey makes him a little nauseated. "Oompf!!"
"What! You said oomph?"
"Huh. Oof!"

He barely understands the meaning of oomph. But seeing her smile he ignores it. She's been smiling all of this evening anyways. The engineer that he is; his English vocabulary is not very advanced and he can be slightly obtuse at times.

Matty knows that she would need to exert more effort to understand this guy. She doesn't mind it provided she sees that he is exerting a similar amount of effort as well. "Looks like that Bailey got the wind out of you!" she smiles.

"All in a day's work," he shrugs. Matty signals to the bartender to bring the check. Inexperienced as he is in bar hopping, he waits and watches what's going to happen in regards to the bill. He has brought a little cash. But is it sufficient to pay the bill? He doesn't know.

The waitress arrives with the check and places it on the bar counter. Matty reaches for it and places a slim blue color card in the check folder. "How much is it?" he asks. "I got it!" she nonchalantly says.

He doesn't force his way, but calmly allows her to do the needful. The Bailey seems to be playing its part in calming him down. "We need to give her a tip right?" he asks.
"You can if you want to, but I already gave her. So you can probably save yours for the next bar," quips Matty.
As he tries to get off the bar stool he feels a little slow and heavy. It's either the drinks or the fact that he is getting more comfortable with the beautiful lass next to him. "The Bailey definitely seems to be bringing out the calmer version of yourself!" says the Inner Voice.

****

Ralph holds open the door for her as they exit the bar. She gently smiles. "Very soon you'll be holding more than just the door," she mutters to herself. She knows what she wants to have him hold.

Around eighty steps away, Ralph sees a trinity of 3 pubs. The one in the center has the biggest sign post. "Which of these are we going to," he inquires.

"I like the one in the middle. It's the biggest and has a terrific music environment."

As they enter, Ralph is awestruck by the environment. They have an 'in your face' kind of blaring music with a coterie of people mixing freely with each other. The women seem to be more skimpily clad than in the previous bar, not to mention the layout of the place seems a lot better. With some wearing hip length shorts, others wearing micro miniskirts and almost all having plunging necklines that go deeper than sea level.

Matty figures Ralph would lose his composure in this sort of an environment. Firstly, because of everyone's dress attire. The Bailey he has had takes a short while to kick in. Nobody can resist the invisible power of alcohol to sweep you off your feet.

She looks at him in a telling manner as he gazes across the bar and into unknown or hitherto unseen territory. He clearly has a 'deer in the headlights' look on his face as he stands there; waiting for Matty to lead him on. There is a tendency to feel lost and he knows it only too well. He is glad that Matty is there, though. Although he is not going to make it obvious that he is taking her lead, he is, in fact, following her.

It helps to have a chaperone that can show you around in a foreign country. More so if you are not independent or smart enough to find out things yourself. Ralph is one of those guys who can shift between being super smart and relatively sluggish.

Mother would always call him 'hyperactive' and ridiculously intelligent when he was a child. As he grew up though the precocious traits were replaced by an unwieldy innocence or rather a sensory delusion. He no longer interacted as astutely as he did when he was a child. In fact, he didn't interact at all. Events at home and school made him despondent enough to shun company. He began to be withdrawn, kept to himself and didn't have as big a circle of friends as before. All that came as a rude shock when he came to the States and realized he would have to interact with all and sundry. Interaction is the key to gaining any type of knowledge in the States.

People use their social network to gain leverage in career, relationships and life in general. Ralph hoped that the developing friendship with Matty would help him understand American culture and customs.

****

As she heads towards a small corner table in the bar, she notices a couple of men staring at her. Feeling uncomfortable and conscious, she looks back at Ralph hinting at him to come closer to her so that the male gaze will reduce if they realize she has a boyfriend with her. Ralph senses this and quickly gets close to her. "Stay close to me kid! Don't want you to get confused and get lost. This is the real world; not the library," she declares and smiles sarcastically.

Not giving her any repartee or resistance, he politely obeys. There is something about their relationship thus far that makes it obvious that she is in control or that he probably doesn't wear the pants. Not that he would want to at this point but knowledge of the country and of what to do next gives people a stronghold in terms of their status in relationships. Why do drop dead gorgeous women go around with ordinary looking men who have lots of cash and power? Why are top directors and presidents of companies respected the way they are even though they might not have the technical skills to back their position? It's all because of situational status and timing. Somebody has the power and position at a given point of time to pull strings or control others either because they are financially capable of doing so or emotionally stronger than the person in need. In a way, emotional status is affected by economic circumstances.

Subtle signs of power are often more easily detected by people than overt indications of dominance. The latter might be reviled and hated while the former is usually accepted without much resistance.

Matilda positions herself in a seat as he waits to sit down after ensuring she is comfortable. "You okay?" he caringly asks sensing her discomfort with the male gaze. He grabs a small chair and cuddles up close to her. They sit silently for some time as though ruminating, contemplating. She seems to be in some sort of daze, almost thinking about some sort of puzzle or conundrum.

"You okay!" he asks again. "Oh yes. I'm fine," she gives a propitiatory smile.

Happy that she is responsive he looks into her eyes to start a conversation. "The layout in this bar is quite different isn't it?" he asks. "Yeah, the atmosphere is different too."

She pauses. "But it's all good," she says seeking to be friendly and collegial.

"So what do you want to drink," she quickly asks.

"Nothing. Let's talk for a while before we get the drinks."

"Sure. The waiter might come and ask us, though. You could tell her why we're not having drinks," she smiles.

"Yeah I sure will tell her that it's because you are on a dry spell."

"Yeah right!"

When a relationship is still in its building phase and trust is still being generated; it is considered better to not be dull and sad or show a down feeling. Often times it causes the person you are with to lose interest in being with you or in not being with you at all. Ralph and Matty were good friends but had still not reached the point where they could count on each other without asking the other explicitly. All relationships take time to foster. The only time when strong relationships are developed is in times of adversity. They were not in any adversity like a war, a natural calamity or any other similar situation. But Ralph's struggle to learn and adjust to conditions in the US constituted a mini struggle. Or at least that's how he saw it. Both of them were trying to build and strengthen their relationship. But the only way to do that was to spend more time together, do things together and have fun together.

A waitress in an ordinary pinafore gown walks up to the calm couple. "Hi, lady and gentleman! I notice you have an empty table. Would you like to drink anything?"

"Well, we're just getting settled. We'll order in a while. Thanks!" says Ralph.

For a moment he is surprised how calmly he addressed the waitress while Matty just looked on without saying a word. My confidence must be getting better, he thinks to himself. She smiles and side glances him realizing he seems to be falling into the groove.

"So what were you doing before you came here today?" he asks.

"I went to the salon, got my hair and nails done. Then went to the Macy's store near my house and got this amazing pair of earrings."
"Oh yeah. I wanted to compliment you on them. But then I feared you might feel flattered to the point of disgust. And I didn't want to get a beating. So I decided to keep it to myself," he smiles slyly.
"Nice try! You just didn't notice them. How's that for a fair assessment!"
"Huh…"
"Say yes buster[16]!!"
"Hahahha! You are always so accurate. But this time I did realize the beautiful earrings. Not all that much, though!"

She shoots him a glare; more intended to intimidate than bite.

****

"So why don't we order some beers this time. You haven't really tried beers have you?" she asks.
"Well, my Dad used to drink beer back home. And I did try it. But not sure what the beer here tastes like. I guess same as there. But not sure."
"Then you should try it," she quips. She secretly hopes that the mix of hard liquor and beer-based spirits will be sufficient to knock him off his feet and get him to loosen up. But then again, his third world resilience is not known to her and sometimes these hardy, despair and poverty hardened internationals have more tenacity that the strongest of Americans. She will have to improvise as the night matures. But even if the doses in the bar are not sufficient, she seeks consolation in the fact that she has a lot more alcohol at home in her room.
"So what else besides going to the salon and doing earring shopping did you do before coming here?"
"Ate a lot of hot dogs at a girls only barbecue," she grins.
"Hahahaha…I didn't know you liked hot dogs."
"There are many things you don't know, kid!" she laughs.
"Yes Grandma! There's a lot I could learn from you."
"Yeah. Once I give your rear a spanking you will learn fast. Got it!"

---

[16] **Buster** is an informal way of addressing a man especially someone you are annoyed with

From the day they met, Ralph kind of sensed that she would be wearing the pants at least for some time in the initial stages of their friendship.

"Absolutely Grandma!" he giggles.
"You asked me what I did. But haven't told me what you did."
"Instead of going to the library I did all my work at home. I completed one assignment and laid the foundation for the other."
"And?" she didn't seem impressed with his choice of work.
"I made chicken xacuti. It's a special dish made in India. It's usually eaten with rice."
"Sounds delicious. Does it taste as such?"
"Yes. Of course. Else I wouldn't be making it."
"So when are you going to teach me how to cook?"
"Whenever you want to and when you are ready to participate rather than be a mere spectator."
(Pause) "Though I doubt you can be a good cook. It takes more dedication than you might be capable of."
"I think you might be getting close to that rear spanking that I was telling you about," she says in a matter of fact manner.
"Haha. I'm just messing around."
She continues to glare.

"Why don't we order the beers and continue chatting," she says hoping to keep the conversation going while the drinks are ordered.

Ralph rises from the chair to draw the attention of the waitress on the bar floor. Waves a hand till she notices him.

"Hey….could you get us two beers please. I will have a Corona. What will you have Ralphie?" asks Matty.
"I'll have the same," he says not knowing what brand of beer to select.

The teetotaler that he is; beer brands don't come to him naturally. Even if they did, they would be beer brands common in India, not the US. Learning the brands, fashions and fads of a new country is a whole new effort and takes time. For some, it might be easier than others. But on the whole, adjusting to a foreign land is no small task. Having friends in the culture makes it that much easier to adjust especially if those friends are born and raised in the same country.

At every small point of interaction with Matty, Ralph would come across concepts, terms he had no clue of; had never heard or just

239

couldn't perceive. At many of these instances, he would unabashedly ask her the meaning or would allow himself to be embarrassed by her. The end result would be that he would learn something new and Matty would have a secret appreciation of his innocence and humility. Sometimes it takes kindness, caring and a little vulnerability to win over another. In Ralph's case, Matty appreciated his forthrightness and ability to take criticism for the sake of learning new stuff.

"This waitress is so tall, isn't she?" he says.
"So you like tall chicks huh! I won't blame you......(pause)" she says.
"What!"
"I said I won't blame you. Most guys like tall girls. They are more substance to hold and just jiggy with it!"
"Jiggy?"
"Yes. You know right. Holding, caressing and fondling a girl!" she bites her lower lip to suppress an obvious smile.
"No I said it just as an observation," he blushes.
"Oh yeah, no, that's fine. Good observation I must say," she just can't seem to have enough of pulling his legs.
He gives a slight smile and looks away; almost embarrassed.
"So what kind of girls do you like?"
He gradually turns to her. "What?"
"Yesssss....what kind of girls do you like?" she asks intently.

He continues giving her the 'deer in the headlights' look, wondering what she is up to. The Bailey still hasn't downgraded his judgment and sense of propriety.

"Are you gay or anything that you don't like girls. Or like only guys?"
"In that case my question would be 'what kind of guys do you like'?" she continues with an air of sarcasm.
"Hunky guys, puny guys, effeminate guys....? And there's no need to feel shy about your orientation. It's all okay here in America."
"I like normal girls," he answers curtly.
"And?"
Pause again.
"And more normal girls I guess!" she grimaces.
"Hey, you don't have to be shy about your likes or about telling me stuff that might sound crazy or embarrassing. Trust me I know everything in these matters. Perhaps I could even educate you if you are in the dark about certain terminologies."

"So it is a great benefit for you considering you have a lot to learn about American culture," she says sensing his hesitation.

"Well, I like cultured girls from a good background. Nice and friendly."

"And boobilicious or skinny or big butt, small tits, long hair; the whole enchilada. You know the normal things that guys like to see."

"Ummhh"

"By the way, are you a guy?" she smiles.

He looks at her with a strange gaze.

"Cause you're shy about saying what you like or don't like. As though it's something top secret. Just to let you know in America all these things are in the open and you don't have to feel shy about it."

"Well?"

"Yes I like a girl with shapely breasts, nice figure, smooth skin and sharp looks."

"I guess you want someone without a butt then!"

"Oh and a nice big butt is always a plus," he sheepishly smiles.

"Kind of like what you look like right now!" he leans forward saying that.

"Oh thanks! So you're checking me out huh!"

"Have you asked permission from your Mum before doing so, you shameless brat!" she grins.

Both of them descend into fitful laughter.

Through her interactions with him, Matilda has begun to understand that the culture he comes from is of a collective type. Wherein permission is needed to be obtained for almost all major things outside of eating, shitting and sleeping. Which is why career, education, marriage, asset creation decisions are all reviewed with elders and near and dear ones before actually taking a step.

In the US or other western cultures, things are way different. Individually driven decisions are valued and highly regarded. In fact, asking for permission is not always looked upon very highly. One might risk being called "slow or non-independent" if everyday decisions require sanction from elders or friends and relatives.

If you find a nice person to go around with and share life, generally people will be happy with it. There will seldom be any opposition from family to that. There are exceptions though and some parents might willingly interfere in their ward's personal life if they feel their future is being threatened. In these instances, it is common for the youth to feel caged and subdued. And they vent it out with friends and close pals; but not always. In the case of Asian youth, it is customary to have parents actively partake in the choice of career, spouse or other major milestones in life.

"So what do you plan to do after we are done with the bar hopping tonight," she rolls her eyes fiendishly as she asks.

He skirts the question by pointing out to the waitress leaning over a customer at the corner of the bar table. "Do they do that for all customers?"

"Well. Depends."

"Depends on what?"

"Depends how good looking the customer is. Or how wealthy he is. Or what else he has to offer. Some guys tend to exude a notion that they have long anatomies which some girls just can't resist. Others just have this drop dead powerful gift of the gab which if anything is just too charming to turn down even if you want to."

"You are charming too!" she smiles.

"Okay," he acknowledges.

A noisy silence ensues. Agitated with the silence, she interjects. "I hope you are not feeling insecure Ralph!"

"About what?" he shoots.

"Uh, about your ability to hit on women or to get a girl to be interested in you!"

"No. I'm fine," he replies curtly.

"Are you sure. You…."

"You seem to be interested in me," he quickly interrupts her.

"You brought me here in your car. Took me to your house. How would that have happened if you didn't find me charming and interesting," he looks at her with an air of cool confidence.

"True. I don't have another explanation to substantiate it apart from the fact that I took pity on you."

"Pity! I am not a creature that needs pity. Though kindness would be a better word to continue good relations."

Their conversation is suddenly interrupted.

****

The slender waitress pushes her body towards them as though she is going to ram the table with her voluptuous flesh. Ralph is a little taken aback by the person that approaches them all of a sudden. From a close range, she is as svelte and real as can be. His carnal hunger suddenly seems to rekindle. Matty seems to sense his captivation and doesn't bother to interrupt. For some reason she prefers trying to understand his sexual desires rather than tease him about it. The waitress places the Corona bottles exactly perpendicular to each person on the table.

"Let me know if you need anything else."
"Sure," utters Matty.
"Enjoy!" she thunders as she leaves the area.
"Liked her didn't you?"
"Umhhh…well yes," he doesn't hide his feelings this time.
"So you like red heads then! Interesting!"
"You mean the hair? I like brown hair, black hair, blonde and almost every other color except blue."
"Brown hair is called brunette, just to let you know. Yes she was pretty hot. I see you like slender girls."
"Well, she was pretty good looking."
"Yes there's a lot of limb to hold on to with slender girls right!" she chuckles.
"Sorry!" he's a little taken aback.
"Nothing!"
"No, but you did say something."
"No. Really it was nothing at all."

Ralph has a slight dimple on his cheeks. The beer seems to be making his initially somber demeanor a little laid back. Matty starts downing the beer in quick gulps. She has reached a level of comfort with the beer cans that Ralph is not sure he entirely understands.

"Do you get high pretty quickly or is your threshold level pretty developed?" he asks.
"I can usually take quite a few beers before I begin to feel lousy. How about you?"
"I don't know. Never counted."

He is embarrassed to admit but this is his first time actually drinking a substantial quantity of beer. He has never had any prior experiences that he can set a precedent against. He prefers not admitting it openly even though he suspects she might know. She seems to have gauged his level of 'bumpkinness' already. In many ways, it might seem like she is wearing the pants in their friendship-relationship kind of camaraderie. At least in terms of knowledge of the US and the social environment that seems like the case.

Ralph is comfortable allowing her to have her way though. At least he can learn from her. He is normally not so gracious in his approach to being dominated and subdued. Matty has carried out the domination in a very subtle manner, though. It doesn't even appear to be domination or that is what Ralph would like to think. Being from a foreign country it is important to have access to information in regards to how American society operates; the cultures and norms and acceptable forms of behavior.

"You don't seem like you could take a lot of beers," she says.
"I don't know. Why?"
"I don't know either," she replies.
"You really meant that?" he asks feeling her dry comment.
"Relax! I was just kidding."

He can't seem to forget the comment but resolves to. It can be rather embarrassing when your endurance capabilities are called into question by the woman you think should be actually admiring and respecting them.

"So you like the party atmosphere here?"
"Umm….it's okay!" he replies curtly.
"Did you like the setting in the earlier bar more?"
"Yup!"
"Well if you don't like it, you don't like it. You don't have to say you like something you don't just to be politically correct."
In reality, she knows that he is still smarting from her earlier comment about his endurance in regards to alcohol consumption. International students can be very sensitive when it comes to discussing their weaknesses and non-existent strengths in public.

"I really like the way you are gradually sipping that beer. Speaks a lot about your control," he says.
"Control?"
"Yes. That's the actual way to consume any alcohol. Slow and relaxed. It goes down better."
(Pauses) "And best of all you don't get high or feel a hangover the next day."

Matty rolls her eyes. She knows that the whole idea behind drinking is to get high and to forget your inhibitions. Because inhibitions are a major barrier to effective communication and to getting to know people. Inhibitions relating to approaching someone, particularly of the opposite sex; fears about telling people about yourself, with the hidden potential of making yourself vulnerable. In America, professional settings are characterized by discipline and a neutral form of conduct. All sexual innuendos, ribald jokes and songs are best kept out of the work setting. At least that's what is recommended since the effect of your actions, however innocuous is judged on impact not intent.

The workplace is considered a place where core attention and a no-nonsense approach is needed. That's why in America socializing is normally done in bars and pubs. People would normally carry their office demeanor to the bar if alcohol wasn't a component of social interactions. That's where a drink or two helps people let their guard down and loosen up a little.

Getting drunk and consequently having a hangover is the byproduct of enabling more open social interactions. Matty finds it odd that Ralph prefers being sober as opposed to letting loose. She doesn't know the real reason though behind his preference for sobriety to intoxication.

"Why don't you want to get drunk and have a hangover?" she questions sharply.
"Because it's not right to get drunk."

She peers unbelievably at him. Almost dumbfounded by his assertion.

"And why is that may I ask?"
"Just that many things can go wrong when one is drunk. You can't drive properly, judge properly and what not."

She falls back into her chair and just wonders, almost disappointed.

"Gosh, this guy is a priest. I need to get him to loosen up!" she thinks to herself.
"But that's the reason you have me. Even if I drink a lot I don't lose judgement. I can drive just as well as when I haven't drunk a drop of booze."

She looks at him intently hoping to see some reaction but doesn't spot any. He merely looks at her non-plussed.

"So? What do you think?"

"I don't think anything," he replies.

"Dude. You got to change some things about you. I know you are from a different country and you have traits and customs you have learned from there. But now that you are in America you need to learn certain customs from here too. And run with it. That's how you are going to gain acceptance and trust," she declares.

"What, you mean drinking is a necessary part of getting to know people in the US?" he stares.

She looks at him with an intent to soothe him; a little surprised at his aggressive question at first.

"You mean people don't get to know each other and make friends without drinks?"

"No that's not what I meant at all! All I meant is that it becomes easier to socialize and exchange ideas and relate to people when you let your guard down. Drinks help you let your guard down. That's all!" she interjects.

"Okay."

"I mean just look at yourself right now. You were not as conversant when we left my place as you are now. The beers are definitely making it easy for you to loosen up. That's exactly what happens when you have a couple of vodkas or pegs. Conversation making becomes easier and the content of the conversation generally tends to become light and breezy."

"Ummmh"

"Makes sense?" she shakes her head approvingly as she looks on for signs of conciliation on his face.

He grabs the Corona and downs it quickly. He's not sure if he's downing it to feel its punch or because he just doesn't entirely comprehend the meaning of what she has just conveyed. A person that has not understood something generally tries to conceal his ignorance by saying yes while sipping a drink.

"So how often do you come to pubs?"

"As often as I can. Why?"

"No. Just wondering that this seems to be a major avenue to socialize in the US."

"Well we have other ways to socialize too. But this one is used most by college students, grads as well as undergrads. I asked you to come along so that you would get familiar with it and get better at this form of socialization as you keep coming."

She knows that it doesn't take too many visits to the pub to make friends with the regulars who frequent it. It is not uncommon to have ultimate gratification with contacts made at the bar. The same goes for lasting connections as well. However, temporary fun is more the norm at bars. Not many people in the US make business contacts at bars meant for students and teens. Unless of course, it's a snazzy bar where a martini can be something like $30 a piece.

"Thanks for that. Hopefully as I get used to this form of socializing I will be able to meet more people."

"Yes. You shouldn't just stay at home the weekends. Go out, meet people and don't feel like a stranger."

"Yup."

She eyes him with a smooth form of admiration. The kind that you normally reserve for a loved one or potential mate. She has plans for this hunk. Only if he would make it easier for her and just go with the flow. His foreign customs and principles are a bit of a hindrance for getting cozy and lovey-dovey. But she knows he has potential. "God knows what love making skills he's got up that Indian, kamasutrian sleeve of his," she wonders.

****

She doesn't mind waiting to find out. After all what's good takes time to get.

"So do you meet lots of different people here every weekend? Or is it just the same people?" he asks.

"It's a mix. I have made quite a few friends with the bartenders and waitresses though!"

"Oh!"

"Do you want me to introduce you to any of the bartenders?"

(Pause) "What about the waitresses then?" she smiles sensing his hesitation.

"That would be great!"

Both of them burst out laughing.

"Now you are learning it!" she quips.
"I guess the beer is having an effect after all," he thunders.
"That's a good sign. See you are beginning to go with the flow. That's how it ought to be!"

Both of them realize their beer bottles are empty.

"I guess the beers disappear with the excitement!" quips Matty.
"How about another one?" she suggests.
"Sure!" he accepts.

Matty makes a V sign to indicate two of the same beers to the waitress who had served them before. The drinks are promptly brought to the table and they decide to gulp their way through the bottles.

"Well, that was quick. Ready to go to the next happening place sunny?" she asks again.
"Lead the way captain!" he seems to give her total privileges to determine the plan for the night.

They walk towards the door and like a true gentleman he opens the door and allows her to exit as he dutifully follows her. They walk a few steps in close unison as he lightly places his hand on her waist.
She grabs his hand with her left palm and places it on her flank very firmly in contact with her body. The alcohol is definitely making the interaction easier. And Ralph is probably too tipsy to notice that. Matty though is aware that a few more drinks and he will be all hers.

They walk 500 feet in the direction of Irish Renaissance; the pub with a colloquially Irish feel to it. All along they are in close contact with each other. Their bodies almost intertwined with hands and shoulders linked like those of Siamese twins.

As they enter they are viewed by all in the pub with an element of interest. It's odd to find a couple already quite intoxicated and of mixed race so much intertwined and into each other. If they weren't in the bar, it would be fair to consider they were either dry humping or dancing the tango. Close contact can be quite an interesting concept in any culture. Especially when the contact is between a man and a woman.

They stagger their way onto the vast wooden floor of the renaissance focused pub. Strangely, the pub has old chandeliers and rather old looking pieces of furniture. But it seems to have an unique inverse polarity with their attire which looks pretty appealing. Ralph is in rugged blue jeans and an immaculate white shirt. Matty has donned on her tight cotton dress with a hemline just below her crotch. Her dress is sea blue colored with a mix of gel-like dark blue. Needless to say, she is hot as a smoldering iron. But Ralph is either too innocent to see and feel her or just oblivious to all the carnal pleasures that abound in his vicinity.

"You need to try their Terrapin Hopsecutioner. It's a special of this place," she screeches as she staggers onto a bar stool.
"What's Terra...r..a.......what!"
"Oh, it's a beer. Sorry I tend to forget that you are not a regular here. Some of my other friends who come here often know the beverages by number on the menu card and by the name."
"What's it called again?"
"Terrapin Hopsecutioner as in Terrapin and then Hop-se-cu-tioner. Easy enough?"
"Yup. I won't try to repeat it," comes the quick reply.
"Well even if you don't repeat it, it will be as charming as it has always been. Remember Shakespeare's saying, 'a rose by any other name would smell as sweet!'"
"This beer is the kind that makes you hit the roof! Just wait till you get it."
"Hey there Matty! Terrapins for 2 is it? And who's the new friend?" comes a quick question from a wide-mouthed bartender.
"This is Ralph. We study together."
"Hey there. How's it going, Ralph!"

Ralph is almost clueless what just happened. He is confused how the bartender knows the pretty damsel so well and also that he just wished him. By the time, he opens his mouth to answer, Johnny is already onto the next question.

"I guess ice cold is the deal right."
"Two ice cold it is!" she emphasizes.

"Hold on. I don't want any more beer. I think I've had enough for tonight," he says with hesitation.

"What? Turning down a Terrapin. Normally people would kill to get a Terrapin. Particularly when it's offered by the lovely lady here!" Johnny reiterates.

"Just get us two Johnny," she says placing her hand on Ralph's.

"Don't worry, it's not strong. You'll be fine. I'm driving anyways."

"I hope I can stand after this!"

"Just chill dude! You are not the only one who is having the third beer in the same night. People through the ages have been doing it and have survived," she quips, sensing his apprehension to downing the third beer in less than an hour.

"You won't be able to enjoy the social scene here if you stick to your 'no-drink' policy. You got to mix and gel with the crowd like how I told you earlier remember!" she advises.

"Yup," he keeps his answer curt and non-committal. Internally he is not confident of being able to withstand the dose of three beers in two days, let alone in a night. There's something about his mental or physiological makeup that suggests an inability to handle alcohol. And Ralph is at a loss to understand where that weakness comes from. *"Is it the conditioning in regards to abstaining from alcohol or is it the fear of violating Mum's instructions in spite of knowing the innocuousness of a certain situation?"* he wonders.

He was brought up to think that Mum's instructions were the final truth and the only truth. Any other instruction would be mere myth and lies. He would have loved to believe it to be so. But the realities of the world had only too often shown him that the ability to critically assess is more important than only being steadfastly loyal to a set of ground rules. Irrespective of the fact if these rules were established by you or someone else. America had definitely convinced him that adaptation to one's surroundings is the key to survival and growth. What other place would adaptation not be valued in?

"Here you are little lady!" says Johnny as he places the beers on the table.

"You're an angel as always Johnny!" she smiles delicately.

"Anything for you my dear!" he points to her as he turns to help his other patrons. He winks at Ralph as he turns away.

"Looks like you two got something going there?" says Ralph slyly.

She looks at him gently and smiles. "I don't have anything going with him. But if you are interested in him, I could hook you up. Then your sexual orientation would be called something else, though."
"Haahahhahaa….you're funny. I'm just kidding," clarifies Ralph.
"Same here," quips Matty.
"But seriously. You two seem to enjoy a very good rapport. You know him for a very long time?"
"As a person who visits this bar often I know most bartenders who work here. I meet him more often than the other bartenders though. So he has taken a liking to me. I am like one of his patron customers. So he serves me every time I am at the bar. It helps to have a nice bartender always taking care of you."
"Especially when you are a regular bar hopper!" Ralph suppresses a cheeky laugh.
"So you are getting into the groove huh," she sips the glass of beer and smiles slightly at him.
"Just learning to go with the flow. You keep saying that you are a 'flow person' right. That's what I am trying and learning to be. Slowly but surely I will get there! What you say?" he smiles.
"I say you got something going for you," she says seriously.

She feels him getting familiar with the way Americans socialize and have fun. She appreciates it and wants to tell him but doesn't; fearing he might get complacent. Americans have a peculiar way of noticing and acknowledging progress made by individuals who they do not consider to be way below their league. They view such progress with pleasure without openly showing it. Matty knows that Ralph needs to go out more often to get real comfortable in his shoes and in interacting with people.

"So you were telling me about the kinds of girls you like. And we never completed that conversation before coming here."
"Okay."
"I mean, continue where we left off," she looks at him as though groping for any reaction from him.
"Ummmm…..I don't remember, had too many beers to remember anyways," he says looking at the glass of beer in front of him.
"You were talking about women with a specific type of hair that you are fond of. I think the last we had spoken you said you liked brunette, blonde, and I forget the other category?"

"Yes, I believe I said I like all women, especially the ones with blonde hair or even brunette. But yes all women would be desirable if I had a chance to have them."

(Pause) He smiles non-chalantly as she looks at him stunned as a deer in the headlights.

"*This guy is getting horny. Time for my next move*," she thinks to herself.
"Instead of just staring at it, it would taste better if you drank it," she says looking at Ralph as he rubs his fingers over the contours of his beer glass.

He obediently drinks without saying a word.

"So what other things about these blond, brunette and 'women in general' do you like?"
"I like those that have a nice, big butt; shapely body and soft, tender breasts."

She is blown over by his frankness and puts up an act to show she is not moved by his statement. The alcohol is obviously having its effect in loosening him up.

"Do you like them tall, short, medium…?"
"I prefer petite, but hot is always desirable."

She notices he hasn't asked her a single question about her likes and preferences as far as mates go. That's a good sign for her purposes. It means he is becoming more focused on what she wants to know rather than pursuing his agenda of obtaining information about her.

"So you ready to try out the bar of all bars?" she asks seeing him finish the glass of Terrapin.
"I am."
"Okay. Let's go then."
"Hey Johnny. Thanks for the Terrapins."

She places a $20 bill on the bar table as she puts her hand on Ralph's shoulder and descends from the high stool; her right stiletto almost coming off. Ralph realizes why many Americans have few savings in spite of having sizable amounts of income. It's probably because their weekend lifestyle revolves around splurging dollars earned during the week. Or maybe not. But seeing Matty lay down dollar bills like pocket change seemed impressive. Especially to his frugal, savings-oriented Asian mentality; spending on beers and shots at a bar was considered unnecessary and wasteful. "You got to get used to American ways of enjoyment," the Inner Voice began to tell him.

Ralph grabs her by the elbow as she stabilizes herself.

"How about a hug next time sweetie?" says Johnny from across the bar. "Yes. And I am going to grab you so tight; it's going to get the wind out of your lungs!" she smiles.
"I thought you guys would be staying longer?"
"We'd love to. But we have a couple of friends to meet. I am just showing him around bar city. He's new here."
"Okay. Well, enjoy buddy. (slight pause) Ralph right?"
"You bet," says the now relaxed and calm Ralph.

Ralph instinctively grabs Matty by the flank as he rolls his palms across her smooth, slender torso. He can feel his male instincts going into action pushing him to embrace, kiss and cuddle her. But the principled Asiatic celibate in him is still at large and cannot allow his carnal instincts to prevail even in free America.

Matty senses his manly traits taking control as well, as she feels his well-rounded arms and relatively muscular body wrapping around her. She feels the gratification of her attempt to seduce the young lad paying off. She can't wait for the final act of human gratification. They walk out the door and into the cool breeze of the May night towards the bar of all bars.

"Crazy River is known for the way it is because of the binge drinking and beer drinking contests they have there. It has a post-Renaissance European feel to it. The drinks are without a doubt the very best and the bartenders are award winners in several bartending competitions."
"You been to this bar a lot?"
"Well, not as much as the one we just came out from."
"You seem to know so much about this one!"
"Oh I'm just babbling. Because I like this one so much. It's a shame. Sometimes this place is so crowded we barely get to enter. But it's the crowd, the conversations and the people that make this place so much fun."

"Oh. Okay."

As they approach the bar, Ralph can clearly see a plethora of people through the tinted windows. For some reason, it seems almost like a can of corned beef with liquid flowing through the perimeter of the can. The liquid almost seeming like it is going to erupt from the can."

Ralph begins to feel the push and pull of the beers and the Terrapins. They seem to be exercising a weird control on him. The sort of control that the conscious mind wouldn't know and which ecstasy cannot reason with. "You probably should have kept the drinks more concentrated to water and lime rather than aerated spirits," says the Inner Voice.

"You always advise me after the fact!" Ralph drools.
"What!" Matilda exclaims.
"No sorry. I was thinking out loud," he quickly tries to shipshape himself.
"Crazy River is a bar with a difference for a reason," she says.
"What's that?" he asks.
"You'll find out."

As they reach the threshold, the rotating doors open up with crispy smoothness. Inside a melee of self-satisfied and indulgent people seem to unconsciously welcome the visitors. The sloping ramp is turquoise colored with designs of mermaids and fresh water fish strewn all over. The floor is very evenly laid out to afford a comfortable standing space; almost devoid of steps and heights. The atmosphere seems to be full of romance with a burlesque vibe of fun and entertainment......,"*a queer combination*" Ralph thinks. The décor all around is of painted mirrors and shiny surfaces. Almost like the moon above a sandy grey floor with a turquoise river flowing into the sandy mass.

The circular feel of the area gives a ship-deck like feeling while being inside of a submarine. As they slowly descend down the aisle, Ralph instinctively grabs her hand. He needs to make her feel that he is a chivalrous man and that they are not just friends. But something more....probably very very good friends. Friends that hold hands and probably even kiss and smooch. More so he wants her to feel protected. To a stranger, they would seem like a couple very much in love. Ralph knows, though, that Mum's home teachings do not allow boyfriend-girlfriend relationships although it is perfectly normal and sometimes necessary to have these relationships in the States.

"Why don't you grab me a little closer on the waist. I might fall you know," she sneers at him suggestively.

He obediently reaches for her waist as his chest touches her shoulder. She smiles slyly. She knows that the loosening up process is beginning to work. Less than an hour ago, it would have been impossible to get him to hold her waist or get this close to her.

"Why don't they have steps here?" Ralph asks seeing the smooth flat land that looks like a sea with hard ground.
"That's why it's called Crazy River; a river with the feel of sea, sand and mermaids."
"That's why people seem to be in love here," she explains.

It seemed so right. Everywhere he looked people were either kissing, cuddling or in emotionally intensive physical lockdowns. The atmosphere, although peaceful, seemed charged with love making electrons. *"Was this Matty's ultimate intention for the night. To get me drunk and top it off with sensual love making,"* Ralph wondered in his semi-drunk state.

The bar area is amazingly empty of people as everyone seems to be crouched up close to the couches and the ends of the bar perimeter close to the windows. No wonder Ralph felt the place looked like an over-packed sardine can from the outside. The center of the bar seems less populated so that's where the Ralph Matty couple decide to camp out while in Crazy River.

"This place is so cool. Don't you think," she avers.
"Yes, it has a nice décor."
"And a nice crowd and of course, great drinks."

(Short pause) Ralph doesn't react.

"Speaking of which, what would you like to drink?"
"Oh, I am fine. Not really thirsty or anything."
"You can't say that in Crazy River. It is a tradition in here to have some drink whether you want it or not. And if you can't pay for it, they give you for free," she bawls.
"For free? Does that ever happen in any bar?"
"Yes. It does here. Ask Jimmy, my favorite bar attendant," she signals to a short, portly man as she smiles effusively.

Her beauty is accentuated as she smiles; the dimples on her cheeks reflecting her smooth skin in an undulating fashion. For a moment, Ralph is taken aback by her goddess-like looks. *"Did the drinks make her complexion so good. She surely didn't look this good at the start of the evening. Or is it just the effect of the lights in the bar. Or probably because the beers have begun having an effect on my senses!"* Ralph wonders and is not able to reach a definite conclusion. *"I hope the drinks have not already clouded my judgement. Probably they have."* He looks for the inner voice and can't seem to find its faintest of rumblings.

****

"Hey Matty. Long time no see. How you been?" says Jimmy delightfully.
"I've been around. Good to see you."
"And this good looking guy is your …..?"
"My boyfriend!!"
"Woah…so you finally have someone special! Time for celebration."

Ralph although a little shaken at first is pleasantly surprised by her forthrightness. But prefers their 'no longer friends but lovers' kind of description. It also shows him her approval of their relationship and indeed her interest.

"How about some drinks then," asks Jimmy almost sounding plainly business.
"2 vodkas would be great. Which do you have?" she asks in a matter of fact fashion.
"Ummhh, I could do with just water," Ralph feebly admits.
"Come on this is celebration time. You must have our traditional vodkas," insists Jimmy. She winks at Jimmy with full approval.
"Yup. He's right. If you don't want to drink it, I will gladly drink your share," she smiles.

Ralph is speechless.

"Which type of vodka would you like? We have grain, potato, wheat and rye and grape."
"One potato and one grape would be great."
"Good choice lady!"
"You're the best Jimmy!" she thunders.

"See how easy it is to get the best drinks ordered. Vodkas are supposed to be the 'everyday special' of this place."

"Oh really!" Ralph winces.

"Yes. I don't know why they call it Crazy River instead of Vodka River."

"Is their vodka very powerful?"

"No, it's like any other vodka. But it's served in style. Have you had vodka before?"

"Well, I've.."

"No you haven't," she blurts without allowing him to complete. She knows he's a fuddy-duddy who hasn't tried anything.

"Well you need to try this and I won't take a no for an excuse. Got it!"

"Umm....yes."

"Here you go sweetie. Enjoy!" gushes Jimmy as he places the silver tray with 2 bottles of vodka on the standup table near the bar.

"Always on target right Jimmy!" she smiles.

The blue and light green bottles are very tastefully set on the silver tray with two immaculately transparent connoisseur glasses.

Jimmy grabs the blue one by the base and pours it into one of the glasses. "I assume you like blue so I am going to give you the blue one first. And which one would you like Sir?"

"I'll try the green one."

"Cool!" he fills the glass with the liquid from the green bottle as he hands it to Ralph.

"Enjoy!"

"Next time Jimmy, we want a toast with you!"

"You bet Matty. I would love that!"

"Cool guy, isn't he," she mumbles to Ralph.

"Seems like a nice guy!"

"He sure is."

"Let's drink to us then."

She raises her glass for a toast as he ponders whether he should make the toast or not. An unsaid rule of making a toast in America is if you make the toast, you have to drink what's in your glass. And Ralph is not sure he can handle the punch that vodka renders. Not after the beers have already had their effect that is.

"To us and our friendship!" she gloats.

"It won't be friendship once we get horizontal," she quietly thinks to herself.

He dutifully raises his glass and carefully gulps down a sip of the potato based liquid from the green bottle.

"This is the essence of Crazy River. Fine vodka with great company and an ambiance to die for!"

"Once you get used to this kind of bar you won't want to come to any other types of bars. I started off going to the bars we went to before and finally ended up with this bar. That's how Jimmy and I are such good friends."

"You visit here often?"

"Absolutely!"

"You like Jimmy?" he smiles.

"Yes. He's a cool guy."

"So why haven't you asked him out!"

"Haha. Not in that way. I like him as a good friend."

"He seems to have the hots for you though?"

"I know. Which is why I told him you and I were together."

"Oh, so that was just to deflect him?"

"Not entirely," she glances at him with a gaze somewhere between a guess and as a matter of fact.

He takes another sip and feels the cold liquid pass down his throat. It feels a lot warmer once it reaches his belly. "I think I'm done with this," he specifies to her.

"What! You've just had like two or three sips. Is that all you can take. We haven't even started getting warmed up!" she looks at him a little worried.

"Umm. I could do one more sip. That's it."

"Well for my sake, try a little more. I will drive you home. You don't have to worry," she reassures him.

"Umm....I don't know."

"Well when I told Jimmy we were together, I meant it. Now will you try it....all of it?" she says hoping to garner his compliance.

"Interesting. You validate your statements so that you get me to try your favorite drink....ummm...now I thought you would want to drink all of it...no?"

"Yeah, I would. That's if I was not so nice and didn't want to give you the experience of having vodka in the best bar in town. But I am nice, sweet and…"

(Ralph interrupting) "And considerate and mellow and kind and beautiful. The most beautiful person I have ever met!" he smiles with a deep admiration.

"Awwww.....that's so sweet," she hugs him her breasts pressing tight against his chest. He instinctively grabs her tiny frame and places his lips on her forehead close to her hairline.

"I think I could drink this bottle. I have become a little 'alcohol immune'!"

"You'll get completely immune to alcohol if you hang around with me!" she quips.

"Oh yeah," he seems to agree instantaneously.

"Vodka is believed to have several health benefits."

"Is that why you drink it?"

"Yes. There are other reasons for which I drink it as well."

"Which are?"

"Vodka is often associated with a kind of love that is very sensual and passionate. And drinking it makes people feel that way."

"Is that good for blood pressure though? Because passion makes the blood pressure rise, doesn't it!"

"Well I'm talking about love here. Why would you be concerned about biology and blood pressure of all things? Get with the times Ralph!" she blurts.

He smiles generously as he drinks some more vodka.

"So how important is love to you. And what kind of love?"

"Oh gosh. You always have a statistical or quantitative question for everything. Kind of love as in?"

"Like sensual or platonic or some other kind of love?"

"Love is without a doubt probably the most important of things. Whether it's sensual or platonic doesn't really matter. Why? What kind of love are you used to?"

"I don't know," he replies curtly.

"Oh, I forgot. You are from India. You guys have a more conservative approach to love back there."

"Don't know about that. But I guess sensual love is always desired in any kind of relationship."

"So you have an interest in that kind of love too, huh."

"Who doesn't?"

(Pause) "Have you ever experienced it?" she asks shyly.

He glances at her with a look somewhere in between surprise and inappropriateness of her question.

"Oh I forgot. It's not appropriate to ask that even though we are together?" she seeks to get his affirmation. Your culture would forbid talking about those things I guess!" she continues.

He keeps drinking his vodka, ignoring her ranting. Long pause. She seems to be thinking if he is all of a sudden in a bad mood or rather what his state of mind is. She hopes it's not the former. Comments which are considered innocuous in one culture might seem explosive in another. She can't tell if the topic about his supposed virginity is within bounds from his point of view or not. But she is feeling the impropriety of having asked him that question.

"Not really. In my culture things are unfortunately done under wraps rather than openly. The people are the same, the urges the same; it's just society and social conditioning that adds complexity or simplifies the platform to interact. Some cultures make interaction easy; others make the same simple process a whole lot complicated," he says sounding almost philosopher like.
"What do you think the culture in America makes it?" she asks seeming interested.
"Too promiscuous," says the Inner Voice.
He conserves his urge to repeat the Inner Voice's words. "I don't know," he mumbles.
"Well, then why don't we find out!"
"Sorry!" he says looking surprised.
She flinches, concealing a naughty look on her face. "No. I was saying it would be nice to find out how the culture in the States makes it easy or difficult to foster man-woman relationships."

He is visibly shaken and tries desperately to show a straight face when in actuality he would love to blush the life out of himself.

She senses his male weakness and virility pull the composure away from him rendering him even weaker to the effects of the spirits. She knows the spirits; the vodka will soon render him a near vegetable. It always helps to have a subservient male when you need to give directions in love making.

"Looks like you are done with that bottle of vodka. Would you like another?"

"Nope. It was good though."

"Why don't you try this green bottle. I don't think I can finish it myself."

"Sure." The initial inhibition to drinking is overcome by a submission to her suggestions.

As he empties the green bottle of its contents and downs the liquid through his throat she looks at him with considerate eyes knowing that she is on the verge of getting even closer to him emotionally and physically.

"Ready to go?" she asks.

"Sure am," he says instinctively. They have had a long night and she feels ready to go home. She wanted to give him a taste of the bar life and get him to loosen up. That done, the other part of her agenda is ready for execution.

****

They stagger to their feet and he seems less stable than fifteen minutes ago. In the tradition of Crazy River couples, she grabs his hand and puts it around her waist. He clasps his fingers tightly around her soft flesh. They walk towards the exit and out the door. They slowly totter down the road towards where her car is. With the exception of a few passing taxis, there is absolute silence. She ponders how she is going to make out with this hunk. Women always seem to have this realm of thought in their head thinking through various matters, issues and concepts.

With the vodka taking effect, he is more like a subservient squirrel. She always liked to be in control of good looking men. But this experience would be even more stimulating. International, brown skinned and handsome; he was quite a cookie to enjoy. They delicately separate as she enters the car and signals him to the other seat. He lands heavily in the seat, the effect of the beers and the vodka seeming apparent.

As they drive, the car running as smooth as a calm river; they say nothing. Matty makes a turn and drives up her driveway. "Come on, let's go upstairs and watch a movie or something," she says as she places her hand on his.

261

He obediently walks behind her; not saying a word. He seems calm, composed and is probably a little tired. He could do with a night of sleep.

She opens the front door and holds it ajar as he enters. She closes it behind her, then grabs his hand and guides him up the stairs into her room. All the while being careful not to disturb the other occupants of the house.

She quickly pulls him into the room, shuts the door and turns the light on to a dim level. "Feel at home. I thought you could spend the night here instead of going back home."
"Would you like anything to eat or drink?"
"No," he says as he slides into the silvery brown couch. He begins taking his shoes off and his belt. Places them beside the sofa and his belt on the charpoy next to the armrest.
"So tired huh?" she says.

He doesn't reply. Just lays down, hands spread out wide.

"Yeah. It can get tiring. But it's fun. With all the work that we go through throughout the week," she continues.
His silence is deafening. She takes off her light overcoat, grabs a white garment and heads into the bathroom inside the room.

"I'll be right back!" she motions to him.

When she is out, he is still deep in a semi-slumber state.

She has changed into a velvety negligee which is semi-transparent. Her party clothes lie hanging on a hook in the bathroom. Her well-shaped breasts and tender curves and contours are conspicuous through the translucent negligee.

"You tired?" she asks again hoping to arouse him a little when he slightly notices her new dress.

Seeing him still inactive she decides to try another approach. She runs down to the kitchen. In her lighter garments, she is fast and her legs move freely. She quickly grabs a bottle of Glaceau vitamin water, a glass and is back in the room in a jiffy.

She places the glass on the dresser and pours some water into it. Vitamin water could make the slumping hunk a little more active. She would need some action from his end for what she wants to do for the rest of the night with him.

She takes the glass and sits beside him on the couch, looking anxiously at him. There is nobody in the room, no distractions, no traffic on the road outside the house; pin drop silence. Just she, him and pin drop silence. He still doesn't stir; not even with the scantily clad girl sitting next to him.

"Ralph, you can't be that tired. We've been out just like three hours."

Still no movement from him.

"Here I bought you some vitamin water. It will make you feel better," she says to a limp Ralph.

She grabs his hand and shakes him to elicit a response. He moves suddenly as his hand hits the glass of water she is holding in her right hand.

"Oww!" she says as the water spills all over her thighs and the negligee she is wearing.

The sound shakes him from his dazed state. "Ohh, I'm so sorry! I didn't mean to ......"

He is dumbfounded on seeing her in her provocative negligee; aroused to the extent of losing his speech. The hangover of the beers and the vodka suddenly seems less powerful. The new hangover is the result of the girl in the negligee. The inner voice can no longer be heard and he feels this is one hangover he won't be able to get out of for a while.

"Feeling better!" she says sensing his captivation and confusion. She knows what can turn on even the most principled and stubborn of men. And past experience has taught her how to break men down and reduce them to their base instincts – creatures of weakness and lust. This Asian male had proven to be more resilient though. Resisting her initial moves, playing ignoramuse or simply not engaging.

He was now in a tender spot though. Under the influence of my negligee and the later foreplay, this hunk will not be able to resist!" she reassures herself.

He peers at her inquisitively. Checking her out without any embarrassment. He doesn't need to feel embarrassed. They are alone in a room and there is definitely a reason why she has brought him here.

"Feeling better?" she slyly says.

He simply smiles.

She places her hand on his thigh. "So how you feeling. Did you enjoy today dear?"
"It was great. Thank you for allowing me to be a part of it!"
"You are always welcome. You should come more often now that you know how it's done."
"Yeah. Absolutely."
"And you were great there. You got along with the bartenders and my other friends just fine."
"Well, I am glad you introduced and stuff. You were very helpful!"

She continues looking at him intently.

"And nice!"
"You are very nice too. And you need to learn to relax better, more often" she says as she gently caresses his forehead. "Else you will burn out quickly and won't have anything to show for it."
"Yeah!" he says as they both look into each other's eyes. She draws her face close to his and looks at his lips greedily. Her upper lip biting her lower lip profusely as she seeks some reaction from him.
He looks at her closely and smiles slightly as she lunges forward, grabs his face with her hands and locks lips with him. The Asian hermit in him doesn't resist. It is rather she who cannot resist the voluptuous hunk. It is already late in the night and the hunk is too handsome, too wasted to think of anything but love and passion. The female courtship drama is too time-consuming now. And she can't afford him to come up to speed in making the move on her. She decides to exhort him to yield to her.

They smooch for almost thirty minutes. His hands reach for her waist, then her torso, then higher, higher until they reach her soft breasts. Her negligee comes off to reveal only a g-string and her bare breasts. She starts unbuttoning his shirt as he squeezes her breasts.

His shirt off, she goes down to his pants. All the while he fondles her breasts as he begins to feel the heat of passion. As the kissing and the cuddling gets more intense she reaches for his underwear and tries to pull it off. She knows exactly where his touch points are. It is a function of experience. The experience of being in passionate dalliances with quite a few hunks. This hunk is more unique and queer though. He needs to be led into every bout of passion. As her fingers dig deep under his underwear, he feels titillated.

"Hunh?" he reflexively gestures and raises his head. She continues probing reaching deeper and gripping the elastic to pull down the flimsy undergarment. "Hunh!" he gestures again; this time a little more forcefully.
"It's alright honey" she flinches.

But he stirs again.

"You can't do this before marriage," screeches the Inner Voice finally arisen from its seemingly perpetual silence.

As she begins to tighten her grip on his pole, he grabs her hand and takes it off his property.

"What's wrong honey?" she says feeling more confused than frustrated about why any guy would resist such female stimulation.
"Ummhh!" he doesn't want to insult her neither does he want to allow this lascivious merrymaking to go forward.

She tries to grab his priced anatomy again. But this time he holds it, protecting it from her. She is a little surprised how the hunk just had one erection and then prevented any more sensual activity. None of her previous sexual encounters have been like this.

"Is this what one should expect from Asian romantic interests?" she wonders.

He keeps his hands over his penis like a protective sheath as he pulls his legs closer to him and tries to get some distance between her body and his. She keeps calm and although a little frazzled by his unloving behavior doesn't lose her temper.

"It's okay if you don't want to get close now. I understand," she calmly says as he begins to pull back his underwear.

Under her calm façade, there is a storm of questions brewing though. "What would make this handsome hunk want to resist her? He was so nice and chivalrous at the bar, all lovey-dovey; what could have changed so suddenly and so abruptly here? Did I do anything wrong; did I move too fast on him; or is it his Asian background that's preventing him from going ahead with what Americans consider as weekend night relaxation?" She just couldn't fathom what drove this guy to pull up his underpants. The size of anatomy definitely wasn't the issue since he had a sizeable length and no guy would feel embarrassed about it. Then why, she wondered.

She respectfully pulled herself away from him and began to put on her negligee. All the while maintaining her calm albeit confused demeanor. A unique trait among Americans is to understate facts so that the person at fault doesn't feel embarrassed or ashamed. Matty didn't want Ralph to feel embarrassed about not wanting or not being able to go ahead with the physical romance. But she was also relatively disappointed that he didn't have the courage to capitalize on an opportunity to get closer to her. She felt that he could have been more forthcoming in regards to bonding with her. She couldn't figure it out. But probably it was a mix of confusion, embarrassment and the fact that she was from a different culture that he couldn't loosen up when with her. Loosen up in terms of intimacy.

"People who hang out with you might not always want to have sex with you," she said to herself.
Feeling a little embarrassed, she puts on her night chemisette and pajamas to cover her voluptuous legs. Not that he would be interested in doing anything more. But he seems to have withdrawn interest in her. Too frozen by the thought of fornicating and getting horizontal before marriage. Too frozen to dare violate the instructions of his Inner Voice. The voice that is symbolic of his Asian upbringing and the parental discipline epitomized by his Asian-European mother.

She comes back to the couch and slowly drops on the far corner from him. Looking at him silently all the while. Trying to figure out what could make this hunk loosen up. Or why is he so averse to having casual sex; when all it does is improve bonding besides giving amazing relaxation.

"So you're tired, I guess," she tries suggesting an excuse to reason out why he doesn't want to go ahead with lovemaking. Being experienced in the art of love making she knows it would be stupid to suggest any other reason for his lack of interest in sex. Least of all celibacy, discipline or impotency. She doesn't suspect impotency as she did see his sizeable erection at the start of their foreplay. "It takes a rare kind of man to come to square one from that level of arousal!" she thinks. But that rarity makes her want him all the more.

"Yes. I just want to lie down," he says as he puts his jeans back on and pulls a sheet onto his bare chest.
He tries to close his eyes prematurely fearing he won't be able to face her after the embarrassing withdrawal and his rejection of her sexual overtures. No girl likes to be rejected when she is the one who makes the first move. But Matty was good at keeping her calm. She continues looking at him as he feigns exhaustion and tries to fall asleep. He knows he can't open his eyes now. Not until morning.

Then she slowly moves away and lies on her bed. Disappointed but hopeful that things will change for the better. That the handsome hunk will, in fact, loosen up sometime in the not too distant future. The fling with Matty came at a good time for Ralph. He was just smarting from the wounds of a raucous dismissal from the social engineering class group. Her attention proved to be a major confidence boost for him after the ignominy of being chucked out of the group.

****

Sitting in the library, Ralph feels the blandness of anything happening on the social engineering team side. A day has passed and no judgment, no punishment. Everything seems eerily inactive. Sensing something brewing, he feels the need to draft an email explaining his side of the story to the professor. Particularly since he wasn't allowed to sit in when they were complaining to the professor. As he types he brings forth the gross lack of concern that team members showed while working out project details and assigning project tasks. His nascent exposure to the work culture in the US leaves him baffled in regards to how unforgiving and callously intolerant executives and personnel can be to people joining fresh in the organization. He was not only new to the work culture but was dangerously new and inexperienced in regards to US work culture. As he types out the email he points out fundamental changes in the way attitudes and work cultures in the US differ from those in other parts of the world.

And then the unthinkable happens. As he finishes the email and clicks the send button; he finds another email in his mailbox. It's from the person he suspected of the double role and double standards. He realizes before opening the email that the painful was bound to happen. He'd rather just go with the flow now and try to salvage some pride rather than get engaged in a pitched battle of revenge. In a peremptory email, Dr. Panini states in a decent fashion a very harsh fact.

"Ralph, after going through the evidence piled against you, I think the fair thing to do would be to remove you from the group as the trust in you is too damaged to be repaired this late in the semester. I will give you another project to work on in lieu of your final project assignment. You will not be graded on this project.

Signed,

Dr. Panini"

Ralph was stunned looking at the short, curt and almost emotionless email. There didn't seem to be any sort of credible explanation about his side of the story in the email. Just a judgment. A pretty strong one at that. *"Was justice always this hard, this direct in the US! Or was it mere discrimination in this case because he was from another country and didn't know the rules and norms in the US?"* he wondered.
There was very little he could do though. The decision had already been rolled out and chances of recanting the decision were not even remotely slim. They were just non-existent. At least that's what it seemed like.

"It is a shocker when you are not even given a chance to a fair trial in a democratic setup like that in the US," wondered Ralph. That mere circumstantial evidence can sway the decision making authority against you. In spite of the horrid news, Ralph had one consolation at least. The days of praying and hoping that the worst wouldn't happen had ceased.

The judgment was out and there was nothing more to do but look to the future and plan next steps effectively.

It's so strange, but sometimes the very act of waiting is more painful than the judgment itself. Several defendants and accused lose control or go insane simply waiting for the judgment. The actual judgment ceases to have any effect on them thereafter. The damage that the judgment was meant to inflict proves too impotent. Long drawn out suffering is worse than sudden shock.

The slowness in understanding what hit you makes the difference between crushing defeat and temporary shock. I would any day prefer the temporary shock to the long drawn out suffering of having to endure a painful eventuality that is coming closer every day.

The isolation created by the expulsion from the team is difficult to bear. But the verdict cannot be overturned since laws in the US fall under two categories: those that are for the poor and those applicable to the rich. All laws apply to the poor. For the rich, though, there are barely any laws that could touch them. Except of course, if they kill or physically hurt somebody. In this case, it was a poor foreign student who wasn't aware of the intricacies of academic decorum in the US. What was the practice in India wasn't considered correct or excusable in the US. In fact, it was regarded as an offense and worthy of prosecution in the States.

Ralph still felt that there ought to have been a better way of going about the whole thing than just running over people and prosecuting them. Well-meaning people who commit innocuous offenses inadvertently need to be given a chance to present themselves before the law and explain their legitimate reason for doing what they did. Not giving them a chance to present their case and over and above passing blanket verdicts amounts to a double penalty. It's an insult to injury.

His earlier email to Dr. Panini and his former teammates receives no reply. He realizes it is futile to discuss or argue with these people since it will only aggravate the situation. There is not much left to do. It is clear that Americans have a long way to go to understand the difficulties faced by international students or simply immigrants for that matter. Just as immigrants struggle to understand the nuances of the American way of life.

As this conundrum of mutual misunderstanding clouds his mind he realizes the factors which are within his control and those which are not. He realizes that he can change his method of studying and working and deliver quality results in breakneck time. He realizes that the strength of his work is only in his hands and nobody else's. That perseverance and determination could get him where others had reached through years of experience and by simply being in a certain place. There was only one way to shorten the learning curve of his America adjustment – dive deep into whatever that he is doing and try to learn it inside out. That was the key to getting things done and achieving success.

Dr. Panini summons him to a meeting in his office. During the meeting, it becomes clear that the professor doesn't want to be lenient or make an exception for the young Ralph. No exception even though he is an international and knows not the rules of the game in the US. Rules governing plagiarism that are virtually non-existent or not as strongly enforced as in the US are a new novelty for Ralph. And he feels amused that these are so seriously enforced in the land of democracy and freedom. Only later will he learn that with freedom comes great responsibility and it is in this bastion of democracy that enforcement walks side by side with freedom. Often times this enforcement can also be overdone. But it's an inevitable part of America.

"Firstly, do you have any questions for me?" asks Dr. Panini.
"No. But I was wondering if the decision could be reversed?"
"No, the decision stands. Once given there is no reversal," Dr. Panini replies curtly.

It is clear the person who committed the offence is looked at from a very negative light, no matter how innocent the offender might be. Often times, ignorance of a law is not considered as a valid reason for breaking it. The offender is looked at in the same light as someone who knowingly broke the law. Even inadvertent violation of the law is taken very seriously. Dr. Panini doesn't seem to be in the mood to negotiate or compromise the reason he has removed Ralph from the team. He is unapologetic and strangely neutral about the whole thing.

Ralph feels the injustice in the way the proceedings were conducted to remove him from the group. Information being given to the professor behind his back without he being there to defend himself. A fair trial is one in which the defendant is allowed to provide suitable reasons in his or her defense. In this case, there was no opportunity to present a defense.

Seeing the professor's lack of reaction he realizes that the email he sent has had no effect on the professor. "An important fact about culture in the US is people don't get friendly or close to you easily. They aren't as welcoming like people in the Orient. Moreover, in this particular group my ideas weren't even taken into consideration," he remonstrates to Dr. Panini. Sporting a blank look on his face, the professor seems either to not understand or feigns not understanding. Ralph is bewildered by the professor's behavior.

Back home teachers were concerned about the welfare of their students and the issues that they faced. Or at least that's the impression they gave. In the States, it all seemed like a mighty hogwash; a smokescreen of 'I like you, but I am not concerned about you. And honestly, you don't matter' kind of thing.

"Here the laws and indeed the people generally don't go to consider the circumstances that motivated a certain response or action. It is more convenient to emphasize that if you are not on the right side of the law you are in trouble. Or rather there cannot be a middle ground where you can hope to survive; unless of course if you are one of those folks born with a silver spoon in their mouth and with a trust fund to their name," Ralph elaborates.
"But you are here. How will you get things done with that mindset!" Dr. Panini questions.
"Well that's the way the world thinks. In the US, things are done differently and I guess I have to accept that because what choice do I have?"

Dr. Panini looks at him with a look of pity and irritation; more pity because he doesn't know how to make the young man understand that life is harder than what he thinks it is or what it has been so far. Internally he wants to let Ralph know that he has got the lighter side of the deal. He wasn't removed from the course nor was he given a very heavy penalty in terms of losing a large part of the grade. But the professor doesn't seem to have the time or patience to discuss these things with the young lad.

"Well, your team is not off the hook either. I am going to look at them with double the amount of scrutiny and check why they couldn't resolve this situation themselves."

Ralph looks at him with no reaction wondering what kind of consolation the professor is trying to give him saying his former teammates are still on the hook. It doesn't change the fact that he has been removed from the team or that he is not being graded on the group project which was deduced plagiarized. It doesn't change the fact that he was publicly shamed through the email sent to the whole class.

"So how does that help me out?"
"It's a good thing that you are not on the team because they are not getting your assistance in doing the project while you are not getting graded on the project," the professor justifies.

Ralph is stunned by the audacity of the professor's efforts to package a horrible thing into something more bearable or positive. He calls excommunication from a team as not giving your assistance to them thereby indicating you are at an advantage and they are at a loss. And he sugar coats you not being graded on a project as a small loss for you. In other words they lose a point, while you lose a point kind of analogy. Though, in actuality, Ralph is the one losing both points. Americans know how to market and package facts – they would market even a difficult fact in a very rosy fashion. Ralph realized the need to learn this skill. The reality though was that Ralph, as the inadvertent committer of the mistake, had been totally on the receiving end of things and had lost the most.

America is all about packaging. Even if you package a hard truth or situation in a positive light you stand to gain from it; especially if the other party is not in the emotional or physical state to combat your claims. Packaging and marketing go hand in hand. The better the tag line and marketing effort the better the sales irrespective of the quality of the product. The product does need to be of a basic quality though. Eventually though people will find out your product or service is not worth the words you associate with it. But before that realization is reached, sleazy businessmen would have made their mini fortune.

"But they aren't losing any of their grades so why should I?" questions Ralph peremptorily.

"Okay. So I can give you another project to do by which you will be graded in place of the one you weren't allowed to do," says the professor seeing the logic in Ralph's question and not seeking to enter into a further argument with him.

Ralph's spirits are uplifted with this move and he gives himself a much needed pat of encouragement. The encouragement is much deserved after all the humiliation of going through an excommunication from the group and public shaming by sending an email to the whole class about his removal.

He walks out of the professor's office feeling energized that there is at least some hope of redemption for him. The idea of burning the midnight oil to attain superlative results doesn't ring any truer than now. These are not the days when he would go to the school chapel and pray to the Lord to give him better results in his exams. These are testing times when actual delivery is what counts, not just theoretical knowledge and rote learning. It's not just about passing a test but providing effective insights into the work done so that the person reading the deliverable feels that some constructive work has been done.

"India wasn't even the frying pan. This academic struggle is going to take a lot of creative genius to put out. I am going to have to think on my feet!" thinks Ralph to himself as he climbs the stairs towards his part-time job as a graduate assistant in the computer science department.

He starts researching and googling several topics as they relate to social engineering, team dynamics and several other topics. The case study given by Dr. Panini is a complex one but not impossible to crack if sufficient research is conducted. As he feverishly works on the case study while simultaneously fulfilling his graduate assistantship duties he can't help but be thankful that Dr. Panini didn't complain to the chair of the department. Could it have affected his employment as a graduate assistant had he complained? One can only speculate. But life is known to have its spill-over effects. And it's best that spills are contained before they snowball out of control. Is he thankful to God or to Dr. Panini? Without a shadow of a doubt to God. His Inner Voice is, in fact, a manifestation of God playing his life out; guiding him throughout.

Matilda texts him from time to time. And he occasionally runs into her at the library as well. But his new focus is not on relationships but on professional and intellectual advancement. She desperately tries to arouse him several times. Her miniskirts, sleeveless blouses and plunging necklines have become commonplace for him. His focus on professional advancement remains steadfast. On one occasion she persuaded him to accompany her to an inter-varsity student party. Dressed in a black micro mini skirt and white tank top she looks her most voluptuous self. She grabbed Ralph's hand and walked with him into the hall.

However, the focused lad felt no impulses or urges from the touch of the smooth lass. His interests are now part of a Pan American international student body that's as competitive and hungry as it is smart. They dance and hang around and eat the snacks at the party. All along he seems uncharacteristically robotic and tight-lipped. His lack of interest in her attempts to seduce him frustrates her.

She tries to make him jealous by flirting with another guy on the dance floor and all along he just appears to enjoy the music. Least bothered by what she is doing or whom she is dancing with.

"So you seem rather occupied with quite a few things these days!" she suggests as they walk to her car after the party.
"Just course-related stuff," he says nonchalantly.
"Don't I fascinate you anymore?" she asks probingly.
"I didn't say that."
(A long silence follows) "But you seem to have this uncanny lack of interest and attention going on. Looks like you are interested in something totally different or someone different!" she manages to squeeze the somewhat investigative statement out of her conscience; honestly not wishing to get into a controversy for doing so.

He seems to silently ponder over what she said. For a moment he seems to brood over it too. She passes a cursory glance at him and sees his face contorted like that of a nuclear scientist deep in thought. She flinches a little.

"What are you doing tonight?" she asks hoping to change the topic.
"You are right. I am more interested in other things and have been concerned with those things for a short while now. They are not to do with someone but with more important topics like studies and work-related stuff."

"Okay!!" she says with an artificial smile on her face.

"You mustn't worry so much about it. It's part of life. You need to get serious about life at some point. I have reached that point."

"I am not worried. I am just disappointed!" she says feeling resentful.

"You seem angry now!" he retorts as they walk farther from the college campus.

"No just disappointed!" her monotonous voice changes in frequency for the first time.

"Well I am not sure why you are disappointed or angry but you shouldn't be!"

"Easy for you to say!"

"What's the matter Matty?" he says turning directly towards her and holding her gently by the shoulders.

She wrests away from his grip and starts walking forward slowly. Ralph senses that she wants him to push and pursue her and make her feel like a million bucks. It's something about women when they don't walk away quickly and walk away by saying something in a low, relatively decent tone; they are not saying 'No.' They want to make amends and they usually want you to initiate it.

Ralph knows this. But the focused student is in no mood to negotiate. Studies and professional advancement are his top priority at the moment.

He feebly tries to grab her hand and make her understand. He understands what she feels but doesn't really want to empathize with her and make her feel like a million bucks. The Inner voice is categorical in its delineation of professional life and personal life. And at the moment it says 'No personal life' for a while. In the struggle to succeed in a foreign nation, there is usually a trade-off between personal and professional life. Invariably, personal life takes a backseat in favor of professional advancement.

She tries to reject his hand and then screams at him. "I don't mean anything to you anymore. Then why did you waste my time from the start? Didn't you have anything better to do?"

"What's this about Matty?" he asks feigning ignorance. When you are an international student or a no name immigrant in this country you have to play your cards well. The last thing you want is to lose a friendly person's help and support. It is no secret that getting help or becoming friends is difficult in the first place.

As he tries to reach out and hold her hand again she breaks into a boisterous fit and yells at the top of her voice. "You keep playing these games with me all the time. If you have some other bitch why don't you just go fuck with her and even dance with her? Why me!"
"What the fuck are you talking about?" he raises his voice, exasperated.
"You know what I am talking about," she growls.
"What!"
"Oh gosh. Stop it. Stop playing innocent. You have been cheating which is why you pretend to be impotent and don't seem to be ready to ever get cozy," she snarls and has glassy eyes. Tears seem imminent but she controls herself.
"So now you are accusing me of going around with somebody else. And also about the other thing!" he says angrily.
"Or no. Maybe you are just gay. You don't feel like it with any girl. You just go about flirting with different girls without doing anything with them!"
"You better watch your mouth, Matty! This is getting out of hand. Don't forget we are still on the road."
"So what, you scared that everyone's going to find out you're gay!"
"Shut the fuck up. I'm not gay."
"Oh yeah. Well, you just go around with some other girls and move with me for some reason."
"That's not the case."
"Well, you just go around with some other girls and go with me to parties but nothing ever happens after that. I guess that's quite a surprise isn't it!"
"That's not the case."
"Oh wait or maybe you feel pity for me since I am living alone here away from family and have had many family issues."
"If you want to fight this out, then I am not going to back down! But I am living away from family as well and wouldn't expect anybody to feel pity for me; let alone feeling pity for someone else who is like me," he explains.

A long silence ensues. Ralph doesn't do anything; no reaction, no attempt at rapprochement. This only adds to Matty's frustrations. Americans are very conscious of facial cues that reveal the behavior or potential attitude of a person to a situation. Not seeing any reaction from him leads her to believe that he is nothing but a limp dick and is only using her to go places and spend a weekend or holiday.

"Well really Ralph. It just doesn't seem to be working and I frankly have had enough of you. You just lamely go around, don't show any enthusiasm, feel entitled and are just not active enough to have sex. You suck! I don't want to have anything to do with you again. Please don't call me ever. Bye!" she says disappointedly and walks away.

He stands there dumbfounded and cool as a cucumber. As she rushes home full speed ahead; her buttocks seem to swell like jellos about to burst.

"*Man I should have at least boned that bitch quite hard. What was I doing!*" he says to himself. The inner voice had kept him under control for quite a while and the difficult situations he faced at school and in the social engineering team ensured his ability to flirt was at its minimum.

He begins walking slowly home. By now her short skirt is only a tiny object along the darkening road of that late Pennsylvania evening. Their relationship seems effectively ended. And Ralph doesn't seem to be in the mood to try to resurrect it. Not to mention Matty is totally crestfallen with his lackadaisical attitude to their interactions. Sometimes with women, even American women; pursuing them when they don't want anything to do with you might be the best way to get the relationship working again. But this was not one of those cases of reconciled love.

He reaches home, says a prayer and resolves that the coming semesters will be better than all the previous ones. He knows one thing – and the Inner voice doesn't have to second this fact. But hard work always pays!!!

THE SMART APPRENTICE

THE SEPARATION WITH MATTY was not nearly as painful as the removal from the group in the social engineering class. Although he did have mixed feelings about that relationship, Ralph does wonder if there could have been anything deeper to that fling with her. *"Probably not,"* he says to satisfy his apprehension.

Firstly, she is from a different culture than he is and secondly her idea of fun is diametrically opposite to his concept of fun and frolic. Still, the two might have been able to be closer than close. But becoming soul mates is an entirely different ball game. For that, there needs to be love between two people. Was love there between the two? The Inner Voice always told him that love could not be easily developed between people from different cultures. Or even if love were able to develop; marriage would be a totally different endeavor altogether.

Probably he was attracted to her because of the physical aspect more than anything else. The preponderance of loneliness and boredom in the US is so great that one needs an outlet to talk and get to know someone other than your own mind. The loneliness and resulting frustration get even more accentuated with the constant rut of having to maintain academic recency and meritorious constancy. The grades need to be top notch; not to mention the need to gel and integrate with a diverse team. It can be quite a challenging proposition maintaining your calm and composure when a great deal of uncertainty and ambivalence about continuing life in the US continues to linger in the mind of the international student. There are so many laws and regulations preventing an international student from working here or even getting a part-time job. Until the paperwork is resolved and equal opportunity attained for these professional, but legally handicapped immigrants a lot of their life continues to remain in limbo.

"Should I continue to stay in the US or go back to India and get a fine job, a fine woman and be with the family?" is a question that regularly

haunts Ralph and which the Inner Voice is remarkably silent on. Sometimes he wonders why the Inner Voice is so non-committal in regards to this major life decision of whether to cut and run or to stick it out in the so-called land of opportunity. For now, though, the decision seems to be left up to him to make.

Winding up and leaving is not a worthwhile option at this point. Not so early in the game and not when he still hasn't obtained the Master's degree he came to the US for. Mum was always very particular about goal achievement. Getting a Masters from the US was an integral part of that goal. It is too common that you come here to achieve educational goals and in the bargain end up being lost in the maelstrom of free-floating ideas and next steps in one's career direction. Feeling lost is not a good state to be in. But every immigrant in the US has gone through it; at least to some extent. Ralph was no different. He wasn't the son of a millionaire or a 'trust fund baby', but a mere lad who had strong sinews and lofty ambitions.

It's amazing where high ambitions can get you. Ralph was a product of unfettered ambition. And his accidental though unfortunate debacle from the social engineering class team served as a catalyst to strive and do even better. He would use the latest techniques, the most innovative approaches and little-known resources to complete assignments and work tasks as best as possible. A man set on a goal is all that's needed for luck to meet opportunity.

During the database class, Professor Alamuddin seems to be a task master. His lectures are fast paced; too fast actually and he packs quite a punch into them. The amount of technical knowledge doled out in these sessions is massive and very industry-related. No doubt it is difficult to understand and absorb all of it. But on the flip side, there is a great incentive if you do well in his class. Ralph had heard of this incentive from a couple of his senior colleagues; the guys he was living with before he moved into International House.

Ralph thought this incentive to be decent enough to work hard towards getting an A in the course and doing well in the subject of databases. Besides, the doctor's tall claims that there are a lot of job openings in the database and data warehousing sector was enough to look forward to the database class and do it well. Well one certainly wouldn't find their future mate in this class since the complexity of the subject ensures that more men than women enroll in it. But the sheer magnitude of competitive students ensures that the course is a high velocity, high learning experience.

Ralph visited the library three times a day now. His study sessions were filled with conscious research at breakneck speeds. *"There has got to be a faster way to master all this information all at once,"* he said to himself. As he researched the ins and outs of the multifarious databases and Google links, he realized the preponderance of eBooks and the difficulties involved in obtaining the complete versions of these books. He used to be an amateur hacker in his 'bachelor's degree' days and was quite hated for it by his peers. *"Why not resurrect those skills for better end results!"* he thought.

Through a combination of prior knowledge, situation based cues and sheer presence of mind he manages to find eBook dispensing websites. One of them provides e-Books for free and is exactly what Ralph was looking for. As the days go by his state of occupation affords him very little time for extracurricular activities and for socialization. So engrossed is he in work that female interests, porn or random thoughts don't even occupy a micro-millimeter of his brain's attention.

He keeps downloading different kinds of books and white papers. Sometimes there are very few ways to succeed except by burning the midnight oil. That is the sure shot way to imbibe learning and knowledge and achieve goals. Thomas Alva Edison was right when he said, "Success is 1% inspiration and 99% perspiration!" Ralph prints the quote on a large sheet of paper and pastes it on the wall in front of his table in his room. The quote keeps him grounded, he feels. But what also keeps him focused is his intense sense of purpose to succeed and to do well after the ignominy of being let go from the 'social engineering' team so unceremoniously.

****

One fine day, as he is sitting in the library surfing the bulletin boards of various clubs, he chances upon a 'corporate internship' announcement. The internship is in premier companies like Siemens, SAP and a few others. His eyes widen with amazement and greed. Having an internship is a faster way to a full-time job than applying from a scratch. "You need to get this internship!" speaks out the Inner Voice. He is surprised listening to it. The Voice hasn't spoken in a long time and he wonders if it is of any consequence at this point. Sometimes when your core being focuses hard, there is no need of a third eye, a sixth sense, or an inner voice. Your knowledge and wisdom become the Inner Voice. The powers of the earth that are; become your guidance and light. The beacon of hope in an otherwise desolate terrain.

Ralph knows that he needs to acquire an internship. The question is how and in which company? An interesting aspect of being international in this land is the sheer confusion that arises from not knowing what to do, where to be, and which activity gets you the most bang for the buck. Confusion arises from the dilemma of being in a foreign country while having the ability to continue with life in your home country. Life as a first class citizen in the home country versus life as a second class citizen in a foreign country, with the hope of a potentially better future with more money, more opportunities and better prospects is the primary cause of this dilemma. The difficulties that one temporarily faces trying to setup in a foreign country are sometimes considered unnecessary as opposed to the wide-ranging openings that are available in a developing country like India. But then again if you do well in the wealthiest country on the planet; the jackpot never seems to run out; unless you do something abnormally stupid.

****

Ralph's everyday routine involves going to the admissions office and working as a database administrator, monitoring the queries and the flow of data between various systems. He tends to come across several students, university staff and stakeholders in his job. Three days after his learning of the internship opportunities he meets Madhu, his old roommate again. "Hello Big Boss Man!" says Madhu with his characteristic Telugu accent. Ralph doesn't fancy speaking to Telugu people a whole lot and generally tries to stay away from them. However, Madhu is a little different. Ralph has had a history of close encounters when he roomed with Madhu. He vividly remembers the day he faced a drunken roommate trying to intimidate Madhu. Madhu barely put up a fight so Ralph had to jump in and resolve matters. After a swift blow to the side of the drunk roommate's stomach, Ralph dispatched him to his room by holding the scruff of his neck and dragging him into the booze-smelling room.

Madhu and Ralph had got tired of the alcohol-infested shenanigans that this aberrant roommate would commit. Though Madhu could not do much to show his displeasure with this behavior except ignore Prasad. He simply lacked the wherewithal to physically threaten Prasad or maintain his own spatial integrity in the shared apartment. Madhu was too soft, too mild and physically too weak to contest the abominable behavior that Prasad so often exhibited to the occupants of the apartment. Prasad, on the other hand, was tall and broad shouldered. He would stomp all over the apartment with his hairy legs. When he got unbearably intoxicated he would just drop on anybody's bed and puke.

Madhu had several such instances and finally couldn't take it anymore. Fortunately, Ralph was there to physically back him up when he contested Prasad. Ralph had helped Madhu in other instances as well. It was for this and his general liking of Ralph that Madhu always shared information with him openly.

"Long time no see!" says Ralph.
"Yes I've been in hiding," smiles Madhu.
Ralph is a little surprised at his use of American parlance. *"Ummhh, could he speak like this before?"* he wonders. *"Surely there must have been some exposure to Americans outside of the university!"* he thinks.
"So what has kept you in hiding?" he asks curiously, seeking more information into his sudden change of demeanor and style.
"I actually got an internship at Siemens so have been doing that for the last three months," Madhu smiles.
"That's awesome man. What are you doing there?" Ralph asks seeming casual.

There is good enough reason to want to seem casual. Excessive curiosity in the professional accomplishments of a colleague can be viewed with suspicion, particularly when both individuals are in the same field. Among internationals in the US, there is always an element of jealousy and competition when it comes to professional advancement and opportunities. Best of friends deny each other information about quality opportunities for the specific reason to avoid competition. Moreover, there is always the idea of one-upmanship over the other. If I am better off than the other person; my friend and rival, I get to show off and he doesn't.

In such situations obtaining information should be done in a very subtle fashion without giving away the slightest indication of data extraction or spying. People can be very cliquey and closed when it comes to providing information to colleagues or people who they feel threatened to interact and share information with. Ralph had been in situations like that before and had learned a thing or two about not opening up a can of worms in regards to generating suspicion about one's intentions.

First rule about not arousing suspicion: Do not ask a direct question!

"I am a student intern working on defect tracking for their Soarian medical management software."
"Man, that's so cool. Now I have to call you Mr. Manager huh!" he says.
"I don't mind being called manager but I am a mere intern. And thanks for the promotion by the way!" replies Madhu.
"So how did you get it?"
"I applied online and got it," replies Madhu. He continues looking at Ralph as though that was the most simple, basic question he had ever heard.

Ralph looks at him and pretends he is not surprised. Internally he wonders how a gulti[17] like Madhu can get into Siemens. "If he can get into Siemens so can you. That gulti ain't better than you!" reinforces the Inner Voice. After a long time, the inner voice seems to have spoken and is beginning to speak more forcefully lately. That's a good omen. Mum would always tell Ralph to see the omens and align his actions with the level of favor the omens afford. It helps to have the cosmos on your side before taking any big initiative.

"That's really cool man. So what brings you to admissions today?" Ralph asks, wanting to change the topic. It is always wise to change the topic quickly when opportunity related information is discussed so that the other person does not feel you are trying to extract information from them. Questioning should be done in a smart fashion without making people feel that detailed information is sought. How much information

---

[17] Gulti - Derogatory term to mean Telugu person from Andhra Pradesh, India.

you obtain from people is a function of how effectively you talk and interact with them.

"I had come to get my transcripts from here so I thought of coming down and saying hi to you!" he smiles.

Ralph is surprised with this guy's forthrightness. "Woah, that's very nice of you Madhu!"

"*Did this guy want something from me or did he just genuinely drop by to say hello?*" wonders Ralph to himself. Gultis were known to make friends with people for two of many things. Firstly, to ask them about how they got a job and the other was to know how much someone's salary was.

Ralph was not interested in speaking to anyone about either of these topics. He considered these off limits to speak to anybody about except Mum. "*Probably this guy is grateful that I saved his ass when Prasad was about to beat him to a pulp!*" Ralph thinks to himself.

"So how have things been going with you? What's new?" asks Madhu.

"Same ol, same old! I have been here for quite a while. Doing the same old thing. Working in this GA office since the beginning of time," he smiles at Madhu.

"It's time to apply for an internship man. I am sure you will get it."

Ralph looks at him with great surprise. For the first time in his short life in the US, someone has approached him with a piece of constructive advice. And that too for future resource and faculty development.

"Yes I have been thinking of that. But the only thing is I am not sure which company to apply for," he winces.

"Apply for Siemens man. We have lots of student internship positions. And I am sure they would need your top notch skills!" replies Madhu. For once, Ralph feels a gulti being genuine. "*It must definitely be because of the help I gave him when Prasad was about to make him lick the floor. And he always liked my work ethic,*" Ralph thinks to himself.

"Oh really. And all these are in computer science is it?" he tries to confirm with Madhu.

"Yes of course. All you need to do is apply!" he smiles.

"Yes, I will."

"Well let me know if you need any help. I am developing my contacts in the company. So networking can also help sometimes. Though I doubt you would need that!" exclaims Madhu. He knows Ralph has the capacity and the ability to prove himself on the job.

"I will certainly apply. Thanks."

"Well it was nice seeing you again Ralph. After such a long time!"

"Thanks for coming over Madhu. Let's catch up at the cafeteria or somewhere outside sometime."

"Yeah yeah. Just call me."

"Sure absolutely."

"Okay. Take it easy man," says Madhu as he pats Ralph's shoulder good bye.

Physical contact between Asian men is very common without any concern of being regarded as gay. In fact, it isn't even a concern. It goes without saying that many of them don't realize that in the States their sexual orientation might be looked upon negatively precisely because of the physical contact with other men. Albeit this physical contact is a mere pat on the shoulder or touch to the back. Being politically correct is an important aspect of living and working in the US. Several people, even the rich and famous have gotten into weird situations just because they failed to observe so-called 'politically correct' sensibilities of the place they were in.

"*I need to stop this now and start applying,*" says Ralph to himself.

He speeds up his work as he figures out a strategy to start applying for internships quicker. In another hour he is done with the admissions office work and requests an early day. The supervisor who happens to be Indian as well is only too happy to grant it since Ralph is one of the most productive of workers he has in that department.

****

Ralph reaches home and rushes to his room. He fires up the 'sleeping' laptop and completes the remaining half of his mission to refine his resume. He had started this immediately after hearing of several people applying for internships but hadn't quite completed it. The fateful meeting with Madhu has his juices fired up now and he completes the resume refinement within half an hour.

As he starts applying for the internship positions listed online, a random thought strikes him. "*How much of a chance do I stand in getting any of these positions?*"

285

"You never learnt to give up even when in Goa and you will not give up now. You will apply and reapply for the same position till you get a call telling you to apply no more!" the Inner voice is louder than it has been in a long time; louder than it has ever been actually. He knows the direction he has to go in now. The omens are pointing in the right direction and he is feeling the surge of strength in him. The barrage of applications begins.

He sees positions like compliance intern, data quality intern and computer engineering intern among others. He applies for all with the one resume. Exhaustion doesn't seem to bother him. In fact he seems to revel in it. Edison's motto posted on his wall is a constant reminder that perspiration and persistent endeavor is the way to a glorious future. There can be no shortcut to achieving the future he wants to achieve. Thomas Alva Edison didn't become great merely by sitting on his ass.

Two weeks pass and still not a single reply. He wishes to believe that he will not get the position. But the optimism of the Inner voice doesn't allow him to believe that. At midday, he occasionally goes to the cafeteria to sit down and see his former workplace. He could afford the $9 lunch but prefers to save and eat home-cooked meals. After about fifteen minutes of relishing memories of his cafeteria work days, he usually walks across the yard and sits under the acorn trees in front of the university chapel. There he thinks about the next steps he would need to take as he eats the mayonnaise sandwich he had packed at home in the morning.

The feeling of loneliness and being lost is always there. But a benefit of being an international student in the States for more than one and half years is the strength that one develops from being constantly on the receiving end of life and misfortune. Eventually one learns to ignore the disappointments and setbacks and focus on what was learnt from those follies. There is no escaping the pain that life in the land of the free and the home of the brave throws at you. The only reason for bearing all this though is with the hope that one day the pain will metamorphose into something sweet; something worth all the efforts taken to come to this country and stick it out.

On one such day as he was biting into the mayonnaise sandwich his phone begins to buzz with the cricket ringtone he had applied to it. It's a number he hasn't saved or seen before but which looks to be from the area. With the morsel of sandwich and ham still in his mouth, he accepts the call. "Hello," he says suppressing the juices from the delicious sandwich.

"Hi, this is Heather from Siemens Medical Solutions. Could I speak to Ralph please," says the sexy sounding voice on the phone.

His heart almost comes into his throat as he spits out the delicious morsel of food and clears his throat.

"Speaking!" he says as he clears his throat.

"How are you doing today Ralph?"

"Great! How about you?" Although he is not all that positive, it is customary policy to put up a brave and 'all good' front to a person you do not know. Especially when the person is possibly calling you about a job. All's well and hunky dory with you when someone calls you with a potential opportunity. No one in America or for that matter in most parts of the world would appreciate a low energy attitude. Successful people are known to pride themselves on high energy, vivaciousness and outreach. Being introverted, shy or low energy is looked down upon and is not generally a quality associated with leadership. Low energy, shy people are not usually recommended for jobs unless it is a heads-down clerical job or research intensive work.

Ralph had had experiences before when he had lost 'easy to obtain' opportunities due to his lethargy in demeanor and outlook. Presentation is a big part of one's personality and what you present is what the external world sees. If the interviewer sees you as not convinced or mentally unprepared for the job opening being discussed, he or she might as well not offer you the job. The Inner voice had been instrumental in keeping him in good order whenever his performance slipped. But this time, Ralph wanted it to be his head that gave him the instructions. Mum had taught him that reaching a stage where more is dependent on preparation rather than chance or luck is a more sought after scenario. Dad was different, though.

Dad believed that luck and chance are God's way of telling you what's meant for you; what's right for you. Dad always believed in the power of divine intercession, the omens. Mum believed in the omens too but not as strongly as Dad. She was a woman of unfathomable courage, wrought iron resolve and a believer in the miraculous power of a 'can-do' attitude.

****

"So I see you have applied to a couple of positions at Siemens. Is there a specific position you are interested in?" she asks with breakneck speed.
"I am interested in computer science positions since I am studying computer engineering."

"We have internship positions for IT students and I think that should match your profile."
"Okay."
"Would you be interested in that?"
"Yes, I would."
"Well, then you would need to resubmit your application for it. Two managers have indicated their interest in interviewing you. One position is for IT student intern, the other is for IT quality assurance intern."
"You could interview for one of the two or I could set you up for both," she offers.
"Yes, that would be great. I would like to interview for both and see how it turns out."
"We've had candidates interview for several positions and depending on if they receive one offer or multiple offers, they make a call in terms of preference and what they like to do the most."
"So as a take away from this conversation Ralph, I would need you to apply on the website again for the two positions. Thereafter I will send you two documents that you would need to fill out and send me."
"Sure. That would be great. I will fill them out and send them back."
"Yes. Make sure you sign them and send them. That way I can put in the paperwork and get started on scheduling the interviews."
"Yes, sure."
"I should have the papers emailed to you in another hour or so," she says.
"I will look out for them."
"Thanks Ralph. Have a great day!"
"You too!" he replies resolutely.

When speaking business with Americans, it needs to be very professional. It is best not to include any sort of emotion or weakness in your dealings with them. Because in the US, any sort of weakness or hesitation is viewed as a sign of being lost or of not being sure. Worse still it is viewed as a sign of being servile and of begging.

288

Caucasian Americans don't like people that beg. They rather prefer those that are strong and self-sufficient; a sure sign that one is mature and doesn't need to be shown the ropes.

****

Ralph quickly grabs the remaining part of the sandwich, his note book and rushes home. The sleeping laptop is fired up and he sits there till evening, learning the basics of Siemens' core business and product and service divisions. With quite a lot of work done, he opens the tiny closet and sets aside a pair of well-ironed pants, socks, undergarments and shirt. A jet black coat is taken from the corner of the closet and kept in the middle of the clothesline in the closet for ease of access. A yellowish tie is delicately slid along a multi-rung hanger.

"Perfecto!" he mutters to himself looking at the extent of preparation he has done.

Life is good when one is dedicated to the work that needs to be completed. When one is focused on the goals that one needs to do and when those goals come closer to fruition. The icing on the cake is when the goal is achieved.

Ralph was a guy who worked on getting things done. The faster, the better was his motto. Which is why he tried to do things as fast as he possibly could.

He walks into the database class the next day as alert and full of enthusiasm as he could be. Dr. Alamuddin looks at the dashing young man in the prime of vigor, pumped and ready to kick some ass.

"Every one of you will be submitting your term end assignments today," he says peremptorily. He receives no reply.
"As scheduled, let's get started on the live programming test." He had emailed details about the programming test the weekend before and expected everyone to be prepared for it.

All the students start opening their printed out question slips and notes to complete the program on the computer. Ralph doesn't do any of that. He simply starts the computer and begins chipping away at the test program. He is done within twenty minutes flat with what was supposed to be a one-hour test. He saves the database he created, the queries developed and the analytics results obtained into the secure drive to enable Dr. Alamuddin to evaluate the test results.

A couple of students look at him full of surprise as he walks out the hall nonchalantly. Dr. Alamuddin sees him literally sprint out of the room and shakes his head in recognition of his speed and supposed accuracy. "Ralph!" he hears a grateful voice as he approaches the end of the corridor. Dr. Alamuddin trots towards him in a seemingly conciliatory gesture.

"How are you man?" he asks seeming friendly.

"Very good Professor" replies Ralph wondering why the professor has suddenly taken an interest in him. Dr. Alamuddin was known to be one of the most nerdiest and egotistical professors you could find in US academia. Or if people didn't find him egotistical they did find him slightly obtuse; even schizophrenic sometimes. His ratings on several websites had rave reviews associated with them.

"How did you manage to complete that assignment and give it two weeks ahead of time?" he asks Ralph.

"You mean the one on the development of AI for database structures?"

"Yes."

"Just the way I handed over the papers for the two assignments before that. I thought it would be good to finish the work in advance."

"Yes but this last one was very complex. And you scored a straight A on it. You are the first student who has done that!" says the doctor expecting a more thorough response to his question.

"Well, I read a lot and try to maintain my level of curiosity to a consistent level. So the additional knowledge helps me complete a lot of work in a relatively short period of time. That's how!"

Ralph doesn't really wish to divulge too many vital details about his research techniques, reference books and key websites he goes to in order to complete work. He knows how difficult a road he has had to tread to reach where he is now. In America, people may give you many things. But what they will generally withhold from you is the knowledge and information that could help you get an edge.

Whoever gives you information and knowledge is your true friend. Because information is power. People make money, earn their livelihoods based on the information they know. Information which the people that hire them might not necessarily know. The idea in America and many other parts of the world is to maintain secrecy of information with an aim to preserve monopoly or power. Having money or owning wealth is considered a pre-requisite to have power.

****

The interview is scheduled three days after the live database test. Ralph is focused and driven to make this happen. However, he is going to have to be doubly prepared. Two interviews with two different managers have been scheduled that day. One position is directly related to computer science, the other related to management and technology. Ralph is typically a technical person and enjoys being involved in core programming or development-related work. He never really enjoyed business or management and the associated politics that goes with it.

Ralph begins covering material he needs to read before the interview. General IT information, programming principles, key aspects of Java and a host of other things. The minute he finishes one topic, the realization that there are ten more to cover comes like a heavy thud on the floor. Preparing for an interview can be intimidating and painful. What does one cover first, what does one consign to the end. How is the preparation to be done? All these conundrum-like questions have situation specific answers. "Perhaps the only way to find the definite answer to them is to actually go through the situation and then analyze if the path you had taken was correct or not," says the Inner voice.

Ralph thinks that real-time analysis of what's yielding results and what is a wet blanket is a better way to ascertain if a particular path is to be followed or not. There is no time to make expensive time and effort investments in directions that are not yielding quick results. "But quick results are not the way nature functions. Things in nature and indeed in life take time," quips the Inner voice again.

The way America operates is based on a principle of 'quick gratification.' Returns and results are wanted in quick succession or in a very short period of time. There is a very short ramp-up time or time to prepare. If you are joining a position in an organization the manager or supervisor there would expect you to ramp up and start to deliver in a matter of a week or two. If you are not able to deliver, that might cast serious doubts on your capability or faculties. It is best to work hard towards delivering on base expectations first and then work towards enhancing your delivery.

In a capitalist setup, it is productivity and gains that are looked at very favorably rather than mere trying. Trying is just not good enough if it fails to yield the appropriate benefits. Solid results distinguish the grain from the chaff.

So many academically astute and intelligent people just don't survive in jobs because they are too esoteric rather than results-oriented. Things get shifted to being done in a theoretical fashion rather than being done in a way in which tangible results can be obtained.

New York City wasn't built by being esoteric or theoretical. It was built with one piece of work getting completed every day. Several times it was more than one piece of work getting done.

****

"I am here to see Mr. Dodworth from the management reporting department," he says as he looks at the receptionist at the front desk. The company buildings are huge and spread far apart. It looks like a maze of big cream blocks.

The cream blocks are facing green undulating meadows uniformly dispersed like dollops of green ice cream. There are picnic tables spread all over. The most attractive table seems to be the one under the tree. Wait a minute, it is occupied by a couple discreetly sharing a close moment. *"Woah, so they do have discreet settings even in the open!"* wonders Ralph.

"Excuse me Sir. What time is your appointment with Mr. Dodworth?" asks the receptionist interrupting Ralph's wanderlust.
"11:30 am," says Ralph feeling a little shaken from his thoughts. Ralph came to the place by train. It takes around 1 hour to get there since it is eighteen miles away from home. It is far but the company is of high brand value and Ralph knows that if he gets even 6 months of work in that company on his resume, he will have great demand in the job market.

The recession hasn't done anything to help new job seekers in the market. Any advantage one can get through work experience or contacts is well worth the effort. Traveling eighteen miles every morning and working there 9 to 5 is definitely an ardor. But if the benefits justify the efforts then there is a light at the end of the tunnel. International students do have to bear quite a bit of burden to achieve even the smallest measure of success that normal American citizen students can achieve with practically very little effort.

"Just have a seat. I have informed him that you are here. He should come get you shortly," she says.

Ralph walks to the chocolate colored seats in the reception area and tries to make himself comfortable. He doesn't look at the grassy meadows outside or at the couple getting cozy. This time he opens his file and gives his resume a glance. Then reads a few post-its with vital facts about the company on his notebook. Twenty minutes later, a petite, blonde woman with slight dimples walks towards him. "Are you Ralph?" she asks.

"It's show time boy!" says the Inner Voice as Ralph feels the thrill of having a potential job offer before him along with a nice, petite damsel by his side. A job offer would be the first preference though.
"Ralph!" she says not finding it difficult to guess. There was another person in the reception area but it was a girl.
"How are you doing?" says Ralph standing erect.
"Great. Did you find the place alright and everything?"
"I'm here," he smiles.
"Well great. All ready for your interview then."
"Yes, absolutely."
"Follow me right this way. So is it far where you're coming from?"
"Yes. Around 18 miles," he says making it sound like nothing.
"Okay. So how did you get here?"
"I took the train."

They reach a room with glass panes and a light wooden door.

"Just make yourself comfortable. Mr. Dodworth will be with you shortly," she says as she shuts the door behind her.

Ralph looks at his watch. Its ten minutes before 11:30am; the scheduled time to meet with Mr. Dodworth.

"Breathe deep," whispers the Inner Voice to him. "It's only a short while before he will be here. And you don't have to worry, you will smash all his questions and dazzle him." Mental visualization is what has helped Ralph in the past and the Inner Voice helps him even more with it.

He knows that Mr. Dodworth will come in prepared to interview him. But he also knows that this man has a reputation for grilling interviewees. His Linkedin profile had read IT & management guru; new tech pioneer. *"That's quite a headline to have for one's profile!"* thinks Ralph. People who are too full of themselves also do not have such a profile heading, he thinks.

He sneaks a peek at his interview post-its. As he sheepishly looks at some hastily scribbled points, a burly, dark image quickly passes by along the opaque glass pane and darts into the door.

"Ralph! I am Mr. Dodworth," the burly, white man says as he extends his hand to Ralph.
"Nice to meet you," replies Ralph with a firm handshake.
"How are you doing today?" he asks.
"Just fine!" replies Ralph. "You?"
"I am good, thank you."

The hefty man adjusts himself into the small seat and positions a slim file and notepad on the desk.

"So what did you like about the position?"
"It is into IT and involves data and information analysis. I am a computer science student so I am interested in the position because of that," says Ralph nonchalantly.
"Well then if you have read the job description you might also know that this position involves quite a bit of business understanding as well, right?"

The man's tone sounded stone cold; very businesslike. There is no emotion or friendliness in it. Ralph feels the pseudo-hostility coming through like a draft.

"Well yes. Being from the technical line I am predisposed to looking at the technical aspects first and then noticing the business nuances," replies Ralph seeking to answer Mr. Dodworth's not-so-question-like question.

****

In one of his several conversations with Mum over the phone, she had told him to always keep his attitude in check. Mum knew that Ralph could be rather short-tempered. He had got into quite a few tussles with colleagues and people back home due to this predisposition. She knew he couldn't handle stress or discord. His way of venting his resentment was to get into fierce verbal duels or physical fights.

Back home, these interactions were not welcome because they led to the creation of grudges and harboring of ill will. It's always helpful when you have very few or no enemies to think about. It makes life that much easier to live.

Ralph would be attentive in listening to Mum's advice but would pay only cursory attention to the part about restraining his vocals. When it came to contesting someone, he couldn't restrain himself. Something about him just didn't agree with the idea of ignoring an irascible or difficult individual; nor the comments that they might have made. Resolving a difficult situation with a confrontation was his preferred method of dealing with difficult situations.

"Difficult situations are always there in life. It's your approach to dealing with them that determines how successful you are in life and what you get out of life," was what Mum always said. Though Ralph knew what she said was right, changing his approach from one of active responsiveness to passivity was a gargantuan, if not impossible task to undertake and achieve.

"Brazen aggression can get you into trouble," the Inner Voice often told him. "You need to learn to ignore certain things which you feel are unjust," was what Mum regularly reiterated.

Ralph was an openly friendly person; particularly sensitive to aggressive posturing and business-like manners. He always felt the need to be more at home and amiable in all his interactions. Probably being from a coastal city made his attitude so.

"Yes this position, although it has a little technical stuff is fairly lopsided in favor of business knowledge and application. It needs a fair amount of business knowledge. How comfortable are you with that?" Mr. Dodworth asks a pointed question.
"Be polite with this guy!" comes the quick advice from the Inner Voice.
"I don't have a great degree of business exposure, but I can learn."

Madhu had once told Ralph that when you do not have a certain skill, err on the side of caution and conservativeness. Admitting you don't know something that you don't know and then saying you can learn it goes a long way in showing your maturity.

"Okay, but for this role, we do need someone who has pretty deep business knowledge and ability to develop metrics. Learning is good but prior experience is what we are looking for," Mr. Dodworth emphasizes.
"I understand," Ralph keeps his cool.

"What would be some of the things I could do to better understand the business aspects that you are referring to?" Ralph asks, seeking to be more accepting of Mr. Dodworth's seeming rejection of his qualifications and candidacy.
"Well Ralph, that's something you would need to know. And I would expect that the candidate who applies for this position already knows that. Don't you agree!"
"Calm, calm!" interjects the Inner Voice as Ralph's temper seems to have a mercurial rise.
"Oh sure. Of course," replies Ralph seeking to maintain the peace.

There is a long stretch of silence.

"So tell me about your technical skills. What have you done?" asks Mr. Dodworth eager to break the silence and lighten the apparent hostility. Ralph's silence suggests something of an affront due to Mr. Dodworth's forthrightness in approaching the topic of his suitability for the position.
"You mean programming?" asks Ralph seeming disinterested. His strong enthusiasm and vitality reduced to nonchalant passivism. Dad knew that if Ralph couldn't get his way through aggression he would sink into despair and helplessness. Aggression and contention were

Ralph's way of restoring balance to an unbalanced situation. He wasn't one of those people who could deal with conflict and try to resolve it diplomatically or politically. Use of force or verbal aggression was his way of restoring normalcy and winning battles. Both Dad and Mum knew that he would need to outgrow this tendency soon enough or risk having life short-change him for his failure to do so.

Mum strongly believed that time would rid him of all his shortcomings.

"I have done Java, JavaScript and PHP programming. I have developed applications mostly using Java though," Ralph says plainly.
"That's great. We could use those skills to develop some in-house applications for our department."
"What did you like most about this position?" asks Mr. Dodworth seemingly just to make small talk.
"I liked the technical part and opportunity to learn about business," Ralph replies. At this point, he doesn't even care if he gets the position or not. He is just going to state his qualifications as they are. No sugarcoating or mollycoddling; plain matter-of-fact manner of stating them. The Inner Voice seems to be in tacit agreement with his policy. Sometimes there needs to be a minimal reciprocation of courtesy from the other party for decency and goodwill to work.

"Do you have any questions for me?" asks Mr. Dodworth.
"Yes."
"Given the fact that the person needs to know about the different business aspects of the job before they decide to interview for it; what business knowledge would be needed to be had to do well in this position?"
"You would need to know business impacts of IT decisions related to purchasing IT equipment, softwares and security-related infrastructure. Besides that, you would need to know the environmental and legal implications of not recycling IT waste and of not having an enterprise-wide recycling policy in place."
"Okay. Thanks. That's all the questions I had."
"Great. Give me around a week. I will get back to you on this position." The words are a nice way of saying 'no you didn't get the job.' And Ralph knows this only too well. Even when Ryan, Ralph's younger brother applied for positions in business back in India; 'we'll get back to you' was an often used phrase in giving candidates the 'no' hint in

regards to selection. Again nothing personal; it's only business as the Americans so often say.

"Sure," replies Ralph.

As Mr. Dodworth rises, Ralph instinctively heads towards the door.

"Thanks for your time Ralph!" says Mr. Dodworth.

"Yours too!"

The manager extends his hand and Ralph emotionlessly shakes it. He knows that this manager is a shrew, a taskmaster without the wisdom to provide training and guidance. Which is why the 'before the fact' knowledge of certain facts was expected and would not be passed down or so it seemed.

"Have a good day Mr. Dodworth!"

"You too Ralph. Call me Nate," he says trying to appear friendly.

"Sounds good."

"Do you know the way out?" he asks.

"Yes, I do. I'll find it if I don't" asserts Ralph.

****

"Your time starts now," said Dr. Alamuddin looking curiously at Ralph sitting in the corner of the classroom.

The journey back home from the Siemens campus although long felt short. It's probably the mix of thoughts about the interview and the trepidation with which he approached it that ran through his mind. He has yet another escapade that he needs to execute the next day, though. This one is more important than this lopsided interview with a defunct Methuselah in a culturally rigid department.

The test the next morning would determine the final grade and/or extra project that one would get in Dr. Alamuddin's coveted database structures course. As he starts reading the details of the test he realizes the truth behind Dr. Alamuddin's claims.

"It's going to be a live project for an actual organization that needs to develop its database infrastructure and potential solution for a few technology issues. And you will have the great opportunity of developing a solution for them." – Dr. Alamuddin had said in an email.

So what was the catch to this. Apparently, the solution was to be derived in 2 hours flat at which time the test would come to an end. There would not be an opportunity to discuss or think too extensively. It would all come down to how quickly an engineer can think on his feet and how versatile his or her solution is.

"Bingo!" muttered Ralph as he reached the end of reading the live case study write up. "*I know this stuff and I could crank this out in one hour flat instead of using up the given two hours for the test,*" he says to himself.

The project involves developing a database to store customer information along with a front end form to access this information. Ralph begins developing the entities and objects that are a part of the database structure for the customer information that is needed to be stored. Having completed the data modeling effort in fifteen minutes he dedicates the next half hour to develop the front end form to access the information.

All done in forty-five minutes, he spends the next fifteen minutes testing the solution he completed. Just to ensure that the I's are dotted and the t's are crossed. Satisfied that everything is working as it should, he saves the project and rises from his desk to notice Dr. Alamuddin, again surprised at his tremendous speed in completing a test.

"All done Ralph?" questions the doctor.
"Yes Professor!" he respectfully says.
Dr. Alamuddin looks at him with a look of amazement and wonder as to how he managed to complete the test so quickly. "Were you able to complete all the questions?" he asks, making Ralph wait from exiting the classroom.
"Yes, of course."
"One second. In order to leave the hall before one and half hour of the allotted test time; the student needs my permission."
"Do I have it?" asks Ralph with an innocent smile.
"I would need to check if you have completed all the questions. Only then am I allowed to let you leave the classroom," he says.

He approaches the slim apple MacBook on his desk and begins accessing it to have a look at the work Ralph has done. Ralph notices his face brightening up as he goes through the contents on the laptop screen.

As Ralph looks on standing close to the exit, the professor begins to rise from the chair and walks calmly towards Ralph. "You may go Ralph," he smiles.

"Thanks, Dr. Alamuddin."

"Oh, one more thing Ralph. We have a couple of companies that have small projects relating to database and application development. You seem to be pretty good at databases and in application development in general. Would you be interested in any of these requirements?"

"Sure. Just let me know what they are?" says Ralph.

"Yes. I think they could use someone like you. And it's good exposure. Not to mention they offer good salaries as well."

"Thanks for that Doctor!" says Ralph as he exits the classroom. He is full of intent and purpose and is very focused on making a difference in his life. He quickly walks towards the stairs on his way to prepare for another interview at Siemens. This time the interview is for a more technical role; Ralph's forte.

Two impatient days pass by and no phone call or email. A day later, Ralph gets the much awaited call from the same Heather that arranged his interview with Mr. Dodworth from Siemens.

"Hi Ralph! How are you doing? This is Heather speaking."

"Good. How are you?"

"Fantastic!"

"I have some good news for you!"

"Oh really! What's that?"

"Mrs. Shurfina of the IT department wants to interview you. She has given us a set of dates."

"Oh great. I thought you were going to give me feedback about my interview with Mr. Dodworth," he smiles.

There is a brief pause. Heather seems to sense his eagerness to know about what happened in the previous interview.

"Oh, I would love to give you an update on that position. However, we just haven't heard from Mr. Dodworth yet."

"Okay. What are the date options with Mrs. Shurfina?"

"We have the 7th, 10th and 12th of March at this point. She is available in the mornings from 9 am to 12 noon on the 7th and the 10th and from 1 pm to 4 pm on the 12th."

A brief pause.

"Which day works for you?" she asks hearing only silence.
"Could I get back to you on this Heather? I just need to look at my schedule."
"Sure. You could call or email me."
"Right-O. I will do that in another hour or so. Thanks so much!"
"You're welcome Ralph!" she says; her smile being heard clearly over the phone.
"I will be able to make it for the interview at 10:30 am on the 7th" reads the email from Ralph to Heather.
"Sure, will let her know and block the time. Thanks," reads her reply the next day.

****

"I think you have some very good skills concerning databases and programming constructs."

Ralph looks at him bewildered.

"Your skills might be of great use to some people I know."
"People you know?" asks Ralph's skeptically.
"Yes. I know a couple of people who have their own businesses that need help developing an IT infrastructure."
"What type of IT systems do they need?"
"Well for starters, I know this lady Mrs. Heffenhoffer. She owns a company called Reike Bridal Services. Over the last two years, their growth has quadrupled both in clients and business value."
"Okay."
"Mrs. Heffenhoffer has been finding it increasingly difficult to manage the details of her clientele and to compare the past business value with potential future demand."
"Sounds like she needs a CRM system," quips Ralph.
"Exactly Ralph! You got it," exults Dr. Alamuddin.

"But they are not as big of an organization to invest in a massive off-the-shelf system. Do you think you would be able to study their company and develop a system for them?"

Ralph remains silent. "Would you be interested in the project firstly? I think that's a more appropriate question!" Dr. Alamuddin quickly asks, sensing his hesitation

Ralph's silence continues.

"Yeah and you can take your time," Dr. Alamuddin's eagerness to work with Ralph continues.
"Is this going to be a greenfield solution? Or do they already have something they are currently using?"
"Well I believe they currently have a barebones system that doesn't have much functionality in it," says Dr. Alamuddin; a little surprised at the level of maturity exhibited by Ralph in asking the question.
"Okay. So I would need to study their current system and then think about a potential solution," suggests Ralph.
"Yes. Absolutely. That's the way it's done traditionally and I typically agree with that approach," says Dr. Alamuddin with an air of confidence in Ralph's abilities.
"Okay!' says Ralph.
"Okay. So you're interested or okay as in okay?" smiles Dr. Alamuddin.
"Yes I am definitely interested, but I would need more insight into the deeper details of the project and who are the people working on it in various capacities," says Ralph peremptorily.
"Oh yes definitely. There shouldn't be any problem in giving you that information," says Dr. Alamuddin with a wide smile.
"Cool. So see me tomorrow at 10 am in my office. I will have all the details for you at that time. And I also want to introduce you to the owner and chief technology officer of Reike!"

****

Fifteen minutes before 10:30 am Ralph stands tall in his trademark black suit at the same entrance of Siemens from where he was ushered in to meet Mr. Dodworth for the previous interview. He informs the front desk person and gets comfortable on the brown couch that gives the place a 50s look. This time there are no other visitors or guests to share the sofa. He is alone. And even if there were he probably wouldn't have been distracted. Today, more than anything else he has an iron focus. The kind that comes only with a clear goal and hardship seasoned direction. As he leafs through some of his notes, Heather walks through the door and presents herself in front of him.

"Hey Ralph! How are you doing today? Guess you didn't face too much problem finding the place this time right!" she smiles.
"This time it was too easy!" he grins.
"Yup, in this case, the second time is a charm." Her demeanor seems flirtatious and racy. Probably the dusky hunk has got the blonde recruiter to swoon over him. And it's not his fault. Ralph has often noticed that many white women have an inexplicable affinity for tawny men with muscular features.

Ralph was not overly built up. But he was fairly muscular. His mix of looks and physical built would make women go gaga over him. He wasn't surprised but he was perplexed as to how to convert initial attraction to a tangible relationship. A question many men face throughout their manhood. In fact women face the same dilemma as well – how do you convert mutual attraction to something involving more love and passion?

There is probably no universal formula to enable this. But a lot depends on your mojo coming into play to make this possible. "Is there anything specific that Mrs. Shurfina wants to talk to me about today?" asks Ralph. The question seems 'out-of-place' since Heather is just into HR and doesn't have any visibility into the subject matter of Mrs. Shurfina's department. But in America anything is possible. Any tidbits of information that might reside with someone and which could provide an edge in terms of the actual interview are always a great help.

"I don't know really. But don't sweat it. Mrs. Shurfina is generally very easy going. The interview should be fun." Her reassurance calms Ralph down a bit. But the Inner Voice is always wide awake and active, deep down in Ralph.
"Make yourself comfortable. Mrs. Shurfina will be with you in a bit. She was very busy today," she says as she leads Ralph into a well-decked conference room. The grey table matches well with all the white background of the room. The large LCD screen gives the room a Star Trek-like feel.

Ralph has always been crazy about décor and looks. His dressing sense speaks volumes of his interest in the visual effects of good clothing and nice things. "I want the best sandals we can get from this store was his regular urging to Mum when they visited the shoe store before the school season was to begin."

After going through several pairs, he would spend a good deal of time thinking about the product. By this point, the sales person attending to Ralph would be so tired showing him the pairs; he/she would just make an excuse to see the next client.

Mum looked at Ralph and smiled silently. Her smile held the exasperation felt by the sales clerk. She knew her son is not a 'yes' man or one who is easily pleased. He always sought the best for himself and could be rather fastidious when it came to most things involving the purchase of a product or a service. On most occasions though he wouldn't settle for any footwear less than Rs. 3000. That's around fifty dollars at a Rs. 60 per dollar exchange rate – a big sum by Indian standards.

He gets into a comfy seat that seems a tad too big for his size. Hurriedly he opens his laptop and a small notebook containing vital details about the company.

****

Knock, knock.
"Come in!"
"Oh hi Ralph!" says Dr. Alamuddin; his stoic countenance suddenly lightening up.
"How are you?"
"Very well Doctor," says an upbeat Ralph.
"Great! I have a couple of materials here that my good friend Mrs. Heffenhoffer asked that I give you."
"These are very confidential documents Ralph; and I am trusting you with them," he says as he hands them over.
Ralph respectfully accepts them. "Once I am done with them I will hand them back to you."
"Take some time and go through them, Ralph! I am always here for questions."

Ralph's reading is fast and his eye is sharp.

"Doctor," he sheepishly mutters in a few minutes of reading.
"Yes. Question?"
"Do you have data models of the existing system in Reike?"
"Isn't it in that bundle I gave you?"
"I don't see it here."
"I don't believe they have a very complicated system there. In fact, I don't think they have anything like an ERD or database system. Anyway, Mrs. Heffenhoffer will be coming in a short while. She can answer all questions you have. Just keep the technical questions to a minimum, though. She is not a very computer savvy person."
Ralph looks at him with a tinge of astonishment. "Okay," he says. In fact, it would have helped him to get technical insights into the current IT infrastructure.
"No sweat!" you know enough of how to get systems up and running says the Inner Voice reassuring him of his technical prowess.

****

"Hey, Ralph! How's it going?" comes the swift voice through the door of the conference room. Mrs. Shurfina is quite the symbol of directorial power and authority. Her large breasts protruding through her coat contrast against her elegant necklace, page boy hairstyle and slender torso. The marks on her nose show clear signs of spectacle usage but on this occasion she hasn't worn them. She could be anywhere between 50 and 65 years. But looks a lot younger. He prefers not to guess, though.
"Fine," he says seeming surprised.
"I am Mrs. Shurfina!" she says as she extends her hand.
"Nice to meet you!" he smiles.
"Same here. Did you find the place alright and everything?" she asks.
"Yes. It was easy."
"Great!"
[Pause] "So I've had the pleasure of reading quite a bit about your profile. You seem to have quite a concentration of activity around human computer interaction and database development."
"Yes."
"So I don't know how much you know about the project but we could certainly use skills relating to database development and design."
"Okay."
"So tell me about your background."

"My undergrad is in computer science engineering and my Masters is also in the same. I have worked on short-term projects and assignments that are database intensive with a fair degree of user experience design features."

"In the university, I am vice president of the computer science club and the German club. A few exchange students from Germany provide a great learning interface for networking and understanding the way in which they use various techniques for better database creation, testing and code generation."

Mrs. Shurfina looks at him with a subdued admiration and interest. It seems as though she didn't expect this gauche local yokel to be able to communicate as effectively. But apparently, he does.

"What are some of the activities you undertake with your German colleagues in the German club?" she asks, seeming to evince a keen interest in his German connection. Siemens was also a German company.

"We've developed programs together; worked on security projects and been partners on white papers for seminars, apart from many other smaller collaborations here and there."

"What do you like most about working with Germans?"

"I never really looked at it from that angle. But some of the overarching characteristics about working with them relates to their level of concentration and dedication. Almost all Germans I have met thus far are very focused on the task at hand and in obtaining optimum results for the same. They have a very high-quality initiative and that is very impressive."

"Okay. What makes you think you are a good fit for this position?"

"I have extensive exposure to databases, development of programs and testing. I think my greatest ability is to learn things I have never done before very quickly."

"What are the steps involved in database development?"

"That's a pretty loaded question. Because depending on the organization and their current application infrastructure, it might need different steps to create databases. Based on the place you start there could be a couple of steps to build a database."

His answer leaves her pleasantly confused.

"What languages can you code in?"

"I have coded in Java and C++ mainly."

"I don't think you have what it takes to be in this internship; why should I hire you?"

"I have the right mix of analytical and technical skills; not to mention communication skills to be successful in this internship role. All I need is a chance to prove myself."

Ralph lays it bare about his abilities and his positive "can-do" attitude. His demeanor makes him seem impervious and least troubled with her question. Apparently, she is impressed.

"I've asked you all the questions I could. Do you have any questions for me?"

"What are you expecting from the person in this role in terms of delivery?"

"Well, I have a team working with me on a medical transcription product. I would need this person to test the product, use it and ultimately get a good enough understanding of it to start suggesting enhancements to the same. You would need to extract data from the database, analyze it and derive meaningful insights from it. Apart from this if there are any other tasks for which we need your help we will request and expect you to help."

"Okay. How soon are you looking to fill the position?"

"As soon as we have the right candidate!" she says. She says this in a way which gives out very little clues in regards to his candidacy. Pure political speak from a relatively seasoned director.

"Ok. Is there any other question I can answer which would help you make a decision in regards to my candidacy?"

"No. I think I have all the information I need."

"Okay. Well if you think of anything you need to know about me, you have my email and phone number for further contact. Thanks so much for your time."

"Thanks Ralph," she says as she waits for him to pack his notes and laptop which he didn't use.

He seems to stumble hurrying the notes and laptop into his bag. "Are you okay? Do you need any help? she asks looking outwardly concerned.

Ralph has only too often seen this ceremonious display of kindness from business connections. He knows that human behavior is pretty much the same all over the world regardless of the culture or upbringing. The

Inner Voice informs him about this as well. The same jealousies, grudges, hate and despondencies exist the world over. The only thing that varies is the extent of these emotions.

Even in terms of competition and peer rivalry; the more the prestige involved, the greater the rivalry. In India, it is more about getting jobs to earn a salary, a living. In the US, there is a different tinge to job seeking and indeed job seekers. Job seekers distinguish their job seeking efforts and results by the jobs they apply for and the type of organizations they apply in. They pride themselves on the exclusivity of their connections and on the extent of rapport they have.

Although similar equations and dynamics exist in other countries; the opportunity to obtain a chance at bridging the gap is easier in the US than in most other countries. All one needs to do is try and try hard!!!

****

As he leafs through the slim file; a characteristic "tick tock" sound seems to emanate from outside the hallway. It draws closer becoming louder and more resolute. "Mrs. Heffenhoffer!" gobbles Dr. Alamuddin. "How are you Mark!" she bursts into his room as he rises to hug her. Apparently, the doctor and Mrs. Heffenhoffer have more of a history than meets the eye. "Are they just friends!!" questions the Inner Voice as Ralph seems a little taken aback by the level of rapport between the two.
"How you been Mark?"
"Better, now that I see you!" he gushes.
"Ohh! Stop it!!" she echoes.
"How are Marilyn and Zachary doing?"
"They're great. You should come home sometime. Marilyn's going to be starting university next fall."
"Woah! Looks like they are growing faster than we can catch up."
"Well before you know it they're adults!"
"You got it, Mark!"
"Well let's not keep Ralph waiting any longer. We can always talk some more later," says Dr. Alamuddin.

Mrs. Heffenhoffer seems to be pretty attached to him. And why wouldn't she? Dr. Alamuddin was of Lebanese origin. His light skin, gravel colored hair, sharp facial symmetry and slender height made him an appealing target for women. Besides, he had a dress sense that was out of the ordinary. Focusing on lighter colors, he wore garments that reflected a texture and hue close to cream and pink.

"One thing to consider if you want to pick up girls!" echoed the Inner Voice stupidly. Ralph knew that dress sense needs to be well developed to impress women. But not always! Women can be the most fleeting, finicky and dubious of creatures in the human-animal kingdom. Predicting them is next to impossible.

"So sorry to keep you waiting, young man! It's just that we are such good friends and we haven't seen each other for a long, long time," she apologizes.

"No problem at all."

"So Ralph here, is the top student not only of my class but probably one I have not seen in a very long time!" says Dr. Alamuddin to Mrs. Heffenhoffer with vivacity.

"Don't believe him. When you see how I work you will find out the truth!" quips Ralph.

"So nice to meet you, Ralph! Mark here has not been able to stop talking good things about you. In fact he had told me about you and your amazing powers several months ago."

"Powers huh!"

"And I'm glad we finally get to meet," she continues.

"Oh, the pleasure is all mine! I hope I match up to all the good things that Dr. Alamuddin has been telling you about me."

"I have no doubt you will Ralph," galls Dr. Alamuddin seeming only too sure that Ralph is way more than the total package.

"Okay, why don't we all take a seat and see what we have!" suggests Dr. Alamuddin as the pleasantries begin to die down.

"Cool," says the graying but attractive lady.

Mrs. Heffenhoffer is nothing of the generic aging business lady. In spite of her seeming age, she exudes a child-like confidence. She has flowing, long locks of hair and the black locks effectively intertwine with the grey and brown ones. It is obvious her fingernails and toes are well manicured and cared for. She has light blue eyes, smooth skin and a slender frame that accentuates a raw sensuality that seems an integral part of her being.

Overall, the woman, in spite of her age is physically attractive. Although what seems most sexy about her is her positive and friendly attitude.

She is immeasurably affable and a true joy to work with as Ralph would later come to realize.

"So Mrs. Heffenhoffer, I briefly went through some of the documents the doctor here provided me with. However, I would need more time to go through them more accurately. What can you tell me about your operations and procedures? I personally don't know much about a bridal service company."
"Are you married Ralph?" she smiles coyly.

Ralph is taken aback and flinches.

"Sounds like a No! Girlfriend?" she looks at him more closely; the dimples on her cheeks lighting up.

Ralph bursts into a rage of laughter.

"Okay. Now that's a mixed response. It seems you may or may not have a girlfriend. But there are overwhelming signs that you have certainly had a couple in the past."
Ralph still grinning – "Well you seem to have multiple talents. You're not just a business owner; you read crystal balls as well!"

There is uncontrolled laughter in the room. Dr. Alamuddin is generous in laughter.

"She is capable of such things. I've known her for several years and she never fails to surprise me," says Dr. Alamuddin.
"I'm sure!" replies Ralph.
"So I was right then wasn't I Ralph!" she purrs.
"Oh Carla. Give the kid a break!"
"It's cool Doctor," he smiles.
"I like when there is humor. It makes work a lot less monotonous."
"So anyways, my point behind asking you about your relationship status is because the bridal services business closely relates to that."
"Oh!"
"Yes. If you know how relationships work you have understood half my business."

Dr. Alamuddin can't seem to get over the laughter.

"Okay. Well, I am definitely not married. So maybe you can give me some tips on how to do that. And then even explain the details of the business," Ralph says with a grin.

"It would be my pleasure. And it always helps to learn some life skills from those who already know them," she coyly winks.

"Thanks!!"

Mrs. Heffenhoffer is certainly not the serious, uptight type of post-menopausal woman one might expect to find.

"So Reike Bridal Services provides all wedding-related services from the dress to the food, venue and decorations. We are the premier wedding planning company in the Philadelphia area," she continues.

"Okay."

"Our operations have brought great delight and help to families and people in the region during their time of need. So we get a lot of repeat business and reference-based business."

"Sounds like fun!"

"Yes. But the problem we've been facing is our business is growing but we are not able to service customers as effectively as before when we had fewer customers."

"Okay. What problems are you facing?" he asks gingerly.

"One problem we faced in the recent past was; we have a policy to provide a discount to a reference-related customer. But because we don't have an effective system to track references and the new customers being referred; we missed giving discounts to these references. This created a little concern to our customers that referred the new ones and thus the relationship got strained."

"If we had a computer system tracking customer details and history we would have avoided this shameful situation. So that's what we want to institute in the business. We can't afford to have disgruntled, frustrated customers if the business is to grow!" she says in a matter of fact manner.

A period of silence ensues. Everyone's looking at Ralph seeking a response. Ralph seems non-plussed and contemplative. He doesn't have anything going through his mind. It is vacant. But his life is dotted with instances of creative genius after such periods of vacant thought.

"So basically, in technical terms what she is saying is she needs a sort of a CRM system by which you can track customer details, transactions and follow-ups with them. Any ideas Ralph?"

Ralph is still in a pensive, semi-hypnotic state. He seems almost like a dummy for a second.

"Well, I would need to think about how to specifically implement this so that it works as desired," Ralph finally speaks.
"Yes, great Ralph. We can find out the detailed requirements about how we want to get things started and how the application is to grow," says Dr. Alamuddin.
"Carla would be more than happy to help you with the requirements."
"Just let me know what you need," says a sparkling Mrs. Heffenhoffer.
"Yep we can probably gather requirements over a two-day period and then I can start developing a potential solution," avers Ralph.
Dr. Alamuddin has a wide smile on his face. "Carla just give him as much time as he needs so that we can get the ball rolling on having a system developed."
"You got it!" she glows.
"Well, I will email you my schedule Mrs. Heffenhoffer. And we can fix two or three days to meet and finalize the requirements."
"Sure. Just email me. Do you have my email address?"
"Yes I think I saw it in the documentation," Ralph says with a light smile.
"Great. Well here's my card just in case."
"Thanks, Mrs. Heffenhoffer!"
"Call me Carla. And thank you!!" she says with a touch of sexy attraction in her tone.
"Ooh looks like somebody's cooking!!" quips the Inner Voice as Ralph graciously nods and smiles suppressing his instincts.

****

The sweet voice on the phone is a welcome break after a morning of intense research and study.

"Mrs. Shurfina would be delighted to offer you the position Ralph!" says Heather.
"Oh jeesh! That's awesome."
"Yup. We will be offering $20 per hour for the position."

"Okay."

"Mrs. Shurfina would like you to start on the first of December."

"Ummm 1ˢᵗ of December?"

"Is that possible?" asks Heather sensing hesitation in Ralph's voice.

"Well, I need to go home to visit my parents at that time."

"Okay. When do you think you would be back?"

"I will be leaving in December before Christmas so will be back in January next year."

"Okay. Let me get that to Mrs. Shurfina and then let you know."

"Sure. Thanks Heather!"

"No problem!"

****

The room is well furnished. The slick leather sofas have well-crocheted covers on the head rest. There is an artificial fireplace. All four walls of the study have elaborate paintings of varied landscapes; predominantly American and of native American culture they seem. The walls are of a plain yellow hue and go well with the soft light filtering through the window.

A long rectangular charpoy[18] in the middle of the room lends a tasteful feel to the décor of dark red teak; it could pass for redwood though. It is sturdy and well kept. The unlit chandelier above gives off a dim glint reflective of cut glass. The room has a soft jasmine smell that gives it a romantic feel. The maid Roza had ushered him into the house and set him on the large leather sofa.

"Tea or coffee," she had asked.

"I already had tea." In keeping with Goan traditions, Ralph was always very regular in having his fill of tea and basic snacks before he went anywhere.

"Okay. Juice then?"

"Sure."

"We have orange and mango juice because Carla likes fresh juice."

"Orange would be fine," he quips.

"Great. I'll be right back," she grins.

---

[18] Charpoy is a bed used in India consisting of a frame strung with light rope

He sits back and views the opulence of the room. *"Women of a high economic strata have special tastes,"* he muses.

As he unpacks some papers, the sweet jasmine scent of the room is interrupted by buttery aromas. A rolling trolley packed with orange juice, croissants and colorful pastries rolls into the living room making a clunky sound. He had to travel several miles by train to reach her house. The light tea and dry breakfast he munched on is all but gone.

"Feel free to help yourself with anything. There's pastries, juice, butter and jam. Carla will be with you in a wee bit."
"Thanks a ton Roza!"

Ralph is a little surprised by the hospitality rolled out to him.

"Why would she be treating me with such kindness and generosity. Juice and breakfast on the first day for the first work meeting!" he wonders.

But then again, he is going to be there for only two or three days max; unless of course Mrs. Heffenhoffer alias Carla gets smitten by his tawny skin and symmetrical looks. But it is also in her interests that he is at his best.

As he finishes up the first glass of orange juice, a svelte shadow begins to approach him. Her silhouette seems to seductively envelop the room bringing with it a semblance of peace and sensual charm.

Mrs. Heffenhoffer is quite the forty, fifty year old something with a touch of grand oomph and sensuality to her. She is lavish in giving affection and combines it with a gentle, motherly touch. She is elder but not elderly; greying but not greyed out. In spite of being in her early 50s, she exudes a kind of vibrant look. One categorized by a firm, toned body; tight, medium sized breasts and a flat midriff.

As Ralph looks back and prepares to stand she reaches him quicker than expected. "Hi Ralph," she says as she grabs his hand and envelopes him in a tight embrace. He wants to flinch but her warm body is irresistible. Her breasts press against his athletic physique.

"Quite a greeting!" says the Inner Voice.
"American attraction to Asian genes!" Ralph thinks.

"Did you find the place alright hon?"

"Yes. It's a train ride and then a short walk."

"Okay. It must be hard without a car."

"You get used to it I guess," he quips.

"Yeah. I guess you have the great qualities of being intelligent and strong. I like that so much!" she says with a twinkle in her eye.

For some reason, Ralph has this feeling of being hit on indirectly. Being hit on by an older woman is a different feeling. Her t-shirt's plunging neckline and tight wrap around don't help things either.

"Thanks!" he says.

"Mrs. Heffenhoffer, I have a set of potential solutions I wanted to discuss with you in regards to automating your business record management processes," he quickly broaches the subject, not wanting to get too cozy with the aged hottie.

"Well, we won't be doing any of the solutions if you keep calling me Mrs. Heffenhoffer. I prefer you call me Carla. I don't call you by a Mr. Last Name. So give me the pleasure of hearing my first name too."

"Absolutely. I forgot you had told me that last time too. Sorry!" he says trying to suppress a blush.

"No problem. You'll learn," she says with a suggestive smile.

"So I have two solutions and I think the first one would be more appropriate given the ease of implementing it. But you can see both and give your opinion."

Ralph had meticulously prepared two possible record maintenance options for Reike Bridal Services. He knew how to implement them and was confident in his ability to explain their value.

"Great!"

"So the first solution involves the creation of an MS-Access database to house all customer details from names, addresses, phone number to emails."

"What's MS-Access?" she asks.

"Oh it's a database management software," he says, trying real hard to keep a straight face.

It is a common occurrence that Americans not in the IT profession seldom know anything about technical concepts if not very little. And it is a common perception among many Asians that people here can tend to be duffers in technology-related matters even if that assumption is not true. Obviously, most major technologies originated in the West and then found their way in other countries. But those people who invented these technologies are the minuscule, so-called "mentally elite" set of people.

"Oh," she says the expression on her face full of concealed doubt. It is clear that she doesn't patronize technology and would be at a loss to understand it. She is a straightforward woman who believes in the lighter side of life. She doesn't do a very good job of pretending that she understands.

"The second solution involves buying a CRM software. I will configure it once purchased. I would recommend buying Siebel," he says with a lump in his throat trying to conceal how expensive Siebel is.

"Ok" is her standard response.

"Rule of thumb with non-technical people – never get into technical details," resonates the Inner Voice. This advice would come in handy at a special time in the future.

A period of silence ensues.

"So would you like to think about which solution you want to go with?" Ralph asks seeking an answer from the seemingly confused Mrs. Heffenhoffer.

"Which one would you go with if you were me?" asks Mrs. Heffenhoffer.

"I would go for the first one at this point, hands down," says Ralph.

"Okay then I opt for that," she says without questioning the logic behind his decision.

"Are you sure Carla?" he gingerly asks.

"Yes, I am sure. If you think it's the best solution then I have full confidence in your abilities and recommendation."

Her explicit trust in his abilities impresses him and makes him like her more. "*If I have a wife I'd like her to be like Carla!*" he says in his mind.

"Don't jump to conclusions so fast! You have just met her," cautions the Inner Voice.

"Well great. I will begin to draw up detailed specifications to implement this solution."

"Okay awesome!" she puts her palm on his hand as she slides closer to him on the sofa.

"I am going to have to tell Mark how great of an IT genius you are," she avers.

"Wait to see the solution, Carla, before you give me a pat on the back," he smiles shyly.

He continues to look at her expecting her to ask him how long it would take or some other tactical question. She keeps viewing him with an affectionate gaze. Her voluptuous body almost sliding along the smooth leather couch towards his torso.

"Would you like to know how much time it would take to get this done?" Ralph throws out the question to get her to start thinking and reduce the gaze upon him. He feels a little out of place with the sexy, aged woman's gaze.

"How much time do you want?" she asks.

"Really, is she that liberal that she offered me the option to select the amount of time I need!" his mind yells.

"I would need around 2 weeks to get all the work done and the application setup for use," he confidently says.

"Take three if you need to. I believe that to do a good job you need time. So take as much as you need!" she chimes.

"There's got to be a catch to why she is so nice," he thinks. "There is always something someone wants from you when they are nice to you!" Mama would say.

In the US, people are good to you either when they know you have something they need or when they have a possibility of attaining monetary or sexual gratification from you. Apart from this, the only other reason many people would want to help is if they see they are not breaking a law to do so or if you are so shit out of luck that they feel sorry for you.

And isn't that how it is in most parts of this market dominated world! People are viewed as prospects and situations as opportunities. Humans are looked upon as a means to an end. And how is all this categorized – "its business!" – a common quote heard in many parts of the world and especially in America.

"Sure. I will take the time I need! But I don't think it should take more than two weeks," he says plainly.

"Have a good night Carla. I must be going now."

"Stay for dinner Ralph. It wouldn't hurt to go on a full stomach."

"Thanks so much for offering. But I need to be home before it gets dark."

It was winter season and it got dark quickly. Ralph didn't seem too interested in getting laid by the older, albeit attractive woman.

****

"Mrs. Shurfina can wait for you to come back after visiting your family," says Heather.

"That's awesome! Thanks Heather."

"Great. Mrs. Shurfina just wanted to ensure you get the time you need to do what you need to do."

"Thanks again!"

"So, would the 25th Monday be a good day to start?"

"Yes, that would be great. One week after I come back from my trip!"

"Look forward to joining you guys," says Ralph with a touch of enthusiasm in his tone.

"Same here Ralph! Mrs. Shurfina can't wait to have you here."

Feeling the exhilaration of a smooth conversation Ralph proceeds to put together the design of his blueprint for Carla's customer management system.

"*It is done!*" he says.

It's 7:15pm and Ralph has completed the wee bit of the remaining part of the solution for Reike Bridal Services.

"She should be satisfied with the results," quotes the Inner Voice as Ralph vigorously tests the product.

"*Now all I need to do is offload this product into the systems of Reike Bridal. That hot bitch is going to flip when she sees this. Will probably give me a hard blow too!!*" he says to himself with gusto.

318

Men of his age are particularly inclined to the pleasures of sexual activity. And which young man isn't! The loneliness in a foreign country combined with the growth in hormones renders a burgeoning supply of pent up sexual energy. One which is seldom spent fantasizing alone. Real-time activity is a good panacea to releasing that desire; not necessarily to realize it.

He completes the work. Sets it aside and then takes a shower. The next couple of hours will be spent at the International House party. He is often asked to come to the parties with his laptop to play some music and add value to the crowd. Matilda though, is not there this time. The demise of the relationship came about gradually and literally unannounced.

While at the party Ralph gets a surprise call from a friend he had met while at a club some time ago.

"Hey Ralph. You want to come to Cupid Freedom today. We're having a bikini party at 11 pm tonight" says Andrew.
"I would love to. But I don't have a way to get there."
"I could give you a ride in my car. That shouldn't be a problem."
"Ummm....well.."
"Come on bud. You shouldn't have to think and analyze so much for this. It's a bikini party which means a lot of half-naked, sexy girls along with their friends. There is just one answer – Yes!!" gasps Andrew at Ralph's lack of overt understanding and apparent hesitation.

"Yeah, yeah!"
"So I'll come get you at 10:00 pm then. Okay!"
"Yeah that's cool," replies a smiling and 'no longer in a dilemma' Ralph.

Decision-making by the self is a crucial facet of life in the US if not in many other Western countries. In India, Mum and Dad would make almost all decisions for Ralph and his brother Douglas. Independence was literally non-existent or rather not afforded. "We know what's best for you!" was a common rejoinder to Ralph's protests to make his own decisions.

Very little was left for self-thought or self-analysis. It was the product of a collectivistic culture. The US is different though. Almost all decisions are to be made by the self. How does a domesticated, tamed lion respond when it is thrust into the wild after six years of captivity and human-assisted feeding. It obviously cannot hunt and wouldn't be able to survive too long in that setting.

The same was the case with Ralph. Arriving at yes or no decisions was particularly difficult for him and his underdeveloped, non-individualistic mindset. In the US, it is but obvious that an individualistic mindset grants you way more mileage than a collectivistic attitude.

****

Half an hour before 10 pm, Ralph excuses himself from the party after wishing well to all the missionaries, lay people converted to missionaries, friends of International House and other acquaintances he has made before heading upstairs. "*That was a pretty good party. The food was good too,*" he says to himself as he quickly goes up the stairs. Thrusts the door open and then quickly bolts it shut.

As he gets his hair gelled and ready to go, his party instincts begin to play out. He dons his white party shirts, cream khaki pants. In less than fifteen minutes, he is fit and ready to go. All trim and fine.

"Ooh, I forgot. I need a shave too." The shave renders his cheeks as smooth as a baby's bottom.
"Hey bro, I am with my bright grey machine outside. Come and get me!" says the Hispanic sounding voice on the phone.

Ralph gingerly tiptoes down the staircase to get to the door. He prefers his party-going escapades to be confidential.

"*Gosh. Going from one party to another!*" he quips to himself.
"Now you're living the American way!" says the Inner Voice candidly.
"Hey, ma man. Come on into my humble vehicle. We're gonna get you to Ibiza!" says Andrew from his car.
"You're the man!"
"Ralph, we're going to go get Ray too."
"Cool. Ray's coming?"
"Yes, we won't be able to enjoy as much without him!"
"Certainly not."

The car cruises at a higher speed to the smooth tunes of La Bamba and Gypsy Kings. Andrew has a taste for smooth Latin songs. And Ralph can only revel in the extent of his friend's acoustic prowess. It definitely helps to have friends with advanced musical tastes. The music can be electrifying, energizing, mellow or soothing and depending on your mood you could appreciate it or hate it. Ralph would have a lot of Latino exposure as the night progressed.

****

The pretty little girl takes two dollar bills and hands them tokens for their coats. As Ralph walks into the fray of electron charged bodies, black flannel dresses, miniskirts and fashionable tunics he feels the exuberant energy of youth and fun. Clubbing in America definitely has a great element of youth to it.

"Hey, so you enjoying the party and all that," he asks randomly to a smoking hot, dark haired girl.
"Yes. The music is awesome!" she says.
"I'm Ralph. What's your name?"
"I'm Cassandra."
"Where you from?"
"I'm from Brazil. You?"
"I am originally from India. But settled here since a couple of years."
"What do you do here?" she inquisitively asks.
"I am an analyst at Siemens," he confidently says. Having a job makes it a lot easier while approaching random women. A job means that you have something to do and of course it means money.

Someone had told him never to say that he was a student or any other word indicating a lack of money or earning. Not with a good looking woman at least. It seemed as though good looking women look for deep pockets in men they meet. And that was the 'hookup' advice his buddies Andrew and Ray had told him.

He had no qualms about quoting his Siemens job as full time as he would be able to justify the truth to a great extent; although it was only an internship.

"Oh nice!"
"What about you?"

"I work in a hospital."
"That's about the information you will need," says the Inner voice cautioning Ralph against being too nosey at the start.

When it comes to women never deliberate too much about the professional side of things. Focus more on not being put in the friend zone and on building sexual tension.

At least when it comes to women in America, they want to have fun. They want a guy that can sing and dance with them, that can take them out and have a good time with them. Boring topics and boring guys are usually kicked to the curb. American women, and in fact, women in most parts of the world today cannot stand boredom or not having anything interesting to do. If you are a guy that knows how to beat this you have beaten a major roadblock.

With increased globalization, a majority of countries and their people are unconsciously adopting a Western sub-culture and mindset. One that involves the likes of Miley Cyrus, Rihanna and Justin Bieber.

"So what brings you to this club?" she asks.
"I like it," is his typical nerdy response.
"Why do you like it?" she quizzes.
"Cause you're here," he surprises even himself with that response. He always had this thought that he was slow at the mouth. But he can apparently hold his own when put in the situation.
She bursts out laughing. "So you knew I was going to come here huh!" she says as she tries to mask the laugh.
"Yes and I even knew the color and size of the dress you were going to wear," he says as he reaches for her hand instinctively.

People from a different culture can say things considered 'weird' or 'creepy' in an American cultural context. But these statements are considered very appropriate and innocuous in non-American settings. Even in other Western settings in fact.

Ray and Andrew are surprised with the rapidity with which Ralph has developed a rapport with the hot dame. They try to reach closer to listen to the conversation. But the racy crowd in between is too thick, too uncompromising to give way or space for two strong, polite men.

"Wow. Well, so you know everything about me then."
"I guess I do."
"Are you a mind reader or something."
"No. But I am a mind reader who can only read your mind," he grins.
"How sweet. I have a mind reader and I don't even have to pay for it. I must be special."
"You certainly are..(pause)....for me at least," he smiles coyly.

She looks at him with adoring eyes, bites a lip and continues staring with a look of affection and possibility. For a moment she looks confused. But the confusion is normal. Women keep analyzing to see if a guy is dating, boyfriend or husband material. Various cues give them the fodder to conduct, complete and confirm their analysis. The way a guy talks, behaves and treats them all contribute to their ideas.

"So would you like to dance," he casually asks.
"Absolutely!" she galls.

They start off with a wild dance and start feeling each other out; slowly and steadily. He touching her more than the other way round.

Time seems to run quickly and they reach a plateau of interaction. He feels it. "You need to keep her interested!" cautions the Inner Voice.

"How about we get a drink," he suggests.
"Sure."
"I'd like to have Coca-Cola. What would you like?" he asks.
"I'll have a Bloody Mary," she asks the bartender.

Ralph grabs his Coke as she looks at him with a queer gaze.

"I'll wait for your drink to come before I start sipping," he says.

She smiles delicately. Women all over the world tend to have an inordinate appreciation for considerate and kind men and the actions that go with such care. But there are also those who would just sideline male attention and care as a façade for being called the weaker sex.

"So do you work out?" she asks.
"Yes I do. But I've not been working out much lately," he admits.
"Why?"

"You seem very flexible and are good at dancing. I figured you were pretty fit and exercised quite a bit."

"Yeah I like to stay active."

"What else do you do for exercise?"

"Umm, pushups, basketball, hockey, yoga."

"Did I hear you say hockey?"

"Here you go Miss. Enjoy your drink," says the bartender as he lays the drink in front of the hottie.

"Thank you!"

"Yes. Hockey I know is a girl's game in the US. But I have been playing it since I was a child. And I have no problem being regarded as gay or closer to the girls by doing this."

His comments put an incandescent smile on her face.

"Wow looks like you know your way around women!"

"I try."

"So what type of yoga do you do?"

"All types. But mostly stretching. Stretching is a major part of any yoga."

"Do you do yoga?"

"What do you stretch?" she asks with a sparkle in her eyes.

"Legs, hands, extremities, torso may be," he says seeming ignorant about her suggestiveness.

"What else do you stretch?" she persists.

"What else is there to stretch!" he smiles seeming to know what she is referring to.

"Umm so many other things," she smiles.

Her demeanor seems to transform from bland to horny in a short while.

"Time to up the ante!" says the Inner Voice.

"Yoga is good for every extremity and appendage of the body" he quips.

"Do you do yoga?"

"Yes I do stretching, but I like to do Kamasutra-based yogic poses," she says.

He almost flinches but maintains an iron control over his instincts.

"The poses aid stretching and enhance muscle strength and flexibility. Flexibility that could be used in everyday life and also in many other activities," she purrs.

324

"She's heated up boy!" the Inner Voice summons.

As she turns to sip her drink, Ralph quickly gulps down the coke.

"You want a sip," she asks after taking a sip of the vodka based drink.

Ralph nods and reaches for the glass of Bloody Mary. Putting his hands over hers, he delicately places his lips on the rims of the glass and lets the cold liquid pass down his throat. It seems to have a calming effect on the energy-charged lad. As though the orgasmic peace of a voluptuous damsel has descended on his persona.

"Pretty good huh!" she remarks.
"Yeah. Heavenly!"

He casts aside the Coke and sits there as though in a trance.

"So how do you know about Kamasutra and the poses?" he asks.
"I am just interested in yoga. And health!"
"Do you know a lot?" he questions.
"Almost all the positions," she says with a twinkle in her eyes.

[Pause]

"Maybe I can show you some!"
"Sure," he says not knowing how to respond. When faced with an offer from a beautiful girl; err on the side of acceptance; is the thumb rule of action.
"If you're done with your Coke we can go home," she says.
If anything he is now surprised. *"Is this the day he loses his virginity!"* he wonders.
"I'm done with the coke!"

She gulps down the remainder of the Bloody Mary and gets off the high barstool. He reaches to support her and puts his hands on her waist. They glide towards the jacket counter and grab their jackets. It is clear these two love birds are in a trance which will end in only one way.

"Hey where are they going," says Ray noticing the hot babe with Ralph in tow.

Andrew turns his head sharply to see how the rookie managed to convince the hottie.

"How did that grasshopper manage to clutch on to that thing?" he says. "Beginner's luck," says Ray looking pleasantly surprised.
Andrew quickly texts Ralph. "Hey bro. Don't know where you are going. But just keep me posted if you need help."

Andrew knows it would blow Ralph's night if he walked towards the couple and asked where he was going. She probably wouldn't feel comfortable knowing that there are other guys with him. Or even that he's attached to them.

****

The porch to the house is large. As she walks up the stairs her large breasts surge forward like rubber balls bouncing on frothing waves of ocean water. Her mini skirt seems a lot smaller than in the club. It's clear the sip of the Bloody Mary seems to be having quite an effect on his imagination. It would hopefully be even more useful as the night progressed.

There are four rooms on the second floor; all with flower vases outside them. The area has a queer wood finishing to it and is well ensconced in a seemingly exclusive and very private part of the house.

"This way hon!" she says.

As he obediently follows her, she deftly pulls out the key from a location in her mini skirt and inserts it into the key hole. With the door open, both of them slide in; her hand firmly on his arm.

"Nice room!" he instinctively says.
"Don't worry you don't have to compliment me. I'd like to get cozy anyway." Her comment comes like a bolt out of a clear sky. Some things look quite certain now. And he figures it's not just a flicker of a doubt.

She delicately takes off her heels and tosses them into the closet. Then she turns around and looks at him seductively.

"So are you hungry or anything?" asks Ralph feeling a little unnerved.
"Yes I am!" she says as she plops into the soft couch.
"Where is the kitchen. I could make you something."
"Come sit here. I will tell you what you can make me."

He feels the surge of accomplishment suddenly. The accomplishment of being close to a woman. He has never had this close of an experience before except with the pugnacious Jessica. He slowly walks towards the couch and sits in one corner of it. She sits upright and looking at him with a slight smirk begins to tap the couch signaling him to get closer. He cautiously slides towards her.

"Don't be so anxious. I won't bite," she says as she raises her legs exposing the floss like lingerie.

Ralph can't seem to bear it any longer. He voluntarily slides closer to her and holds her by the hips.

She puts her arms around his neck, rolls her palms along his cheeks and his nose. All along feeling the symmetry of his face. The handsome lad is quite a handful.

He reaches for her shoulders as he gently pins her down and starts rubbing her neck with his lips as pillows. She purrs and relaxes as she gently hugs him harder. As the neck kissing gets more intense, he progresses to kiss her deeper down the neckline. His hands instinctively reach for the straps of her top. He coolly lets the top slide off.

The callow lad senses a sweet jasmine aroma as he kisses her down her cleavage. She rubs his back hard and wraps her legs around him. "*I wish I had studied and remembered more about the Kamasutra positions from that book,*" he says to himself.

The night is vigorous and full of energy. Midway she slides a condom on his manhood and they make mad, passionate love. The pushing and the friction are robust but the air conditioner is noisy and the other girls in the house are either absent or fast asleep.

With two tired bodies side by side, Ralph falls into a deep slumber. Until the feeling of an alien room and a warm naked body close by makes him bat an eyelid a couple of hours later. "Read your phone!" says the Inner Voice.

"Hey bud. Make sure you leave before everyone wakes up if it's a one night fling. Just a rule of thumb," reads the message from Andrew.

Exactly forty-five minutes after reading that message Ralph heads out of the calm house towards home. His senses are at their optimum level and he feels recharged from the smooth exercise of the previous night.

He remembers kissing Cassandra on the forehead after getting dressed before leaving the house. Though he could just walk out he had preferred to be more decent and kiss the sleeping beauty goodbye.

He is grateful his pants still contain the change he had put in the night before. Catching a bus won't be a problem with this. He doesn't have a credit card anyways. Being an international student was like being a newborn baby in the US. Brand new social security number, no credit history, no background, very few friends or no friends.

****

"Your hardware systems here could also be rearranged to save on power and reduce cleaning costs," says Ralph emphatically as he winds up the installation of the IT solution in Reike Bridal services.

"Groovy! I guess you know that too!" says Carla.

He smiles.

"Is there anything you don't know!"

"Yes. I don't know how to watch TV, how to dance and how to bake," he quips.

"Don't know to dance. Well, I think I can teach you that. The rest we can pray for divine intervention!" Both of them burst out in spontaneous laughter.

"So this system should work like a charm. All you need to do is enter relevant information, that's it."

"Awesome! – you're awesome!" she smiles.

"You enter information the way I showed you earlier. Just use it for a couple of days and then let me know how you find it. If changes are needed we can always do that," he says reassuringly.

"I trust your system is very strong and I am sure I will like it," she says.

"Let's hope so," he smiles.

****

"Excuse me, does this bus go to Lowerbrook avenue?" Ralph asks.

"Yes it does," replies the kindly old black man.

"Why don't you have gloves young man. It's the beginning of the year and it's still quite cold."

"I forgot to carry them."

"Well, that's something you just can't afford to miss. Health is something which once lost is difficult to get back."

"I hear you on that Sir," says Ralph as he reaches for his pocket while climbing the bus.

"So where you from kid?" The old man appears interested in talking to the young man.

"Where do you think I am from?"

"Pakistan (pause)…may be."

"I'm from India actually," smiles Ralph. "Why did you think Pakistan?"

"You're lighter than most Indian people I've seen."

"Okay."

"Well, I might have a distant relative from Pakistan then."

"So you're new to the US is it?"

"Yes. Just came around 13 months ago."

"Wow. How are you finding it so far!"

"It's an interesting place. But very different from where I come."

"It sure must be."

"What did you come here to do son?"

The bus comes to a sudden halt and Ralph looks outside to see the derelict neighborhood. Two rough looking African American guys jump into the bus and go to the back of the bus without paying the bus fare. The driver doesn't protest. Ralph looks at the old man surprised.

"Yeah. Regular occurrences in this neighborhood!" the driver explains. "I've lived in this area for twenty-three years and almost every month we have some sort of shooting, killing or homicide here. Not a week goes by without some sort of trouble."

[Pause]

"That's the reality here. Keep yourself safe wherever you happen to pass in this neighborhood," he cautions the young Asian.

"You mean keep running or stand and fight when attacked?"

"I meant if you can avoid going through this neighborhood do so!" the old man gawks at him seriously.

"Okay!!"

"You see those two guys at the back there. They didn't pay to ride the bus. You don't see a lot of that in other neighborhoods not too far away from here. But had I argued with them we probably would have had a fight or probably even a dead person on the bus."

"Really? Is it that serious?" says Ralph looking perplexed.

"Yes. Guns and bullets are easy to obtain in this country. You can even obtain them without a license if you know people. Again, it's who you know."

"Is that why the killing and homicide rate is so high?"

"That and also that the new generation lacks patience and they have easy access to all lethal weapons possible. Even civilians can get their hands on certain military equipment which would be a lot harder, if not impossible to get in other countries. Moreover, the value system nowadays is not the same as when I was young."

[Pause] The old man glances at the two men speaking loudly at the back of the bus. It is obvious they are speaking obscenities concerning a drug deal.

"The new generation of African Americans has few role models and a greater number of delinquents from broken families. The virtues which were part of my growing up as a boy are not something they have the benefit of knowing. Though I doubt they would want to learn those values. Those values lack fashionable appeal among the youth. They are considered boring and fuddy-duddy!" he says giving Ralph a suggestive look.

"What do you do when two or three guys come after you in a neighborhood like this, carrying guns or knives?"

"First rule of thumb; do not resist! These thugs are known to kill at the slightest sign of contest. They are already under pressure from the police. So they generally focus on soft targets expecting the victim not to retaliate much. Neutralizing a soft target is considered way easier than a hard target anyways."

"It's better you give them everything you have when they ask. You might lose a few dollars or even a lot of money. But you will escape with your life to live, fight and love another day."

"Ok...!" Ralph says looking concerned.

"You don't really have to fear son. Just watch your back in this city. There are a lot of places here you wouldn't want to visit after a certain time. Or in some cases not at all. And be aware of your surroundings."

"Yeah. I think that's always important."

"I am sure in your country too, there are good and not so good neighborhoods and also good and bad people."

"Yes, it's the same in my country too. Only thing we don't have as many guns there as they do here," Ralphs says plainly.

"Yeah, it's a big country son. And it's definitely different from yours."

"So have you made friends since you've been here?"

"Yes, I have a few. Though it hasn't been that easy."

"Yeah. People can be quite superficial and transactional here. They generally want to have something to do with you only if you are doing business with them."

"So is there a way you can become good friends with them in spite of the business-like approach?"

"Yes. In some cases. Always start with a business approach first, though. As you gain their confidence and trust go in for the meat."

"Meat?"

"Yeah. Invite them over to parties or movies. Accept their invitations to parties! As you get closer to them feel free to take a larger role in their lives depending on the situation."

"How do you know when to push forward in terms of getting more friendly?" Ralph asks looking curious.

"It all depends on your judgment. You need to know when to get closer or work towards getting closer in life. That's something that comes with experience. I understand you are young. But you just learn some things by getting your knees skinned in life."

"Knees skinned?"

"Yeah not everything can be told or taught," says the old man plainly.

Ralph listens carefully to the old man's advice.

"Do you have a girlfriend?" the old man asks.

"Had. Not anymore."

"Okay. Having an American girlfriend might be useful in giving you a couple of tips about how to develop close relationships with people here."

"Okay."

"So you are currently single then?"

"Yep. And enjoying it."

"When you are young and single you have a lot to look forward to."

"There's a lot of stress these days, though."

"Stress is a normal part of life. And I am sure it exists as much in your country as it does here."

"So what do we do about it?"

"You cannot stop it, but you can change your attitude towards it. It's all attitude. Attitude helps you deal with the unexpected twists and turns of life."

[Pause]

"The best way to fight stress is to first know it exists. The next step is to look for ways to eliminate the situation that is causing the stress."

"What if you don't find a solution?"

The old man pauses and gives it a thought again.

"Well, then you just need to figure out a temporary placebo that can reduce the difficulties you are facing. Particularly when eliminating the difficulties might not be possible."

"Sometimes in life, it is not entirely possible to solve problems. You just need to develop the resilience to outlast them."

"Only God can solve problems if your prayers are strong enough."

Ralph notices a glint in the old man's eyes as he says this. And wonders.

"With God all things are possible!" says the man as the bus reaches Lowerbrook Avenue, Ralph's stop.

****

"So this your stop?" says the old man noticing Ralph stir.

"Looks like it…it is," smiles Ralph, feeling the relaxation that comes from being on home turf.

"Home sweet home! East or west, home is the best," serenades the old man.

"Absolutely Sir. It was a pleasure meeting you!"

"I regard it as a great opportunity to talk to a younger soul. If I help them it's a bonus."

"Take care," he says as he draws out his hand to shake Ralph's.

"Thank you Sir. It was a pleasure," says Ralph with a smile more genuine than many the old man had seen in the recent past.

The conversation with the old man was enlightening, to say the least. *"Wish I got this illiterate black man lecturing me regularly. At least he's way more smarter than those overpaid, fucked up professors in the university,"* quips Ralph as he rolls down the stairs of the bus.

The morning sun is pristine and the air fresh. After the night of romantic revelry and the bus ride of wisdom, Ralph feels a new mojo in him. A new purpose to achieve old objectives and goals with greater vigor.

Ralph gets freshened up and heads to Carla's home office to implement the final part of the database solution he has been working on for her.

"So in case Dr. Alamuddin asks you about it, you can tell him it's implemented. This is the final stage. And I can give you a run-down of how to use it today," he says to her.

He gives her a detailed walk-through of the system. All along she looks at him with sensual delight. His facial features, skin tone, hair and physique are worth dying for. And she can't begin to get enough of him. She controls her actionable desires though in the interests of maintaining propriety and in order to allow the work to get done.

Two days later Ralph visits Carla on her invitation to inquire how she finds the new system.

"The system works great. In fact, the connections between customer history and current need are amazing. You did an awesome job!"

"I am glad it's working the way you wanted it to."

"Well, it's working even better than that. You seem to have read my mind."

"Oh. So I have mind reading skills now."

"You must! I need to pay you or give you something for this," she says with a glint in her eyes.

"Your good recommendation should suffice!"

"Ralph why don't you come work for me. We have enough work here for a lifetime."

Ralph remains silent.

"Oh and we can sponsor you, the visa you need to start work and live here," she says sensing that the international student would need legal permission to work and continue to live in the US.

Ralph's face lights up with respect and gratitude.

"Oh Carla, that's so very nice of you. And you can't believe how much I appreciate it now and will continue to appreciate it all my life."

She looks at him with anxious expectation.

"However, I have an offer for an internship at a medical device company. And I am scheduled to start in a week."

"Oh that's awesome," she tries to conceal her disappointment regarding him not joining her team but tries to show she is happy for him.

[Pause]

"So when do you join them?"

"Next week," he smiles.

"Okay," she works very hard to put on a happy, non-negative face. It's difficult to hide your displeasure when you want something real bad and you know you are not going to get it.

"Sounds like you are all gung-ho about the position at the company!"

"Well, it's good experience."

"I'm sure it is. I will miss having you here. But I am glad you will be at a place you like and would grow at."

Ralph senses a forlorn feeling in Carla. For a moment he feels the strain that has put some of the clearly visible wrinkles on her otherwise vibrant face. He feels bad.

"Well, the opportunity will be of great significance to my career and ability to get future jobs in a better profile. But I would love to continue to help your company and the IT systems grow in whatever way I can."
"Oh that's so nice of you Ralph. I don't know when I have last come across a man of intellect as high as you and character as profound. Surely, God must have spent a lot more time creating you than the rest of us!" she holds his palms in hers and caresses them affectionately.

He smiles and no longer feels the sensual urges he would when she would get close to him. This time it's more of her affection that he feels. It is evident their relationship has matured from one of mere 'lustful suggestion' to 'genuine caring and concern.' When relationships reach that level it is evident they have matured.

"Hey Ralph," she looks at him intently as though wishing to tell him something he already knows. She draws her eyes closer to his. "If you ever need a reference in any job process don't hesitate to ask okay!"
"Oh, you're too nice."
"No. I'm serious. I would be honored to provide you the highest recommendation you need. At any time in your life," she says.
"Oh. I'm honored, Carla. I will keep that in mind for the rest of my life!"
"Please do Ralph. It would help me to repay some of the debt I owe you."

They hug and he lightly kisses her on the cheek as they bid farewell. It's not the last time they would cross paths.

****

Sitting in his room on the couch that night, Ralph feels the hope in life written all over the walls of his room. Never-the-less he knows the uncertainties and tragedies of life are always around the corner. Being watchful is a trait he could not have learnt sooner in the US. The US, a crucible of situations, happenings, discoveries, talents, tragedies and triumphs. So disparate yet so united in the fabric of its being that people who enter it learn to change. They learn to change their approach to life and their idea of success and quality of life.

There is little to be rigid here except values. Values don't change – not even in the counter-cultures that constantly erupt in this wellspring of a country.

Fashions and fads keep changing to enable retailers and organizations to continue doing business and earning profits. What remains constant though is people's desire to live in peace, happiness and prosperity. Ralph had the same urge. To live a successful life, with love and hope of a better tomorrow.

The phone buzzes with a name he doesn't have to read to know. Mum is always close at hand when nonchalant thoughts prowl his mind, he thinks.

"Hello Baba!"
"Hello Mama," he almost interrupts her.
"How are you?" she asks.
"I am fine!"

[Pause]

The silence is rife with telepathic thoughts about what the latest happenings are. For some reason, there is always this overwhelming feeling that Mum always knows what is happening.

"I start my internship at Siemens tomorrow," he smiles.
"Oh great. That is fantastic."
"You have kept your clothes and everything, pen, paper, etc. ready right," she suggests peremptorily.
"Yes, I have. But this will be the first time I will be in a formal company setting."
"Yes. There is nothing to worry about. Be steadfast in your efforts, warm in your reach and strong in your hope. Companies are like groups of people; only more organized. Or at least they are required to be."

[Pause] Ralph wonders what she is getting at.

"There is always a leader. The person doesn't have to be the smartest or most intelligent. But he might be the most vociferous. Group dynamics play a great part in teams in companies."

[Pause again]

"Whatever happens, remember that perseverance and hard work always pays off. Never take sides or indulge in office politics. Because people who do that are insecure and unsure of themselves. Focus on producing a good work output."

"Never maintain grudges either. They will consume you before you know it. Only remember whom to watch out for."

"Just like in any workplace; even the ones here in India; there are cobras and vipers everywhere. In any part of the world, you will find them. Always be neutral when it comes to office politics. Help people out. What you give will come back to you two-fold."

Ralph could feel the weight in Mum's voice.

"Such earnestness comes only with experience and frontline exposure to the vagaries of life," he says to himself.

"I wonder how it is going to be! It's a German company so people there are bound to be hard working and very precise."

"If you work diligently every day you will also become strong in what you do. There is no deep secret to being smart. It's all hard work and discipline."

"I will work hard Mama!"

"I know you will."

"Go to bed now son," she says with a smile of approval. "You have a long day ahead tomorrow."

****

The next morning he puts on his best shirt. The morning is cold so he pulls out his heavy jacket. The previous winter his light windbreaker had proved useless against the snow. In his hurry to get home, it had got caught in the door jamb of the train. A lateral movement resulted in it getting torn beyond repair. Mama had told him to try and repair it.

But in America, broken things don't get repaired. They are just replaced. That's just the nature of life in the US. Things and relationships that don't work out just get sidelined. Ralph would later come to understand that things and projects in the US get discarded because it is cheaper to buy new stuff then to invest time and energy in replacing old equipment.

There is an element of frustration and disappointment that sets in when trying to fix broken stuff. At least that's the feeling it gives people who want to get the job done. Americans, for the most part, are a hard working bunch and look to get work done on time most of the time. Ralph had seen before that when working with Americans it is best not to get them irritated or disappointed even by mistake. Not that they are not forgiving. But every poor performance reduces your chances of getting business from the same person again.

****

As he heads to the office; his first day at work, he ponders the situations he is going to face and what he is going to need to get done. His thoughts are in line with most newbies on their way to the first day of work. *"What might American people be thinking though on their first day of work!"* he wonders.

"Do they have some different, special thoughts? Is their preparation extra solid and different? Do they get help from other people who are their contacts? How do they manage their onset into a new gig?" He knows his questions are many and he is callow. At this point, he has more questions than answers. But he knows those questions are going to be replaced by answers and more questions once he joins active duty.

The Inner Voice seems to be inactive this early in the morning. Normally it doesn't become active until later in the day. Probably because the hum of the train is drowning it out. Maybe the dull reverberations of the engine and the bogies of the train have created a separate incantation that's producing an alternative transcendental reality. The hum seems perfect; so constant, so rough, yet so boorishly smooth. Almost like a trance-inducing chant. The Inner voice probably feels the competition but prefers not to disturb the existing trance-like situation. But then again, maybe it is confident in the contemplation that the train's chant is kindling. It doesn't feel the need to disturb the thoughts that nature brings to Ralph. For Nature is a creation of the Almighty just like the Inner voice itself.

Mom used to say that things will figure themselves out. Indeed, he hopes and prays that this stint at the medical device company is smooth and full of learning. There are fifteen stations that the train needs to cross to reach the final destination. From there Ralph would need to take a bus to reach the company building.

He feels the exhaustion ebbing away as he peers through the sleek glass doors of the company building. He can see small reddish yellow lights blinking; almost like police sirens minus the blue light. There seem to be a few people but not a whole lot. As he approaches the threshold of the building, the portly countenance of the receptionist becomes evident. "Hold on, this is the main entrance isn't it!" says the Inner Voice. "*Yes. I need to report at the other entrance I guess?*" he says to himself. "*Gosh why do I make these crazy weird mistakes!*" he admonishes his common sense.

"Well that's why you have me right!" says the Voice from God. "I am here to see Heather. I had an appointment with her at 8:30 am."

The front desk assistant contacts Heather as he takes a seat, finally relieved that he is in the right location. A few seconds of rest seem like an hour of relaxation. The extremes of travel and effort make any sort of down time seem like a godsend. He needs to get used to a lifestyle of long travel and quality work. He seems to sense that the current situation would necessitate a shift in operational tactics and probably even thought process. He still has one semester of school to complete so moving his residence closer to the company would not be possible soon.

"When the going gets tough; the tough get going!" was something he always believed in. It would play out again; at least he hoped so.

Heather greets the handsome lad and guides him through the maze-like network of office cubicles and rooms. They first get him an office badge; then walk towards the laptop inventory department and obtain the laptop that had been assigned to him. "Wow looks like you are getting famous here signing requisitions for laptops and all," says the Inner Voice almost cheering him up for the day ahead.

Her demeanor is very mild and motherly and she seems to be very concerned about him being able to understand the way the organization functions. As they walk, he feels relaxed and calm. Not in a romantic way, but in a way resembling an angel holding a child; protecting it with its every being.

Heather escorts him into a room where another HR person seems to be busy at work on her laptop. "Hi Ralph! Welcome to Siemens."

"Ralph meet Joyce. And she is our very knowledgeable and inspiring HR policy person."

"Hahaahahhha….you Heather you!!" says Joyce trying to deflect credit onto Heather.

"Well, we are just going to give you a brief about the company, its policies and some do's and don'ts as an intern."

"Sure."

The session moves at a brisk pace. And Ralph feels that it is just another set of routines until they come to the don'ts.

"We have an office communicator program but always watch what you write on it as everything is monitored by company network communications. You are allowed two breaks – one in the morning and the other in the afternoon. Each of ten minutes."

"We are an ISO certified organization so we ask that you follow the cleanliness and information security procedures set by your department."

"Apart from this, I don't have anything more. Your department manager might have a few more things to cover with you. Do you have any questions for me?"

"Umm…yes. What day do I fill up my timesheet? Does it have to be Friday only or can I do it the coming Monday as well?"

"You can do it the coming Monday. Though we prefer you do Friday as that helps us process payroll quicker. And your manager might have more to cover with you in that regard; more specifically relating to your department."

"Thanks!"

"Any other questions?"

"No. Thanks for the information."

"Great. So if you don't have any more questions, I will take you and introduce you to your manager Mrs. Shurfina."

"Sure."

Ralph could have sworn he saw Heather blush all throughout the meeting in the room. Joyce was totally professional, though. As Heather hands him over to Mrs. Shurfina, she shakes his hand and wishes him the best.

"Welcome to Siemens Ralph! How was your holiday?"
"It was nice. My father was not in the best of health so I had to rush home." Ralph knows that a health reason would be the most valid and legitimate when it comes to justifying delaying a start date or for that matter most other work tasks in corporate America. Little did he know that the trip to Goa would be one of his last in a long time. He had taken Dad kitchen items which he had obtained from the thrift store. He bought Mum a special bag from the duty-free shop at the airport. And also some Godiva chocolates.

Mrs. Shurfina is quite the uncharacteristic manager. Her large breasts and sprightly stride give her more of an athlete's look. Probably she was an athlete at one point many years ago though Ralph doesn't ask.

"How is he now?"
"He's better. So we are happy"
"Great! We did have some highly qualified candidates for this position that we didn't choose just because I felt you had a lot of potential. We have a lot of work to get done so we will give you some basic training and then you can start delivering."

Her approach seems very curt, direct and practical. He wonders what to expect going forward.

"Stay positive! First days are always high pressure," says the Inner voice.

****

It's a typical corner office and has a nice view of the outside greens. She begins showing him a few sheets of the type of work they do in her department. It looks very rudimentary and numeric; alphanumeric to be precise.

"So these are some coordinates of the kind of reports we generate from the marketing and warranty database that we have here," she says handing him the papers and charts. He seems clueless about these. But remains calm and composed. Experience has taught him not to reveal his feelings and opinions too soon lest it be misconstrued. Moreover, revealing your true feelings at the very outset too overtly can have the

341

added danger of revealing your ignorance or the lack of understanding about a subject area.

"We already have an intern here. She has been here for over a year and knows how things work around here. I will put you in touch with her."

"Okay."

"Let's head to her cube. This way." Mrs. Shurfina leads him towards the cube of her most prized intern.

"So, Lois will show you around a few things as she has provided terrific service to our department for a year now. Learn as much as you can from her," she advises.

"Sure."

"Hi Lois. So this is our new intern Ralph. He will be helping you with some of your most vexing duties. I have shown him around the place but being how new he is please help him around when he needs it."

"Hi!" says Lois in a very robotic tone.

"Hi Lois!" Ralph extends his hand.

She flinches at first and reluctantly extends her palm. Mrs. Shurfina smiles sensing Lois' behavior. Lois is not particularly the social kind. She is more the introverted, heads-down analyst.

"Okay, so I will leave you to her Ralph."

"Sure. Thanks, Mrs. Shurfina!"

"Sure. Call me Judith from now on," she smiles. Mrs. Shurfina is definitely not the friendly Mrs. Heffenhoffer. But using first names is a common norm in corporate America. A norm that facilitates stronger working relationships and a better work ethic.

"Umm...first it was Carla from Mrs. Heffenhoffer; now it is Judith from Mrs. Shurfina," titillates the Inner Voice. "Wonder what's next....Love from Lois!!"

****

"So you have a lot of work to do to match the requirements of this department. We have been having a backlog for the last several months and it is imperative that we clear up this load. The success of our department depends on it," she says looking coldly serious.

Her look and demeanor seem one of cruel concentration and callous disregard to gradual learning of the business and system infrastructure. Evidently, empathy is not one of her best traits. She looks focused;

almost artificial. When she dictates the coordinates of a task her demeanor is so robotic it seems realistically unreal. Ralph wonders how such a creature could get selected through an in-person interview. What do you do when a person gives you memorized, zero personality, clear cut answers as quickly and continuously as a tape recorder! "I guess you hire them," says the Inner Voice.

Is that correct? Or is it just that a German company would hire these so-called geeks on the premise that maybe they can get the job done regardless of their personality. Whether they are boring, robotic, rude or drop dead serious simply doesn't matter. Make them work is the catch phrase. And in all good stead.

"Okay. So what are the tasks I need to perform?" he asks.

"Actually we have a set of tasks per the main task!" her voice crescendos.

"So you mean like a task within a task."

"Yes and we could start with cleaning the Soarian database."

"What is Soarian database?"

"It's a database we use here," comes the curt reply.

"Why is it called Soarian?"

"We'll come to that later. But first, we need to have you do some cleaning work on it."

Ralph would realize in due course that when working with a less than ideal co-worker, relegate questions to a later time if the context of the discussion doesn't help explain their meaning. A lot of professional offices can have recalcitrant and obstructive cultures when it comes to entertaining newbie questions.

Although a little concerned with her presumptuous behavior in regards to questions, he maintains his calm. "Get her to answer questions gradually. She will yield," says the Inner Voice.

"What cleaning needs to be done?"

"We have a database housing 'customer data points.' This database has several columns of gibberish data. You need to spot this data and clean it up."

"Is there a script we need to modify to get this done?"

"No. It's to be done manually."

"What's the size of the database?"

"Several million records, possibly." For the first time in their ten minute interaction, she seems vulnerable and unaware.

When newbies enter the workplace, existing members try to put on a show of knowledge and power. The idea is to make the newcomer feel intimidated and thereby deliver respect. It's ultimately an exercise intended to have the newcomer toe the line of the temporary caretaker for an inordinate amount of time or for as long as possible preferably. Organizations have their pecking order inherently placed in the hierarchy.

"How could she not be certain about the size of the database," he wonders. *"Probably besides being a robot she is also a robotic dunce!"* Don't get intimidated by her show of unbridled efficiency and knowledge" says the Inner Voice.

He has worked with databases before and knows that scripts make life easier when it comes to data cleaning or refreshing. He refrains from questioning the bespectacled dork just yet.

"So these are the details of the database. Connect to it and start the cleaning asap," she says as she shoves a set of papers onto his lap.

He looks at her confused but smiles none-the-less. Agreeableness is important even when confronted with a disagreeable boss or co-worker. American professional standards necessitate trying to get along with the boss as long as the boss' behavior doesn't trespass into the forbidden territory of sexual harassment or abuse.

Over the next two days, he spends half his time trying to manually clean the database and the other half trying to develop a script to automate the cleaning operation. The work is difficult as there is very little guidance. The churlish Lois is busy doing her own tasks, most of which revolve around scheduling meetings for Judith. This pseudo administrative job is important as it lends vital face time with the boss. And what does vital face time with the boss finally lead to – room for favoritism or favor! No wonder administrative assistants tend to be very close to the boss and have special favor when it comes to various privileges.

The work is intense and he tries multiple ways to resolve the database cleansing issue. After much effort and grind, he gets a brainwave to change his approach. "Data is governed by quality parameters. You understand the parameters of quality; you understand which data is good

344

and which is bad and what makes the data dirty. You then develop a script to automate cleaning of the dirty data."

He is not sure if this is a random brainwave or a vision from the Inner Voice. Regardless he decides to give it a shot. Far from welcoming them, Lois doesn't seem to be a person who takes questions kindly. She tries her best to brush him off, rebukes his approaches for building a rapport and refutes his suggestions. Ralph though believes in the principle that "when at work, leave all your pride and ego at the door." "Hey Lois, I think we can clean up the database in three weeks flat if we use a script I have developed. It would get the work done so much faster in addition to making our lives easier."

She sighs and looks at him with scorn.

"Would you like to see how it works?" he continues, not showing any signs of being affected by her demeanor.

She still doesn't respond, continuing to look at the screen.

The positive Ralph is undeterred. "It is an amazing script and maybe you can represent it to Judith when we meet her end of the week." (Lois looking peeved) "Ralph, I thought I already told you. We just need to manually clean up the database. We don't need all these fancy techniques to get it done."
"These techniques might be fancy. But they sure reduce the amount of time it takes to complete the job. Not to mention the level of accuracy it brings into the work output."
"I am actually very busy right now so will not be able to see your stuff."
"How about tomorrow then?"
"I'm super occupied tomorrow too and won't be able to spare any time."
"That's okay," Ralph walks away even more determined to make his finding a success.
"If she doesn't want to cooperate in doing the right thing for the organization; I will keep pushing till the discoveries are noticed by management."

****

"How was the database structures test?" asks Dr. Brack to the class.

Silence.

"Well, I take silence as being positive."
[Pause] "Or maybe not. Though I was pleased with the answers to the programming questions for the most part."

He begins the class solving questions from the quiz. Towards the end of the class as students begin exiting the room; he lightly calls out to Ralph.

"Hello Ralph! How are you?"
"Pretty good Doctor."
"I thought the manner in which you solved the data sorting issue in the quiz was quite creative and ingenious."
"Thank you, Doctor. Glad you liked it."
"I think you have some great potential to work in a database-related field as an analyst and maybe even administrator."
"Oh. I'm flattered."
"If you ever need an internship feel free to reach out to me. I always have people from industry asking me for capable people to fill their jobs and internship openings."
"Thank you Doctor. But I currently am in an internship with Siemens."
"Oh nice. When did you start?"
"A couple of weeks ago."
"Do you like it?"
"It's interesting. And there's a lot to learn."
"Keep your eyes and ears open. It will all come together in due time. And I know your capabilities – you have a lot to look forward to young man."

Ralph smiles.

"Yeah. But let me know if you need an opportunity. Not that you would."
"Thanks so much Doctor. I sure will."

In America, people want to associate with capability and strength. If you're really good at what you do you will have people wanting to help you and be associated with you. On the flip side, if you are mediocre you probably would not obtain references or people to vouch for your capabilities too easily. It's just the hard reality of how capitalism works.

****

"What's the latest and the greatest Lois?" asks Judith looking at Lois directly.

"A lot. I set up those meetings with the Soarian development lead and key developers. Also prepared an agenda for the weekly touchpoint."

"Great! What about the Soarian database cleaning?"

"Ralph is doing that," she says looking at him with an expression somewhere between a smile and a smirk.

"Yes so I started cleaning the database and have been documenting the types of bad data prevalent in the repository," says Ralph.

"The hope is as I continue cleaning it manually, I will come across enough bad data patterns that I can eventually write a script to automate the cleaning."

"Wow. Awesome that is so cool. Automation is great!" says Judith.

"But I thought we were to only do the cleaning manually!" interjects Lois, surprised that Judith prefers Ralph's approach to getting the work done.

"I said no such thing. I only said that since manual cleaning is simple you can go ahead with it. If there is faster, better way to do it, it ought to be used."

"But wouldn't a script be confusing the matter," she interrupts Judith again.

"How would it confuse things?" Judith questions.

[Pause]

"If anything it would make things a lot more efficient. Our processes need to be streamlined and if automation can do it; then so be it. Great job Ralph!" Judith praises Ralph.

Lois no longer has either the smirk or the smile on her face. The color on her face changes from pale to blue. Judith's approval of Ralph's direction spells a foreboding of job insecurity for her. She had suspected this spring chicken, although callow, had a strong element of capability and will in him. But the extent of this result was quite unexpected.

"I have actually already developed a script and it did work wonders on the last few sectors of the database that I was working on."

"Oh! You are definitely ahead of the curve Ralph," Judith resonates. Ralph smiles. Lois is shell shocked.

"Yes, I will continue to test and perfect it till it can be deployed and used without even thinking what it is going to do."

"Great. Keep up the good work Ralph. I'd like to hear more about this in the coming week."

As they prepare to leave, Judith asks Lois to stay. Ralph takes leave.

"You didn't tell me about that magazine item you have been working on since the last two months Lois!" she asks looking concerned.

"Umm! Yes Judith, I am still working on it."

"That's like a one week job isn't it," Judith interrupts her looking at her with playful suspicion.

"Yes. I will have it by the coming week."

"Please do that. We need to have it ready for the VP of the department. She has been asking for it and in fact asked me for it this week."

"Yes!"

Lois exits Judith's office without another word. She literally stumbles on the way to her cubicle. Then hurries to the bathroom. When she looks in the mirror in the washroom she sees an image wrought with fear.

Ralph continues to work tirelessly in developing new forms of automation. His database cleansing program is a grand success in the department. And he gains not only Judith's recognition but the director, Mrs. Neumeister's attention.

Ralph's work in the classroom is impeccable. Aided with the real-time implementation experience in the Siemens internship he feels emboldened in developing better code; taking more coding risks and getting better quality results. In the database class, he earns an A- and overt recognition of Dr. Brack.

Lois' attitude no longer serves as a limiting factor or stressor for him. He knows that hard work and faith will take him where no one or no amount of partiality can ever stop him. All the limiting factors are only temporary in nature. God has a way of smelting the purest steel from iron and finding the most well-shaped diamond from coal. It all depends on whether you are willing to surrender your life to Him. Whether you are an immigrant, a student or a person in any other walk of life; God provides everyone with the struggle they need to learn respect for the world, for others and for Him.

The greatest form of revenge for those trying to put you down is unbridled success! Ralph realizes this and goes about trying to prove it.

****

1 month later

"Hey Ralph, we have a party for Siemens interns tomorrow. Why don't you come?" asks Ken, the German intern from Mr. Dodworth's department.

Ralph's interaction skills and knowledge of the German language have gained him wide popularity. His reputation now spans across most departments dealing directly or indirectly with marketing data. He is known in certain circles as the "dark German."

The march from 'international student turned intern' to reliable go-getter has had its share of difficulties but has been worth it.

"Sure. What time are you leaving?"
"I leave at 5:00 pm. Today is Friday," Ken says with a glint in his eyes.
"Most Americans would leave by 4:00 or 4:30 pm," Ralph thinks to himself.
"We could bring Lois too right?" he asks.
"Yes. Sure," says Ken.
"Okay. I will ask her."

[In a few minutes, at Lois' desk]

"Hey Lois. We are going for a German intern party to celebrate the end of the third quarter. Would you like to join us?"
"Thanks. But I have stuff to do."
"Really. It's just for three hours."
"Nope. No time today."
"I understand. But think of it this way. You spend one to two hours socializing and having fun. That down time will give you way more energy to get your work done faster and better."

She sits there shaking her head. Ralph approaches her and with a gentle touch to her shoulder, whispers.

"Lois, I know you are busy and dedicated. And that you would prefer doing your work rather than socializing but also think of what you are missing out on. You could make new friends, new connections. Connections that could change your life, give you new perspectives and make you feel good about yourself."
"I am not coming Ralph and I don't want to hear any of your advice," she screams.

Ralph flinches.

"Well. Suit yourself. Remember though, that time you said automation of the database cleansing work wouldn't work. You said Judith would reject it. And she ended up approving it with open arms. In fact today every team using that database thanks me for the level of automation I introduced into it. Automation which would not have been existent had I listened to you and not gone ahead with it."

[Pin drop silence]

"I hope this decision of yours to stay in your cubicle is not like that career limiting move you were trying to impose on me."
"You can try to destroy the careers of others but please don't destroy yourself, your life. That's all."

He begins to walk toward the corridor towards the Exit sign.

"Ralph!" comes the shrill voice from far aback.

He is taken aback to hear the bespectacled churl scream in a kinder tone. He suspects a probable change of heart. Though it could be a brick bat coming his way too. There were times when the girl used a soft touch to deliver a stronger message. Ralph had grown accustomed to Lois' rather unpredictable and capricious personality. She hurries towards him, a little breathless not from oxygen deprivation but a sort of change of heart.
"I'm sorry I was so rude to you back there. I didn't mean to be uncouth."

He looks at her, bewildered.

"I'd like to come for the party."
"Ohh! That's nice to hear," Ralph says still looking at her surprised.
"What time did you say it starts?"
"6:30 pm at the Roundhouse Apartments; 1st floor."
"How are you going there?"
"I don't know. Maybe hitch a ride with Ken or somebody."

Lois knew that Ralph used the train and then the bus to get to work. She sometimes wondered how he would survive such a commute day after day, week after week. Except for one time in the winter, he was never late. Whenever she entered he would be busy plugging away at the keyboard. He would come in early and leave late.

His urge to learn and understand the work seemed intense. Even Lois' "closed book information behavior" did not prevent him from pushing forward with learning what he needed to learn to execute his job. What kind of faith drove this young man to keep fighting the seemingly insurmountable odds to achieve the results he desired. It was desire and faith in a better tomorrow probably. The same faith that drives immigrants to cross oceans, deserts, barbed wire and fences to reach lands with milk and honey.

Once they cross these barriers there are a few more barriers to cross. Crossing people's mental barriers and their objections is another major obstacle. Getting people to accept an immigrant as an integral part of American society and culture is quite a herculean task. Ralph was going about this task with great vigor. He seemed to be on the verge of success with Lois.

Sometimes opening up closed minds is more strenuous than crossing borders or covering miles of daunting terrain. Ralph knew he was facing this challenge and would probably continue to face it as long as he did not make a name for himself in the US of A. He had only his wits, his strength and his will to fight against all the prejudice and hate that had and would come his way.

"I could give you a ride you know."

Ralph is stunned. In six months of being on the job, she had never offered him a ride. Obviously, there is some détente going on here.

"That's if you are okay going with me," she smiles playfully.
"That would be great," he smiles graciously. He informs Ken that he would be driving with Lois to the party just so he doesn't have to wait for him.

As they drive, Ralph tries to make small talk about her family, brothers, sisters and her former love interests. Being as guarded as she is in her normal setting; she resists discussing her former flames. He perseveres and learns that she has had a series of rejections in her personal life. Being abandoned by her father; then by a number of boyfriends; and not having any close friends either.

He understands the reason behind her closed, guarded nature. Being hurt by so many people in the past; she just doesn't want to make herself vulnerable to anybody; not any woman, definitely not any man. Showing love and concern for such individuals are important. They need emotional healing to help them cope with the pain of abandonment and loss. And when they receive that from you, they open up to you like never before.

As he flirts with the German females all over the place in the party, he notices Lois in the corner, isolated and alone. She has a glass of punch in her hand and is looking around plainly, not knowing who to approach or interact with. "Go approach her, she is all yours," comes the unexpected voice from his subconscious.

He goes next to her and gently places his palm on her shoulder. "So you enjoying the party?" he asks softly.
"Umm, yeah."
"You don't have to say yes if you are not. Just be yourself," he reassures her.
"No, it's nice," she says, not wanting to come across as a spoil-sport.
"So do you go to parties often?"
"Sometimes."

Something about her demeanor makes it sound like she just doesn't go for parties at all. In fact, she seems to be out of place at the party.

"There is a saying – that the more things change the more they remain the same!"

"Okay….aha"

"And that you are a sum of your experiences."

"So where is this getting at?"

"It's getting at you!" he smiles.

They both stare at each other. She is obviously very confused with his statements.

"You were never very social. You prefer being aloof, to yourself and reserved. People think you can be quite a snob sometimes."

"What do you think of me?" she interrupts.

"I think behind that hard exterior you are kind and nice at heart. And that you long to have the right company, good company or rather a companion."

He stares at her. She takes a deep breath and then winces. Almost giving away a feeling of resignation. Resignation to the vagaries of her attitude; her loss and seeming loss of hope.

"You have your whole life ahead of you though. And there is a lot of hope in life," he encourages her.

"How did you read my mind?" she blurts.

"Mind reading is a quality of those who have favor with the Gods!" he smiles again.

As her comfort level with discussing deep personal issues increases; Ralph senses the impossible becoming possible. He knows that she normally doesn't let her guard down and doesn't open up. But is open to new ideas when she opens up about her personality. What other way is there to make people open up even more than having them down a couple of vodka shots?

As he brings her the third vodka mocktail, she is visibly happier and less stressed out. Her personality begins to flow better. She lets loose her long locks of hair. Ralph's flirtatious element is at its peak. He swings his hand around her waist as they get closer. As he touches her hair; he plants a quick kiss on her lips. Two more follow along with the seemingly endless barrage of mocktails and pseudo-margaritas.

For the first time in a decade she feels the warmth of a man; delicate and nice. The intoxication seems to dispose of all her inhibitions. Makes her enjoy the attention and company a lot more. Not that she wouldn't have enjoyed it had she been sober.

Ralph quietly grabs her hand and leads her into a small private corniche and shuts the large door behind them. They kiss even harder as they plop onto the tiny bed…..he knows his way around her after that.

****

He wakes up early, kisses her on the forehead and walks out the door. She is still pretty intoxicated. Teetotalers find it hard to get over hangovers. Often it's the hangover that's more persistent than the lingering smell of beer and vodka. He takes the bus back home and reminisces the experience of boning his internship nemesis. "*Quite a hot cookie,*" he tells himself grinning. "Geeky girls can be hotter than they look. Which is why you need to marry a smart one," suggests the Inner Voice.

The next day is not the same. "Good morning Lois!" he says when she enters their work area. She simply nods her head and rushes to her desk. She used to derive power and strength from her barriers and professional relationships with everyone in the office. But now the so-called grasshopper whom she sought to control has broken down all her barriers and seen her most intimately. All of her assets and flaws were exposed to him. It is evident that with her barriers and secrets opened to him she no longer feels the same level of potency and strength as before. For the first time in several years, she feels vulnerable, exposed.

But he is not one to take advantage of this situation. He goes beside her, puts his hand on her shoulder and tries to make small talk with her. She participates in the small talk for a while; then quickly returns back to work. He senses she feels the shame of opening up to him. When in effect there should be no shame. It was a night of passion.

A week later she puts in her resignation. Ralph senses the cause to be a disruption in the environment after their intimate encounter. He is now the lead intern in Judith's department. Through all the turbulence things are finally looking up for him. In spite of all their professional differences, he didn't wish Lois to leave though.

H1 No. 1

THROUGHOUT RALPH'S INTERNSHIP IN the marketing data department, Lois had maintained an attitude of coldness and kept her distance. She would go to the cafeteria alone or sit along with a few other senior managers. Even if Ralph asked if she wanted to sit with him she would plainly refuse him. The cold treatment she meted out to him pushed him closer to the German interns. He sat with them and tried to brush up on his German language skills. He had studied German before but sitting with them gave him the opportunity to practice it.

In particular, he developed a close relationship with Ken Rueger. Ken worked for Mr. Dodworth's Medical Information Management department as an intern. He and Ken got along very well. Mainly because both of them enjoyed soccer and would play together quite often and partly because of his ability to learn and speak quite a bit of German. And that's what endeared him to several other German students interning there as well.

As they share quite a bit of quality time together, Ralph discusses the complexities of being a first generation immigrant in the US. "It's difficult to get a full-time job here because people shy away from sponsoring a work visa. Without the right papers, getting a job is hard unless you are a rocket scientist!"

"That would even be the case for me since I am from Germany and not a citizen," smiles Ken, raising an eyebrow to emphasize his point. But Ralph knows that being white opens more doors in the US than being the tawny color of his skin. Although the US is officially a religion and race neutral country; actual ground situations defy constitutional principles. Over the years the issues of race and color, not so much religion, have come to provide a tainted image of the country as being covertly racist.
"Maybe!" quips Ralph.

"Well you got one thing on your side....you are a programmer."

"Fair enough!"

"Do you have any openings in your department?"

"As a matter of fact, we do. Mr. Dodworth was saying he needed a JAVA programmer a few days ago. I would have applied for it had I been in programming. But had I been in programming you wouldn't have heard of this position," he grins clearly indicating competition is always prevalent.

"Okay. Do I apply online?"

"Nope. Send me your resume and I will forward it to Mr. Dodworth's secretary. She will pass it on to him so that he can review it."

"Cool. Hope I get some good news from this," says Ralph.

"Be positive man. Good things come to those who try and don't give up."

"I'm sure they do," he smiles.

****

"Hey Bob, you got a quarter?" says the middle-aged man outside the grocery store.

Ralph looks at him and wonders what to do. He doesn't have a lot of cash as he has used his currency to buy vegetables, eggs and milk at the produce center. He rummages into the deepest corners of his pant pockets and finally comes upon a nickel. He hands it over to the African American man, feeling a little embarrassed to hand over such a small amount.

"Giving any amount is better than giving none!" reminds the Inner Voice.

The African American man is evidently living on the streets. His stuff seems to be piled up some distance away in the corner, not far from the pavement. In the subprime mortgage crisis that hit America hard, almost ten percent of all homeowners had lost more equity in their house than the purchase price. Due to unrestricted lending to buy homes; demand spiked and prices of homes temporarily increased. The artificial price increase came crashing down when the lending diminished and people who could never afford the houses in the first place defaulted on their payments. The result was a massive crash in housing prices as cash-strapped banks began to look to sell off whatever remaining value they had in mortgaged properties.

What do you need to do to sell off mortgaged properties? Well firstly, you need to evict the current owners or people living in the house; then refurbish the place and finally place an ad for it on the open market at a competitive price. The hope is it will get sold for a price less than what it was originally purchased for and the bank will not face a complete loss. Sounds like a lesser of two evils, doesn't it!

But what about the untold suffering and hardship brought upon those who have to leave their home lock, stock and barrel. Imagine families leaving with their possessions, not knowing whether they will have a roof over their head that night or in the days to come. Families with children are the worst hit. Children come with expenses; whether it's education or clothes or food or some other tidbits of convenience. More than anything it is the psychological burden of not being able to quit and run because there is the responsibility of a child. An innocent child that knows nothing, has seen nothing. All they know is you as their world. You can relegate responsibility to your employer, to your job or your spouse but not to your child because God has assigned you to them. They are a gift which came without the option of "return after purchase."

The economic downturn had hit not just lower middle-class folks. Upper middle-class families, college graduates and recently laid off workers were all struggling under the strain of decimated employment and loss of positions that would probably never come back due to the significant contraction of the economy. The wars in Iraq and Afghanistan were a huge drain on the economy as well. God knows why presidents and rulers look to fight wars when it is clearly evident that there are millions who can barely scrape a decent meal a day.

Although there is very little you can do with a nickel, the aged man gratefully smiles at Ralph. "Never allow your happiness to be determined by extraneous factors. Happiness is a state of mind and you should keep it that way!" quips the Inner Voice. The old man has tremendous grace and tolerance in the light of oppressive, almost crushing misery.

"What happened Sir?" asks Ralph, seeming oblivious to the old man's situation. When you don't understand a situation you are bound to ask very basic questions.

"I lost my home son. Couldn't pay the dang mortgage!" he says, a guttural cry of pain seeming to emanate from his words.

Ralph looks on. "But I have no regrets. On any given day I could be a dead man, six feet under. God has a plan for me which is why he has kept me alive and will continue to till I achieve that what I am supposed to achieve," says the old man with a smile so characteristic of deep resilience and courage. Ralph is taken aback by the man's defiance in the face of unforgiving odds.

"I am Wallace. What's your name son?" he asks extending his hand.

"I am Ralph. Nice to meet you," says Ralph as he staggers trying to move the grocery bags from his right hand into the left one.

"Same here! I used to be a young man like you once."

"Oh....hahaha."

"Yes. Sure feels like the world is your playground when you are that age," smiles Wallace.

[Pause]

"This recession seems to be taking a toll on everyone though. My grandson has been struggling to find a job since he got let go 3 months ago. He is on unemployment. Don't know how he is managing with that. He might be a little older than you. How old are you?"

"I am 24."

"Good age to be. When I was 24, I used to work 16 hours a day in a car making factory. Those guys also seem to be going out of business in this economy."

"Do you receive any assistance from the government, Sir?"

"Well only if I get so sick that I fall dead. Then they would wait for me to die before they take me to the hospital. Transport and even their paperwork cost money. They know I have none of that so they prefer I die than use up any of their resources. All they do with a dead body is probably hand it over to the church or the family or in other cases use it for some weird research. In my case, I probably wouldn't have any family member come forth to claim my body except maybe my job-hunting grandson. But he'd probably dump me in the river once he realized that even dead bodies cost money to dispose of," he says sounding morose.

"In my country and even in Europe, senior citizens receive help and food aid in many cases."
"Not here son!" Wallace clarifies. "It is prevalent but not very widespread."
"But you are a citizen. Right, Sir? You would receive it if you applied," he continues looking at the old man incredulously.

Wallace clears his throat. He sees that the kid is a greenhorn from a different country and doesn't clearly understand the intricacies of financial aid in the US of A.

"If I had the option to get help from the government, I would be the first to jump at it. But this government is a capitalist lover. A friend, crony and slave of capitalism. Helping a poor, old man with very little business or monetary value is not part of their agenda. They don't care about us. The poor are a liability here. You are only of value if you have something that they want. Once they get it out of you and have no use for you, they bid farewell to you. That's the nature of capitalism in this country," he says plainly.
"The only thing I ever got here was some help from the church I frequented. They say the new president is going to bring in many reforms to help the underprivileged and the poverty-stricken. But I do not know when that is going to materialize. Till then we have only God and ourselves to rely on. And of course kind people like yourself. Thanks for the nickel," he smiles seeming amused that Ralph provided that small of an amount to him.

Capitalism is a brutal system if you are not the capitalist owning the land, the factories and in effect the workers. Many times even wage workers are on the receiving end of this system as their rights and wages can be trampled on. Which is why they have unions. And these too are being increasingly sidelined. Capitalism provides more wealth to the wealthy. It makes the rich richer and poor poorer. But ordinary people have no option but to follow it; as it is too powerful to be overthrown by force, cunning or subterfuge. At the end of the day, normal people are just cogs in a wheel that is churning huge profits for the rich and the famous.

****

"So what did you do in the Marketing Data department?" asks Mr. Dodworth, noticing a familiarity with the intern he had interviewed around 9 months ago and not selected.

"I was engaged in data cleansing, streamlining the report delivery process and also developed scripts to automate bad data elimination. I also completed other tasks and processes as required."

"Okay. So what are you looking for in your next opportunity and why is this opportunity of interest to you?"

"I am looking for a programming job profile and this opening provides the opportunity to code and learn new languages. Moreover, I have worked in various kinds of scenarios before which provide me a good platform to handle all the responsibilities of this position."

"So what makes you think you can contribute to this team?" Mr. Dodworth asks curtly wanting to evoke a gut feeling from Ralph.

Ralph maintains his cool. "Firstly, I am a pretty flexible person and can adjust and learn new ways and techniques. Therefore, learning departmental processes is not an issue at all. I am a quick learner and am very good at JAVA and other types of coding. My educational track record shows that I can deliver quality code in record time. That's why I feel confident about my ability to be able to contribute to your team."

Mr. Dodworth smiles slyly; almost amused at the young man's calm response. Throughout the remainder of the interview, he quizzes him on the details of his work profile, his attitude to work, mindset and work ethic. Needless to say, he is amazed at the young man's resolve in putting forth his candidacy in such a forthright and crisp fashion.

"We will get back to you in a week," says Mr. Dodworth at the end of the hour-long interview.

"How did the interview go?" asks Ken.

"Went pretty well. It was very detail oriented."

"Did he indicate any potential action after the interview?"

"He just said he would get back to me after a week."

"Mr. Dodworth is generally serious about timelines. If he says he will get back to you after a week, he will definitely get back after a week."

"Well I hope his department does."

"They have a need there. They will definitely get back to you," assures Ken.

"I wanted to congratulate you on getting the job as a junior programmer with the Medical Information Management team Ralph," says Diego from HR placement services a day later.

"That's great to hear. Thanks," replies Ralph. Diego gives him a few instructions on what paper work is required and congratulates him again.

Ralph knows that when the job starts he will have to be a sponge and absorb and learn as much as he possibly can.

****

Visits to the store are always a course in sobriety and penance. At the height of the 2008 economic crisis, also called the Great Recession, Ralph sees single mothers, old destitute men and young lonely kids outside the store looking for scraps of free food that the store might be dumping into the trash dumpster or just offering to the public. But these items are seldom offered to anybody. Ralph would later learn the reason for this. Giving food that is to be discarded to someone poses the risk of them getting sick after consuming it. Food that is to be discarded typically does not carry any insurance. Hence, if someone gets ill after consuming it; there is no medical assistance that can be provided to them what-so-ever by the company that made the food. But the person could still take the organization to court on whatever charges, thus greatly jeopardizing the reputation and brand value of the organization. This is why organizations generally don't give away food to be discarded to charity unless they are cleared of any potential liability.

On one such occasion, Ralph sees a mother with a child beside her. She is Caucasian and looks impoverished and worn out. Though young, the strain of life is evident in the wrinkles on her face. She is visibly stressed with the daily battles she seems to be going through, taking care of the cherubic child not being the least of them. She purchases only cucumbers, looking intently at the other fruits, vegetables, milk and egg assortments in the shelf displays. But cucumbers are the cheapest food in the whole grocery store. He would like to go up and talk to her and offer assistance. But he fears she might feel offended or embarrassed. Poverty is generally a very sensitive topic in almost any part of the world.

Even in India, the government is very concerned about the rest of the world viewing the major problems the country faces. Poverty casts the prestige of the country in a negative light and is a soft underbelly.

Ralph reaches the counter and a young African-American kid is holding a can of milk. He seems too weak to carry it and staggers as he tries to balance the weight of the can. He places a ragged plastic bag with coins in it at the counter. The clerk winces and reluctantly goes through the bag with coins in it. "It's not enough to buy the can," she says sounding a little irritated.

"Your chance to earn some grace!" says the Inner Voice.

"I will buy that for him. Return his coins please," says Ralph quickly. She gives him the can and the coins as Ralph hands over two dollars to her. "Say thank you," she prods the kid before he leaves.

"You are welcome!" smiles Ralph congenially.

Doing charity never felt this good. Because you get to see and feel the change it brings to people's lives. Ralph saw the change that a small act of kindness brought to the life of a young kid. "When he goes home his mother will ask him how he got the milk can without spending the coins he had taken with him. She will be happy to know that there was some kind Samaritan out there who noticed that the coins were not enough and decided to pay for it. Helping the needy, helpless and oppressed is the essence of life. God has a way of raising the downtrodden and the meek," quips the Inner Voice.

Ralph always wondered where the Inner Voice derived its wisdom from. Was it his parents or God talking to him through the voice? One day he would find out.

****

The sound of the train moving along the moist June rails was symbolic of progress. He had to travel eighteen miles to get to work. Without a car, things were tough. But he didn't mind the weekday commute. He was gaining valuable experience and learning a great deal about how organizations operate. Had the commute been eliminated though, he would have an entire hour to himself to read or do research or any other valuable activity. He did read while on the train though.

A marginal tiredness set in after the commute that involved a train and a bus to the destination. The medical information management team had four work groups. He was placed with Dharamraj as his mentor. Dharamraj was an experienced programmer who had been on that team for a little over two years. He was therefore, a good resource to obtain information from. He went about instructing Ralph on the intricacies of office politics and work processes. Ralph asked questions and Dharamraj was only too happy to answer. Towards the end of the week though Dharamraj informed Ralph about something unsettling.

"I have already spent more than two years in this company and department Ralph. I had asked them to process my green card. But that request was met with cold indifference. They wanted to have me continue working here on a visa and when that expired they would simply roll me off and hire someone else. I didn't like that idea."

Ralph listened intently, his eyes widening in dismay and a mild sense of worry.

"I recently received an offer to work for another medical device company in a better position. They even offered to do my green card."
"Where?"
"I am keeping that confidential for now Ralph. But will let you know as soon as I am out of here. Maybe we can meet for lunch sometime after I join there. I will be living not too far away from here anyways," he smiles gently.
"Since I am leaving; your new mentor will be Chang."
"Ooooo...," Ralph groans.
"Yes. He is known for his erratic and rude behavior but he is very knowledgeable about the processes in this department. He is a terrific programmer too and would be a great mentor," Dharamraj consoles Ralph. A lot of people in the team did not like Chang because of his peculiar ways.
"But I have heard that he barely ever helps anybody even if they have helped him in the past!" Ralph remonstrated. Ralph had observed office politics and had heard a thing or two about Chang; not so good things.
"He has his hang-ups, no doubt. But don't let that get you down. Keep asking questions and trying to understand more about the department and how it functions. Try to understand the way processes work. If he begins to deny cooperation keep sending him emails and meeting invites. He can't keep denying those."
"And now smile my man! Life can't be all that bad. Even if the whole world were to instantly get filled with evil people there would still be hope. God is always there watching us," he pats Ralph on the shoulder.

363

All his closest colleagues give Dharamraj a small party in the Indian restaurant nearby as a send-off. Chang is invited but arrives late and stays aloof. He exchanges neutral stares with Ralph and Dharamraj and is content to leave first at the end of the lunch.

****

A few weeks into the job Ralph receives his H1B visa. The daily commutes are difficult and impose a strain on Ralph. He still doesn't have a car. But feels blessed that he at least has a job. The current state of the economy has made it almost impossible for anyone without a decent amount of experience to get a job. Even people with experience are having a tough time finding an interview, let alone a job.

"When times are tough or times are good, any benefit is a blessing. And blessings are to be respected, cherished and valued. For life is so much better with them rather than without," quips the Inner Voice.

Ralph is grateful he has managed to find a job that has eluded so many of his friends. But he does feel the homesickness that comes from not having visited home for almost a year and a half. Mum and Dad are physically so distant that it gives him a feeling that he might never be able to meet them should something happen with his visa or job situation in the US. This is a situation many young professionals on a work visa face in the US. Issues faced in entry and exit in and out of the US are always a major roadblock to any travel plans for people on a visa; be it a student, work or any other type of visa.

It is common knowledge that there have been multiple horror stories of people being made to return to their country of origin from the airport itself. This happened even though they had valid visas to enter the US. Ralph has obtained his H1 work visa but has not got the stamp on his passport. Without the stamp, he couldn't possibly enter the US even though he had a legal H1 work visa.

Cases of people on a work visa being made to turn back are a dime a dozen. But Ralph hopes he will not ever be in their situation.

"I don't know that," says Chang in a rude overtone. "You can ask someone else."
"Who would you recommend I ask this question to?"

"I don't know!" comes the curt rejoinder.

Ralph goes to his desk and sends Chang an email asking for the information needed. Chang was his de facto mentor now that Dharamraj was no longer with the company. Ralph knew that if the mentor wasn't living up to the expectations of his role he would need to do everything in his power to obtain the support needed. Even if it meant seeking managerial help in the process.

A day passes and Ralph receives no reply. He follows the next step. He emails Chang again; cc'ing Mr. Lechtenberg, their immediate supervisor this time. Chang replies within an hour of sending the email with Mr. Lechtenberg on it. He comes to Ralph's desk and asks him not to include Mr. Lechtenberg on future email requests. Ralph informs him that he will not add Mr. Lechtenberg in future communications only if he agrees to cooperate more readily. After all, he was assigned to be his mentor after Dharamraj left. Chang grudgingly agrees.

Ralph keeps playing the brinkmanship game for about a month or so trying to extract information and knowledge from Chang in regards to the job that he is required to do. Working with Chang is not always easy, but at least he is not as malicious as Lois. He is one of those people who approaches work as a curse of pain and helping his coworkers as a curse to humanity. It is evident he doesn't enjoy his job all that much and is against cooperating with colleagues unless it would benefit him.

As the work related issues begin to ebb away, Ralph begins to feel more comfortable executing his daily duties. However, the commute is always a drag. But there is only so much satisfaction work can give you. As a single international student turned work visa enabled software developer, he is alone in this large country. His family is thousands of miles away. Only the Inner Voice goes everywhere with him keeping him company. Loneliness is an ever-present facet of living and working in the US. Several people do meet a boyfriend, girlfriend or significant other and rid the loneliness away. But then again, many are torn between attachment to the country of birth and getting adjusted to life in the US.

Humans, as social animals, were meant to be in the company of others. The loneliness transforms into a kind of morose and surly feeling. Ralph often feels bad that he doesn't have anyone close with whom he can confide his most intimate feelings. Even Matilda seems to have changed her phone number. Probably she wouldn't have taken his call even if she knew he was calling. Their breakup hadn't been on the best of terms.

Ralph is no shrinking violet though. "You owe it to yourself to get yourself out of this lonely plight into one of hearty company!" quips the Inner Voice.

****

[AT THE SUPERMARKET/GROCERY STORE]

"Do I know you?" asks the glowing girl in a cute white dress seeming surprised.
"Of course you do. We used to go fishing together when in the university. We went to St. Paul's together remember?"
"You used to help me with my computer science assignments. You were so intelligent that you would always be at the top of the class," he says trying to appear distracted looking at some items in the supermarket isle. "But…"
"Come on Janice. How could you forget?"
"But I am not Janice. You might have got me confused with someone else."
"What really!"
"You certainly look like her. Exactly!"
"No. I am not Janice."
"What's your name then?" he inquires trying to appear surprised.
"I am Betty," she smiles appearing to conceal a blush. It's not often that handsome, tawny young men walk up to her and proclaim friendship. Although they have asked her out quite directly before. Ralph knows the direct approach has greater chances of failure though. At least it hasn't worked much for him before. But he still decides to do it as hope beats desperation, in his book. A lot of people who come to the US do so with an overarching sense of hope that they will be able to work and be a part of the American economic miracle. Several continue to chug along in spite of failure. And what keeps them going – it is hope!!
"Do you have a twin sister or anything?"
"No!" she screeches seeming a little frazzled and worried about not wanting to offend him.

366

"Wow, you look exactly like her. Gosh if she saw you she would think you guys were twins."

"So what do you study?"

"I am studying to be a nurse," she says appearing a little embarrassed to be discussing personal stuff with strangers. Though he appears so friendly and of such good nature that she fears coming across as rude and distant to him.

"Well even if you are not Janice, I am glad I met you…umm..uh…," he flounders.

"Betty," she gushes.

"Yeah. Betty…nice name"

She has an inkling that he is trying to hit on her though she cannot be certain for a fact.

"So would you like to meet for coffee or fishing sometime?" he coyly asks.

"Ummm….I would love to but I am very busy," she tries to finagle out of it.

"Everybody is busy. But since you look just like one of my best friend's, I thought maybe we could get to know each other."

"Oh, I would love to. But I have a boyfriend."

He tries other persuasion techniques to try to obtain her number. But the young damsel is too wary of handsome strangers. This is not the first time he hasn't been successful at obtaining female contact details. Nor the first time she has been approached by good looking men.

An overarching trend that he has noticed points to the fact that you need to know people and develop a relationship with them gradually. Only then can you get their phone numbers and other contact details. Moreover, the media is very strong in America. Incidents of rape, molestation, kidnapping and other crimes are broadly advertised on the radio, news and other forms of television and mainstream broadcasting. Wary parents make it a point to inform and educate their daughters and other female members of their household to be alert and vigilant to unwelcome advances by unknown people. These could be either male or female. It definitely helps to have a long history of acquaintance with someone before you can ask them out. Ralph was barely two years in the US. No chance of a history for him here.

That's where the so-called 'lack of friendliness' from women comes. Strangers trying to be too friendly are increasingly viewed with suspicion and doubt. "Why is he trying to be so friendly? What does he want?" are some of the things people wonder about.

Ralph keeps trying to make friends with girls in the supermarket, on the train and bus station; practically anywhere he sees a good-looking female. Lady luck doesn't always shine on him though. He is faced with rejection after rejection. When you have a non-American accent, a brown face and don't entirely know the culture, it is more a factor of luck fraternizing with the local women than anything else. Knowledge of dating norms and fads is important in order to enhance your chances of meeting with success when approaching women born and brought up in this culture. All that changes when he visits Temple University for a software engineering conference.

"What is this charming man doing here?" says Jessica from a seat away as he rises to leave the conference.
"Woah. Is that you, ummm….airport girl!"
"Yes I am the airport girl. Glad you remember hotshot. Though my name is Jessica….even though I like the airport girl synonym," she gushes.
"Long time no see….almost a year and a half right?"
"Yes around that much time."
"How are your studies going? Almost done by now I guess?"
"Yes, I am done with the course. Working for Siemens in their software engineering department now."
"Congrats. You're kicking it handsome!"
"Trying to. The job is going well so far. And I am trying to keep it that way. Which is why I came for this conference as I was sure it could teach me something."

[Pause] She looks at him admirably; almost sizing him up and trying to get a feel for his body. It is easy to tell when American women have the hots for you and fancy you in bed.

"So what are you doing here?" he asks seeking to steer clear from her seductive gaze.
[She is momentarily stunned] "Oh, I work for Temple. I had a friend who was going to present a paper at this conference. But he pulled out at the last moment. Since I had the ticket pass, I came anyway. And I am

glad I did. We wouldn't have met otherwise!" she says looking concerned. Women can be very particular when it involves missing out on a key opportunity to meet a good man.
"I am glad you did too," he smiles gently.

They walk shoulder to shoulder into the atrium outside. She grabs a 7up and gives him a coca cola.

"Thanks. But I just had lots of water," he specifies not wanting to indulge in the sugar heavy soda concentrate.
"So now that you are working you must be having quite some time to yourself right?" she asks.
"Yes, definitely more time than when I was studying," he sighs with a sense of relief on his face.
"So what do you do on the weekends?"
"I sleep and cook," he laughs.
"Man…that's boring! You need to get out there and into the groove!"
"I sure do," he acknowledges.
"How about you join me this weekend. I am going dancing," she quickly fills in.

He pauses to think.

"I recall you telling me you knew a few moves. It will be fun!" she continues.

He is silent.

"Come on. Don't overthink this. It's a simple yes or no. And honestly saying 'yes' wouldn't do any harm," she blurts.
"Hey you still remember your dance moves right?" she sheepishly smiles.
"I am a little rusty. But there is nothing some practice can't help resolve," he says plainly.
"Oh, but I don't have a car still."
"No worries. I will come get you."

Ralph begins a new chapter of romantic adventure and discovery in a whirlwind romance with Jessica. This relationship seems like it is going to be several times more intense than the one with Matilda.

During his time with her, he learns the pleasure of multiple blowjobs and naked joint baths. He feels the satisfaction of sleeping on soft breasts as pillows and of kissing delicate, pale hips and voluptuous, burlesque thighs. On several occasions, he simply grabs her naked body as tight as he would his teddy bear when he was a child. Both of them lock on with amorous rapture. Though whenever they have intercourse he ensures he wears protection. He knows that he wants to avoid getting her pregnant at all costs.

He wouldn't want to have an unwed mother or an illegitimate child coming out of their romantic involvement. Moreover, he is not sure about her reliability as a potential spouse. She has indicated her overt interest in pursuing something long-term and serious with him several times. But he has reserved his comments to 'just friendship' without quoting a 'friends with benefits' kind of arrangement. In fact, it is not a friend's with benefits kind of arrangement. Nor is it just friendship. But something in between.

As weird and 'anti-family oriented' as it sounds; he prefers focusing on work for now. He doesn't mind the female company as a vital distraction from the stress of work. In the US, people begin to learn to be selfish. If it serves their character traits they don't mind incorporating certain facets of the culture into their lifestyle. There are tons of cases of ultra-conservative, religious individuals from distant nations coming here and living like 'good ole Casanova and Lothario's' for the duration of their stay. As soon as their period of stay comes to an end, they return to their respective countries and resume a life of domestic penance and prayer as prescribed by the customs of their place.

Ralph was not an ultra-conservative person. Nor was his household in Goa. But he didn't mind the little freedom his American adventure was giving him. While he seemed to enjoy this he often felt the pain of the dichotomy of being from a different country, but living and making a life in another. His heart would be in Goa where his parents were while the physical Ralph was in the US. A major issue was bridging this dichotomy of heart and body. A conundrum of being both mind and body in the same place. This is something he, along with so many other international students, grappled with on a regular basis. Trying to build a home away from home is no easy task.

SORRY GOODBYE

AS HE TRUDGES ALONG trying to bring some meaning to his friendless, family deprived life in the US he knows that there is always some possibility of a disaster looming. The US is a very dynamic place. There is always a possibility of sudden change in fortunes. Extremely wealthy people can have their wealth diminish; poverty stricken folks can receive a windfall. People considered secure can get shot or mugged and policies and rules can change overnight. The US is known as the land of the free and the home of the brave. "It ought to be called the land of immense change as well," quips the Inner Voice.

Ralph was working hard trying to understand the ins and outs of everyday tasks at work. Being a German company, there was a ton of work to be done. But being the novice he was; there were a lot of areas for a potential slip. Moreover, the dastardly mentor that Chang was, if Ralph never asked a question he never got an answer. Chang was not open to volunteer his time and knowledge to Ralph. No question, meant no answer; therefore no knowledge. Chang was notorious for not volunteering information unless explicitly asked for it. He usually preferred email over verbal communication it seemed. That was the only way he would provide help anyway. Verbal requests got lost somewhere in the chasms of his self-centered, egotistical mind.

At everyday standups, Chang would elaborate a litany of things he did single-handedly. Ralph was the only newbie in the department and delineated only what had been assigned to him and what he got done. Since it was Chang who assigned work to him most of the time; there wasn't much to speak about to that extent. Chang was trying to take his sweet revenge by not assigning Ralph any work. As always there was an overarching agenda of trying to show himself as more smart, knowledgeable and diligent than everybody else. How on God's green earth could he allow Ralph to steal any of the spotlight!

371

Ralph had informed Mr. Lechtenberg about the situation. He only promised that he would talk to Chang about the situation. Given his workload and lack of interest to the concerns of the newbie, he only paid overall lip service to the issue. Chang remained resolute in his behavior towards Ralph. Ralph's cache of accomplishments and tasks began to dry up. He would barely have anything to talk about at the morning stand up meetings and in review sessions.

Over a period of a couple of weeks, Mr. Lechtenberg began to feel a little distressed about Ralph's performance. Chang's reviews, even though he didn't take them seriously, were creating a negative leaning in Brett's (Mr. Lechtenberg) mind about Ralph. But being the hard driven company that it is, Mr. Lechtenberg would prefer to hear of results at all costs rather than constraints and roadblocks; even if they were genuine. To make matters worse, the economy was in a recession. Hence it made more sense to keep employees who were most productive and let go of the rest.

After some deliberation with Mr. Dodworth; Mr. Lechtenberg obtained the green signal to put Ralph on a performance improvement plan. The goal is to develop conditions that would force rapid improvement in work performance from the employee while at the same time setting the stage for a possible termination if the performance does not improve. Ralph wondered which of the two Brett was more in favor of. Performance improvement plans or PIPs remove all liability from the organization and divert it solely onto the candidate.

Mr. Lechtenberg seemed rather belligerent while serving Ralph with the performance improvement plan. And not very much in the mood for negotiation. The performance improvement plan was to be spread over a period of 4 weeks. He would be assessed on a number of factors including but not limited to his social skills with colleagues, understanding of work tasks, work delivery, consistency, timeliness of completing tasks and in coming and leaving the office, readiness to accept correction and overall congeniality in the office.

The warning also delineated that violation of any of the company's rules would result in immediate termination. He knew he needed to get through this predicament successfully. And to do so he would need to dedicate himself to every task given to him.

The first few days he receives relatively simple tasks. As the days wear on the complexity begins to increase. He is given tasks as simple as tabulating data right up to creating complex database relationships and advanced scripts for data manipulation.

His sheer dedication and urge to get through the PIP (performance improvement plan) enable him to
successfully navigate the exercises and complete the month-long initiative. Now it's the final evaluation week of the plan.

****

"Who are you seeing these days. Found a new crush I guess!" says Jessica angrily over the phone. The performance improvement plan had afforded Ralph very little time for extra-curricular activities or to attend to his personal life. He could barely call Jessica, let alone see her during this time due to his work related pre-occupation.

"I have been crazy busy at work!"
"Oh, so she is your colleague. That explains it. It is easier to screw her. She is more available. Anyways she might be better at squeezing out the stress after a long day isn't it!" she says in a shrill tone.
"Jessica stop it...I haven't been seeing anybody else. I have just been very busy. I was put on a performance improvement plan at work to improve my performance."

[Silence] She doesn't seem convinced.

"If I was going to cheat on you I would not have taken your call today."
"But you didn't take my call last couple of days either."
"See, my boss wasn't confident of my performance so he put me on a performance improvement plan to see if I can meet the requirements of the job and if not, use it to fire me."
[Feeling bad now] "I'm so sorry to hear that honey. I didn't know you were in such a difficult situation."

He winces on his side of the phone.

"I apologize for being so rude to you!" she literally cries over the phone.
"That's okay. What's the scoop on your side of the world?"

"Just work. Going to clubs and dance bars alone. You've been missing out!!" she gushes.

"Yeah. I know. I have been so focused on work that things haven't quite been kicking for me. This performance improvement plan that I am on is sucking the life out of me."

"When does it get done?"

"End of April."

"So you got like another week and a half to go?" she sighs.

"Yes," he says grimly.

"Don't worry Ralph. I know you will get through it well. I have faith in you!!"

He feels a surge when she says that. It is not easy getting moral support and someone's goodwill in any part of the world in modern times. Ralph is glad his romantic escapades have at least yielded him someone he can confide in. It is the closest thing he has to a support system in this country.

"Having relationships is better than any other type of resource. For relationships give you a springboard to regenerate other resources; be it money, a job or simply another relationship. Without knowing people first it is difficult to convince them of your worth and capacity," reaffirms the Inner Voice.

"To grow relationships, be trustworthy. Be convivial!" Ralph knows the Inner Voice can't be wrong; it cannot be lying. Relationships are like plants and the more emphasis and value you place on them the more value you get out of them. The stronger they become.

****

"I feel so anxious!" he says to Jessica after she is done giving him a gravity-defying blowjob. She had come home to check on him and rekindle their dying romance.

"I hear that performance improvement plan shit bothering you," she asserts as they lie naked on the couch.

"Yes, it's the last three days of the performance improvement plan. I don't know what is going to come out of it."

"At the end of the day, if they have to remove you they will remove you. No matter how good of a job you have done; if their original intention was to get rid of you, they will."

374

She waits for him to process what she has said. He is somewhere in between relaxed after the blowjob and marginally concerned about his work situation.

"A performance improvement plan is only meant to provide the organization with legal cover to justify your removal in case you decide to sue them. It is not actually to improve your performance; rather to give you a chance to think if you should continue in the organization or voluntarily leave. A real trial."
"Okay!" he says, seeming resigned to the fact of his probable removal.

But he seeks consolation in the fact that he has completed the work assigned to him to the best possible extent. He knows it is quality.

The said day comes and he has second thoughts about leaving the office early or just clutching the laptop and running away. He has heard notorious stories about workers being walked out and escorted to the exit in US offices. Madhu, his former roommate would always speak about such stories. It particularly concerned Madhu as he wasn't entirely confident of his skills and abilities. He always thought that in a weak economy or in the case of performance issues he would need to be ready for the termination scenario if it played out.

Ralph knew that his communication was top notch; comparable to many Americans if not better. But he knew that he could better it if he just persevered and continued to learn. How could he learn more? By interacting with Americans who were willing to talk to him? Who were willing to share ideas and information with him?

"Not all people are friendly. Not all Americans are friendly. The only way to find out if people are friendly is by trying to talk to them even if they don't seem like they want to converse. To try to figure them out. Sometimes the quietest people have the most vivacious personalities," reminds the Inner Voice.

There are a lot of things in the US that people don't talk about or even don't ask about. It might be difficult for people from a different culture to know this right off the bat. Generally, you go through several permutations of hit or miss to arrive at a cohesive understanding of what is considered acceptable and what is derided in US social interactions.

"You should continue to keep up the same level of effort. You have done well during this period. If you continue like this you will do well here. Let me know if you come across any roadblocks along the way. You are officially off the performance improvement plan!" says Mr. Lechtenberg, giving a slight smile.

Ralph pauses seeming puzzled. "Have I completed it successfully?" he asks.

"No need to be so perplexed. If you had not completed it successfully you would be looking for a new job now and not be sitting in my office," Mr. Lechtenberg says in a semi-sarcastic manner.

Ralph gives a slight guffaw and takes Mr. Lechtenberg's leave.

People can be brutally direct and blunt in the corporate world. It is capitalism at its height. But then again if they aren't that way, their performance is called into question. The pecking order is defined by the hierarchy on the totem pole. The lower you are the more often you are pecked at. The people high up on the totem pole get high salaries, benefits and stock options. But they are required to face up to the pressures imposed on them by the chairman, board of directors and whoever else that is above them.

Many people think of beating the pecking order and going it alone. If they succeed they are called "genius entrepreneurs." If they don't they are regarded as intelligent resource persons for a new venture.

Ralph knows that he is going to have to keep his socks pulled up if he is to survive in this company. Day after day he comes early to office. Leaves late. Tries to be as productive as possible. Hoping that he won't be put under the microscope. Hoping that things will keep getting better. And then the unthinkable happens.

****

Sept 15, 2008, a date that will go down in infamy as one that broke the bank. The day that Lehmann Brothers filed for bankruptcy started the chain of events that would eventually lead to the Great Recession. A recession which destroyed nest eggs and took the wind out of people's savings. Thousands of workers were laid off and an equal number of jobs were not coming back. It is estimated the US economy itself lost

8.5 million jobs. Worldwide other countries also lost several jobs and countless businesses had to shut down.

Among the hardest hit were junior level IT workers and fresh college graduates. With very little experience and knowledge about the industry they could barely manage to compete with industry hardened employees who had either been let go or were looking for higher wage jobs. Underemployment was another issue encountered by experienced industry workers. Not having a need for regular, permanent employees companies began contracting workers to fill temporary positions, requiring seasonal work.

Not just financial companies and banks but companies across the board began taking action to safeguard their financial positions and interests. Being the cash conscious company it was, Siemens took preemptive action to ensure it wasn't jeopardizing its fiscal strength. The first step was to eliminate non-essential overhead. This essentially translated into eliminating junior level positions and bottom level performers. Although a good performer, Ralph was regarded poorly after being put on the performance improvement plan and the perennial negative reference from the churlish Chang. His perceived performance was considered lax. His actual performance was not so.

But in corporate life as in so many other things; perception is reality. "We are giving you a month to find another job. Because of the economic situation, we are laying off several people in the company. You are one of them. We are sorry we have to let you go, but we have no choice."

It had been a little over two years in Siemens. Ralph had worked his butt off and had not anticipated that things would come to this. But life never tells you before it throws a curve ball at you. But the signs are always there. However under pronounced they might be.

"The best recourse to all these uncertainties is to keep praying and to keep God in your heart. God is never uncertain. And He knows everything about you from the beginning to the end. He will never fail you. If He brought you to it; He will get you through it," reassures the Inner Voice.

The key to knowing that God is with you is to keep praying and doing good. For without God's blessings, all and every effort is equal to naught. The next day onwards, Ralph braces himself for the rigorous application process that he had followed immediately after he graduated from St. Paul's University. He would need to put in a lot of effort and a great deal of luck to beat the odds this time. The economy was not the best. Nor were his chances with a mere two years of experience. "Never give up!" said the Inner Voice.

****

"I can't believe this bitch!" she says as she wipes the viscous cum from Ralph's thighs after one of her heavenly blowjobs. Ralph and Jessica had reached such a comfort level that the minute she came to his place she would lay her bag down; literally, rip off his pants and start giving him a blow. All other matters would be spoken about after that. "Talk about free ones!" quipped the Inner Voice.

"What happened?" asks Ralph seeming calm.
"That bitch Tamara Cuttle has just let two of my colleagues go. And now I have to do my work along with the responsibilities of two others. She encourages me by saying that I will be promoted in three months' time!"

Silence in the room. He looks at her perplexed.

"That's if I survive three months" she laments.
"Why were they let go?"
"Cost cutting apparently. Though I wonder why she let senior people with more experience and knowledge go away. I am way junior to the people who were sent away."
"Cost cutting apparently. They probably drew a larger salary and benefits than you did. So it made sense to keep someone cheaper on and let the more expensive ones loose," he quips.
"Umm....however cruel it sounds it is the truth. The bitter truth!"
"This recession has bitten everyone's ass pretty hard. I didn't think it would happen to an educational institution too. But it has," she continues.
"Yes it's surprising how the economy affects literally every institution; be it product or service related."

Ralph knew the cause of the Great Recession was the lax bank lending rules. Essentially it started with the near collapse of the big banks and then moved on to other industries and businesses. Things are so interconnected in America. And for that matter in the rest of the world. When the economy begins to dip in America; a whole bunch of other nations begin to lose confidence and stop investing, stop spending. The economies of the free world are so interdependent and interconnected by free trade and globalization that a sneeze in one economy has the potential to have grave repercussions in so many others.

The farmer grows food, the food is bought by customers, they eat the food and gain energy. They use the energy to work and do well in their jobs. Their employers gain value from the work they do and invest in the economy and pay taxes. The taxes collected by the government are used to build roads, bridges and other vital infrastructure and services. These services and infrastructure are used by the farmer to educate his or her kids and transport his produce to the markets where it is sold. So it is a self-sustaining structure that enables people to live and flourish. A practice in symbiotic living and sustenance. The way God had meant for humans to live, to be.

"Which is why it is important to be ethical and fair in all dealings. A banker misappropriating and not following the rules in one place can have repercussions in other places; other sectors of the economy. And many a times on the life and livelihood of the banker too. If it doesn't affect him it will certainly affect his conscience. And guilt is a very bad thing to be carrying in your heart. It destroys you from the inside, deprives you of all hope and renders your efforts meaningless and ineffectual," the Inner Voice emphasizes.
"You need to start applying for other positions so that in the event that she suddenly decides to chop your position as well you have something to fall back on. Or at least have something in the pipeline," quips Ralph as a symbol of pragmatic thinking that he so often prides himself upon. "Umm!" she ponders.
"Yes. Start applying because in these uncertain times you need to be proactive so that the economy doesn't catch you on the wrong foot," he emphasizes. She keeps his advice in mind as she takes his leave that evening.

THE FIGHT BACK

RALPH KNOWS THAT HE has only one month of paid time to get a job. After that, it would be another month until his work visa becomes invalid. So essentially, just eight weeks of time until he is deemed illegal in the US. He has two options – one is to sit down and feel sorry for himself and wonder what went wrong with the Siemens job. The other is to mold his setbacks into determined resistance and work fiercely in search of a job. The idea being to not stop till a job is found and he gets settled in it. He opts for the second option because it is rife with hope. "When all is lost never lose hope! That is the only thing that no one can take away from you. Everything else can be taken," says the Inner Voice.

With his new found strength and hope driven by the Inner Voice and God's direction, Ralph goes about applying for job openings. He saturates the US job websites within a week. He wakes up at 6am in the morning every day. Has a quick breakfast of bread with egg and tea. Then sits continuously till 12:30 pm applying for jobs. He only leaves the chair for a leak or a drink of water. His resilience in the face of a rotten economy and the 'difficult to reach' recruiters is remarkably unyielding. His lunch is usually for 15 minutes. It consists of either noodles or chicken and bread and sometimes rice. He gulps it down and gets back to his job application station. His approach to job applications is unique though tedious to implement.

He applies to the same position on every job portal and website that he finds. In effect applying for it several times and inundating the employer's email box with his resume. The idea it seems is to get the employer's attention by any means possible at all costs. This 'no prisoners taken' approach of applying for a position through all venues that it is advertised on and inundating the recruiter with his information seems to be paying off. He receives multiple calls and emails from recruiters regarding his situation and background. A few even ask him about his availability for an interview but recant the interview offer once

380

they realize he needs a work visa. Such is the nature of the job application process when you are an immigrant or international student in need of a visa.

Employers always frown upon the need to sponsor a visa because it involves several legal procedures and documentation to be filed with the US Citizenship and Immigration Services. Moreover, in a severely depressed economy, there is already a sizeable chunk of citizens who can be hired for the same position. The supply of workers is always greater than the demand in a depressed economy. Because jobs are at a premium. Then comes the category of people on a green card and those capable of working without the need for a work visa; namely those on some type of refugee status.

The one thing that Ralph knows works for him is the fact that he has programming skills in JAVA and has the capability to learn a new software language rather quickly. This capability of his is sufficient to enable him to stay in the mix for a fighting chance of getting a job in the US of A. Were he a non-technical professional, he probably would not have had as good of a chance to get a job.

****

"She has been trying to fuck me over several times in the last couple of days. Today she gave me three files that typically were to be given to three different people. But considering we have lost two very experienced people; I was given their share as well," Jessica gasps over the phone.
"Which…?" he is interrupted before he completes his question.
"I received a file of low-income students, at-risk youth and physically challenged students," she gasps, her exasperated breathing coming strong over the phone.
"And what…." he is interrupted again as she continues her rant.
"And I need to go through each of these files and mix and match students who we could select. The selection favors those who need the least amount of help and who, we as an institution, can claim that we are helping while providing the least amount of support. Talk about social service and public help and brand propaganda. Companies and corporations seem to be moving in the direction of publicizing their so

called 'charity' rather than doing charity in the spirit of charity. It's strange but true."

"Well it serves their purpose as more the perceived charity that you seem to do; the more the actual charity is considered as done. People are endeared to organizations with a charitable or perceived charitable background. Therefore such organizations get more business. Even if in actuality they are only faking charity," he seconds.

"Right!!" her voice seems exceptionally loud over the phone. Probably it's all that job frustration getting to her. He had recommended her not to visit him in person for a few months after the day he was given notice at his job. He didn't want to get distracted or disturbed by female company. Female company can be very distracting, particularly if you are a young, virile man with a lot of energy and libido.

Job applications necessitated total concentration or rather very little distraction. Having her call him over the phone meant he didn't have a visual on her and therefore it avoided the physical distractions which are a weakness of most young men.

"How are your job applications going on?" he asks.

"I haven't really started," she says after a pause symbolizing regret for not having heeded his advice a few days ago.

"I would encourage you to start sooner rather than later. A few more of my friends who everyone thought were not going to be let go were in fact given notice and we are expecting a lot more surprises in the coming days. It is best not to hedge your bets that the current job will keep you on even with all the hardship you take upon yourself. Tamara might one day walk up to you and ask you to pack up. It has happened before in many places."

"Yes, I will start today I guess."

"Not I guess. You should!"

"Use Monster, Career Builder or any other job site. But start the process either way. You have an updated resume right!"

"I have to update it," she laments.

"Gosh! Why is it taking you so much time to get it done? These things should be done quickly so that you can move to the next phase of applying!" he avers.

"So when are you going to get it done?"

There is silence. Very indicative of indecision and lack of will. Ralph hates it. After all, there is another strong force guiding his determination to carry on and succeed. It is the Inner Voice that he himself hasn't managed to decipher the source of. Is it God speaking to him or his ancestors? His tiny human mind just can't seem to tell.

"Well, I would start doing it immediately after you get off the phone with me. Complete it and start randomly applying for jobs. You need to start now because you never know when that Cuttle bitch might pull the carpet from under your feet. It's best that you are prepared to reduce the blow to you if not to beat her to the punch. The best thing is to be ready by applying for as many jobs as you can and in the event you get an opportunity; do tell that slut boss of yours to jump off a cliff."

Still silence.

"Got it!"
"Yes. Thanks doll!" she says smiling incandescently.

The force of Ralph's positivity imbued in Jessica a will to fight and survive in spite of all the odds. She puts down the phone and gets busy with working on the resume. Ralph returns to his job application effort.

****

"This is a solution architect position. Have you done it before?" asks the soft voice on the other side of the line.
"I am a JAVA developer and I have mostly done development related work. No solution architecture work as such."
"Well the position you applied for was in solution architecture. You should look at the title before applying," came the curt recommendation from the recruiter.

Ralph was doing mass applications. He did not see or have time to be selective about job applications. Whatever job he found that was related to development in any way he applied for it. No wonder he got calls for positions he was not at all suitable for. But that is the nature of the game. Ralph had opted for the game involving numbers over specific applications. In other words, quantity over quality. But then again quantity has a quality of its own.

Dr. Alamuddin had always told him that quality is way better than quantity. "In difficult times if you can't get a job through contacts or connections; inundate the job sites and recruiters email boxes with hundreds of applications so that they sit up and take notice of you. That is the key to getting traction on your goal of getting a job," emphasized the Inner Voice.

He comes across several positions needing varied experience and exposure. "PHP front end developer with 5 years of experience; JAVA architect with Hybris expertise; solution architect with experience in HVAC systems software; and a host of others."

He knows that a shot gun approach will get him farther than a rifle approach. The more energy he puts in his overall effort, the more the possibility of a positive outcome. He believes that mass application of one resume to multiple employers can get you noticed. And could potentially land you a job as well. Instead of being specific and trying to apply only to a select few set of positions, he decides to bombard recruiters with several applications. Sometimes even applying to the same job multiple times. Many recruiters begin to hate his repetitive application style. But, over time some recruiters grow to see the eagerness in his attitude and approach.

He gets several interview calls, phone interviews, skype interviews and in-person interviews. But none seem to materialize a great deal. He begins to worry and despair about his ability to find a job. He shuttles from motions of hope to dejection to despair to downright frustration. He cycles through these motions regularly. But what never crosses his mind is the thought of giving up. He knows that he cannot give up. Not now. Not after he has come so far in this country.

****

"I can't believe I actually got a call from a recruiter with another university!" says Jessica.
"Really!"
"Yes. She was asking me about my background and what kind of work I do in my present job. I couldn't believe my ears."
"Well, you are that good after all then!" he smirks.
"Shut up. You think only you can apply for jobs!"
"I'm just pulling your legs. Chill! I am very happy though that you got a response to your applications."
"Yeah. I was ecstatic when I received it," she thunders.

"How many did you apply for?" he asks.

"Three," she smiles.

"And you got a call from just that!" he says sounding surprised.

"Yep!"

"Man how come you are so lucky. In my part of the world, it would be difficult to get a response based on just three or four applications."

"And how is your application scenario going on?" she inquires sounding concerned.

"I have got many calls and interview requests; just no jobs at this point."

There is a stoic silence. She evidently feels the dejection and loss of confidence he is going through in not being able to secure a job after all the applications.

"Well, I am sure you will get something pretty soon. You are the hardest working engineer I have ever met!"

"Yeah. Please pray for me. Let me know if you come across anything."

She knew he was hardworking; a great kisser with a strong body. But she had never been able to experience his love-making abilities. She wished she could since she desperately wanted a serious relationship with him. Jessica was a typical American girl. She has had her share of crushes and breakups and wants something serious and long-term now. She sees a lot of promise in Ralph. He is educated, focused and so full of life that he seems like the total package. She doesn't know what she could get that would be better than him.

What drives her to court him more than he courts her is the utter failure of her previous relationships. One of the relationships was in fact marriage. Her husband used to be an ironworker. They had met at a club and fallen in love. The marriage lasted for a year until he met a hotter looking woman when on one of his work assignments. After the divorce, she looked to find love wherever she could. Hooking up with men from the club, from work, or any other place that she met them.

All of these encounters and relationships didn't materialize into anything serious. After her acquaintances got what they wanted from the relationship; they were quick to dump Jessica and her long-term goals. They probably just saw her as a means to an end; not a relationship with her as an end in itself.

"Is she being so nice and considerate because she wants something from me or is she normally like this?" Ralph often wondered.

"Most people, whether in America or anywhere else have an ulterior motive to making friends or wanting to talk to someone courteously," reminded the Inner Voice every now and then.

"But then there could be worse things in life in the form of hostile people. At least that's not my problem now," Ralph thought.

He knew Jessica wanted a stable relationship with him as she had indicated her interest in something solid several times. But he wasn't ready to rush into things. He had his career in which he needed to find a job and get settled in. And then, of course, there was the H factor. The H1 visa needed to culminate into the filing of a green card which would enable him to work for any employer he wished. Essentially making him legal in the US just below the status of a citizen. The only privilege he wouldn't have with the green card is the right to vote. But then again he could get full citizenship if he married the '*eager-to-settle*' Jessica. No privileges or rights withheld. The straight path to American citizenship.

"Is that what you really want!" asked the Inner Voice. Mum was totally against marrying a divorcee or for that matter a white American girl. Not because she was a racist. She just didn't believe that an American girl could stick with a man as husband 'till death do them part.' Be it an American man or a man from any other culture.

Mum always dreaded divorce as a major probability in case of Western women. Which is why she had constantly drilled into Ralph the need to marry a local Indian woman and more so a Goan woman. An American woman and a divorced one at that would be anathema to her. She couldn't allow her eldest, strongest boy to fall victim to this.

Getting a job was the biggest conundrum facing him now. The H-1B work visa would become invalid in another 30 days and he needed to find a position that would sponsor him before that. The predicament here is that the filing of a new H-1B visa takes a minimum of 30 days if everything goes as per plan. 'Goes as per plan' alludes to getting a job and the employer agreeing to file an H1 visa quickly enough. Which means that even if he gets a job; there is always the risk that the H-1B status he holds might be invalid even before he gets transferred onto the new H-1B.

The goal is to get the new job as soon as possible and then begin the new H-1B visa filing as soon as possible. That way the new H1B goes into effect before the old H1B expires. Thus obviating the need to provide extensive explanations to the immigration authorities.

****

"I am not sure we can file your H-1B so quickly Ralph," said the sweet looking woman in the demure office decorated with pristine white flowers and silverware. Being an university office it was tastefully decorated; very representative of the Burlesque era of office décor. "You have lawyers working for this institution full time right?"
"Yes but they have other priorities. It would not be fair to burden them with more work."
"Even though you are getting a reliable resource who is willing to stay here long term?"
"I understand you are a terrific resource but we have limitations at this point of time. Our budgets are already over-stretched on other things. So for the filing of an H1 we need to present and get another budget proposal approved. So that's a bit of a process. It's not like we don't want to do it or anything. It's just the volume of work that we are dealing with right now."

Ralph was not ready to give up just yet. He had invested quite a bit of time in the interview process and had done two tests for the purpose.

He was first given an online test to evaluate his JAVA skills. The coding test was simple but tested all the basic JAVA concepts. Then, two days later, he was given a live coding test which was a little more complex. This was to test his scripting skills. He passed both with flying colors and was finally called in for the second round to talk to the hiring manager.

It was essential to have all these rounds as they were offering a full-time position and needed to ensure that the person they were bringing on not only knows his stuff but is also a nice person and easy to work with.

The tests were each about two hours. He had to do four hours of preparation for both of them. The interview went on for about two hours. This was a big investment of time, effort and of course the time to go and come to the interview venue. He didn't want to let this effort go to waste by not negotiating well enough or by not pushing people hard enough. When it came to persuasion he used his genes to push ahead. Mum and Dad were always very persuasive when it came to trying to convince people. He hoped it would work.

"I understand your obligations but can you see if it would be possible to pull some strings and try something. Because I only have one month to get the work visa and the job. After that, I am afraid I have to return to my country."
"Yes. Sure, I will definitely look into it and will also talk to the director about your situation."
"Thanks. Whatever you find out let me know. So that way both of us are on the same page and I can increase or reduce my job application efforts."

His outlook to approaching a 'No' was not very smooth and courteous. In fact, it was more engineering and mechanical oriented. In the US, employers prefer candidates that are smooth and emotionally intelligent about handling difficult situations. "You need to learn to be more suave," the Inner Voice always reminded him, without delving into any details.

"Yes, maybe next time. Now I just need to get home and continue my stream of applications," he says to himself as he scoots down the stairs of the university building where he went for the interview.

****

"Hey, they called me in for an interview on Thursday," Jessica screeches over the phone.
"Awesome!" he says in a lackadaisical fashion.
"Yes. And the HR person really likes me. She says that the manager also likes me based on the phone conversation with her."

As she goes on and on about her good fortune, she notices a kind of slump in his response.

"Why are you sounding so down?" she inquires.
"Umm…I am okay. Just too much of work!" he laments.
"Ok. What's up Ralphie. There's something you're not telling me," she decides to investigate.

Silence ensues.

"Come on. I owe my recent interviewing success to you and that is why I am telling you all about this. If it wasn't for you I would still probably be struggling with that Tamara Cuttle bitch making my life a nightmare, day in and day out. I owe all the interviews and offers coming my way to you. You encouraged me through my periods of disappointment."
"It is only natural that I return the favor by helping you out in your difficult times!"

Silence again.

"Could you at least tell me what's the matter?"

Ralph is a very macho, chauvinistic kind of guy. He prefers not telling people his problems; least of all a woman he is having a romantic liaison with. Telling her your problems is a sign of weakness he feels in his mind.

"It's ok to be vulnerable with people you are close to honey!" she reminds him delicately.
"Thanks!"

She waits.

"Ralph please tell me what's up! I am really worried about you because I care about you a lot," she says, sensing the seemingly endless silence.
"Well, the interview I just had ended up in a stalemate. And the other interviews are taking too long to materialize," he finally relents.
"So it's not all that of a rosy picture right now but I am keeping on trying."
"And that's what's needed. You keep pushing and trying till you get it. Remember what you told me once – don't let others decide your fate. You work hard so that you can engineer it for yourself. So much so that others cannot have too much bargaining power against you. But that you have bargaining power yourself as well." Bargaining power comes with confidence and strength in the US or for that matter in every other part of the world.
"Yes. I know. I am trying other places as well."
"Other places?"

"Yes. I have begun applying to other countries too. And looking for jobs on Linkedin as well."

"Why would you want to leave the US?" she says sounding worried. After all, you can't have a relationship across the oceans.

"Well, it's just where I can find a job. If there are opportunities elsewhere and I can get them, then I need to. At least it's better than staying unemployed!"

"Yes. I hope you get the opportunity that is right for you in the US itself though. That way you don't have to move countries. And we get to be together!" she says seeming worried. It is evident that having his love is more important to her.

He doesn't comment on her last statement. He is really not concerned about any relationship with her. He sees the interaction with her as mutual company and stress relief; although in not as blunt of a sense.

****

In the coming days, he intensifies his job hunt on Linkedin and even Facebook. His updated profile on Linkedin looks a lot more professional than when he started 4 weeks ago. On Facebook, he searches "jobs in JAVA; JAVA jobs; programmer jobs;" and so many other permutations and combinations of job titles to get to positions that normal websites like Dice, Indeed and Monster do not have.

According to estimates, only 25% of the vacant job openings are advertised on job portals. The others are either internally advertised or are just not vetted enough by management to judge if they are needed to be advertised or not. In fact, the job market is not even a market. Nobody really knows how many openings are out there or if there are other openings which have just not been recognized enough to prod organizations to create a requisition for them. All open vacancies are not necessarily known and hence are not on the market. And one can't apply for a position that is not advertised.

He works Linkedin like a charm applying for jobs that are ordinarily not advertised on regular job sites. He also ends up making quite a few valuable connections. Though he hasn't had the kind of success that people with an extensive array of connections might have. Being an obscure international student comes with its downsides. Not having the connections and network that make life easier is one of them.

The response rate is agonizingly slow though.

"We regret to inform you that we are unable to proceed with your application as we have other suitable candidates that are better suited for the position. We tried our best to push a proposal to get your visa sponsored but the governing body has its budget occupied with other more crucial tasks at this point," reads the reply from Dalinda, the sweet looking girl from the University of Sciences who had spoken to Ralph after the interview.

Ralph is flabbergasted on seeing this email. But realizes this is capitalism. If their finances cannot manage it; you don't have a job. If they don't have a genuine need they don't create a position. No position, no interview process, no job.

He resolves to push no matter what.

"Would you be open for an interview at 11 am UK time, 6 am US time?" reads the question from Elise, the recruiter for tech positions in the UK.
"Yes, I should be available at that time. Please confirm it. Thanks."

He attends phone and skype interviews with European companies on a very frequent basis. The urge to get a job and survive is strong and very robust. "Even God will be impressed to see how hard you are fighting. Keep it up!" says the Inner Voice.

The calls and interviews from Europe get increasingly frequent. Ralph uses amazing levels of prioritization to deal with interviews from both America as well as Europe. To maintain his voice and throat he uses lozenges and hard candy, chewing them down every so often.

The calls require him to be at the top of his game and he seems to be holding the fort rather well. "It's a matter of time before you get a job," reassures the Inner Voice. When all human company is absent he knows that the Inner voice will never leave him alone to fight and fend for himself.

****

"Hey I got the offer for the position at Grindstone University!" says an ecstatic Jessica. "I met this lady at a networking event from the same university and she said she would recommend me for the position. I was so elated when she actually did and I got the call for the interview and then the offer."

"Wow. Great!"

"Yes. They are asking me to start in 3 weeks. I can't believe it."

"Well, congrats. Now you can tell that Cuttle bitch to fuck off!"

"Yes. But I will give her a two-week notice. I want to depart on a positive note."

"Great. I need to run Jessica. I have to prepare for another set of interviews and calls. Let's talk later this evening."

"Oh yes sure," she says, wanting to hide her disappointment at not being able to speak to him for a longer time. She wanted to celebrate with him with a bottle of wine and some cheese. And then maybe some 'no-holds-barred' romance. He doesn't seem to be in the mood for any of that though.

"Thanks for your support and help throughout," she says wanting to encourage him to continue to talk to her.

"Bye!" he says in a matter of fact manner.

"She is a citizen; so that makes it a whole lot easier for her to get jobs here!" the Inner Voice reminds him.

A major issue with getting a job in the US is the fact whether you have the proper paperwork or not. Paperwork meaning the right to work; which is either a work visa or a green card as a minimum. All international students in general experience the need for paperwork as a major stumbling block to finding a job in the US. Almost all employers are e-verified now. Which means if you don't have the right to work in the form of proper documentation in the US; they would not be able to give you a job here. Even if you are the right candidate for the position.

"Gosh if I marry her, I can get that paperwork in no time!" he says to himself. "Gulp!"

But Jessica isn't the type of girl he wants as a wife. She is too brash, too aggressive, too American for him. He wants someone who will listen and agree with him. Not necessarily contest him all the time. He wants a wife with good looks, Asian values and a good nature. That's a combination which is not easy to come by. Or let's just say you need to be richly blessed to come across that kind of person.

"You are richly blessed! You just need to go out more often and meet people," says the Inner Voice. It always seemed like such a conundrum that when the question of whether he is better off or worse off in the US came up, Ralph never had a direct answer. He would always be in doubt. It never occurred to him, or at least not quick enough, that the job he had and could get in the US would be hard to come by in most other countries. As the population and subsequent competition for the same job in other countries are much higher, it is normally more difficult to land a job in those countries as opposed to in the US.

Moreover, the earnings in US currency translated to heftier sums when converted to Indian rupees. A year of work in the US earned you two to three years' worth of income in Indian currency in a similar profession. The perks of working in the US were definitely very clear. One just needed to have the clarity of mind to see them. Ralph very often tended to get clouded by homesickness, depletion of enthusiasm and general lack of motivation. His negativity would sometimes overshadow the positives that could be found in any situation if one looked closely enough. The Inner Voice would come to his aid quite often in such situations. So often he felt that the Inner Voice was, in fact, God talking to him.

But it was important that Ralph see the good fortune of his situation rather than just griping about the misfortune that he was privy to. Many international students and indeed people from foreign countries become very anxious and worried about their future in the US all too often. There is always a means to an end and they fail to realize that worrying is not going to solve anything. Targeted and specific actions will. So instead of working hard and trying new things they sit back feeling sorry for themselves. This is the exact behavior to orchestrate a failure.

On the flip side, in order to bring about a change in your circumstances, you need to take heart and think what you are going to do next. What is your response going to be to the situation that you are in? How are you going to change the status quo and go from a position of idle desperation to constructive movement? It's definitely not by worrying about things but making constructive changes in your life through directed action.

Ralph's job application effort was in a state of semi-gridlock with many things still in the pipeline or in process. Nothing had really materialized. "Do not lose hope at this time!" said the Inner Voice. And the unthinkable began to happen.

REDEMPTION IN THE NICK OF TIME

RALPH LOOKS AT MONDAY morning with a lot of anticipation and a bit of dread. Anticipation, because two days of applications over Saturday and Sunday are going to result in him being inundated with calls from recruiters. Dread, because in the last four weeks he has received a ton of rejection letters which start coming in on Monday and continue right up to Friday of every week. Applications are reviewed on weekdays so the rejection letters pour in on the same days. Generally, no one works on the weekend.

He wakes up early on Monday; gets ready and then says a short prayer asking for God's help in getting through the rigor of the day. Ralph has a strong belief in the power of the occult and indeed in fate. He believes God can drive his fate in the right direction and lead him to greener pastures and riches he could never comprehend. And he believes this is not just a possibility but something that will one day come true.

Mum had always referred to the omens to make important decisions in life. Ralph too, believes that omens tend to indicate things that are to come before actual facts begin to reveal the truth. Although, he prefers if his actions could determine reality. But life is not that simple or straightforward. There is always the unseen element that affects life and the direction of it. These unseen forces are the forces of nature, of the cosmos and of God. We are all a part of the Cosmos and the God that made the Cosmos and directs its every move who also controls the destiny of every person on earth. It is only natural that first respect is given to Him and everything else comes later.

He gets on his computer and starts going through his emails first. By this point in the application process, he has two laptops. One is for applications and email checking purposes. The other is just for having Skype interviews. He keeps Skype running on the other machine continuously while it is on. As he goes through the mountain of emails showing application confirmations, his eyes remain peeled for something that looks a little different. Different would be an email that looks like a specific, personalized communication from a recruiter or an email inquiring about his background. Four weeks of continuous applications have trained him to spot such emails in a jiffy. Prior to that, he has several years of internship applications to his credit as well.

"Not a single personalized email this morning!" he says to himself. But it is only the beginning of the day. Recruiters generally come in at 8:30 or 9 am and start looking at their email box. They go through resumes after that and start contacting eligible candidates.

"Be patient and positive!" reminds the Inner Voice to pacify the 'easy-to-agitate' Ralph.

He puts on his white shirt and black tie and gets ready for the 8 am Skype interview with a software company from Austria. He has already had one phone interview with them and it went well. Instead of HR, he will be talking to the hiring manager today. Mr. Krackenhoff seems like a well-educated, versatile individual who has been in a number of roles in IT. His LinkedIn profile is richer than most Ralph has come across. *"This interview is going to be intense!"* he says to himself. *"But I am ready!"*

Exactly at one minute before 8am Mr.Krackenhoff's skype id comes online and starts calling Ralph's skype id.

"Hello Mr. Krackenhoff?" says Ralph turning his camera on.
"Hello Ralph."
"Wie geht es dir?" asks Ralph mustering together some of the skeletal vestiges of German phrases he still remembers from his time learning German at Max Mueller Bhavan.
"Hahaha….so you know huh!" says Mr. Krackenhoff.
"I had studied it for some time a few years ago," smiles Ralph.

Mr. Krackenhoff is quite the well-groomed, well-dressed gentleman his profile specified him to be. His gold-rimmed glasses, clean white shirt, simple face and light gray hair present an image representative of a seasoned executive with a touch of divine calm to him. He seems very focused and his gaze seems to peer into Ralph's past like a shining light from a distant star.

"So Ralph, this position is for a mid-level JAVA developer in our company. It is a very dynamic role and needs someone who can learn and deliver on the job quickly. We are currently dealing with social welfare applications coding and development."

"Okay."

"Could you give me a brief summary of your background and the different software languages you have worked on."

"Sure. I have a certification in JAVA and have primarily worked on JAVA and SQL most of my career. I worked in Siemens Medical Solutions for two years as a JAVA developer. I worked on a medical billing application for them and learnt the business rules governing billing."

"Okay. So you have hands-on experience with billing software then?"

"Yes. I worked on the backend and the connections between the database and the application."

As the interview progresses, Mr. Krackenhoff's calm face gives way to a smile. He thanks Ralph for his time and says he might schedule another session to go over some other aspects of his background along with a colleague of his.

****

"*I am so hungry today!*" says Ralph to himself as he quickly heads down the stairs to have some rice and chicken. He sets his lunch plate down and starts munching through it, feeling relaxed that he finally got to the lunch table. Lunch is always a good time of the day as it gives him a temporary respite from the hustle and bustle of job applications and job hunting.

He hears a heavy thud as Kuda, the caretaker and director of International House enters through the heavy door. He is followed by a slim, clean shaven, handsome-looking man behind him. The man is dressed in brown trousers and a white t-shirt. He is pulling a big suitcase behind him.

Kuda peers through the dining hall into the kitchen to see who is there.

"Hey Ralph!" he says with a broad smile.

"Paresh is going to be joining us from this month onward. He is moving to town for a job and wanted to rent with us."

Paresh gives him a wide smile.

"Oh. Awesome. Welcome Paresh!" says Ralph in a subdued tone.

Ralph wasn't the best at welcoming people or even in terms of his soft skills. He was a typical programmer and engineer. A little uncouth, almost bordering on rude in his conversation style. He didn't really have a knack for making people feel comfortable. He'd probably be an utter failure had he entered the hospitality profession.

"I won't shake your hand right now as my hands are a little messy," he tells Paresh as he tries to wind up his lunch. He generally preferred eating alone.
"Absolutely. Please take your time. We can always talk later."

Kuda looks at their interaction and realizes a fact he has often noted. Ralph is not the best host you might find. "Yes, Ralph is a great cook. In fact, I can't resist his food many times. Someday we will have a party and have him cook for you as well," smiles Kuda.
"Haha," smiles Paresh sensing a borderline hostility. The kind of hostility that is usually shown towards newcomers but ordinarily shouldn't be.
"Why don't I show you your room and everything. Get you settled," suggests Kuda.
"That would be great!" replies Paresh.
"Nice meeting you Ralph!" says Paresh.
"Same here," says Ralph in his traditional subdued welcome to newcomers.

Ralph never liked new additions to the house from the outside. He seemed to feel that it violated his privacy and current control over things. Having a new person start in the house meant training them on the various norms and rules of the house and getting them assimilated. Being how quick and impatient he was in giving training, Ralph hated providing training or help to new members. The attitude came from a tendency to learn things quickly. He was quick to pick up and learn things. He expected others to be that way. And if they weren't he would get very angry and impatient. He probably would not have made a good teacher, coach or even guide. Dad had regularly brought this issue up with him and hoped he would learn and change his behavior in regards to this.

Ralph finishes lunch and rushes to his room not wanting to have to interact with Kuda or Paresh. He preferred to grind himself down on his chair in front of the computer and apply for positions rather than have small talk with Paresh or Kuda.

****

"Hiya, I started my new job!" beamed Jessica's voice through the speakers of his phone. The voice is not in real time, though. It is the voicemail she left as Ralph didn't pick the call when she was calling. He let it go to voicemail as he was too busy and didn't want to get disturbed with her jabbering.
"Maybe we should meet this weekend for a celebration at Rittenhouse or my place. I have special wine with me, not to mention your favorite steak. All you have to do is bring yourself! Let me know."

He knew he wouldn't reply to that voicemail. He had way more important things on his plate for now. And even if he did have the time to go he probably wouldn't. He didn't want to do anything that would suggest he was interested in having a long-term relationship with her or have something real serious.

As the day wears on he begins to get a little grumpy and sullen. The day was kind of slow and he received just two calls from people inquiring about his background. This is now the fifth week and no job in site. He has three more weeks before his legal status becomes invalid in the US.

He opts for an early dinner at 8 pm and goes downstairs.

"Hey Ralph!" smiles a dazzling Paresh. He is holding a cooker in one hand and spoon in another, pouring a gooey substance on a plate.
"Would you like some dal fry and roti?" he asks Ralph.
"Thanks. But I have my own dinner in the fridge."
"So how was your day?" he continues as Ralph hurries to the fridge to begin heating his dinner.
"It was okay," Ralph says in his characteristic subdued tone.

Paresh senses he is not much of a friendship monger. So he decides to turn his selfless charm on.

"I am a system administrator at UPENN. I have my Masters in Information Systems and Networking. What do you do?" he asks.

Ralph is a little taken aback that this tall, unassuming guy works for UPENN. He thought he was the most well-educated and accomplished guy in the whole of International House. Now there is someone who matches him. "Definitely somebody you could learn something from!" reminds the Inner Voice.
"I used to work for Siemens Medical as a JAVA developer. But I have been laid off and am currently looking for a job," he replies sounding a little down and desperate.
"Oh, sorry to hear that man."

Except for the 'cling-clang' of Ralph's dishes, there is an awkward silence.

Paresh musters some more courage to converse hoping he might be able to help Ralph out. "How is the job hunt going so far?" he delicately asks. He knows job hunts can be mentally and physically exhausting. Moreover, they are a constant drag in the back of one's mind in regards to what the future holds.

"Umm, lots of calls and interviews but no offer in sight yet!" he laments. "How did you get the job at UPENN?"
"I applied through an educational jobs website to several universities. UPENN called and offered me a position first. So I took it."
"Was the selection process very rigorous?"
"Well, I underwent two phone interviews. And then came and had an in-person interview. They paid for the transport and cost of staying. So it was cool."
"Amazing. So where did you come from?"
"I moved here from Miami, Florida."
"That's a nice place. Why did you leave?"
"Just the job. More jobs here."
"Okay. Are they paying for your relocation?"
"They said they would cover half of it."
"Good policy!"
"Yeah I thought it was good. One of the few places that covers relocation expenses."
"You could get in there too. If this guy could do it so can you," prods the Inner Voice.

"You should try out UPENN as well. I am sure they have a lot of JAVA developer vacancies. And they always want good people too."

"Yes, I will start applying there."

"Let me know if you need any specific help," offers Paresh.

"Thanks so much man," says Ralph as he hurries up the stairs with his plate of sliced ham, bread and butter slices. Ralph is not the kind to ask for help. His ego pushes him to do more and push himself harder to work and create. He is an engineer and builder at heart.

He begins applying on the educational website for positions in UPENN first and then in several other universities. His fingers move at lightning speed. He barely takes a breath to bite into the sandwich still lying untouched on the plate.

As the sun's rays come shining through the windows of his plush room on the second floor he realizes he is hungry. That's when the sandwich almost deprived of all moisture, the butter a lot softer gets consumed. He feels the joy of biting and eating it. The feeling is even better with the accomplishment of having completed so many applications online. "*I didn't know this website he told me about...man!*" he says to himself.

For the first time in a long time, he realizes that he doesn't know quite a few things. And he wouldn't know what he didn't know had he not spoken to different people. "You need to be more social and talk to people. Being hard working and self-driven is good. But there is a component of talking to people and learning and exchanging ideas that you need to understand and do. That will make you smarter than you currently are!" counsels the Inner Voice in a message that has been repeated several times but he doesn't seem to understand or implement it for whatever reason.

****

"Happy Tuesday!" says Paresh as he sees Ralph pop into the kitchen for a morning bite.

"Hey buddy!" says Ralph, way more friendly this time around. He acknowledges Paresh with a pat on the back. When someone is better than you and has contributed to your knowledge and understanding; you are generally more inclined to respect and value them.

"So did you apply through that website?" asks Paresh.

"Yes. Very good website man!"

"It is probably one of the best websites I have seen and used," reaffirms Paresh. "Moreover, it gives you access to positions in non-profit organizations like educational institutions, government and quasi-government organizations, and a host of others. These positions cannot be found on just Monster, Dice or Indeed."

"Yes. How did you find this website?"

"I was reading a newspaper in the university library where I came across this information. So I thought of giving it a try."

"That's amazing. So you read a lot of papers too!"

"Umm…I just like reading in general. And I think it helps you stay informed and current. Besides, it helps in interviews or any type of endeavor which is knowledge intensive."

"Yeah. This H1 work visa is a major issue for us guys. If I had a green card it would be so easy to get a job here!" laments Ralph.

"Which is why you need to apply to non-profit organizations. You can get a work visa way faster through a non-profit organization than through a corporation."

"How is that?" he put his bread cutting knife down to listen intently.

"Yes. Visa applications filed for by non-profit organizations don't come under the quota category that other applications filed by regular corporations are subject to. Hence, they are not subject to a lottery or picking. They go through directly from stage to stage. They are subject to priority dates though."

"Woah! Amazing. That is something."

"Yes. Which is why I can only emphasize bud….apply to non-profits if you want your work visa and green card done quickly."

"You bet!"

"Well, I am done with my cereal. I am going to go get the train. Keep up the applications!"

"Thanks man. See you in the evening," smiles Ralph.

It is difficult to see the smile on his face in the mornings. But today is different. Ralph feels that there is great hope and great things to look forward to. Someone is actually helping him in his efforts. And who else might have sent Paresh his way….It is God!

"When the whole world caves in on you, God's got you bud!" says the Inner Voice resoundingly.

Ralph continues to apply to every position in UPENN whether it is a junior, mid-level or senior position. He applies directly on UPENN's website as well as on the website Paresh told him about. He provides Paresh' name as a reference.

His logic behind these mass applications is that the chances of his name getting noticed increases every time a recruiter opens the email box and sees his details. Even if it's for a position not at all relevant to his background. *"You begin to love the dog you see every day; even if you didn't love it in the beginning. Let's follow this principle to make yourself famous with the recruiters,"* says Ralph to himself.

****

"Good Morning Ralph!"

"Good morning. Who is this?" Ralph says as he painstakingly rises from his sleeping mat. Waking up the following morning after a long day's work is always difficult, particularly in cooler weather.

Although he had a couch Ralph preferred sleeping on the mat as it kept his back and spine in shape and ensured he got a sound sleep without disrupting his posture in any way.

"This is Elise. And I have some good news for you!"
"Oh really. Hi Elise!"
"Yes. Mr. Krackenhoff would like to schedule a last round of interview with you along with one of his directors."
"That's great to hear!" he says rubbing his eyes to ward off the sleepiness a little. It was still 6:30 am and he had pulled a late night to get some job applications in.
"How does Friday at 7 am your time sound?"

He didn't have time to go to the desk and check his calendar. But he figured he wouldn't have any appointment at that time. So he answered in the affirmative. You normally don't try to reschedule or postpone an appointment for a job.

"Great. I will send you an invite and any other information about the other person who will be in the interview."
"Thanks so much! Appreciate it!"
"All the best Ralph!" she says cheerfully.

He quickly rises from the mat, folds the bedsheet and says a quick prayer. After ablutions, he brings his cobbled-up breakfast of ham and boiled eggs to the room and gulps it down slowly as he goes through the mountain of emails in his email box.

The day is pretty uneventful until he receives calls for a phone interview for one position in UPENN and an 'in person' for another. Paresh had advised him to apply on the UPENN careers website directly as well as through the non-profit website for UPENN jobs. He would have done it that way anyway. The results of this strategy are clear to see now, though. And the results confirm his belief. "Listen to your inner logic and the voice of God!" said the Inner Voice every so often. And listen he does as it has put him in better situations so many times in the past.

After lunch, he receives a third call. This time to UPENN as well. They select a phone interview date for the coming week; not immediately. *"One of those slow coaches!"* he says to himself with a snigger.

Immigrants to the US typically get very strong and astute working on a regular basis executing various efforts. In regards to international students, the dedicated ones get very strong in marketing techniques as they continue to apply for jobs and network for career opportunities. They learn about new recruitment and training consultancies; new techniques of making connections with recruiters and headhunters. The benefits that accrue by working towards finding a job are immense and transcend mere job connections. These efforts help you connect with people, build bridges and learn professional interpersonal skills.

However, there is also a tendency to grow disenchanted and cynical about the whole process. This particularly happens to people who are looking for quick results and are just not patient enough to work through the slump in the job market. Generally, depressions in the economy require workers to put in more time to find work. With a larger pool of applicants wooing a smaller number of total jobs in the market; the competition is obviously fiercer and the window for rejection at the disposal of the employer is larger. Great patience and resilience is needed to weather the slump in jobs creation and indeed the pace of recruitment and selection.

Many people dedicate their time to learning a new skill and others join university or some other program to learn something new during such times. There are several ways to avoid becoming negative or morose with the lack of movement on the job front. The smart thing to do though is to keep getting and staying as positive as possible. When one is positive you give an opportunity for God to work in your life and orchestrate miracles. You beat frustration and keep negativity at bay.

****

There is a temporary lull in calls from Jessica. She probably understands that Ralph is in no mood for sweet talk. After two sets of voicemails don't create a call in return she realizes that something else is top of his mind. His razor focus can be strong and very rude at times. She doesn't want to get on his wrong side by continuing to push him to call her.

Ralph spends the whole day applying for jobs and being available for phone interviews, Skype interviews and attending in-person interviews when the situation demands. He waits for dinner time as that is when he meets Paresh. Paresh Krishnan, a free spirited, good looking guy from the southern part of India has earned the respect of hard-driving Ralph. He has an uncanny style of looking for jobs or learning a new skill or pretty much doing anything of relevance for a young professional.

Ralph realizes he could learn a ton from Paresh in all aspects of life; not just professional. For now, though, he prefers sticking to the professional aspect of things till he gets suitable employment.

"Have you ever tried to get a job in other countries Paresh?"
"Yes I did apply a couple of times to Germany. But then stopped that once I started getting calls from companies in the US. That was when I was in India. I did apply to a few other countries when I graduated in the States. But that was for a very short period of time."
"Okay"
"Why? You not happy with the applications in the US?"
"No. It's just that I have applied for positions in the EU. And I am kind of confused what I am going to do if I get an opening there. Should I leave the US and go there or let that opportunity go and continue to look in the US? It's very confusing at this point."
"That's an interesting question you ask. I have also faced a dilemma like this a long time ago. But not in such depth as you. As I had not received any offers from a foreign country."

Paresh pauses to think. "I would say keep the decision-making simple. You are in the US and I know we are in a recession. But should you get a job here, I would recommend staying here. The expenses of relocating to the EU are immense and besides, you don't have citizenship there. So it would take time to file your work visa and what not. At least here you know the way the system works and the learning curve is not as much as it will be if you go to the EU for good."

Both of them look at each other silently.

"I know what I am saying to you sounds dead simple and easy to say. But I understand it is easier for me to say it than for you to be in it. Being in a predicament or dilemma is always way more difficult than being in no situation or in a stable situation which is what I am in. So, kind of easy for me to say; but difficult to execute. I understand the difficulty of your situation but you need to take some objective, decisive action."
"If you get a job in the EU very easily and your visa and everything is taken care without a hitch then only that place might be worth considering. Otherwise, for all practical purposes the US is a better place to work and settle. In fact, I have heard that things are way cheaper in the US than in the EU. And there is a lot more opportunity here than in the EU. This is a larger market with a lot more businesses and a lot more going on. All you need to do is to ride out the economic recession at this time until things become better."

Silence again.

"Okay."
"Yes give it a thought. And as I said, focus on non-profit organizations for now. Because that is one avenue that is not affected by the economy or recession as much as say a for-profit corporation."
"Did you get any calls from UPENN?" he asks.
"Yes, I got three calls. One in-person interview was today and then a phone interview is scheduled for the coming week. I had a phone interview for a position yesterday. Haven't heard back from them yet."
"Okay. Cool. Being a university they are almost like a government organization. Slow but not as slow as a government organization. They do take their time so don't let that bum you out."
"Sure thing. Thanks man!" says a grateful and smiling Ralph.

"Absolutely. Don't hesitate to ask me anything you like. If I can help I will."

"Yeah yeah. I will. Thanks."
As Paresh turns to head upstairs to his room, he stops and asks Ralph.
"By the way, what questions did they ask you in the interviews?"
"The first interview was relatively simple and they asked me relatively simple questions about JAVA and some scripting languages. However, for the in person interview today they asked me pretty tough questions which I couldn't handle. And a few questions which needed me to use my memory. I just couldn't remember many things we did in undergrad. On the others I did ok."
"When you are required to use your memory to remember things and you just cannot, don't sweat it. How you handle this scenario is; you just let them know that 'I did this or studied this but I would need to refresh my memory about it as I do not remember it in great detail', " interrupts Paresh.
"So when you tell them the truth about what you know of the concept or the question they are more likely to believe and like what you said about it. So it's not that you are not answering the question or that you are answering it wrong. It's just that you are stating the truth about it. One person cannot be expected to know everything about everything. Being human it is but natural that you have to go back and refer to stuff. Your brain can't possibly remember and recall everything you have studied and read like it was yesterday. At least not for a normal person."
"Moreover, they will appreciate your honesty and forthrightness in letting them know what you know and don't know. Many a times it is not what you know that gets you the job but your overall attitude to the interview and how you deal with the people in the interview. I can't tell you how many times I have come across people who have their jobs just based on their positive and forthright attitude and personality as opposed to just technical information and knowledge. In fact, people who are technically smart end up having a tough time finding a job merely because they scare people away just by their brash and haughty attitude."
"Ring a bell!" says the Inner Voice to Ralph.
"So don't worry if the interview was tough. As long as you didn't freak out or start abusing the interviewers there is every chance that you could be in the running. And even if you do not make the cut; no problem. That job was not for you. I look at things that way. Whether it is in the case of jobs or in the case of relationships."

Paresh's advice feels like a god-send. He can't remember, but the last time someone told him this was when he was back home in Goa. Dad used to have candid conversations with him on a range of topics. He appreciated Paresh giving him a dump on the real knowledge that textbooks and class lectures and courses do not. A kind of vicarious advice from Dad.

****

"Hello Ralph. So this is my colleague Ivan. He is the solution architect on the team and for many years was the technical lead. He will be interacting with you today to understand your background from a technical stand point," says Mr. Krackenhoff over Skype.
"Hi Ivan. How are you?"
"Fine Ralph. What about you?"
"Great! Thanks for asking."
"Cool. So I wanted to know a little more about the languages you have programmed in and the different types of projects. Could you give me a summary of what you have done so far."
"Sure. So I have mostly been a JAVA programmer and have worked on medical billing software in my professional experience. Prior to that, I worked on geographic information systems designing the backend and the interface for the operability of the software."
"Okay. So have you designed systems from a scratch?"
"I have designed the blueprint of software applications and the functionality besides doing the coding. I have worked on JAVA but have also used Python for scripting. Which by the way I must say is a very powerful language."
"What have you done in Python?"
"I have prepared small scripts to automate functions and routine tasks. Integrated the scripts with Excel and Access, as well as automated database functions using the scripts."
"Okay. How would you say you handle difficult work tasks or even situations when they arise and you need to deliver results quickly?"
"I have not been in a lot of situations like that so far. But whenever I have, I have ensured I document what I am doing. I always aim to learn as much as I can about the topic so that I can invest that learning in my work. Once a proof of concept or base functionality has been developed, I demonstrate it to the person in charge and get their feedback. Then I seek to improve it based on the suggestions from my manager. I don't

use one specific way to resolve difficult situations. There are many I resort to based on the situation. Most importantly I focus on learning the work and getting clean code developed. I refrain from spaghetti code at all costs."

"Great. Personally, I would try to avoid spaghetti code as well. So definitely good to meet another developer that resists the ease and convenience of spaghetti code," seconds Ivan.

As the interview progresses, Ralph gets to know more about the job and indeed about Ivan and Mr. Krackenhoff. They end up on a promise to get back to Ralph as soon they have a decision made. Europeans like to take their time when decision making is involved.

Later in the day, he receives a few more calls about his background. But what hits him the most is when he receives the email saying he has not made the cut for the first phone interview he had with UPENN. Rejection intimations are always a pain point when one is applying left, right and center for jobs and trying to be positive in spite of all the disappointments and dejections that are a part of daily life.

That same day he realizes that he hasn't made it in the second in person interview at UPENN either. He prays to the Lord for strength to help him fight this surge of rejections and intransigence on the job front.

That night he calls Jessica and has a candid chat with her. "I joined the new job and it is going really well!" she says.
"Glad to hear that!" he says plainly.
"How is your job hunt going? Haven't heard from you in a long time. You must be very busy," she inquires.
"Lots of phone calls and lots of rejection letters or 'on hold' email messages. So it's been a crazy last couple of days. But I still feel I am closer to a job today than at any time in the last three weeks."
She is surprised to hear a ray of positivity in him. A far cry from the gloomy, grim and morose Ralph she is used to dealing with. She wouldn't have been dealing with him had she not had affection and a deep liking for him.
"Well I will see if there are any positions available at my organization in your line....software developer right?"
"Yes. Any type of software engineering, JAVA development; I am the man for it."

He thanks her for her consideration and help and tries to wind up the call. She tries to see if she can get him to meet with her. But he politely turns her down. When a woman is interested in a man she wants to have as much face time with him as possible. They want to meet and spend time with him; have a romantic night and learn more about him. However, if a man is not interested in a woman he would generally not show any excitement in meeting her. In fact, men tend to be more interested in physical satiation from their company with women than the emotional aspect usually. If he is not into the woman mentally; he would not want to have anything more to do with her after his physical needs are satisfied. Physical needs could either mean cuddling, kissing or sex; the final frontier of physiological satiation for most people.

****

The weekend is spent applying for positions and going through unsent emails. He likes to see what was left incomplete during the week – be they incomplete applications, emails still left incomplete in the drafts folder or any other maintenance activity involving cleaning up of files, folders or reformatting of resumes.

Maintenance activity is very important from the point of view of starting off the week on a strong footing. Proper maintenance of files and other documentary artifacts leads to organization. This organization helps in the deployment of effective job applications. Multiple job applications can be made in a very short period of time if you are organized and ready to go with all the data that is needed.

"So what are your plans for tonight?" asks Paresh during lunch time on Saturday.
"Job applications and data cleansing and maintenance as usual. Nothing spectacular," says Ralph in a matter of fact manner.
"Man. I know you have applications to make and job research to do. But you should take some time off. You should go and enjoy so that you get to unwind. It will help you concentrate better if you do. All work and no play makes Jack a dull boy remember!"
"Umm….but there is such a lot of work to do," he says.
"See. Work will always be there. Difficult times will always come. You need to be able to live life in spite of these things. They are just tests that God sends your way to see how you react to them. Do you end up getting depressed by them or do you live life with even more vigor?

410

God would always want you to live life with more vigor and enjoyment no matter what the circumstances. Don't let the sharp thorns of survival stop you from living the flowers of life!"

Paresh's kind words resonate with Ralph's sense of life and sanity. He wishes he could have such an outlook to life; such an approach.

"Now tell me Ralph. Do you really not have any plans today?"

"Still 'no' ma man! My plans didn't change in 20 seconds," he smiles.

"Well, you need to spice up your plans then. You don't need to do anything spectacular to unwind or get some air. Something as simple as going to the park or to the college campus and walking or even meeting a friend would suffice."

"Okay."

"If I were you I would probably go to the strip club; get a lap dance or see some babes. But you don't have to do that if you don't want to. You can be modest to start off. And remain that way. But you must do something to unwind. It is important for you to continue to function at the same pace and power as when you started your job application effort."

Ralph looks at him intently and nods.

"It is proven that as you keep working continuously on a regular basis, day after day, week after week without any significant outing you begin to lose energy and more importantly motivation and enthusiasm for the job."

"If you don't get an outing, you might end up totally screwing up your performance. In this case, it is job applications. In the future, after you get a job it will be at work. You need to keep your motivation up. Performance is always dependent on motivation and enthusiasm for the job."

Paresh knows Ralph is very focused. So focused he can be a fuddy-duddy sometimes. But that drains quite a bit of his creativity and imagination. So much so that it can unknowingly reduce his productivity. Paresh knows this because he was like Ralph a very long time ago until one fateful day he met his first in a string of many girlfriends. His transformation made possible a lot of the success he achieved later.

411

"Let's do one thing bud. I am going to the Saint Paul's track today. Why don't you join me. I would like to suggest some interview techniques; if you are interested."

"Certainly!" says Ralph seeing the benefit of going with Paresh on the track.

Paresh knew Ralph probably wasn't the best of interviewees, which is why he wanted to give him some tips in an informal setting. What better way than when he is in a sports arena or on a track. A bar would have been a better place. But then again, bars can be noisy.

****

"So tell me how you go through your interview normally?" Paresh asks Ralph while they stroll on the track of St. Paul's University.

"Well, there is no real way as such. I just go to the place, introduce myself and then listen to the introduction they give me. They start asking me technical and non-technical questions. I answer them. That's about it." He looks at Paresh wondering what else to say or whether he was looking for anything specific.

Paresh doesn't seem to show much reaction. He just stares at the open track in front of him and seems to ponder. At first blush, Paresh comes across as a very friendly, straightforward kind of person. No baggage, no complications sort of guy. And that is probably true. But he does give a genuine thought to anything he does or on how he interacts with people. He does show concern for people and values them. At least that's the impression that Ralph got.

"That's great that you answer the interview in the best possible fashion and listen to them intently. But do you direct the interview in the direction you want or do you just go with the flow that they direct it in?"

There is pin drop silence for a minute. Ralph feels like both of them are in separate airtight bubbles totally disconnected from the world. He is not sure how to answer the follow-up question so he maintains his silence.

"I don't really follow?" he says.

"That's alright. I was just wanted to know if you do it or not."

"Do what?"

"Okay. Well I follow a certain technique of interviewing that is designed to give better results and an outcome closer to the desired result. I call it 'leading the way.'" Paresh looks at Ralph and smiles.
"Leading the way!" Ralph repeats.
"Yes. So this particular strategy is designed to make the interviewers ask you the questions you want them to ask you. And you obviously have the picture perfect answers you would like to give them. It helps to focus attention on the strengths that you want them to focus on rather than on any underlying weaknesses. In other words, it is the ultimate strategy for better interview performance. It ensures you transition from an interview turkey to an interview tiger. You crack the interview head on."

Paresh's face has the glow of a halo. His wheatish, symmetrical face has a wide smile that accentuates his good looks and personality.

"Okay. So how do you do this? This special interviewing strategy," asks Ralph sounding a little confused.
"It's simple!"
"Before going for any interview, you make a list of your strengths relevant to that particular job. List out at least five strengths. Of the listed strengths, make a super list of the top strengths from that list. Now focus on what kind of sentences or conversation topics you can delve into around those key strengths."
"Ummm...!" Ralph still sounds confused.
"Hold on. Don't get confused. I will answer all your questions."
"So for example, let's say one of your strengths is scripting. You could answer a question in regards to your background and as you are near the end of that subject you could say something like 'I have done scripting in many different languages. But I am particularly good at Python and VBA scripting. I am relatively quick at understanding new scripting languages and implementing them in my day to day work.' Getting it?"
"Umm...okay."
"Yes. So when you say something like that; their attention automatically goes to your scripting abilities and indeed to your technical strengths. And you are good at that. So then you further steer the conversation by answering their questions concerning your technical strengths."

Paresh looks at him to read the reaction on his face. He decides to go into more detail.

"Let's say they ask you what type of scripts have you written? So, when you answer you can give a bit of a look of thinking and then say you have written scripts to automate functions and routine tasks for the department. Or you have written scripts that serve as code modules for future development. Spice up the information you give them and say it in a way which is believable."

"Whatever you do be genuine in your outlook even if you might not entirely be telling the truth. Remember you have nothing to gain from telling all white lies. When you start doing the job you might be caught unaware because they will remember your tales but you won't. And that will create doubts in their mind about who they have hired. Never give room for that to happen."

"Woah!" Ralph's attention is briefly shifted as a hot looking girl runs past them.

"Yeah, and you will see a lot of those in the office too. Make sure you don't get distracted in the office. Because in an official environment women can complain of sexual harassment if they want to. And the onus is on you to defend yourself and prove them wrong. Don't mix flirting and work."

[Paresh continues. He sounds more aggressive now that he has already developed a substantial rapport with Ralph] "Anyways coming back to the interview topic. So you got what I am trying to say – lead the flow of the conversation rather than just answering their questions and having them direct the flow. Lead the flow without making them feel that you are directing the flow. When you are eloquent and smooth in your conversations, people tend to like you and believe you. Aim for that. It is very difficult to find technical people who have good soft skills these days. For some reason, they tend to be mutually exclusive. So a technical person with good soft skills is an even higher priced commodity than someone with only the technical or only the soft skills side of things. Always remember that and aim to raise your game in those two core competencies."

Silence again.

"I think you already have most of the skills required of those two competencies right. I am sure you do. But you can always up the game a little. And keep raising it till you have heads turning."

"Any questions my friend?" asks Paresh sensing Ralph's head is already spinning.

"No. But I appreciate the deep hands-on information."

"Cool. I am not done yet, though. We need to analyze how you take interviews to really figure out how you do in them. What do you do right? What you could maybe improve on."

"Yeah yeah," Ralph turns his head toward Paresh for only the second time in the whole conversation. He sees definite value in what Paresh is saying.

"This is the kind of friend you need!" beams the Inner Voice.

"Why don't we discuss this over dinner this evening?"

"Yeah absolutely!" Ralph almost can't believe his ears that someone is interested in giving him solid knowledge and information. He didn't ask him; didn't cajole or coerce him to share his information. But this dashing chap seems to want to help him.

"Only God knows all that humans can think and guess about! It is best you just take the help and not worry about the logic behind why you are being offered the help!" counsels the Inner Voice.

****

"So you say this guy is providing you with tips and ideas on how to go about interviewing and presenting your case is it?" asks Jessica.

"Yes and he seems to be so confident and amazing at what he does. His understanding and knowledge are so deep! I wish I was as smart," he avers.

"You're smart! Trust me. You just need to see yourself as that," she encourages him.

"Yeah. But there's a lot to learn from this guy. He seems very mature and stable."

"Yes. Learn from him but don't think you are chopped liver." Her words make him feel like she already thinks he is her man.

[Knock on the door] "Okay Jessica. I think somebody is at the door. I will call you later." He quickly winds up the conversation with her and rushes to the door sensing he knows who it is.

"Hey Ralph let's get together sooner. I have plans for tonight. So maybe we can discuss the interview techniques now and then you can prepare over some of the things we discuss," says Paresh as he holds his orange juice on the door jamb.

"Absolutely. You head on down. I will get my pen and paper and be right there," says Ralph as he shoves the phone into his pant pocket.

415

"You are welcome to bring a notepad. But let me be honest with you; you don't need it. What we will discuss is designed to stick to your head," says Paresh looking rather serious.

Ralph has seen that look a few times before. His professor in engineering design had a similar look when he gave the students a test preparatory class. He would always encourage them to not be so worried about their performance or results as long as they were 'true to themselves.' "If you do the work required of you and invest the effort that is needed no one in this world can change what is destined to you!" he would repeatedly say.

He is grateful that he has a housemate who is so mature; yet as young.

"There you are!" he says with a smile as Ralph totters into the kitchen, pen and notepad in hand.
"So tell me Ralph. How do you answer the question 'tell me something about yourself'?"
"So I first tell them about my education, then my work experience and why I feel the role is a good fit for me."
"Anything else?"
"Umm....that's about it!"
"Okay. So can we do a dry run of it – 'tell me something about yourself?'"
"So I am Ralph Cazeema. I have completed my Masters in Computer Science engineering with a 3.8 GPA. And have two years of JAVA development experience in Siemens Medical. While there I worked on a medical billing system. I like this position because I think it will allow me to advance my knowledge and skill in JAVA."
"Done!" says Ralph to indicate to Paresh that he has completed his response.

Paresh doesn't seem to be too satisfied but does a rather remarkable job of masking his feelings.

"Great. Your answer is good. Short, sweet and to the point. However, if I was answering the same question I would do it a little differently. So a different way of doing it would be to first tell them what you do; you are a JAVA developer. You don't need to mention your name as it is already on your resume. They couldn't care less what your name is. Then I would proceed to tell them what my experience in JAVA

416

development is presuming that you are interviewing for a JAVA developer position. Finally, I would say my educational background in computer science strengthens my position as a JAVA developer as it helps me to think critically and solve problems."

Ralph looks at him in respectful wonder.

"So in one go, it would be something like 'I have been a JAVA developer for the last three to four years. I have extensive experience working on medical billing applications as I worked for XYZ company as a developer on their medical billing software. During this time, I was privy to the requirements and changes needed in the system. I developed the requirements in accordance with the expectations of end users and other stakeholders. All in all, I think my Masters in computer science engineering places me at a great advantage in terms of understanding code and analyzing it critically.' "

He looks at Ralph to see his reaction. "So did that sound good?" he asks looking at Ralph intently.
"Yes. Much better than mine in fact."

He slowly nods and shakes his head to indicate that he should answer in that way too.

"Wow. Now I see what has been hampering my interview efforts. It's the brevity with which I answer probably. They don't find the answer clear enough. And are probably so confused with what I say that they feel I don't know what I am talking about."
"Yes. And all of that is in the past. You can't change the past but you can change the future. So what you need to do now is think of interesting, detailed ways to answer questions and keep it simple while doing so. Keep practicing the answers till you make them a part of you; internalize them. Then if somebody wakes you up at midnight and asks; you will be and should be able to answer."
"Yes."
"Also as a developer, I don't know. Has anyone ever asked you for a live demonstration of your skills?"
"Live demonstration?"
"Yes, like to code and show them your skills?"
"Well, sometimes people ask to write some code on paper or on the board. But not a live demo on a computer."

"Okay. Well, I suggest you use a different strategy. Make a presentation of why you think you are a good fit for the job. And include things like your abilities, education and the requirements of the job. Show how your abilities match up against the requirements of the job. Show the interviewer why you would be able to add tremendous value to the role and the organization."

"Umm."

"I know you have probably never done this before. But you must try it and see how it does. After you do it you will believe what I say. A presentation yields tremendous value to an interview and is often times a game changer. It can get you the job as opposed to another candidate who might be equally good if not better."

"Umm...unique concept. I will definitely try it. By the way, which software do you use for this?"

"Use Microsoft PowerPoint. It is the best presentation tool that at least I have used."

"Okay."

"Well, this is all I wanted to communicate to you today. Please allow some time for the information to sink in. If you have any doubts you have my number or just knock my door. You can ask Kuda, our beloved house caretaker for the address if you don't know where my door is." Both of them share a laugh knowing that Paresh has a smart sense of humor to be used at the right time.

As he leaves the kitchen area; Paresh wishes him all the best. "When you get a positive result using these tips, let's go and have a drink. Or go to the club. There are lots of people you could meet and get to know at the club. It will be good for you. Trust me, being social helps." Paresh smiles as he points to Ralph positively.

****

"The more I prepare the luckier I get!" hums Ralph as he prepares notes on how to answer the upcoming phone interview. He knows this is probably the only chance left for him to get a job in UPENN and maybe even in Philadelphia.

On several other occasions he has come across some situations which he would like to forget; others which he would like to remember and yet others which he would regard as plain old neutral. Along the way, there were distasteful interviews during which he was interviewed by nutcases and sycophants. Others in which task masters sat across the table from him. Yet others in which they just didn't have a need for an employee, but were interviewing as a fall back option. Or just to show HR that interviews were being conducted although they already had a candidate from a friend or a relation to fill the position.

Ralph hopes that what will come in the future will be positive and good. He hopes that the pain of applying and trying will be replaced by the joy of success and gainful employment.

"Good things are destined to come to you!" says the Inner Voice.

Ralph knows that this is the final hour. From the end of the current week, he has two weeks left before his H-1B work visa expires and renders his legal status invalid. *"Whatever risks I need to take I rather take them in these remaining three weeks. Because if I am unsuccessful I will live with the regret that I never took the chances that had the potential to give me a job."* At the back of his mind, he knew he was referring to Paresh's techniques and any risks associated with them.

"But that guy is too thorough to not have considered all the risks associated with any techniques that he recommended to me!" Ralph reassures himself. It's always such a boon when someone else has already experimented with different things in life and you get to learn their wisdom without having to go through the effort of reinventing the wheel.

As other random preparation thoughts cross his mind he sees the summer sparrow sitting peacefully in the shade of one of the boughs. He wonders what life would be if he were like that sparrow going through life without a care in the world. The only concern being where to get the next morsel of food from.

The randomness of the passing thought gives way to the purpose of his worldly goal. In one hour he was scheduled for the phone interview with UPENN. He keeps his notepad handy with tips and advice to address any questions that might come forth.

"So, could you give me a brief about your background," says the shrill sounding woman's voice on the phone.

"Sure. I have been a JAVA developer for a couple of years. I have worked on medical billing software building the engine for the last 3 years with Siemens. The experience gave me exposure to all types of syntaxes and coding styles within JAVA. I also learned to integrate with varied scripts and enhance the functionality of JAVA based applications. In doing so, I learned about the business rules of the system and of the medical billing business process in general. I have a Masters in Computer Science engineering and this provides me with a critical mindset to analyze and develop code."

"Great!"

"So tell me about your ability to work under pressure."

"Pressure is the factor that teaches a professional how to be even better at their work. In fact, many times after going through pressure situations we begin to display greater qualities of patience, tolerance and magnanimity. The same has happened to me. In so many pressure situations, I have increased my capacity and delivered more in terms of quality and quantity. And that by no means implies that I do not work enough when there is no pressure. It just means that in pressure situations, while some people may shut down altogether, I go the extra mile and continue to keep working. So pressure has taught me a lot of things. Foremost among them is the ability to embrace change and the need for effort."

"Does that answer your question?"

"It sure does. Thank you!"

The interview goes by as smooth as knife through butter. No hiccups. Answers are on dot, up to the mark. And most important of all, Mrs. Dillmann is happy with his replies.

"I really enjoyed talking to you Ralph. I would like to qualify you to the next stage of an in-person interview at our office."

"Oh. I am glad you feel that way. I really enjoyed talking to you as well."

"What does your availability look like this week?"

"I am available most days from 9:30 am onwards." He says 9:30 am onwards so that he has time to take the public transport and get to where he needs to be or if not, borrow a ride from a friend. When you don't have your own car, travelling can consume quite a bit of time in the US. This is particularly the case when the city or town you live in does not have a reliable and efficient public transport system. Philadelphia was a city with a varied public transport system. Some areas of the city had good, frequent public transport. Others were lackluster.

****

"So how did the phone interview go today?" Paresh peers through Ralph's room door and asks.

"Come on in man! Don't be shy!" says Ralph with a smile. He trusts Paresh enough and is grateful for his help to not be backward with him. "It went really well. I got to say your recommendations were right on the money. I answered according to them and she was thrilled to hear it. You rock man!"

"Great. Has she said anything about next steps? Or did she indicate anything to that extent?"

"Yes, she said she would get back to me with a date this week for an in-person interview."

"Superb! Keep me posted on that. If you wish we can have a dry run of the interview one day before, so that you are confident before you go for it."

"Absolutely. That would be great. I will ping you when I receive notification from her and we can conduct the mock at a suitable time."

"We're kicking it bud!" says Paresh with a smile of cool satisfaction as he exits the room.

"Dear Ralph, Would you be available for an in-person interview at around 11 am on this coming Thursday?" reads the email from Mrs. Dillmann, the next morning.

"I need to craft a short, clean, yet courteous reply," he tells himself. "Dear Mrs. Dillmann, I should be available at 11 am on Thursday. Let me know once you confirm it. Thanks. Ralph."

There is a reason Ralph doesn't object to morning time for an interview. Generally people tend to be at their most positive in the earlier part of the day. Often because they have slept the whole night, are rested and have lots of energy. As the day begins to wear on and they lose energy; they tend to get tired and less willing to negotiate and reason out. This is why it is always better to approach your manager or boss with a proposal or request in the morning. As there is a higher likelihood of it getting accepted at that time. "Better mood makes for better dealings," Dad would always say.

If you want a positive outcome with the boss your chances are best in the morning. Though this is not a guarantee. A salient feature about winning with the boss though is to try to build a strong relationship with him or her whatever their demeanor might be.

"Paresh, do you have time now for a mock interview? I have received notification for a potential interview with UPENN," texts Ralph to Paresh.
"Let's do it in half an hour," replies Paresh.
"Cool!"
Ralph puts on his shirt and tie. *"Even the mock needs to be professional,"* he tells himself.

****

"So we have seen you have some impressive credentials and thought you would be valuable to some efforts we are going to launch in the coming weeks and months."
"Thanks. I'm happy to hear that."
"So what would you say is your strongest quality among all these you have mentioned in your resume?"
Ralph ponders a little and then responds. "My ability to communicate effectively and empathize with people is probably the best. Because when you listen carefully you understand. And when you understand you can bring greater value to your work and what you deliver to the end client."
"I also think my analytical skills are pretty well developed and I could easily attribute my coding proficiency to them."
"Okay. So in terms of performance what would you say was your proudest and most important achievement?"
"I have quite a few of those. So it would be hard to point out any one specific achievement. But the one that really stands out would be when I completed a data migration which hadn't been done for more than a year due to various complications. I worked through the complications to get the work done."
As they look on, Ralph understands he is going to need to provide more substance. "The manager was very happy about the way I completed it because it was done as per specification and within the scheduled time frame."
"To complete it I had to go and talk to many 'not-so-easy' to work with people. Senior people as well as people from a few other related

422

departments. It was a very different experience and a great learning opportunity."

"So if I were to give you a difficult problem and you weren't able to solve it, how would you go about handling that situation? In other words, how would you tell your boss that you haven't been successful?"

"Well, my first step would be to try as hard as possible to try and do the work given to me as best as possible. If after substantial effort I am not able to do it then I would note down the steps I have taken to complete the work. I would go to a colleague and present these steps to them and see if I can get any help or tips from them. If I cannot then I would go to my manager and talk to him or her."

"So essentially I would say this is what I have done. And these are the results I have got. Could you provide me with a resource person to help me get through the remainder of the task or do you have some other suggestion?"

"Okay. Do you think the manager would look down upon such an action?" asks Paresh.

"Well, people can be unpredictable sometimes. But generally, if you go to them with a clear intention, good thoughts and a specific purpose, I don't see any reason why they wouldn't respond positively."

[Pause]

"Besides being the manager he or she would need to set an example by providing some mentorship and advice to help a worker get their job done."

"Great!"

"So do you have any questions for me?"

"Yes. What is the main quality or qualities needed to be successful in this job?"

"Okay. Any other questions?" says Paresh not wanting to actually answer Ralph's (interviewee's) questions. The main purpose of the mock was to assess Ralph's answers to interviewer questions rather than the other way round.

"What is the work-life balance that the job provides?" Ralph looks at him wondering what else he could ask.

"Any other questions?"

"That's about it!"

"Okay. Good job on the mock interview Ralph," says Paresh looking moderately happy with his performance on the interview.

"I have noted a few points I could suggest as improvements, though."

"Okay."

"So the foremost improvement I would suggest is in regards to the questions you ask to the interviewer. Never ask about work life balance or vacation or any of those things. It only causes the interviewer to feel that you are more interested in the vacation or benefits and perks rather than in the job itself. That's a definite no-no for the interviewer."

"It would be great if you could sit straight and show a slight smile when answering questions to show you feel positive about the job. That you like it and would want to have it. When you show such a positive demeanor it means a lot to the interviewer. They want to see someone who is positive and values the job. Someone who respects the job a lot rather than someone who needs to be prodded and pushed to get the job done."

"I mean wouldn't you like someone who is a self-starter as opposed to a deadbeat who needs to be pushed and prodded for everything?" Paresh says suggestively.

"Okay. Yes. Thanks so much buddy!" says a grateful Ralph.

Paresh seems happy to have gotten the opportunity to conduct the mock interview. He feels gratified that he can help someone in need.

"Anytime man! If you get the job it's good for you, for me and for the world. You are a good man and I want a good man to succeed!"

"That is the philosophy you need to practice! It's good karma circulating around the atmosphere and definitely around you," says the Inner Voice.

Ralph had not thought much about karma and about the omens. But Dad would always talk how good things would come to those who did good to others. "You do one good action and it will be returned to you manifold!"

He would say these things with a wide smile on his face. No amount of negative feedback or misfortune would change his outlook on life. He remained as positive and steadfast in his efforts and conduct as humanly possible.

Ralph had never thought much about Dad's belief in the power of the Divine or the cosmos. His American adventure was increasingly changing his viewpoint on this though. Even though there was so much technology, automation and other comforts of life here; not everybody was content. Not everybody had genuine peace.

With all the comforts came additional worries of earning a certain amount or maintaining a certain lifestyle or doing a certain difficult activity. Genuine peace and the hope that good things would come seemed non-existent. People functioned very mechanically in the US of A. "Almost like robots!" Ralph felt so very often.

Even he had begun to operate in a similar fashion. "When in Rome do as the Romans do!" He would wake up in the morning; get ready, have a bite and rush to the office to get stuff done. Not for a moment pausing to see the green grass or take a deep breath of fresh air. The routine was mechanical. Though routine is a word that describes a mixed bag of feelings and emotions it can have a negative connotation as well. "Be grateful you at least have a routine to wake up to. Many people don't even have that in a recession!" reminded the Inner Voice every so often.

****

He heads back to his room and starts putting together a blueprint for a presentation for the in-person interview on Thursday. Paresh had forgotten to mention it during the mock, but Ralph knows that he needs to have that ready. It's going to make the difference between just another candidate and a terrific candidate; the candidate.

His work on the presentation almost done, he heads to the kitchen to grab some culinary delights. But not before a cursory glance at his email box.
"Hello Ralph. I am happy to inform you that Mr. Krackenhoff has confirmed he would like to offer you the position. Please reply to this email confirming whether you would like to accept the offer."

The email from Elise is a major boost to Ralph's efforts. The only downside is that it's in Europe. He feels the surge of fulfillment after all the investment of efforts in finding a job in the EU.

"Well done! Now its decision-making time. But don't rush into a decision," warns the Inner Voice.
He decides to wait 2 days before emailing Elise of his intention whether to accept the offer or not. His top priority is the in-person interview on Thursday of that week. Wednesday night he keeps his wardrobe aside

and polishes his shoes. Takes a deep breath and feels ready. "You will do it!" says the Inner Voice with conviction.

****

"Hi there. Second round is it?" smiles the receptionist as she hands him the visitor badge. A certain familiarity had developed between her and Ralph after his first visit to the same office a week ago. Over the years Ralph had noticed that it was rather easy to develop a relationship with African-American people. It was easy to start a conversation and make a connection with them than it was with folks from many other ethnicities. Black people had a unique charm about them. Now that didn't mean that all black people were congenial and easy to talk to but the majority that Ralph had come across seemed friendly.
"Is it because they are slow to judge or is it because they have seen a fair bit of tragedy, poverty and tribulation in their lives?" he wonders.

A lot of immigrants coming to the US notice the same fact. "Who has suffered more is more happy!" claims the Inner Voice in Dad's trademark style of sharing pearls of wisdom with Ralph.
"All the best!" she smiles as he heads towards the elevators. Black women seem to like tawny light-colored Asian men. He was always quick to observe that. He didn't need the Inner Voice to tell him that.
"Thanks," he smiles back. He is fifteen minutes early for the interview, which is always good. It speaks volumes of the candidate's time management skills.

As he reaches the third floor, he feels the same unique rush of vitality he felt the first time he interviewed with Mrs. Dillmann, the hiring manager at UPENN. *"Hope I am as lucky this time,"* he says to himself hoping for the best.
"You will be successful!" reminds the Inner Voice.

He enters the office with renewed vigor as the office manager looks on.

"Hi Ralph. Mr. Rashtenburg will be with you in ten minutes."
"Great! Thanks."
"Would you like a glass of water or anything?"
"A glass of water would be fine," he says as he takes a seat in the waiting area.
"Hello Ralph!" says Mr. Rashtenburg arriving a few minutes earlier.

"Hello Mr. Rashtenburg!"

Mr. Rashtenburg is a tall, thin and well-dressed man. He appears to like black. He is dressed in a black shirt, black pants and black coat. To top it all, he even has a shining blue tie. He seems like one of those people who would like to comb his hair using his shoes as mirrors. Stylish would be an understatement to describe him it appears.

"How's the day been so far?" he asks.
"So far so good. The weather is good too. So a lot to be thankful for," smiles Ralph.
"The weather has been amazing! I might even have to stop wearing this suit in the office if it gets warmer."

Ralph smiles as a sign of agreement. They settle into his office. It's not a corner office but more of a corner and a little more. It has an area like a narrow galley to keep umbrellas, coats or shoes. And the adjacent room is the main office. It has all chocolate brown leather chairs, elegant Chinese wall hangings and even a tiny wall lamp with a purple drape around it. His table is neat with tiny Chinese figurines placed at the edge. Papers are neatly placed in a bin on the table. A small pen holder looks like a bouquet of pens.

"Sarah (Mrs. Dillmann) has told me a lot about you."
"All good things I hope," smiles Ralph.
"Oh yes. Very good things."
"She says you are technically very sound and your application is very effective. This round is actually to have a chat with you to see if you are a personality match for the organization."
"So tell me Ralph. Have you been in a difficult situation at work before? Be it with the boss or a co-worker? What did you do? How did you handle it?"
"Yes. At this previous place I worked, a co-worker wasn't sending documents that were needed to get some work started. I had emailed him and also requested him to send them in person. That's when I decided to send a follow-up email cc'ing his manager. I normally don't do that. But I decided the only way to get movement on this is to try something new."
"And what happened after that?" asks Mr. Rashtenburg sounding interested.

"I got a response from him. He sent the documents. And then also came in person and requested me not to cc his manager. I didn't say anything about me cc'ing his manager because of a delay in his sending the documents to me. Just agreed not to cc his manager. The problem never reoccurred."

"Okay. Good job!"

"In regards to a problem with the boss; not faced any so far. Nothing major at least!"

Ralph doesn't wish to mention information that could jeopardize the work he has done so far in making a good impression. Mentioning stuff that would portray him in a negative light could potentially harm his chances of landing the job. He elects to use his judgment and knowledge honed after considerable time investment in interviewing skills. No mention of performance improvement plans or any other profession jeopardizing issue is made.

"How would you handle or have you handled a difference of opinion with a colleague when it comes to getting something done?"

"There are always disagreements or differences of opinions. The key to resolving these is by talking about them and negotiating. I generally prefer working on issues together rather than letting things slide or not talking about them and hoping they will take care of themselves."

****

"Great. Now we have a situation here that we are a small shop. We have two more developers and this position will be the third. So typically even if there is a disagreement between anyone; you have to come the next day and work together. That's the reason I am asking these questions. You seem like you're a pretty sociable person. You would do well in this environment."

"Yes. It definitely seems like it is a family type of setting. And a lot of opportunities to learn new things," smiles Ralph.

They continue speaking. Mr. Rashtenburg speaking more about the place now than Ralph. Ralph listens showing overt signs of attention.

"So do you have any questions for me?" asks Mr. Rashtenburg.

Ralph knows he has gotten through the interview when Mr. Rashtenburg asks this. "Be cautious!" reminds the Inner Voice. It is easy to slip into a lackadaisical attitude. Ralph knows he cannot allow this to happen. "You will hear from Raisa, the recruiter or Sarah (Mrs. Dillmann) in regards to next steps," he says.

Ralph gives him a strong handshake and departs the office. He is glad that the final round went through picture perfect. Too smooth to be true in fact.

****

"Hey homeboy! How did it go?" asks a smiling Paresh.

Ralph puts the plate of mashed potatoes and fried chicken aside to speak up.

"It was great. He was very happy with my responses. And we basically got along very well."

[Pause]

"So did he indicate when he is going to get back to you or any of that stuff?"
"Yes. He said Raisa would call me in regards to next steps."
"Did he sound positive when he said that?"
"Yes. Very. He was smiling as we shook hands."
"Okay. Well, keep me posted and good job!" Paresh flashes a thumbs up sign with both his hands. He grabs his orange juice and heads to his room.
"I need to continue applying," thinks Ralph as he finishes the remaining portion of his mashed potatoes and fried chicken dish.

On reaching upstairs he puts on his cardigan and fires up the laptop. He would spend the larger part of his 'awake time' applying for new positions.

It would be strange for Americans, but being an immigrant in the US comes with a diverse bunch of duties, responsibilities and obligations. Keeping one's options open is one of them. Cause there is always this uncertainty of when one door might close. *"Will the other ever open?"*

wonders Ralph sometimes. "*It will if I am proactive!*" he says to himself.

"God helps those who help themselves!" seconds the Inner Voice.

And so goes the modus operandi for most immigrants or at least for an immigrant called Ralph. "Keep looking for opportunities; keep applying even after you are fairly certain of having got an opportunity. Particularly if you have the time to do so. Don't squander the time away relaxing. Put it to productive use. You never know when situations change," Dad would say.

"Be confident and have faith," the Inner Voice would recommend. "Not everything has to be uncertain!"

Ralph was one of those people who was hyperactive and always over prepared in whatever he did. He preferred exhausting all options to doing nothing.

****

"Sure I would like to accept your job offer. Let me know the next steps," Ralph replies to the email from Elise for the job in Austria. He is not a hundred percent sure if he has got the job at UPENN so he might as well accept what offer he is closer to getting. A job in hand is anyways worth two in a bush.

They get back to him the next day offering to file an EU work visa. Ralph begins emailing scans of his passport and other documents needed to file the visa. He is a little concerned that he still hasn't heard from UPENN and it is Friday already. Only two more weeks before his legal status in the US becomes invalid.

"Never lose hope. For when you lose hope you have lost everything. Thinking you have lost doesn't mean you have lost! Not till the final result is declared. God can turn the tables at any moment!" the Inner Voice would say so often. Ralph had begun to believe in the power of the omens and in the occult. Dad would always say that God has control of your final destiny. He will never fail you.

The weekend is spent practicing code and filling out job applications. This weekend though he attends the Saturday Bible study that Theresa of International House used to conduct regularly. Ralph didn't have a penchant for attending Bible studies. But for some reason he ran into her in the kitchen at tea time. And lo and behold she gave him an open invitation to attend the study. She has urged him to attend the study several times before as well. But his interests were more towards his computer and women of course. This time though, as in so many others, she invited him without the slightest whiff of judgment in her tone.

His mind had been preoccupied with too many worldly worries; too many non-sublime thoughts. Except for his nightly prayers he had not dedicated any time to God. He decided to go to the Bible study and dedicate some time to the Lord that made this world possible.

The scripture she reads today strikes Ralph like a bolt out of a clear sky. "Humble yourselves under the mighty hand of God, while you throw all your anxiety on Him; because he cares for you" (1 Peter 5:7). Ralph definitely needed someplace to throw his anxiety; a shoulder to cry on. Who else than the Lord.

"He has been with you when you didn't even know it; when you weren't thinking about Him and even when you felt you were all powerful and glorious," says the Inner Voice.
Throughout the Bible study Ralph focuses on the deep topics of letting God into your life; putting all your worries on Him while working hard at what you need to do. Not being anxious or worried about things that you come across in your life. But just working hard to resolve things as they come. Never giving up in the face of all odds but putting your faith in the one who can make everything better. That is God's message to the world.

"Come to me, O weary traveler, come to me with your distress, come to me you heavy burdened, come to me and find your rest," reads Theresa from a Bible verse.

Ralph feels the stress and pain flowing out of his system and peace coming to dwell on him. For whatever reason he feels recharged, strong and courageous. As he sips the last round of mint tea made by one of the cute looking Chinese girls, he realizes there is a lot more to life than just work. Work only enables you to earn a living to sustain yourself. Living life is an entirely different ball game. Living life is more an art than a science.

431

"Well even if I'm busy there's always time for a good looker," he says to himself as he approaches the atrociously cute Chinese girl sitting diagonal to him.

Lily (American name) is studying international marketing and sounds very sweet and kind. She is probably the most beautiful Asian girl Ralph has seen in a long, long time. Chinese names tend to be a tongue twister and might be difficult to pronounce for people not directly exposed to Chinese culture or to the Chinese language. Hence many Chinese people give themselves an American name when they live or work in America.

As he delights in talking to her he realizes she is here for a very short period of time. This being her last semester, she will be graduating and flying back to Shanghai after that. She doesn't have any intention to look for a job in the US. It would be difficult anyway to get a job here considering her English was not the best.

"I could take her on a date. Maybe start something with her too. But that would consume quite a bit of time. And right now time is at a premium," he thinks to himself.

As he hugs her and bids farewell leaving the general group to head upstairs, he has no idea what is going to happen the coming week. That's a secret that time preserves in its unbreakable vault. The only thing that can decipher the secrets that time has in store for us is time itself. Father time holds knowledge of the future to himself until the future becomes the present. "Wait for your turn!" is his eternal motto. But Ralph is glad he could use the time at his disposal to learn the gospel today. "God's time moves slowly but surely!" reminds the Inner voice.

****

Sunday night he dreams about Lily, her sweet smile and of him walking down the aisle with her. He dreams of his first night together with her and of the amazing love they make. Her skin is like soft velvet, her breasts like juicy pillows. As they cuddle, roll and 'connect' with each other his slumber gets deeper till he is engulfed into an abyss of nothingness.

A shrill, mechanical sound wakes him to the reality of Monday. He turns off the alarm and pulls himself out of the bed. His short pants have dark emblazoned marks on them. All the signs of a passionate night of fantasy and love making. He gives a slight smile; pulls the bedsheet away from his body and just sits still.

He says his customary morning prayer with solemn devotion. Thanks the Lord for a brand new day; another day to live and learn and contribute to the world. Pulls the gunk away from his eyelids and takes a deep yawn. He is ready for Monday!

Though he couldn't pursue anything with Lily due to the limitations of time and availability he realizes that had the circumstances been a little different he would have had greater potential to enamor her. There are some things that being on a work visa doesn't allow you to do. Pursuing relationships effectively, traveling widely or even trying to start a business are some of them. But then again it also depends on how well one is settled in their job or career. Even on a visa, there are people out there that are emotionally secure and financially well off. They feel strong and confident and invigorated that they are in a country that gives them the opportunity to pursue their dreams without the hassle of political pressure or needless red tape and corruption.

Except for a call from Jessica which he ignores; Monday and Tuesday pass by uneventfully. The same old dull routine of opening up the laptop and applying for a ton of jobs; taking inquiry calls from recruiters; calling back numbers that he couldn't receive calls in time on. Keeping up the game and the effort; he is a Spartan by any stretch of the imagination.

"Hey Ralph, I am happy to inform you that we'd like to offer you the position," says the female voice on the phone. Rachel had received the news from the hiring manager and promptly called Ralph to ensure he didn't accept any other offer.

In America or elsewhere, if you get a glowing recommendation from someone you are good to go. External validation is crucial to receiving a job offer quicker. So maintaining relationships with your manager, boss or superior is of critical importance. You always want to be able to go back and get a job at the place you worked before so don't burn bridges.

433

Try to build bridges so that you have a chance to go back. You need to have a face to go back.

"Would you like to accept the offer?" she asks.

That was one of the easiest decisions in his life. He didn't have to think much about that. With no other offer in the US, it's a no-brainer as to what to do. The other option would be to select the job in Europe which would involve moving there and getting adjusted to a new lifestyle and culture.

"That's great! Well, I'll send you an email and if you can confirm your acceptance by email that would be great."
"Absolutely," says Ralph, now almost on seventh heaven on hearing what he just heard. This feeling is quite similar to the one he had when he got a full-time job in Siemens. Only ten times more wonderful as he combated a layoff and a shitty economy to reach the goal that few had the stamina and perseverance to attain. He feels the joy of actually working through a raw "online job application, phone call, phone screen, in person interview," process. He didn't have any references, no help, no support from anybody. It was raw effort, raw force and pretty helpful luck. But without the work he put in there would have been no luck at all.
"But maybe it was serendipity too. If Paresh hadn't come along and given you those tips; you would never have thought of applying to UPENN or other non-profit organizations. Your interviewing skills would not have been as good. I think you owe a lot to the Almighty Lord also," says the Inner Voice in a somber tone.

And yes indeed he had got the position because of the omnipresent hand of God in his life.

"Ralph, are you there?" she asks again; only hearing silence from the other end.
He breaks away from his soiree with the Inner Voice. "Yes Rachel. Sorry I was, umm, I was just …busy thinking," he says for want of a better explanation.
"It's okay. I understand. You're elated! Congrats again and wait for my email," she says.
"Have a good day!" he smiles as he symbolically kisses the phone. The phone of good news!

He can't believe a crazy two-month effort is ending with a crowning success in the midst of the Great Recession of 2008.

****

"Thanks for the email Rachel. I appreciate it. I hereby do accept the offer," writes Ralph with a feeling of splendid delight.

With the click of the Send button Ralph breathes a deep sigh of relief. The crazy six weeks and a little more were ones which he had never experienced before. He experienced great hope, immobilizing despair and surreal strength during this period and at the end of it he witnessed a crowning glory. He liked to think that he would remember this titanic struggle till the end of his years. But more so he would remember the constant encouragement provided by his mother and the Inner Voice during this time.

The hand of God never left him. Backing him every minute and providing solace and comfort, every hour, at every step till the very end.

"I have a lot to be grateful for," he says to himself as he reclines on his swivel chair.

The next day he sees several emails from Elise, the recruiter working for Mr. Krackenhoff regarding more papers and documentation for his EU work visa filing process. He ignores all the emails and starts typing an email to Rachel. His interest still lies in staying in America rather than moving to Europe. The logistics involved in such a move are anyways more elaborate. And he knows he is short on the resources and wherewithal to make such an extensive move.

"Hi Rachel. I forgot to ask you about the work visa filing process now that I have accepted the job offer. What is the process for filing? I only have two weeks before my H-1B visa from the previous company goes out of status."

H-1B work visas are probably one of the most sought after visas by IT companies looking to hire scarce IT talent. The overwhelming majority of this talent being non-American, they need a work visa to legally work here. Normally companies start filing these visas in the beginning of

April. As per United States customs and Immigration services, the allotted H-1B quota of 65000 runs out on the first day of April itself. Companies, lawyers and people are very proactive in filing the visas rather than waiting. The US work environment is much sought after as it boasts a rather open environment, with a non-oppressive management and supervisory approach in many companies.

Ralph knew this fact and was worried that he might not make it in time to secure a work visa. He didn't want to miss out on a visa allotment just because his employer was late in filing the visa papers. Or because they dragged their feet or because of some other non-talent related reason. There have been a myriad number of reasons why visa filing is not successful and virtually all these lapses could have been prevented with a little more care and attention to detail.

"I need to inform Mr. Rashtenburg about this. As director of the department at UPENN, his approval is needed for dedicating budget to visa filing processes. Will loop back with you after I touch base with him," she replies quickly over email.

His calls and emails receive no replies. He thinks he will get a reply by Friday that week but receives nothing. A morose type of worry begins to engulf him. *"Have they decided to rescind the offer because of difficulties involved in filing the H-1B?"* he thinks to himself.

America was in the throes of the Great recession. Employers were looking to cut costs and what better way to do that than to cut employees; reduce salaries and avoid expensive immigration fees on specialized foreign workers. If there were expenses that could be eliminated; organizations were only too keen to take advantage of them. In an environment where organizations don't make a lot of profits due to an economic slowdown, it is but natural that 'cost cutting' is the primary resort to continue to keep the company fires burning.

"Life and all its situations are not just a function of one action. But a collage of multiple factors pulling and tugging at each other. These diverse and divergent factors are important and needed to maintain a balance in the world," said the Inner Voice every so often. In the end, it is divine luck and indeed divine intervention that matters more than anything else.

Without luck and serendipity many things would just be left by the wayside; stationary like the stones at the bottom of a deep sea. God controls luck and no matter how much man tries; without God's blessing nothing would be possible; no substantial result would materialize. This reliance on God and indeed luck is the perennial reminder of man's subservience to God.

****

Monday morning comes and he is all charged up. He doesn't allow any of his underlying anxieties and fears to distract him. It is hard to control your feelings when you know there are a lot of factors affecting or going to affect the way your life turns out in the near future. But fears and feelings can be devastating if allowed to go out of control. Fear has the ability to dent and greatly diminish concentration if it is allowed to run loose and pervade the mind.

Fear and self-doubt eats into the soul and destroys initiative. It saps the person of vitality and zest for life. He shoots another email to Rachel asking her for an update on the H-1B visa filing. This time though he cc's the director Mr. Rashtenburg. Within an hour of sending the email, he receives a call from Rachel informing him that they are proceeding with the filing.

She also asks him not to cc any more non-HR people on his emails. Asking the hiring manager or director about HR related work reflects her in a bad light. And in many ways can mean she is not doing her job well.

But Ralph knows that the only way to get people moving on his case is to ask their bosses or managers. Without a little pressure, he knows HR will tend not to work. "And isn't that the case with so many other things in life. Imposing pressure brings about an urgency to complete tasks which would otherwise be languishing in limbo," seconds the Inner Voice.

He calls her again and lets her know that Saturday of that week his legal status in the US becomes invalid. The filing would need to be done by Friday. She nervously agrees. Knowing that if this doesn't go through, the hiring managers would hold her responsible for not acquiring the candidate they interviewed and liked. The next morning she directly calls him asking that he send all required documents needed for filing the visa. He quickly complies by email.

Fortunately, he has proactively scanned all necessary immigration documents. When you are an international you have to be proactive and think ahead a bit. He had seen his friends scan some of their documents. And thought that it would be useful for him to do the same as well. "Then I don't need to run to the library to scan mine at the nth hour."

Having emailed the documents to her he just keeps his fingers crossed and says Amen; hoping for the best. By some quirk of fate, he happens to look at his bank account. "Thirty thousand dollars in the account," he says to himself. Just enough money to plan a return trip to India with some savings. "But I am not giving up so quick! I hope the UPENN visa filing process goes through!" he cups his eyes to feel the warmth of his palms.

Situations can be rather dire and serious when you are an international in a foreign land trying to make it happen with limited resources. Having one disadvantage is bad enough but having many is a recipe for resourcefulness. Because without tragedy, shortcomings, disadvantages and misfortune one would never be motivated to think out of the box; to plan and innovate. Things would be the same as they always were. There would be no growth. And although we want things to be smooth and be the same, life doesn't accept the status quo. Variation is the law of life. Things that were a certain way yesterday are no longer the same today. They change. "Nothing is permanent; the only constant is change!" said the Buddha. That proverb holds true even today. The only things that remain static for a relatively long period of time though are values! Your values and your morals are what keep you from straying away into an abyss of dread and despair. And that is what even the Almighty; whatever your religion might be says as well. At the end of the day, every hurdle is an opportunity to get better.

WEDNESDAY

"Ralph we are currently working through a backlog of pending visas. Our lawyers have triaged them to finish the most important first. Hence your turn is at the end since we just gave you the offer a few days ago," writes Rachel.

Ralph didn't quite understand what she meant by "most important first." But he suspected it was an excuse mechanism. When people cannot or don't want to do something they formulate an extensive excuse to say why. The way to debunk this is to ask another why in regards to the excuse. Why does what they say have to be true! Or why does it have to be the way they see it? Further probing their rationale behind a "matter of fact" helps you to help them change their mind. And that means the new decision favors you.

"Thanks Rachel. May I know if you can push my case. I understand that I am at the bottom of the pile. But that situation notwithstanding, I must inform you that if the paperwork for the work visa is not submitted to USCIS on or before Friday; I will be deemed out of status and might not be eligible to take the position with UPENN. Any help would be greatly appreciated," reads the email.

Ralph had learnt from prior experiences at International House and indeed during his classes that nobody likes a kill-joy. Hence, he always tried to tone down the intensity with which he approached any topic involving work from another party.

Americans can be stingy when it comes to the investment of effort. They prefer convenience more than most nations and cultures. And they work towards establishing that level of convenience. Whether it's building wide, safe roads or effective public transport or buildings which take into consideration all aspects of safety. Most, if not all things in the US are well planned, clear cut and clean. At least that's how the rest of the world perceives them. But Ralph had no doubt in his mind that building effective and efficient systems were very much a legally enforced practice in America.

This time though he would need to push even if it meant discomfort for Rachel. The cause was definitely worth the struggle. If he didn't push hard enough, he would live to get old with the regret that he had a chance to continue in America. But his hesitation to disturb Rachel from her convenience prevented him from completing the last step that could have changed his circumstances.

He just didn't want to live with this regret. He knew once he got the job; he would barely come across Rachel. "For a transactional relationship,

439

you can push harder! You don't have to worry too much about fitting in or preserving relationships," reminded the Inner Voice.

He calls her and leaves a voicemail. He knew she would be occupied with stuff. So voice message is the best way to let someone know you are very eager and interested and keeping tabs.

****

That night as he takes a breather walking on the porch of International House, he notices a milky white BMW enter the parking lot of the neighboring Humberto's house across the street. A young couple with a small child come out of the car and are greeted with open arms by the elderly couple who own and live in the house.

The Humberto's were nice people who had migrated from Spain in the 70's and made a fortune selling Catalonian and Galician wines. Rumor had it that they even owned a mansion in West Palm beach, Florida. The younger man looked regal. His girlfriend or wife seemed curvy and figurative. In her long, light cotton sarong she looked voluptuous to say the least. But Ralph only got an angular view of her face.

How much he wished he had a car like that. "*With a car like that a girl like her would not be far behind,*" he said to himself. "Or maybe not!" corrected the Inner Voice.

If he were to get the job at UPENN he would need a car to drive back and forth. Maybe not like a silky white BMW but just an ordinary car that would get him from point A to point B.

"*If I can, one day I'd like to be as successful as the Humberto's!*" he resolves.

"And you will cause you have the will in you, the desire and the strength," emphasizes the Inner Voice.

Life is all about positive reinforcement. The more you keep telling yourself positive and healthy things about your future; the more the cosmos will collaborate with your being to generate positive results.

"Always believe in the power of the cosmos and the omens!" Dad would say.

Ralph knows that his dreams are his passport to great things. His hard work is his ticket to that destination.

THURSDAY

In spite of all the upheaval, he wakes up Thursday with a deep sense of hope. The laptop though is not as enthusiastic. In fact not enthusiastic at all. As he tries to get it to start, the engineer in him realizes that its RAM might be burnt out or the operating system might be short on critical updates or might just be infected with a computer virus.

He doesn't have a smartphone to access his email but fortunately, he has an older laptop through which he can satisfy the task of checking for any urgent messages.

"No messages. Great!" he says after having checked his email box using the older system.

The customer service agent offers to send new RAM sticks signaling that his laptop is under warranty and RAM damage is quite certain. In the meantime, Ralph is going to have to make do with the older laptop.

Remarkably, he has stored all major files including resumes in a pen drive. "Be prepared!" is the scout motto that he has made his own in America. He sends a customary email to Rachel asking how things are going in regards to the work visa processing and receives a positive reply from her. Pushing the matter had done the trick of having her be more responsive to him.

The older laptop, although a little clunky, works like a charm. "Old is gold; never to be sold!" Dad would always say to Mum when she criticized his parents and relatives and their lackadaisical ways.

****

"We have everything Ralph. But we need your transcripts in hard copy form to complete the filing process. The lawyers are asking for it," says the frantic sounding Rachel.

"Sure. Let me try to get them."

Ralph knows that Friday's are generally sleepy for people in the university. But he is confident he can use his charm to work magic.

The most convenient thing of all is he still lives close to the university. He makes a sprint to the campus and reaches the office of student affairs where he asks for a copy of his transcripts. They demand cash payment for the sealed documents. He only has his credit card and quickly hands it over. The clerk makes an exception this time as she asks the others to provide the swipe machine.

Not everyone makes exceptions when it comes to established process. But people in a low stress, easy going job tend to be happier. Hence they tend to want to make other people happy as well. That's where the motivation to cooperate and help others out comes from. When you are happy you want to see the world happy and indeed make others happy!

"Here you go Rachel!" he says as he hands the transcripts over into her hands.
"Thanks! This should suffice. Mr. Rashtenburg came to me this morning and said he was keen to get this process rolling as soon as possible. Looks like he likes you a lot. You must have done something really right!" she blushes.
"Oh! Thanks. I think God just wanted me here," he smiles graciously.

She gives off a mixed reaction bordering amazement and something sounding politically incorrect. Matters of faith, religion and grace are generally not openly spoken in a professional environment in the States.

On Friday, he receives an email from Rachel confirming the filing of the work visa. He is asked to provide a date when he can start work. He feels the exhilaration and joy a man just released from prison would feel. The passion of a newly married couple. More than two months of back-breaking toil have reaped benefits beyond his imagination.

He is not going to have to relocate to Europe or for that matter to any other city in the US. He is not even going to have to change towns within his beloved state of Pennsylvania. Philadelphia would continue to remain his home. The applications to Europe were a mere fallback option. As were the applications to other parts of the US.

Sometimes in life, God makes you go down a long and tortuous path to attain realization. Not because he hates you or that he wants you to suffer. But because true wisdom is obtained when the mind is so focused that no distraction or hype can shake it. Suffering and agony make man realize his subservience to God and that every human has a purpose in life. They enable you to crowd out the distractions and know the truth and purpose. God's purpose!

Those doing things against the greater purpose of the Almighty are all but succumbing to their distractions. Distractions serve to impede the course that God has planned for us. But God doesn't prevent them. For he seeks to allow man to make a choice. Because He is a fair and loving God and wants man to know the value behind a good decision and the dangers behind a bad one.

However, man doesn't make choices on his own. There is serendipitous help from the universe. Ralph recalls Dad's perennial advice to him to remember the spirits and the omens. And realizes that God has been with him throughout all his great and small ordeals. That without the Lord nothing would have come to fruition.

He knows that God spoke to him through the Inner Voice and continued to speak to him until the very end of his gargantuan struggle in the 'new world.' He feels secure in the knowledge that the Inner Voice will continue to speak to him even till the end of time.

In so doing, he understands that what life has been trying to teach him is that the Inner Voice is, in fact the voice of God that has been speaking to him all this while. The power that has always guided him at home and even when he left home to explore adventures in a different world. The same power that guides all of us millions to do the right thing when there are overwhelming temptations to stray away.

His story is not one of illegal immigration or a search for wealth or even a story of rags to riches. His is a tale of sheer grit and unyielding will in the face of overwhelmingly lopsided odds. A story of divine presence when human weakness seems preeminent. "Go home for a few days! Relax and then come back," he hears the Inner Voice say.

"I am coming Mama!" he says tears welling down his eyes.

443

ABOUT THE AUTHOR

Joel Mendonca was born and raised in India. He pursued higher education in the US. His experiences as a student advisor and mentor gave him first hand exposure to the daunting challenges faced by international students in their quest to build a career and a new life in the United States. He witnessed the troubled job market during the 2008 recession and very poor prospects for career building. Not only were internships hard to come by but even part-time campus jobs were difficult to get. With his two Masters degrees, he set about on an arduous path of applying for jobs that he was qualified for. And along the way also helped out colleagues who were themselves looking out for career opportunities. But in so doing came face to face with a firewall of work visa sponsorships and cost-cutting employers. This book is based on an adaptation of some of his personal experiences during those challenging times.

BOOK SUMMARY

It's 2008, the post 9/11 internet era. Millennial Ralph arrives in America seeking to obtain a degree and a shot at the American dream. Contrary to expectations he encounters the travails of a country steeped in recession; the economy anemic and opportunity sparse. Deeply committed to a culture of hard work and lofty achievements, Ralph refuses to surrender to the circumstances of fate. His unmitigated quest for success and achievement takes him down a long, dreary path of back-breaking toil, stupendous innovation, profound self-development and disappointing love affairs. In the end all this hardship of life by himself, metamorphoses the person in him from a student into a resilient personality unmoved by the massive ups and downs of life.

This book resonates the thoughts, feelings and aspirations of the hundreds of thousands of students that come to the US to study and make their career and financial dreams come true. It reflects their daily challenges and profound struggles to find identity and success in a melting pot of perennial change.

www.ingramcontent.com/pod-product-compliance
Lightning Source LLC
Chambersburg PA
CBHW051433260626
47162CB00001B/69